Advance Praise for *Chaucer's Canterbury Comedies*

"There is no more important living Chaucer critic than Peter G. Beidler. Everyone who has taught, written about, or even studied the *Canterbury Tales* in a scholarly way knows his work and has benefitted from it. Before other critics dared to take Chaucer's *fabliaux* and other comedies seriously, Beidler showed that they rewarded close analysis, and his effect on the course of Chaucerian scholarship is hard to overstate. Now, in *Chaucer's Canterbury Comedies: Origins and Originality*, he draws together twenty of his most influential essays with new (and very handy) headnotes that outline the context and main points of each.

"The essays themselves exemplify the energy, creativity, humor, and good sense that have always marked Beidler's work. Many have noted his talent for close reading, and the riches he has revealed through this technique are myriad in this volume. Only Beidler would ask what a foot-mantle is and then embark upon a quest worthy of medieval romance to discover, among other things, that the Wife of Bath may not have large hips after all, but that the word *large* could easily refer to the fit of her leggings. And only Beidler would set out to reconcile the wildly disparate assumptions on the worth of the 100 French francs that the monk of St. Denis in the *Shipman's Tale* pays for the wife's favors. While an earlier critic did bother to ask whether Damian in the *Merchant's Tale* reaches a climax in the pear tree with May, only Beidler, in apologizing for the aggressive tone with which he disagreed with the critic's conclusions, could say, 'I shot off this refutation ....'

"Beidler's light, unpretentious tone renders his scholarship as accessible to our students as its solid argument renders it persuasive to professionals. This volume will therefore be welcomed by Chaucer teachers, who will want to recommend it to their students and use it in lesson plans. For many years, Beidler has illuminated areas we did not even notice were dark. Now he has performed an invaluable service by drawing together many of his most important insights in a single, affordable volume. Every Chaucerian will want *Chaucer's Canterbury Comedies* on her bookshelf."

—Leigh Smith, East Stroudsburg University

"*Chaucer's Canterbury Comedies* gathers together some of Peter G. Beidler's most well known arguments about the intersections of the writings of Geoffrey Chaucer, John Gower, and Giovanni Boccaccio. But Beidler's book also does so much more. As the brief narratives that introduce each essay make clear, this volume assembles writings that cover a lifetime, the career of a medievalist. As such, *Chaucer's Canterbury Comedies* enable us to catch a glimpse of the thought processes of a medievalist whose dramatic performances at conferences and in his classroom have captivated at least two generations of Chaucerians. In this volume Beidler answers questions that readers of Chaucer may have wondered over but never had the chance to pursue: Can Chaucer's tales be rendered into dramatic skits? What *is* the Wife of Bath's foot-mantle? Are there alternative ways of punctuating Chaucer's tales than what the editors offer? How much did the work of John Gower and Giovanni Boccaccio affect Geoffrey Chaucer's creative imagination? Since the 1970s, Beidler has introduced us to these enduring questions, and now with these essays—some reprinted, some new—Beidler provides readers with the answers. The work of a scholar who has made it a goal of his lifetime to assemble clearly his complicated ideas, *Chaucer's Canterbury Comedies* distills complex points in readable, and sometimes colloquial, prose. Ever the comedian, Beidler loves Chaucer for being funny, and the essays in this volume immortalize his deep affection for a medieval poet who sought to add a little humor to the world."

—Miriamne Ara Krummel, University of Dayton

"*Chaucer's Canterbury Comedies: Origins and Originality* collects in a single, accessible volume almost four decades of interior dialogue between the master-teacher and the master scholar inhabiting Peter G. Beidler. His (twinkling) eye sees the overlooked detail, the clue that provides persuasive answers to the common-sense questions we have asked ourselves and then brushed aside in our recent stampede to theorize complexly. Yet these puzzles precisely drive our students' curiosity, and Beidler, in essay after essay—most reprinted with slight changes, some written fresh for this compendium—never lets them down, nor loses us in the process. Reading through these pages is a profound reminder of the importance of Beidler's intelligent, learned voice to contemporary Chaucer and Gower studies, as well as a full immersion in the joy of the scholarly life."

—R. F. Yeager, University of West Florida

"Beidler's compelling, interdisciplinary, close analysis is invaluable for students, teachers, and scholars seeking to look with a fresh eye at the originality of Chaucer's adaptations and revisions of his sources.

"Beidler's close reading of Chaucer's comedic narratives is as close as it gets: looking at scatology as a humorous, realistic aspect of Chaucer's artistry in the *Miller's Tale*; reconstructing the Wife of Bath's foot-mantle; finding out how much 100 francs might have been worth in 1385 to determine the worth of a night of pleasure with the merchant's wife in the *Shipman's Tale*; revisiting Damian's climactic copulation with May in the *Merchant's Tale;* re-examining references to the bubonic plague in the Pardoner's *exemplum*.

"The short lead-ins to each essay are not only inspirational, but they also give the book a delightfully refreshing voice."

—Gila Aloni, Société des Anglicistes de l'Enseignement Supérieur

"*Chaucer's Canterbury Comedies* brings together a comprehensive selection of Peter G. Beidler's works on the *Canterbury Tales* for an accessible and entertaining volume. The twenty essays collected here string together pearls of wisdom from more than forty years of Beidler's best, and at times controversial, works on the *Canterbury Tales* as comedic art. This volume captures both the humor of Chaucerian poetry and the hallmark humor of Pete Beidler. It is a must-read for scholars and students of Chaucer alike."

—Larissa Tracy, Longwood University

"*Chaucer's Canterbury Comedies* collects in one place many of Peter G. Beidler's most trenchant essays. Although never theoretically naive, Beidler's work has always emphasized the formulation of specific critical questions and the pursuit of similarly specific answers to whatever extent they are possible: Did Chaucer read the *Decameron*? What is a foot-mantle? What sources did Chaucer use for his poetry, and to what ends did he use them? How might we best resolve textual cruces in the *Canterbury Tales*? Refreshingly aware of the contingencies that shape his responses to such questions, Beidler here provides consistently insightful, useful, *good* answers to them. Even readers who feel they have not learned *the* answer to such issues will learn much from his essays, and all scholars are better off for the well-formed arguments he has contributed to their discussion."

—Tom Farrell, Stetson University

Chaucer's Canterbury Comedies: Origins and Originality

Chaucer's Canterbury Comedies: Origins and Originality

by

Peter G. Beidler
Lehigh University

cp
coffeetownpress
Seattle, Washington

Published by Coffeetown Press.

Library of Congress Cataloging-in-Publication Data

Beidler, Peter G.
Origins and Originality: Chaucer's Canterbury Comedies / by Peter G. Beidler

Reprinted and new essays on Chaucer's Canterbury Tales. Include bibliographical material and index.

ISBN 978-1-60381-075-3 (pbk.: alk. paper)
1. Chaucer, Geoffrey (1340?–1400). 2. Essays on Chaucer's Miller's Tale, Wife of Bath's Tale, Shipman's Tale, Merchant's Tale, and Pardoner's Tale. 3. Sources for Chaucer's tales. 4. John Gower's Confessio Amantis. 5. Giovanni Boccaccio's Decameron.

Designed in Times New Roman font by Publishing Plus, Yardley, PA

Cover design by Sabrina S. Beidler

The paper used in this publication meets the minimum requirements of the American National Standard for Information Sciences—Permanence of Paper for Printed Library Material, ANSI Z39.48-1992.

Coffeetown Press

Contact: info@coffeetownpress.com

CONTENTS

Shipman's Tale

Merchant's Tale

Pardoner's Tale

Preface

This book brings together twenty of my essays on five of the tales told on the journey to Canterbury: the *Miller's Tale*, the *Wife of Bath's Tale*, the *Shipman's Tale*, the *Merchant's Tale*, and the *Pardoner's Tale*. I call these tales comedies because, like most comedies down through the ages, they involve clever deception and happy endings. Of course, the tales of most of the pilgrims fit that definition: those of the Reeve, the Friar, the Summoner, and the Nun's Priest leap most quickly to mind. Only the *Prioress's Tale*, the *Monk's Tale*, the *Second Nun's Tale*, and the *Parson's Tale*, do not readily fit my broad definition of comedy.

Why, then, do I focus on these five tales? I do so because they are the ones I have been most drawn to down through the years, ones that have caused me to raise with my students at Lehigh the most interesting questions. For example:

—Is the *Miller's Tale* really smutty?

—If periods and commas and question marks and quotation marks had not yet been invented in Chaucer's time, who inserted them into Chaucer's texts, and on what authority?

—Why have scholars been so eager to deny the obvious, that Chaucer knew Boccaccio's *Decameron*?

—What is a foot-mantle?

—Is the Wife of Bath really fat?

—Is Gower's *Tale of Florent* better or worse than Chaucer's *Wife of Bath's Tale*—or is that not a useful question?

—Does the fact that we find owl similes in both of those tales give us a clue as to which tale came first?

—When the wife in the *Shipman's Tale* sells her sexual services for a hundred francs, is she overcharging or practically giving it away?

—Who is that maid child in the *Shipman's Tale*, and why did Chaucer insert her into the plot?

—Does January in the *Merchant's Tale* interrupt Damian before or after Damian reaches sexual climax with May, and why does it matter?

—Who the heck is that old man in the *Pardoner's Tale*?

—Why did Chaucer—and only Chaucer among the many tellers of the story of greedy men who find death in pile of gold—set the *Pardoner's Tale* in a time of bubonic plague?

To me those were engaging questions. I had a lot of fun and learned a lot trying to answer questions like those in the twenty essays I present in this book.

Two broad concerns unify these essays: my interest in Chaucer's sources (the *Origins* of my title) and my interest in the changes Chaucer made as he adapted the plots and characters in those sources to new fictional purposes and new fictional tellers (the *Originality* of my title). In my writing about the *Canterbury Tales* I have tried to make clearly defined claims, present clear evidence for those claims, and draw most of that evidence from a loving attention to the words that Chaucer wrote. I'd like to think that while readers will not all agree with my conclusions, they will understand both my arguments and the textual basis for those arguments.

Readers familiar with my work on Chaucer may wonder why I say nothing here about my work identifying the sources of the *Reeve's Tale* and the *Miller's Tale*. I decided to leave that material out because it is readily available in my chapters on those two tales in the *Sources and Analogues of the Canterbury Tales* (Woodbridge, Suffolk: D. S. Brewer, vol. 1, 2002 & vol. 2, 2005). I left out most of my work on pedagogy, my articles on Criseyde, the Man of Law's prologue, the *Knight's Tale*, the *Franklin's Tale*, and so on, either because they did not fit the purposes of this book or because they seemed hopelessly outdated if not downright juvenile. I also left out some of my recent work on the *Miller's Tale* because, as this volume grew larger, I decided to incorporate that material into a new book tentatively entitled *The Dramatic Progress of Chaucer's Miller's Tale*.

As I indicate in the bracketed headnotes below, most of these twenty essays have appeared previously. I am grateful for the generosity of the various publishing houses and journals—particularly the *Chaucer Review* where the majority first appeared—in granting permission for me to reprint my work here. I am especially grateful to Penn State Press for letting me reprint nine of my essays from the *Chaucer Review*. I have slightly reworked most of the essays I that I reprint. I emphasize the adverb "slightly": I have changed an occasional "which" to "that," changed endnotes to footnotes, regularized section headings, and so on. I have in no case altered my basic arguments.

I must express also my gratitude to Laurel Broughton for organizing two panels of papers in my honor at the 2008 International Congress on Medieval Studies in Kalamazoo, for encouraging me to publish this gathering of my essays, and for her eagle eye in checking over the galleys; to Cristin Miller for help with proofreading and with the index; to Holly A. Crocker for her perceptive and generous foreword; and to Marion Frack Egge for scanning the various essays, for bringing them into editorial consistency, and for helping me in so many ways to bring this book to completion.

Foreword

It has been a great pleasure to examine the important contribution Peter G. Beidler has made to scholarship on Chaucer's *Canterbury Tales*. In these twenty articles, which span over forty years, Beidler has been one of only a few voices to argue consistently for the comedic originality of Chaucer's *Canterbury Tales*. By employing a capacious conception of Chaucerian comedy—"tales that involve clever deception and happy endings" (vii)—Beidler argues for the artistic seriousness of the *Canterbury Tales*, including those stories that were traditionally passed over because of their ribaldry. After taking a long view of Beidler's work, I was amazed and inspired by the boldness of this position, particularly when he initially articulated it in the early 1970s. If many of us take for granted the structural and thematic significance of Chaucer's *Canterbury Tales* as a whole, it is because scholars like Beidler have cleared the ground for a broader interpretive consideration of comedic narratives within the *Canterbury Tales*. But it is not just *what* Beidler did with Chaucerian comedy that is important; equally exciting is the *way* he moved critical opinion, for his method of analysis also illuminates many features of Chaucer's originality. Taking a lesson from comedy itself, Beidler's work refuses to draw a line between language and the body; instead, he traces the ways the witty pleasures of Chaucer's comedies move between and through bodies, of characters, texts, scholars, and students.

Beidler attends to the bodily connections of Chaucer's comedy, in simplest terms, by paying close attention to what the characters are actually doing in these stories. In the kissing scenes of the *Miller's Tale*, he ponders the sensory affronts involved in Absolon's humiliation. What would it feel like, smell like, to be subjected to the double-trick that Alisoun and Nicholas play on the besotted parish clerk? He looks at the Wife of Bath's portrait in the context of horseback riding habits. How would the Wife of Bath ride, and what kinds of clothing would she use to protect her "hosen . . . of fyn scarlet reed" (I 456)? In the *Shipman's Tale*, he traces the complex dynamics between daun John and the wife of the merchant of Saint Denis, carefully attending to the transactional interplay that sets up the adulterous liaison between wife and monk. What does it mean that the wife is up so early, and how does daun John turn the conversation to sex so readily? In the *Merchant's Tale*, Beidler examines what is actually going on in this pear-tree story: does Damian reach sexual climax or is he interrupted by Pluto's meddling miracle? If January thinks May is pregnant, does it matter whether she actually is with child at the close of the narrative? And if Chaucer was the only author who used the plague as a backdrop for the more familiar *exemplum* that the Pardoner performs, how do medieval beliefs about this epochal disease intensify the impact of the *Pardoner's Tale*?

With each of these tales, Beidler scrutinizes important details that Chaucer uses to establish relations between characters: a smock that rests on a lover's chest, or a beard on a face that is supposed to be radiantly smooth; an outer riding garment that fits over the hips, or a maid child who plays a role of silent accompaniment. All these features of Chaucerian comedy, under Beidler's critical eye, reveal the originality of character in these tales. He is not squeamish about thinking through the full (bodily) consequences of the details he notices in each story. The base sexual relations of the *Merchant's Tale*, or even of the respectable household of the *Shipman's Tale*, emerge through his exacting and relentless readings of these (often overlooked) features. In most general terms, therefore, Beidler is a consummate close reader. But, more than that, he uses a savvy familiar from comedy itself to demonstrate the narrative coherence of seemingly disparate details. Rather than treat tales as comparatively superior or inferior, Beidler reads the particular conditions that make different narrative strategies effective and original. And while he is recognized for his vast body of Chaucerian scholarship, Beidler argues convincingly for Gower's poetic mastery, acknowledging his influence on Chaucer, and distinguishing the *Tale of Florent* from the *Wife of Bath's Tale* using a detailed reading of each in light of the disparate purposes of the *Confessio Amantis* and the *Canterbury Tales*.

To achieve such detailed analysis, Beidler does not separate his own perspective from the scenes he describes; instead, he fully connects with the matter of each tale in a way that offers a refreshing and unique way of seeing it. In other words, he looks closely at the characters and their relations, but he manages to do so without a distancing appraisal that demarcates his own separation from the feelings and situations on show. In considering the plight of January, for example, Beidler manages a measure of empathy even for a character that the tale seems to portray as irredeemably odious. Rather than seeing the old knight as a pathetic, repulsive, repressed element of the Merchant's embittered consciousness, Beidler considers the frail, limited, and alienated perspective that ultimately isolates January. Much of Beidler's work seeks causes for vindictive, narrow, or cynical characterizations, without applying totalizing or disparaging judgments in his evaluation. To stay with the *Merchant's Tale* a bit longer, Beidler refutes the idea that January's antifeminism is somehow a product of, or a justification for, the Merchant's bleak outlook on women and marriage.

Instead, by resisting the antifeminism of both teller and tale, Beidler demonstrates the ways a selfish model of marriage is defeated by the very fantasy of femininity required for a masculinist marital ideal. May is not a shrew, a drunk, a spendthrift, or any of those things against which Justinus warns. Even so, she is a far greater threat to January than anyone anticipates. By shifting critical attention away from the "winner *vs.* loser" dynamic of the tale, and by paying careful attention to Chaucer's competing characterizations of different men, Beidler calls attention to May's power without censuring her agency. Beidler's readings demonstrate Chaucer's consistent lack of sympathy for characters who use positions of cultural privilege to exploit others. Just as January and the Merchant seek to imagine May in ways that gratify their self-aggrandizing fantasies, so Absolon and Nicholas in the *Miller's Tale* attempt to use Alisoun to prop up their self-enabling fictions. Particularly with his reading of Alisoun of Oxford, Beidler shows that the body is fundamentally equalizing, for it allows Alisoun to exhibit her autonomy against every male player in the tale. Similarly, the wife of Saint Denis in the *Shipman's Tale* is able to enter into the world of commercial transaction inhabited by her husband the merchant and his friend the monk, using her body as capital rather than allowing the men to barter for command over her very tangible goods. Equally important, then, Beidler's work demonstrates the ways traditionally dispossessed characters get the upper hand in Chaucer's comedic narratives.

He does so by investigating another form of corporeal connection. By paying attention to Chaucer's comprehensive engagement with continental comic literatures in the vernacular, Beidler is able to show how the dynamics of these tales arise from a broader focus on social upheaval, which emanates from the body's expansive unruliness. From *Lippijn* to *Heile van Beersele*, Beidler's work traces the myriad connections between Chaucer's tales and other comic stories. While Beidler does not insist on the direct source value of these continental texts, he examines the analogous relations between such forms as a way to broaden our appreciation for Chaucer's innovation in his comedies. Considering the difference between what he calls a "hard" and a "soft" analogue—a story that was possibly available to Chaucer as opposed to a story that he probably could not have accessed—Beidler figures an extensive comic corpus that crosses regional and linguistic boundaries. By noticing Chaucer's indebtedness to this larger tradition, he refines interpretation of key relations in Chaucer's individual stories. From the "naked knees" of the adulterous wife in *Lippijn*, to the "Pinnochio-like nose" in *Heile van Beersele*, Beidler makes a convincing case that Chaucer's economical methods of comic characterization in the *Merchant's Tale* and the *Miller's Tale* were influenced by the detailed renderings figured by such continental works.

His investigation of the *Shipman's Tale's* resonance with a large number of Old French fabliaux—wherein he examines the genre's extensive use of animal euphemisms—unpacks this tale's erotic dynamism with outrageous precision. His varied examples certainly demonstrate the richness of the genre's investment in sexualized animal euphemisms, but, as in much of his work, Beidler presents his evidence as a means to demonstrating a continued connection to the forms of bodily expression so abundant in the fabliaux. As he avers, "There is, of course, nothing surprising in the use of animals to identify human sexual parts. We do it still in English: pussy, beaver, cock, lizard, one-eyed snake, and so on" (201–02). As he makes clear, the fabliau is not a rarefied genre that can be isolated for critical analysis; instead, it remains vibrantly alive to the possibilities of the body, for its humor cannily exploits the continued intimate relations between our language and our bodily expressions. Acknowledging this sustained connection is important to analysis of the *Shipman's Tale*, because keeping modern familiarity with animal euphemisms in mind prevents anyone from expressing prudish surprise at the celerity with which the wife of the story picks up on the monk's sexual cues. Although we might act like we do not have access to these forms of innuendo, and consequently condemn the wife for her supposedly overdeveloped sexual instincts, to do so is simply to deny our own connection to this form of erotic dynamism. As Beidler demonstrates, the petty hypocrisies of prudish sentiment, however understandable, however universal, are also a prime target of Chaucer's comedies.

It is not, however, that Chaucer is exclusively indebted to a comic vernacular tradition; he frequently draws from other common forms of expression, albeit for comic effect. Through a careful reading of Middle English Marian lyrics, Beidler shows how everyday devotional practice subtends the erotic obsessions of the *Miller's Tale*. He demonstrates that Absolon's overtures to Alisoun, specifically his initial supplication at her bedroom window, are scandalous reformulations of late medieval songs to the Virgin. Although Beidler recognizes the ways Marian lyric and erotic praise are intertwined, taking both courtly love longing and religious devotional intensity out of their original contexts sheds new light on Absolon's character. Not only is it clear that Absolon misdirects his affection, Chaucer also uses this consonance to reveal the extent to which the parish clerk exploits his position for selfish motives. Yet, as Beidler also points out, this commonality explains some details that some readers have found puzzling. Why, we might wonder, does the jealous old husband John tolerate Absolon's serenade outside his bedroom window? Although we realize that John *should* be more circumspect, the fact that Absolon performs religiously-inflected verse outside their window defuses his suspicions, demonstrating more comprehensively John's ignorant reverence for ecclesiastical authority.

While much of his work teases out the general atmospheric resonances of Chaucerian comedy, Beidler also argues for more direct and specific comic connections. One of the first modern scholars to argue that Chaucer knew and was influenced by Boccaccio's *Decameron*, he mounts in these pages a sustained argument for interrelations between *Decameron* 8.1 and the *Shipman's Tale*. That Chaucer might have known the *Decameron*, Beidler argues, is extremely plausible given the influence Boccaccio exerts over his other works. Through a careful intertextual reading, Beidler outlines Chaucer's possible borrowings from the story of Gulfardo, the German soldier who gains the sexual favors of the greedy wife, Ambruogia. As he makes clear, Chaucer's departures from this tale are as important as the basic continuities of plot. By making the wife more sympathetic, Chaucer valorizes women's agency. By making daun John more predatory, he critiques those who abuse their religious authority for sexual gratification. Chaucer's use of the *Decameron*, however, is not limited to the *Shipman's Tale*. The *Pardoner's Tale* and the *Merchant's Tale* also have close alignments with several of Boccaccio's stories; even where Chaucer was more directly influenced by other comic (and Italian) sources, Beidler makes a convincing case that Chaucer was familiar with many of the narratives included in Boccaccio's frame collection. On account of the broad perspective that

Beidler provides for the comedy of the *Canterbury Tales*, therefore, it is less surprising that Chaucer devoted so much energy to forms that show the upheaval of traditional formal affinities.

Not only does Beidler urge us to view Chaucer as an international poet; he also shows that many of the priorities of the *Canterbury Tales* are furthered by the irreverence of comedic narratives. He does so most crucially through the pedagogical impetus that motivates so much of his work. Here again, it is clear that Beidler refuses to separate himself from the texts he studies, for he makes no distinction between questions that might be asked in a classroom and questions that might be asked in a scholarly essay. Not only are many of the questions he asks spurred by classroom interactions, many of the details he brings to bear on interpretation emerge from his vigorous engagements with students. For Beidler, there is a direct continuum between the kinds of thinking he does in the collaborative environment he shares with his students and the collective scholarly community that seeks to understand more fully the array of Chaucer's comedic narratives. He freely admits that his students make him a better reader of Chaucer's comedies. It is also easy to see, however, that he makes his students better readers, too. Indeed, he involves his students in Chaucer's comedies, asking them to think through the dynamics involved in each tale. Besides asking students to act out carefully selected key scenes, he encourages them to think through the bodily contacts developed through each narrative. His stress on formal rigor—which in some cases involves a detailed consideration of the punctuation of different tales—teaches us all to think about Chaucer's comedies as artistic expressions that merit the most exacting scholarly attention.

Even so, for Beidler, studying Chaucer is not a dusty, distant topic—this is something he has shown scholars, as much as he has shown many, many students. His willingness to put himself in the place of the reading he performs—*making* the foot-mantel he saw in the Ellesmere portrait of the Wife of Bath to see if his theory of its fit would be accurate—consistently evinces a commitment to reading as a bodily practice. As the essays that follow demonstrate, reading with such intimacy issues a call to empathy, which is continuously directed at Chaucer's new audiences. When considering the impact that the *Pardoner's Tale* might have upon its immediate audience of Canterbury pilgrims, Beidler directs attention to the common markers of historicized significance. But he does not use the copious evidence he gathers from historical chronicles, medical lore, and moralists' writings simply to argue for the importance of the plague to the meaning of this tale. Rather, and more deeply, he shows that cultural beliefs about the plague—which are certainly important to determining the meaning of the tale's enigmatic old man—also galvanize the tale within the framed context of the *Canterbury Tales*. If medieval men and women believed that the plague was related to sin, mortality, and even punishment, how might the Pardoner's telling of his narrative activate fears about the dreaded disease? Is the plague so terrible that pilgrims might be willing to pay the Pardoner for his wares, even if they know they are fakes? Or, if plague was thought to be spread by touch, would the circulation of an "olde breech" (VI 948) signify the potential of corrupting disease? While Beidler does not answer all the questions his investigations raise—indeed, with respect to the *Pardoner's Tale*, he wonders if we will ever get a firm handle on all the potential motivations behind Harry Bailly's aggressive attack—he continues to investigate those attitudes, which others might overlook or assume. In teaching readers of Chaucer's comedies to ask unflinching questions of these tales, while also emphasizing our intimate implication in the very questions we ask, he has opened up the unruliness of these stories through his original influence.

Holly A. Crocker
University of South Carolina

Art and Scatology in the *Miller's Tale*

[J. Burke Severs was my graduate school mentor. I was happy to be able to acknowledge my debt to him in an article that appeared in a special issue of the *Chaucer Review* in his honor. I confess that I got a kick out of dealing with ass-kissing and farting, two subjects that most scholars were reluctant to take seriously. In this essay I took them seriously as contributing not only to the humor of the *Miller's Tale*, but also to its thematic depth. I was amused to read in a 2008 essay that someone named Erica L. Zilleruelo wrote of the passage in which Absolon kisses Alisoun's "naked ers" (A 3734) that "Beidler credits Chaucer with exclusive use of the female posterior." Golly, did I really say that? "Art and Scatology in the *Miller's Tale*" first appeared in *Chaucer Review* 12 (1977): 90–102.]

Although the topic of my paper may not appear to be a highly appropriate vehicle for doing honor to so distinguished a scholar as J. Burke Severs, I do not think he will be offended. He has—and he always encouraged his students to have—a loving respect for all aspects of Chaucer's artistry. If it ever occurred to him to doubt whether Chaucer's scatology was an aspect of his artistry, Burke certainly never let his students doubt it. Indeed, the subject of this paper grows out of some introductory comments that Burke himself made in an article he wrote for another festschrift a decade ago. In an article honoring Margaret Schlauch, he wrote of the artistic effectiveness of the "unsavory jest of anal osculation" as punishment for the fastidious Absolon in the *Miller's Tale*.[1] My own paper is really no more than an extended footnote to that remark.

When Chaucer offered his well-known warning-in-advance about the churlish nature of the *Miller's Tale*, he could not have anticipated how many giants among his future admirers would advise others to take seriously his invitation that they might "turne over the leef and chese another tale" (A 3177).[2] In 1700 John Dryden omitted the *Miller's Tale* from his retelling of the Canterbury stories because he did not want to "offend against good manners" by telling a tale in which there were obscenities "very undecent to be heard."[3] In 1900 Robert Kilburn Root proclaimed it "unfortunate" that Chaucer had written the tale. Although he admitted that, despite its "nasty features," the tale was told with "consummate skill," Root was forced to conclude that "it is certainly a pity that such excellent skill was expended on a story which many of Chaucer's readers will prefer to skip."[4] In 1928 John Matthews Manly, openly proclaiming this "vulgar tale . . . not fit to be read in a mixed comp11any,"[5] included in his edition of the *Tales* only a few selections from the *Miller's Tale*. As recently as 1968 we find Edward Wagenknecht's rather embarrassed discussion of what he calls "the problem of the fabliau stories." Wagenknecht points out that, despite the apparent evidence of the *Miller's Tale*, "Chaucer's mind was not corrupt," but the best he can finally say of the tale itself is that it is "(as we sometimes

[1] "Appropriateness of Character to Plot in the *Franklin's Tale*," in *Studies in Language and Literature in Honour of Margaret Schlauch* (Warsaw: PWN-Polish Scientific Publishers, 1966), 386.

[2] All quotations from Chaucer are from F. N. Robinson, *The Works of Geoffrey Chaucer*, 2nd edn. (Boston: Houghton Mifflin, 1957).

[3] "Preface," *Fables Ancient and Modern*. The passage on Chaucer is readily available to Chaucerians in *Geoffrey Chaucer: A Critical Anthology*, ed. J. A. Burrow (Baltimore: Penguin, 1969), 60–73.

[4] *The Poetry of Chaucer: A Guide to Its Study and Appreciation* (Boston: Houghton Mifflin, 1900), 176–79.

[5] *Canterbury Tales* (New York: Henry Holt and Co., 1928), 558–59.

say), 'good clean dirt,' redeemed, if at all, only in the 'riche gnof's' bumbling affection for his unfaithful young wife." Wagenknecht apparently feels that the tale ought, indeed, to be skipped, for he speaks with disapproval of the "perversions that are now spoken of openly in college classrooms and in mixed company."[6] And in 1969 we find Haldeen Braddy excusing "the Miller's smutty short-story" as Chaucer's necessary pandering to the tastes of an unsophisticated audience: "he had to reproduce the broad tone of the genre to please contemporary tastes." Finding that Chaucer's "facility with fabliaux was the shallowest aspect of his genius," and finding himself "gagging" on the most scatological parts of the tales, Braddy nevertheless reminds us that, after all, "this discreditable sort of filth, Chaucer at his worst, figures small in the total."[7]

While they could not quite bring themselves to be specific about what these "undecent," "nasty," "unfit," "dirty," and "smutty" elements were, these critics were apparently thinking especially of the two unexpected affronts that Absolon receives in successive window scenes on that fateful Monday night: Alisoun's bared buttocks and Nicholas's thunderous fart. And while most recent critics have only praise for the wonderful humor,[8] realism,[9] artistry,[10] and morality[11] of

[6] *The Personality of Chaucer* (Norman: University of Oklahoma Press, 1968), 115–17.

[7] "Chaucer—Realism or Obscenity?" *Arlington Quarterly* 2 (1969): 128, 136–37.

[8] What goes on in the *Miller's Tale* "is supremely good fun for those involved directly. . . . We readers, the indirect participants, enjoy the comic ribaldry too"—Thomas W. Ross, *Chaucer's Bawdy* (New York: Dutton, 1972), 16.

[9] "The Miller is unabashedly, vigorously, a realist. . . . In real life women are women, not Emilys; virile young men don't act like Palamon and Arcite—they go after their wenches"—Bernard F. Huppé, *A Reading of the Canterbury Tales* (Albany: State University of New York, 1964), 76.

[10] "It stands first among the fabliaux, and from the point of view of narrative skill, perhaps first in the whole canon of the *Tales*"—Paul G. Ruggiers, *The Art of the Canterbury Tales* (Madison: University of Wisconsin Press, 1965), 56.

[11] In the *Miller's Tale* Chaucer "was quite consciously criticizing some of the Church's teachings on sexual love"—Trevor Whittock, A *Reading of the Canterbury Tales* (Cambridge, England: Cambridge University Press, 1968), 91.

the tale, very few of them make any direct comment on the kiss and the fart. Most scholars have not yet faced up—at least in print—to those two humorous, realistic, artful, and just affronts that the squeamish Absolon faced up to.

We do not know Chaucer's specific literary source for the *Miller's Tale*, though it is clear that the main outlines of the kiss-and-burn story were not original with him. A close look at the "sources"[12] of the tale shows us, however, that we cannot excuse the two "undecent" window scenes as being merely derivative, merely necessary aspects of the humorous story he was retelling. Comparison with these sources reveals that Chaucer significantly altered the window scenes in ways that made them, in some ways, more shockingly scatological than they were in his originals. The best way to appreciate Chaucer's artistry in these scenes is to try to analyze why Chaucer made the precise changes he did make. By doing so I hope to show that Chaucer included the scenes for more than the laughter they have been evoking for nearly 600 years, and that the *Miller's Tale* is successful because of those scenes, rather than in spite of them.

Perhaps it will be helpful to have before us a brief summary of the Middle Dutch verse fabliau which is the only analogue old enough in its extant written form to have been known to Chaucer. He probably did not know this exact version, but it will serve to remind us of the kind of story Chaucer had probably read or heard:

> Heile, an Antwerp prostitute, makes appointments with three different men for different hours of the night. Willem, a miller,

[12] I shall use the term "sources" to include the several analogues of the *Miller's Tale* known to have existed in Europe in the Middle Ages. These are conveniently gathered together by Stith Thompson in *Sources and Analogues of Chaucer's Canterbury Tales,* ed. W. F. Bryan and Germaine Dempster (New York: Humanities Press, 1958), 106–23, and by Larry D. Benson and Theodore M. Andersson in *The Literary Context of Chaucer's Fabliaux* (Indianapolis: Bobbs-Merrill, 1971), 3–77. I shall ignore for the purposes of this paper the three recent analogues collected in the United States and discussed by James T. Bratcher and Nicolai von Kreisler in "The Popularity of the *Miller's Tale*," *Southern Folklore Quarterly* 25 (1971): 325–35.

> comes first. After he has enjoyed Heile's favors for a time, the second man, a priest, comes at his appointed hour. Heile tells Willem to hide in a trough that hangs from the rafters, then lets the priest in. After thrice satisfying the priest, she (and Willem in the trough above) hear him preach a little sermon on how God will soon drown all the people in the world with a terrible flood. Then comes at his appointed hour the third lover, a smith named Hughe. Heile tells him that he cannot come in now, for she is not well. When Hughe begs for at least a kiss, Heile tells the priest to let the foolish smith kiss his behind. The priest puts his behind out a little window and Hughe kisses it with great zeal. When he realizes from the feel and the smell what has happened, the angry smith runs home and heats an iron. When he returns and insists on a second kiss, the priest assumes his former position and Hughe strikes. "Water! Water! I am dead!" cries the priest. Hearing this cry, Willem thinks that the flood the priest had spoken of has come, and he cuts the rope that holds up his trough. He breaks his arm and his thigh when he comes crashing down. The priest, thinking Williem must be the devil, runs into a corner and falls into a privy. This story shows what happens to men who deal with prostitutes.[13]

Chaucer's story, of course, is considerably different: Alisoun is not a prostitute; the man in the trough is her husband; she accepts only one lover; the priest replaces the smith outside the window; and so on. And of course we can see immediately that Chaucer's plot is better, for the Middle Dutch story offers no clear explanation of the existence of the hanging trough, of the necessity to hide the first lover, of the priest's prediction of the coming flood after he enjoys the promiscuous Heile, of Heile's rejection of the third lover (and presumably his money) after she has already told him to come at a certain hour. If

[13] From *Sources and Analogues*, 112–18.

we look specifically, however, at the first window scene to see what Chaucer has done with it, we see that Chaucer has made one very important change. In the Middle Dutch analogue—as well as in all of the other European analogues—it is the male lover who presents his buttocks out the window for the kiss, while the woman stays in the shadows. Chaucer is unique among early tellers of the story in having the woman execute the trick. Chaucer must have made the change for some other reason besides humor, for the scene is funny in both versions. There must be a better—and more serious—explanation for Chaucer's wanting to have Alisoun directly participate in this highly unladylike activity.

One important reason for Chaucer's change was precisely that—it is "unladylike" for Alisoun to play so active a role in the scatological trick. The Miller, we should recall, has just heard the courtly romance of the Knight and has been annoyed by it. He insists on telling his own tale to "quite" the Knight's. Emily, the noble heroine of the *Knight's Tale*, is a highly idealized young woman. She is distant and aloof from worldly concerns like sex and excrement. She is tearfully naïve about love and would rather serve Diana, goddess of chastity, than any man. The Miller, apparently annoyed by this highly idealized portrait of womankind, is eager to show in Alisoun Emily's realistic counterpart. Alisoun is not distant from worldly affairs, is not naïve about love, very much likes men, and very much despises chastity. What better way would the Miller have had of demonstrating his rejection of Emily's refined values than to have Alisoun present her bared buttocks out the window at, in effect, both the Knight and his idealized Emily? The action may be unladylike, but it is very womanlike—at least according to the realistic Miller's conception of the true nature of womankind. I do not suggest, however, that the Miller means to present a derogatory picture of women; indeed, Alisoun is far more attractive than her promiscuous counterparts in the sources, and is in most ways the most sympathetic character in Chaucer's tale—the only one, at any rate, who is not ultimately punished. The Miller wanted, not to be critical of Alisoun, but through her to take woman down from Emily's pedestal and to show her in all of her delightful realism. Alisoun's bared buttocks thrust out of the window showed to all the world how the Miller felt about the nature of real, live, sensual women. Alisoun's action, then, provided the Miller with an effective rebuttal to this aspect of the *Knight's Tale*.

More important, Alisoun's actions at the window also demonstrate the Miller's contempt for Absolon, the dandyish, fastidious, effeminate, squeamish parish clerk who is the direct recipient of her trick. Absolon's devotion to his role as clerk is open to question, for he is a frequenter of parish taverns, a singer, and a dancer. He spends much of this time courting the pretty young barmaids and wives of the parish. He fancies himself a courtly lover. In contrast to the bold Nicholas, the refined Absolon serenades Alisoun at her bedroom window and asks, not for sexual favors, but for pity and a kiss. Can there have been a better way for the Miller to convey his scorn for Absolon than to have Alisoun shove her buttocks into his face? The insult would have been effectively conveyed if Nicholas had (as in the analogues) presented his buttocks, but how much more effective is the rejection if Alisoun, the object of his unholy desires, presents hers.

One of the most important reasons why Chaucer gave to a woman a role that in his sources had been played by a man is that Chaucer wanted to show this parish clerk worshipping, not the Virgin Mary whom he should have been worshipping, but an earthly woman. Perhaps we should recall that the first window scene takes place shortly after "the belle of laudes gan to rynge" (A 3655)—the time when truly religious men would be singing praise to God. And it is no accident that, as he prepares himself outside her window to receive Alisoun's kiss, Absolon "doun sette hym on his knees" (A 3723) and asks for Alisoun's "grace" (A 3726). Surely this is meant to be a reminder that as a Christian and, especially, as a parish clerk, Absolon ought to be kneeling before, and asking for grace from, another woman. This point would have been lost entirely if the male lover had been the one to play the trick on this clerk who has chosen to devote his attentions to a worldly woman rather than to Mary.[14]

It is important to note, in connection with the first window scene, the images of taste and of eating that are associated with both Alisoun and Absolon. In the first place, Alisoun is described in consistently food-and drink-oriented images. Her apron is "as whit as morne milk" (A 3236); her eyebrows are as black as the fruit of the blackthorn tree; she is as blissful to see as a pear tree; her mouth is as sweet as honey ale or meed, or as apples lying on the heath. In short, Alisoun is as tasty a morsel as any man could desire.

Absolon, on the other hand, is consistently described as a man who associates love with eating. If Absolon were a cat, Chaucer tells us, and if Alisoun were a mouse, "he wolde hire hente anon" (A 3347); and cats, of course, eat mice. As part of his courting of her, Absolon sends Alisoun wine, meed, spiced ale, and hot wafers. His mouth itches all day long in anticipation of her kiss, and the night before the window scene takes place he dreams that he is at a feast. He refers to his lover as "hony-comb" and "sweete cynamome" (A 3698–99). He even tells her that he yearns for her as "dooth a lamb after the tete" (A 3704), and that he is so full of love-longing that he "ete na moore than a mayde" (A 3707).

[14] Jesse M. Gelrich, in "The Parody of Medieval Music in the *Miller's Tale*," *Journal of English and Germanic Philology* 73 (1974): 182–85, has shown that Absolon's speech to Alisoun beginning, "What do ye, hony-comb . . ." (A 3698–3707) strongly echoes expressions used in liturgical songs sung on certain feast days of Mary or in daily masses: "As a 'parissh clerk' he is singing a song that is composed of lyrics he would have sung in his Office and at Mass. As he is led away from his Church duties by Alisoun, he is directing to her in the 'wyndowe' a medley of the music he would sing to Mary in the 'paryssh chirche.' His song is a comic misdirection of his ministerial singing." See also R. E. Kaske, "The *Canticum Canticorum* in the *Miller's Tale*," *Studies in Philology* 59 (1962): 479–500. This "parody"—if that is a strong enough word for what Chaucer is doing here—is given special meaning only if it is Alisoun rather than Nicholas whose buttocks this silly and confused clerk is immediately afterward made to kiss.

This eating imagery—none of it to be found in Chaucer's sources—all culminates in that magnificent scene where the delectable morsel presents through the "serving" window to the starved dining patron, not her sweet lips but her buttocks. The hungry Absolon, of course, kisses her "ful savourly" (A 3735). It is deliciously appropriate that this famished lover should fully savor the foul meal he has so persistently asked for, and that the insult he so richly deserves should come from the Alisoun whose edible sweetness he has been yearning for.

With his customary care in selecting details, Chaucer tells us that Absolon is a barber as well as a clerk: "wel koude he . . . clippe and shave" (A 3326). This fact is particularly significant in that it helps to prepare for and make appropriate Absolon's punishment in the kiss scene. Absolon is particularly fastidious about his own hair. It shines like gold, is curly, and spreads out long and wide like a fan. He is especially careful to keep his part straight and even. Chaucer's description of Absolon's hair tells us, for one thing, that Absolon is a very imperfect clerk, for in Chaucer's time clerks—even ones in minor orders—should have worn their hair tonsured.[15] It also, however, helps to set Absolon up for the coarse trick to be played on him, for he soon comes face to "face" with hair that is not so neatly manicured. That Absolon is a barber suggests that his concern for beautiful hair extends to others as well; that he shaves patrons suggests that he may find beards as offensive as he finds unkempt head hair. In the kiss scene, of course, Absolon's first clue that he has kissed, not a miss, but amiss, is that his lips have encountered, not a smooth female face, but a rough "beard." Chaucer puts it this way:

> Abak he stirte, and thoughte it was amys,
> For wel he wiste a womman hath no berd.
> He felte a thyng al rough and long yherd.
> (A 3736–38)

[15] See Ruth H. Cline, "Three Notes on the *Miller's Tale*," *Huntington Library Quarterly* 26 (1963): 140–45.

We should recall that it is apparently Alisoun's smooth and clean facial complexion that first attracts Absolon to her. Her complexion shines brighter than a "noble yforged newe" (A 3256); the day he first sees her she has just washed her face so well that "hir forheed shoon as bright as any day" (A 3310). Her only facial hair, her black eyebrows, are "ful smale ypulled" (A 3245). In showing Absolon so concerned for his own hair, in making him a barber, and in causing him to be attracted to a girl with such a face, Chaucer creates in Absolon just the sort of character who would react most violently to the hairily offensive trick played on him. Clearly, Chaucer changed the plot available to him so that a woman's, not a man's, buttocks are presented to Absolon. I trust that I need not be overly explicit here about the anatomical appropriateness, considering the position of the person being kissed, of having a woman's posterior presented out the window. A man in the same position would not present what might so readily be mistaken, in the darkness of the night, as a beard. In the sources, of course, no hair is mentioned; it is merely the feel and smell that signal to the kisser the nature of the trick that has been played on him.

Surely it is clear, then, that Chaucer's putting the female lover at the window in the first window scene was a carefully considered change on his part; so, we will find, was the major change he made in the second window scene, the addition of the fart. The only extant analogue which also has this element is a German story by Hans Sachs. Written a full century and a half after Chaucer's, however, Sach's story probably derived from the *Miller's Tale*. In any case, it appears that Chaucer was the first author to introduce the fart into the story. This may seem a dubious distinction for a writer, but Chaucer had good reasons for making the change, more good reasons, certainly, than previous critics have acknowledged.[16]

[16] Robert O. Bowen, in "The Flatus Symbol in Chaucer," *Inland* 2 (1959): 19–22, sees the fart as Chaucer's means of conveying his theme about "the vulnerability of man's ego and his inability to rise above the human situation." Earle Birney, in "The Inhibited and the Uninhibited:

Most obviously, the addition of the fart helps Absolon to locate his target in the pitch dark of that Monday night: "Spek, sweete bryd, I noot nat where thou art" (A 3805). The addition of the fart also allows Chaucer to provide greater variety. We recall that in the sources the same person—the priest in the Middle Dutch analogue, for example—twice presents his buttocks out the window for a kiss. Chaucer varied this not only by having the woman present her buttocks in the first scene, but also by changing the nature of the affront in the second scene.

In addition to helping Absolon locate his target and to providing greater variety, the fart also served to help join together the two plot lines in the *Miller's Tale*. It has long been recognized that the tale consists of two separate plots, each of which is complete in itself, and each of which is extant as a separate story in medieval literature. The first is the flood plot: a lover, by predicting a coming flood, gets rid of a husband so that he can

Ironic Structure in the *Miller's Tale*," *Neophilologus* 44 (1960): 333–38, speaks briefly of Nicholas's "blast that blows [Absolon's] scentedness away." More recently, Janette Richardson, in *Blameth Nat Me: A Study of Imagery in Chaucer's Fabliaux* (The Hague: Mouton, 1970), 165, finds that Chaucer's comparison of Absolon to a goose is particularly appropriate in view of the fart, for "no animal is so sensitive to the smell of man as is the goose." Thomas J. Hatton, in "Absolon, Taste, and Odor in the *Miller's Tale*," *Papers on Language and Literature* 7 (1971): 72–75, finds that, since adultery was sometimes associated with foul smells in Chaucer's time, Nicholas's fart serves as an apt reminder of the spiritual and moral wrongness of Absolon's lecherous desires. Gellrich (186) speaks of the fart as a "comic inversion of Scriptural music sung by Absolon." Roy Peter Clark, in "Squeamishness and Exorcism in Chaucer's *Miller's Tale*," *Thoth* 14 (1973–74): 37–43, treats the subject at more length. Clark believes that Absolon plays a "symbolic role as squeamish devil" in the tale and that Nicholas's fart is part of his attempt "to purge himself and Alisoun of their squeamish intruder." Beryl Rowland, in "Chaucer's Blasphemous Churl: A New Interpretation of the *Miller's Tale*," *Chaucer and Middle English Studies in Honour of Rossell Hope Robbins*, ed. Beryl Rowland (Kent, OH: Kent State University Press, 1974), 43–55, finds the fart to be one aspect of a "blasphemous parody" of the Annunciation in which John plays Joseph, Alisoun Mary, and Nicholas the Angel. Roy Peter Clark again mentions Nicholas's fart in "Christmas Games in Chaucer's *Miller's Tale*," *Studies in Short Fiction* 13 (1976): 277–87, where he suggests that it may have been a reminder to Chaucer's audience of the symbolic sodomy that Absolon performs with the hot coulter.

enjoy the sexual favors of the wife. The second is the kiss-and-burn plot: a promiscuous woman and her lover are surprised by a second lover who, after he is tricked into kissing the buttocks of the first lover, returns to burn those buttocks with a hot poker. Chaucer was not the first to combine these two stories into one story by having the flood prediction be the means of getting rid of the woman's husband so that she can then entertain her lover or lovers in her bedroom—thus initiating the kiss-and-burn plot. And Chaucer was not the first to bring the two plots back together again by using the second lover's anguished cry for "water" as the signal to the husband that the predicted flood has come. It has not been pointed out, however, that Chaucer added Nicholas's fart to the story to give additional warning to the husband that the flood has indeed arrived.

Let me review the flood-plot briefly. Nicholas has told John that on Monday night a hideous rain will come. It will fall so wildly and madly that in less than an hour the world will all be under water and all of mankind will be drowned. The gullible John believes this absurd prediction and busily prepares the tubs, ladders, and food that are to save him, his wife, and his lodger from the deluge. On Monday night he crawls wearily into his tub. Before going to sleep he says his prayers, then crouches nervously in the tub listening for the rain:

> This carpenter seyde his devocioun,
> And stille he sit, and biddeth his preyere,
> Awaitynge on the reyn, if he it heere.
>
> (A 3640–42)

He finally drops off to sleep, still waiting for the sound of the terrible flood. What he hears next, of course, is Nicholas's fart, a fart that, Chaucer pointedly tells us, is as loud as a thunderclap. This noise, followed immediately by Nicholas's cries of "Help! water! water! help!" (A 3815), is surely interpreted by the slumbering John as the thunder that announces the terrible rain. Chaucer's addition, then, by making more believable John's misinterpretation of Nicholas's cry for water to mean that the predicted flood has arrived, helps to precipitate the climactic comic action of the tale.

The most important reason for Chaucer's addition of the fart is that by making it Chaucer greatly intensified the punishment meted out to Absolon, for instead of receiving merely a foul kiss for his troubles, he now receives also a foul fart. The authors of the sources were not so concerned as Chaucer was in heaping punishment on the lover outside the window. Hughe, the smith in the Middle Dutch analogue, for example, gets far less punishment than either Willem or the priest. Indeed, he comes out on top by getting his revenge. Similarly, in Masuccio's fifteenth-century story of Viola and her lovers,[17] the smith is clearly the hero of a story that seems to have been told at least in part to demonstrate his cleverness in getting revenge while also escaping serious punishment himself. He clearly deserves his reward of a fine capon dinner and prolonged sexual pleasure with Viola after the other two lovers are carried off. Chaucer, however, put the corrupt parish clerk outside the window to receive the kiss, and made him the least attractive, rather than the most attractive, of the lovers. The addition of the fart, then, is very much in keeping with Chaucer's purpose, for it intensifies Absolon's punishment.

This punishment is especially appropriate in that Nicholas's fart completes the sensual assault on Absolon that began in the first window scene. In that scene Chaucer showed Absolon effectively, and deservedly, offended in two of his five senses. His exquisite sense of taste is offended when he applies that kiss "ful savourly" to Alisoun's buttocks, and his appreciation of the smooth texture of a clean-shaven face is offended when he brushes up against that "rough" beard below Alisoun's nether cheeks. He immediately rubs his lips with dust and sand and straw and cloth to wipe away the foul affront to taste and touch. In composing the second window scene, Chaucer saw to it that Absolon was offended in his other three senses as well, for he clearly wanted to complete the pattern he had begun in the first scene.

[17] See *Sources and Analogues,* 108–11.

Absolon's sense of smell is the most obviously affronted. Absolon, of course, is inordinately concerned about smells. Before he goes to see Alisoun on Monday night he first chews liquorice and aromatic grains, then places a "trewe-love" (A 3692) under this tongue, all so that he will have sweet-smelling breath for his nocturnal encounter with Alisoun. He has already been specifically said to be "squaymous / Of fartyng" (A 3337–38). Chaucer has obviously set him up as the sort of man who would be most offended by Nicholas's olfactorily abusive fart.

Similarly, Chaucer sets Absolon up as the sort of person whose sense of hearing would be most offended by the noise of the fart (as loud as a "thonder-dent" (A 3807]). Absolon, we recall, is a vocalist and a musician. He plays music on a "smal rubible" (A 3331) and on a "gyterne" (A 3353). To his own musical accompaniment, he sings songs in a voice "gentil and smal" (A 3360). When he serenades Alisoun his voice quavers like a nightingale's, and just before he speaks to her on Monday night he coughs with a "semy soun" (A 3697) to get her attention. To a man so given to soft musical sounds, the sudden discordance of a fart as loud as a thunderclap is the perfect auditory put-down.

Less obviously offended than his other four senses is Absolon's sense of sight, for of course both window scenes take place in the dead of night. Still, it is important to notice that Chaucer was careful to round out his pattern of sensual affront to Absolon by violating this fifth sense as well. The force of Nicholas's fart in Absolon's face, Chaucer tells us, nearly blinds Absolon:

> This Nicholas anon leet fle a fart,
> As greet as it had been a thonder-dent,
> That with the strook he was almoost yblent.
>
> (A 3806–08)

This affront to Absolon's eyes is convincing evidence that Chaucer was eager to complete the pattern of sensual violation.

In the two window scenes, then, this fastidious, dancing, singing, sweet-smelling, finely-dressed barber-clerk is insulted through all five of his senses. Chaucer's purpose, surely, was to suggest that the worldly Absolon is far too sensual in his orientation:

> This Absolon, that jolif was and gay,
> Gooth with a sencer on the haliday,
> Sensynge the wyves of the parisshe faste.
> (A 3339–41)

Whether or not Chaucer intended a pun on "sencer," his elaborately complete affront to all of Absolon's senses later in the tale is a reminder that, as a parish clerk, Absolon ought not to have been preoccupied with his senses. Far from being merely humorous jests, Alisoun's presenting of her buttocks for a kiss and Nicholas's farting in Absolon's face were Chaucer's means of underlining a serious theme, the inappropriateness of behavior like Absolon's, especially in religious officials. They were Chaucer's means of demonstrating that the reward for such worldly behavior is not heavenly bliss, but scatological, as well as eschatological, unpleasantness.

In emphasizing Absolon's sensuality early in the tale and his sensory punishment later in the tale, Chaucer was reminding us that he who lives by his senses shall be punished by them, both on earth and in hell. Indeed, as a result of those two window scenes Absolon is really already in a kind of earthly hell. The Parson's remarks about "delices"—one of the three principle kinds of "defautes" punished in hell—are particularly appropriate:

> And forther over, they shul have defaute of alle manere delices. For certes, delices been after the appetites of the fyve wittes, as sighte, herynge, smellynge, savorynge, and touchynge. / But in helle hir sighte shal be ful of derknesse and of smoke, and therfore ful of teeres; and hir herynge ful of waymentynge and of gryntynge of teeth, as seith Jhesu Crist. / Hir nosethirles shullen be ful of stynkynge stynk; and, as seith Ysaye the prophete, "hir savoryng shal be ful of bitter

> galle"; / and touchynge of all hir body ycovered with "fir that nevere shal quenche, and with wormes that nevere shul dyen," as God seith by the mouth of Ysaye. (I 207–10)

Nicholas's fart, then, in completing the sensual affront to Absolon, gives the sinful Absolon—and the reader—a preview of hell.

The Parson's remarks about the futility of trying to escape or hide from the pains of hell are worth quoting:

> For certes, as seith Seint Jerome, "the erthe shal casten hym out of hym, and the see also, and the eyr also, that shal be ful of thonder-clappes and lightnynges." (I 174)

That "thonder-dent" from Nicholas's rectum is a preview of that "thonder-clappe" that shall signal the final punishment of the likes of Absolon.[18]

Whether or not modern students of Chaucer take seriously the two scatological tricks in the *Miller's Tale*, Chaucer himself clearly took them seriously. He added to his source materials both the kissing of the female buttocks and the fart, and he had good artistic reasons for doing so. Lest I be accused of irresponsibly making earnest of game, perhaps I should point out that I do not wish to deny the game, for the scatological tricks are first and eternally funny. I wish only to show that they are more than funny, for Chaucer added them to develop his characterizations, to advance his plot, and to convey his themes. I wish only to demonstrate that we must move beyond Root's statement that the *Miller's Tale* is just a churl's tale "which no sophistry can elevate into true art."[19] Even at his most churlish moments, Chaucer was a consummate artist.

[18] Edmund Reiss, in "Daun Gerveys in the *Miller's Tale*," *Papers on Language and Literature* 6 (1970): 115–24, suggests that when Absolon visits Gerveys to get the hot coulter he is really visiting the wrathful devil.

[19] Root, 176.

The *Miller's Tale* in China

[In the late 1980s I was privileged to be selected as a Fulbright Professor in Mainland China. I was sent—with my wife Anne and four teenaged children—to Chengdu, a thousand miles from any Chinese city I had ever heard of. Although at Sechuan University I taught only courses in American literature that year, I became acquainted with Professor Xiao Anpu, who taught British literature. Together we wrote this little article on the way Fang Zhong had translated Chaucer into Chinese. I was particularly interested to see how the translator handled—or avoided—the scatological parts of the *Miller's Tale*. "The *Miller's Tale* in China" first appeared in the *Chaucer Newsletter* 11 (1989): 3, 8.]

It will come as no surprise to readers of the *Chaucer Newsletter* that the People's Republic of China is not a hotbed of Chaucer studies. Still, Chaucer is read and appreciated in China, thanks almost entirely to the work of a Chinese scholar named Fang Zhong (sometimes written Fang Chong). Fang Zhong, who also styles himself Lu Lang, has translated most of Chaucer's poetry into Chinese. The purpose of this little article is to give some notion of the state of Chaucer studies in China by reporting briefly on the reliability of Fang Zhong's translation into Chinese of one of Chaucer's *Canterbury Tales*. We have selected the *Miller's Tale* because it is short, accessible, and bawdy.

Fang Zhong, sometime president of the Shanghai Foreign Literature Association and professor of English at Shanghai Institute of Foreign Languages, studied at Stanford University and the University of California from 1923 to 1927 and was for a time a student of J. S. P. Tatlock. He then returned to take up his academic career in his native China.

Fang Zhong began publishing individual translations of *Troilus and Criseyde* and of some of the Canterbury stories in the 1930s. The first translation of the tales (including all but the *Parson's Tale*) in book form came in 1955. He published *An Anthology of Chaucer* in 1960, and this was reprinted in 1980. A two-volume revised edition, comprising the complete works except the *Parson's Tale*, for which Fang Zhong provides a detailed summary, was brought out in 1983 by the Shanghai Translation Publishing House.

Fang Zhong's translations are based on Robinson's second (1957) edition, but in the preface to the 1983 edition he mentions John H. Fisher's new edition of Chaucer (1977) and says that he had "originally intended to revise my translation according to this new edition, but it is hard to have my wish fulfilled because I am old and infirm, and suffer from eye disease." At this writing Fang Zhong is 86 years old. We have used Fang Zhong's 1983 edition and the 1957 Robinson as the basis for our comparisons.

Fang Zhong's translation is prose. In making our comparisons, then, we were not interested in the translation as "poetry," but in the translation as "meaning." All we wanted to know was whether Chinese readers were likely to be getting, through Fang Zhong's translation, a reasonably accurate understanding of the basic plots, characters, and themes of Chaucer. The answer is that they are. The translation is essentially faithful to the Chaucerian Middle English. That it is so accurate is surprising enough, given the special problems of translating Chaucer into Chinese (see M. Chan, "On Translating Chaucer into Chinese," *Renditions* 8 [1977]: 39–51). There are, however, some discrepancies.

Our method for analyzing those discrepancies was simple enough. Xiao Anpu, a professor in the Foreign Langauages Department of Sichuan University in Chengdu, had read Chaucer only in Fang Zhong's translation, but never in Middle English. Peter G. Beidler, a Fulbright professor at Sichuan University in 1987–88, knew Chaucerian Middle English, but did not read Chinese. Xiao "back-translated" into modern English Fang Zhong's Chinese translation of the *Miller's Tale*, and Beidler then listed the more significant discrepancies between the back-translated modern English and the Middle English. We then analyzed the list and concluded that the discrepancies fell into two general categories: 1) elements changed by Fang Zhong to make the Chinese translation more vivid to a Chinese audience; and 2) elements omitted because they were deemed to be too bawdy for publication in a China which, even today, does not permit translations of *Lady Chatterly's Lover* and *Catch-22*.

Adjusting for a Chinese audience

Chaucerian ideas or words are changed to make the text more vivid to a Chinese audience in these instances:

Nicholas's songs. Fang Zhong apparently thought Chinese people would be unnecessarily puzzled by reference to two songs that Nicholas sings on a typical evening: "And *Angelus ad virginem* he song; / And after that he song the the Kynges Noote" (3216-17). Quite aware that a Chinese audience would not know what the *Angelus* was, and that modern scholars are puzzled about what the "King's Note" was, Fang Zhong renders these lines in more general terms, but in such a way as to emphasize Nicholas's penchant for the obscene: "After singing a hymn for prayer, he always sang some obscene songs."

Bathtub. Nicholas sends John to get himself, Alisoun, and Nicholas each "a knedyng trogh, or ellis a kymelyn" (3548). A kymelyn is a tub used for salting meat or brewing liquor. Such tubs are not often used in China. Fang Zhong came near enough to the mark by translating the term "bathtub."

First wife. Pretending to be worried about the terrible flood that Nicholas has predicted, Alisoun tells John that she is "thy trewe, verray wedded wyf" (3609). Fang Zhong, apparently wanting to make her case more convincing for a Chinese audience, has her tell John that she is "your faithful wife by the first marriage." First wives in China are considered more likely to be faithful than second wives. Second wives were sometimes called concubines in the days when men were permitted more than one wife.

Big mouth. When Absolon first comes to Alisoun's window on the night of his undoing, she rejects him outright: "Go forth thy wey, or I wol caste a ston, / And let me slepe, a twenty devel wey!" (3712–13). Fang Zhong, apparently knowing as little as most modern editors do about how to render a way of twenty devils, simply changes the meaning to emphasize Absolon's wordiness: "Shut your big mouth, or I will throw stones at you. Let me sleep. Get out of here!"

Softening the language

More interesting, perhaps, are the changes Fang Zhong made to eliminate or soften the sexual and scatological aspects of the tale. These are the parts that most modern readers find so delightful and so central to any informed understanding of Chaucer's purpose in the *Miller's Tale*. Below, are a number of such changes Fang Zhong made in his translation:

Cuckold. Chaucer tells us early in the tale that John was jealous and kept his young wife in a cage because he "demed hymself been lik a cokewold" (3226). For Chinese readers reading Fang Zhong's translation, John was afraid that "he would be a tortoise."

Queynte. Just after he proclaims his love for Alisoun, Nicholas "caughte hire by the queynte" (3276). Fang Zhong, he "held her tightly by the waist."

Fart. Chaucer tells us that Absolon was "somdeel squaymous / Of fartyng, and of speche daungerous" (3337–38). Fang Zhong allows the fart to disappear into thin air by telling us merely that Absolon "was rather reserved in conversation."

Hole. In the famous window scene, Alisoun is eager to get rid of her second suitor and at the same time to have a little fun:

> And at the wyndow out she putte hir hole,
> And Absolon, hym fil no bet ne wers,
> But with his mouth he kiste hir naked ers
> Ful savourly.
>
> (3732–35)

Fang Zhong skips the direct reference to "hole" and "ers," and refrains from mentioning the savorousness of Absolon's attack: "She projected her private parts out of the window, Absolon, keeping his mind on her, pressed his mouth near to her and kissed her naked hip without any hesitation." The Chinese have words for "queynte," "fart," and "hole," but those words rarely find their way into print, and certainly not from the pen of a fine scholar like Fang Zhong.

Burn. In the second window scene, Absolon gets a second reward in the shape of a hot coulter: "And he was redy with his iren hoot, / And Nicholas amydde the ers he smoot" (3809–10). Fang Zhong translates the coulter into a less phallic "ploughshare" and has Absolon aim it less directly: "He had prepared a red hot ploughshare. With it he poked the place between Nicholas's hips."

Alisoun's nether eye. Chaucer closes the *Miller's Tale* with a little summary of the punishments meted out to the three lecherous men:

> Thus swyved was this carpenteris wyf,
> For all his kepyng and his jalousye;
> And Absolon hath kist hir nether ye;
> And Nicholas is scalded in the towte.
>
> (3850–53)

Fang Zhong politely renders the verb "swyved" as "cheated out of," quietly drops the "toute," and alters the moral balance of the closing by totally neglecting poor Absolon's punishment: "Thus, the carpenter was cheated out of his wife, no matter how closely he watched her. And Nicholas's burn was by no means a light wound."

Given the censorship laws in China, it is not surprising that certain passages in Chaucer were altered in the only Chinese translation of the *Miller's Tale*. After all, certain of the so-called modern English "translations" of the tale do only slightly less violence to Chaucer's story (see *Chaucer Review* 19 [1985], 290–301). Indeed, it is surprising, and fortunate, that the *Miller's Tale* has been published at all in China, and we are delighted that Fang Zhong has made it so readily available, even in slightly altered form, for the enjoyment and edification of the Chinese people.

“Now, deere lady”: Absolon’s Marian Couplet in the *Miller’s Tale*

[This very short article is somewhat different from my usual work on the *Miller’s Tale* in that it deals with the deeply Christian associations of a two-line song that the love-sick clerk Absolon uses to serenade Alisoun. Perhaps to protect himself from the suspicions of Alisoun’s jealous husband John, Absolon sings her a couple of verses that sound very much like verses sung in praise of the Virgin Mary. In doing so he not only envisions an adulterous carnal sin inappropriate to a parish clerk, but also commits soul-endangering blasphemy. “ ‘Now, deere lady’ ” first appeared in *Chaucer Review* 39 (2004): 219–22.]

Every Chaucerian knows that both Nicholas and John in the *Miller’s Tale* are connected through Alisoun to Mary. In *Angelus ad virginem* Nicholas sings the role of Gabriel announcing to the Virgin that she will have a child, and the comedy of old John the carpenter depends in part on his similarities to the biblical and theatrical old Joseph the carpenter, husband to Mary. And, while previous scholars have noted certain Marian associations in Absolon’s singing to Alisoun,[1] they have not talked about the extent to which there are

[1] In “The *Canticum Canticorum* in the *Miller’s Tale*” (*Studies in Philology* 59 [1962]: 479–500), R. E. Kaske focuses on the later window scenes and particularly the parodic associations of lines 3698–3707 with the biblical *Song of Songs.* Of Absolon’s couplet in the first window scene

phrases that echo medieval lyrics to Mary in the couplet that Absolon sings to Alisoun the first time he visits her bedroom window:

> "Now, deere lady, if thy wille be,
> I praye yow that ye wole rewe on me."
> (I 3361–62)[2]

Teachers of the *Miller's Tale* have sometimes been challenged to explain why John is not suspicious when he hears Absolon serenade his lovely young wife. After all, John is said to be "jalous" and to hold his wife "narwe in cage" because he is aware of the difference in their ages and "demed hymself been lik a cokewold" (I 3224–26). I propose that John is not suspicious here because he hears Absolon's couplet to his "deere lady" as a song to the Virgin asking for her mercy. It is more significant than has been supposed that Chaucer describes Absolon's delivery of the couplet as singing (I 3360) and that John describes it as chanting (I 3367)—the kind of vocalizing that clerics would have done to honor Mary. It would not be surprising that a parish clerk (I 3312, 3348, 3657) would know a number of songs to Mary and use them in his courtship of Alisoun, particularly if he wanted to keep from arousing her husband's suspicions.

Kaske says only that it is "a little masterpiece of banality" (492). In "The Parody of Medieval Music in the *Miller's Tale*" (*Journal of English and Germanic Philology* 73 [1974]: 176–88), Jesse M. Gellrich locates the various references to music in the tale, among them songs to Mary. Of the couplet I speak of here he says only in the most general terms that Absolon sings "lyrics and epithets that are popular praises of Mary" (182). More recently, Susanna Greer Fein, in "Why Did Absolon Put a 'Trewelove' under His Tongue?: Herb Paris as a Healing 'Grace' in Middle English Literature" (*Chaucer Review* 25 [1991]: 302–17), shows that the herbal sprig that Absolon puts under his tongue before a later visit to Alisoun's window clearly associates Absolon's "devotion" to Alisoun with his devotion to Mary. Fein does not specifically discuss the couplet Absolon sings in the first window scene. In "Nicholas's 'Angelus ad Virginem' and the Mocking of Noah" (*Yearbook of English Studies* 22 [1992]: 162–80), John B. Friedman talks about the complex biblical associations of Nicholas's song to the Virgin at the start of the *Miller's Tale*. Friedman does not discuss Absolon's couplet. The copious notes in these four articles will direct readers to other references to Mary in the *Miller's Tale*.

[2] This and subsequent quotations from Chaucer are taken from *The Riverside Chaucer*, ed. Larry D. Benson, 3rd edn. (Boston, 1987).

Karen Saupe's recent anthology of Middle English lyrics to Mary offers us a convenient means by which to examine the similarities in phrasing between Absolon's couplet to Alisoun and the phrasing of several of the lyrics.[3] Absolon's opening address to the "deere lady" has echoes in many Marian lyrics of Chaucer's time, where Mary is referred to not only as "mooder," "mayden," "flour," and "queene," but also as "lady," "levedi," "ladi bright," and other such variations. Chaucer himself used the epithet "lady" for Mary in his more obviously Marian lyrics. In line 16 of "An ABC," for example, he refers to Mary as "lady bright" and in the next line as "ladi deere." He uses variations of "lady" in reference to Mary eight other times in the poem.

It would not have been lost on readers that Absolon is said specifically, in the second line of his song, to "praye" to his "lady" for mercy. Praying to the Virgin, of course, was what a cleric did if he was in a pious or contrite mood. The second part of the first line of Absolon's song, where he politely tells Alisoun that he wants her help "if thy wille be," would not have seemed unfamiliar to readers who knew Marian lyrics. For example, in the lyric that Saupe numbers 75 in her section on "The joys of Mary," the speaker asks for help from his "Ladi, Seynte Marie, yif that thi wille were."[4] And as for Absolon's prayer in the second line of his song that his lady "rewe on me," that phrase echoes another line in Saupe's chapter on "The Joys of Mary," in lyric 74: "Levedi, for that suete joy thu reu on me."[5] Several lines in one of the Annunciation lyrics sound remarkably like Absolon's prayer. Consider these from Saupe's lyric 8:

> Mi swete levedi, her mi bene
> And reu of me yif thi wille is.[6]

[3] Karen Saupe, ed., *Middle English Marian Lyrics* (Kalamazoo, MI, 1998).

[4] Saupe, ed., *Middle English Marian Lyrics*, 144 (line 61).

[5] Saupe, ed., *Middle English Marian Lyrics*, 140 (line 25).

[6] Saupe, ed., *Middle English Marian Lyrics,* 52 (lines 7–8).

In his song the supposedly lovesick Absolon[7] plays with the tradition of the love lyric to Mary, both to lead a woman to break her marriage vows and to mask to her husband his true motives.

Absolon's couplet conflates the language of prayer with the language of seduction, just as the Marian lyrics were sometimes romantic, if not erotic, in tone. Consider other lines in Saupe's lyric 8:

> Swete levedi, of me thu reowe
> And have merci of thin knicht.
>
> . . . . .
>
> Levedi milde, softe and swote,
> I crie thee merci, ic am thi mon.[8]

Saupe has a section that she calls "*Chansons d'Aventure* and Love Quests." We find these lines in her lyric 77:

> Ase y me rod this ender day
> By grene wode to seche play,
> Mid herte y thohte al on a may,
> Suetest of alle thinge.
>
> . . . . .
>
> Of alle thinge y love hire mest:
> My dayes blis, my nyhtes rest.[9]

Are we in a medieval romance here or in a Marian lyric? We are in the latter, of course, but there is sometimes a fine line between them, and we can understand why the pious old John would not be suspicious of Absolon's love-couplet.

[7] This is not the place to indulge in any detail my suspicions that Absolon's heterosexual orientation is somewhat dubious, but I do wonder why Absolon seems to think of women in the plural (see, for example, I 3336, 3341–42) as often as he thinks of Alisoun in the singular, and why he seems more comfortable with the real Gerveys, his "Freend so deere" (I 3775), than he does with the idealized woman he takes to be Alisoun, his "lemman" (I 3705, 3719, 3726). Absolon's romanticized attraction for an imagined Alisoun contrasts starkly to the earthy lust of Nicholas for the actual Alisoun.

[8] Saupe, ed., *Middle English Marian Lyrics,* 52 (lines 15–16, 21–22).

[9] Saupe, ed., *Middle English Marian Lyrics,* 147 (lines 1–4, 19–20).

In my reading of the tale, John is still a foolish old man who should know better than to marry a pretty young woman, to take as a boarder the lusty Nicholas, to accept so gullibly Nicholas's prediction of a coming flood, and to cut his rope without verifying the rising waters. But we can perhaps forgive his failure to be suspicious of Absolon's prayer to the Virgin. Certainly we need see no contradiction between his jealousy of his wife in general and his failure to be made jealous in particular by Absolon's song to his wife.

It is less easy to forgive Absolon for using the powers and prayers of his clerical office, lowly though the office of parish clerk was, to seduce a married woman. Any reader of Marian lyrics would have known that many of the prayers to Mary were prayers for forgiveness of sin and for help in avoiding sin. Saupe's lyric 75 is a good example:

> Ladi, Seynte Marie, yif that thi wille were,
> As thou are ful of joye and I am ful of care,
> Thou help me out of sinne and lat me falle namare;
> And geve me grace in erthe my sinnes to reue sare.
>
> . . . . .
>
> Y praye thou her mi stevene and let my soule nevere spille
> In non of the sinnes sevene. . . .[10]

To any reader familiar with the real Marian lyrics, in which sinners prayed to Mary for pity and for help in avoiding sins, the blasphemy of Absolon's false prayer would not have been lost. Absolon, after all, prays not for forgiveness of his sins but for Alisoun's pity as he attempts to seduce her into sin. He prays not to avoid the seven deadly sins, but to get Alisoun to join him in lechery, the seventh of those sins.

In a later window scene Absolon kneels as he prepares to receive Alisoun's kiss: "This Absolon doun sette hym on his knees" (I 3723). Has he so convinced himself that the woman he thinks he loves

[10] Saupe, ed., *Middle English Marian Lyrics,* 144 (lines 61–64, 67–68).

really is the Virgin that he feels justified in blasphemously kneeling before her as he begs for the kiss that is to be his undoing?[11] Perhaps not, but later, as he rushes through the night to get the hot coulter of his vengeance against the real woman he had idealized as his own private Virgin, Absolon proudly proclaims, "My soule bitake I unto Sathanas" (I 3750). If his blasphemous misuse of a prayer to Mary is any measure of his sinfulness, his soul's journey to Satan may not be a long one.

[11] It may be significant that Absolon gets down on "knees" in the plural. It was apparently common English practice in the Middle Ages that a two-kneed kneel was reserved for doing honor to saints and God, while a one-kneed one was for noblemen and noble women. J. W. Robinson refers to "the custom of the English, who knelt on only one knee to man, reserving two knees for God" ("The York Play of the Slaughter of the Innocents and the Play of Herod the Great," in *Studies in Fifteenth-Century Stagecraft,* ed. J. W. Robinson [Kalamazoo, MI, 1991], 144–75, at 155). Robinson gives in his note 32 supporting references to *Dives and Pauper* and the *Lay Mass Book.* A painting of Matthew Paris on two knees before the Virgin and child appears in London, British Library, Royal MS 14.C.vii, fol. 6.

New Terminology for Sources and Analogues: or, Let's Forget the Lost French Source for the *Miller's Tale*

[Frustrated at the lack of precision in the way we Chaucer scholars have come to use the terms *source* and *analogue*, I decided to offer some definitions that we might all agree on. And while I was at it, I challenged the notion that there was a "lost source" for the *Miller's Tale*. The "Just Say Yes" article referenced in the second sentence appears below in this volume (see pp. 161–90). "New Terminology for Sources and Analogues" first appeared in *Studies in the Age of Chaucer* 28 (2006): 225–30.]

We have grown sloppy in our use of the terms *source* and *analogue,* sometimes even using them as if they were synonyms. In an earlier essay,[1] I urged that Chaucerians should refine our use of the terms by agreeing on definitions of three terms: *source* for a work that we are sure Chaucer knew and used; *hard analogue* for a work that would have been available to Chaucer, that has strong plot and character connections with the Chaucerian tale under consideration, but that lacks the verbal parallels that would let us be sure it was a

[1] "Just Say Yes, Chaucer Knew the *Decameron*: Or, Bringing the *Shipman's Tale* Out of Limbo," in *The Decameron and the Canterbury Tales,* ed. Leonard Michael Koff and Brenda Deen Schildgen (Teaneck, NJ: Fairleigh Dickinson University Press, 2002), esp. 41–42.

source; and *soft analogue* for a work that, either because of its late date or because of its narrative distance from the Chaucerian tale, Chaucer almost certainly did not know. In this essay I want to propose a further refinement of our terminology and then lay to rest the notion of a lost French source for the *Miller's Tale.*

Whatever our reasons for wanting to identify the various models for Chaucer's work, we need to be more precise than most of us have often been in the past. Different scholars, of course, have different reasons for wanting to identify the specific antecedents for a Chaucerian work. Some of us who seek to locate sources are driven by a desire to know more about Chaucer's biography: where he traveled, what languages he knew, how widely he had read, how well he remembered what he had read, and even whether a given work can be dated to what might be called his "French period," his "Italian period," or his "English period." For most of us, the interest is less in Chaucer's life than in his literature. Whatever our theoretical orientation, we seek to establish what Chaucer's most likely sources were, or at least what the closest analogues were, so that we can attempt to measure the distance from them of Chaucer's own work. We seek to identify patterns in the kind and number of changes that Chaucer made in transferring old literary wine to a new bottle: his purposes, for example, in adding a scene or a character, or in cutting the first hundred lines of a narrative, or in making a certain character less likable, or more independent, or more full of pride. Sometimes we seek only to identify what elements Chaucer chose not to change.

Volume 2 of the Boydell and Brewer *Sources and Analogues* contains my chapter on the *Miller's Tale.* While working on that chapter, I found myself frustrated by the limitation that the two standard terms *source* and *analogue* gave me. There were, after all, lots of analogues for the *Miller's Tale,* but none of them had yet emerged as an undisputed source. There had been talk about a lost source, but I concluded that such a source, if it ever existed, could not help us because we could not know what it might have been like or how Chaucer might have changed its characters or its narrative line. I found myself needing a refined terminology to do what I thought was my duty in helping Chaucerians talk about the antecedents to the *Miller's Tale.* In the end, I decided that only one of the various analogues is both old enough and close enough to the *Miller's Tale* in plot and language that it could have been Chaucer's actual source: the Middle Dutch *Heile van Beersele.* The story of Heile is not precisely a source, since we cannot be sure that Chaucer knew it, but it is surely more than an analogue, at least in the sense that the other, post-Chaucerian tales are analogues. The term that works best for *Heile van Beersele* is hard analogue with near-source status.

Amending my earlier list, I therefore propose the following five terms and definitions:

hard source: a specific work for which we have an extant copy and that we know, from verbal similarities, character names, and plot sequences, that Chaucer used. An example would be Boccaccio's *Teseida* as a hard source for the *Knight's Tale.*

soft source: a literary, historical, philosophical, classical, religious, mythological, biographical, anecdotal, proverbial, musical, or artistic work that Chaucer almost certainly knew and probably remembered (consciously or not) as he wrote and that provided at least a general or distant influence upon some elements in his own work. Examples would be Boethius's *Consolation of Philosophy* and Statius's *Thebaid* as soft sources for the *Knight's Tale*, the biblical account of the Annunciation for the *Miller's Tale*, and the *Knight's Tale* itself as a soft source for the *Miller's Tale*.

hard analogue: a literary work that is old enough in its extant form that Chaucer could have known it and that bears striking resemblances, usually more narrative than verbal, to a Chaucerian work. We should normally speak of a hard analogue when we do not have a hard source. If it is an especially strong candidate, we might use terminology like hard analogue with near-source status. Examples would be

Decameron 8.1 for the *Shipman's Tale* and *Heile van Beersele* for the *Miller's Tale*. On this last, see my argument below.

soft analogue: a literary work that, because of its late date or its remoteness from its Chaucerian counterpart, Chaucer almost certainly did not know, but that may provide clues to another work that Chaucer may have known. Examples might be Sercambi's *De avaritia et luzuria* for the *Shipman's Tale* and a nineteenth-century Portuguese tale that sounds a bit like the *Merchant's Tale* and that may even have derived from it.

lost source: a literary work that is not extant but that may have existed at one time and that Chaucer may possibly have known, if indeed it ever did exist. The concept of a lost source should be advanced only with the greatest caution. Any argument for such a source will be strengthened by manuscript or historical evidence that it once existed. Positing such a work should be done only with the full knowledge that if such a work did exist, we have almost no idea what it was like.

The idea of a lost source has featured prominently in discussions of the *Miller's Tale.* These discussions have often demonstrated considerably less caution than the case warrants. In the rest of this short essay I want to argue specifically against this once-prevalent notion that there was such a source.

We know that Chaucer knew at least some French fabliaux. There is no question, for example, that the most likely source for the *Reeve's Tale* is the Old French *Le meunier et les .II. clers.* Since Chaucer probably knew that fabliau, it seems quite possible that he knew other thirteenth-century French comic tales as well. There is not a scrap of manuscript evidence, however, that a French source for the *Miller's Tale* ever actually existed. I have read widely in the Old French fabliaux to see whether I could find French counterparts to three of the physical properties of the *Miller's Tale* that are fundamental to its story line: (1) the suspended tubs, (2) the bedroom window, and (3) the hot poker. So far as I can tell, none of these properties plays in any extant French fabliau a role parallel to the one it plays in the *Miller's Tale.*

1. *The suspended tubs.* At Nicholas's urging, old John hangs three tubs from the beams in his house. These are variously described a "tubbe," a "knedyng trogh," and a "kymelyn" (I 3564, 3620–21).[2] To be sure, we do find the occasional tub in the French fabliaux, where it typically serves for bathing with one's lover or for hastily hiding a wife's lover from a suspicious or suddenly returned husband. In none of the French fabliaux, however, is a tub suspended from above, and in none is one used as an ark to escape a predicted flood. Never, indeed, in any of the French fabliaux is there a predicted flood.

2. *The bedroom window.* The window in the *Miller's Tale* plays an important role in the plot. It appears three times, first when Absolon serenades Alisoun, next when Absolon kisses Alisoun's buttocks, and finally when Absolon returns with his hot coulter and gets his revenge, not against Alisoun, but against Nicholas. I have found no French fabliau in which a window plays any important role. I find passing references to a few windows here and there, but in none of these does a man serenade a woman on the other side of her bedroom window or ask for a window-kiss from such a woman, and in none of them does anyone present her or his buttocks out the window for a kiss.

3. *The hot poker.* After being insulted by Alisoun, Absolon rushes to the shop of his friend the blacksmith Gerveys and borrows a hot coulter. We do find a couple of references to a hot poker in the Old French fabliaux, but there it is quite different from the one we find in the *Miller's Tale. De l'aventure d'Ardenne* is a tale about a man too stupid to know how to make love to his wife and who has to be shown how by his mother-in-law. Near the end of the tale is an

[2] Quotations are taken from the *Riverside Chaucer,* ed. Larry D. Benson (Boston: Houghton Mifflin, 1987).

absurd sequence in which the stupid husband finds an awl with which he thinks to puncture a wine-bag to collect some wine to take to his wife. He stirs the fire with the awl to make some light. In the faint light he sees the exposed bottom of a sleeping knight and strikes, thinking he is puncturing a wineskin. The only other hot poker in an Old French fabliaux appears in *De la dame escoilliee,* in which a woman insists on bossing her husband. She is eventually "castrated" by a count who has his knights hold her face-down on the ground and then makes incisions and pretends to remove the testicles from her buttocks. Near the end of that troubling scene, the count threatens that he will cauterize the roots of her testicles so the testicles do not grow back, and he tells one of his retainers to go and heat up an iron coulter. No such mission is necessary, however, because the newly gelded lady swears that she will henceforth be fully obedient to her husband. In neither of these tales is the hot poker similar in function to the one we find in the *Miller's Tale,* where Absolon purposefully goes to a blacksmith, asks to borrow a hot coulter, then runs with it through the streets to punish someone for an insulting humiliation.

It does not appear, then, that the suspended tub, the window, and the hot iron used as a weapon of punishment can be found in the Old French fabliaux or that these three props are in any important way associated with French fabliaux. Wouldn't it be nice if we could locate a medieval comic tale about a woman who is accosted at her night-window by successive lovers and who hides one of them in a tub suspended from the roofbeams? Wouldn't it be nice if that tale included an ass-kissing at that window and, later, a man's buttocks stuck out that same window? Wouldn't it be nice if in that same tale the one who did the kissing then avenged himself by burning someone at that window with a hot iron? And wouldn't it be nice if that tale was old enough that Chaucer could have known it, was in a language that Chaucer probably recognized, and was available in a country he is known to have had connections with?

There is, of course, such a tale: the Middle Dutch *Heile van Beersele,* dating probably from the third quarter of the fourteenth century. That is the only tale that I include in the chapter on the *Miller's*

Tale in the new *Sources and Analogues.* It has been known to us for more than eighty years, but has been largely ignored as Chaucer's likely source because A. J. Barnouw, the man who brought it to the attention of the scholarly world, claimed that he had found not Chaucer's probable source but merely a Middle Dutch adaptation of a lost French original that Chaucer would have known.[3]

Why have scholars been so reluctant to take seriously the idea that *Heile van Beersele* was, of all of the analogues to the *Miller's Tale,* Chaucer's most likely source, preferring to chase after the chimera of a lost French source? Perhaps they were reluctant to challenge the experts, the scholars who stated with such assurance that there must have been such a source. Perhaps they wanted to posit a French fabliau with ass-kissing and farting so they could blame the scatological elements of the *Miller's Tale* not on Chaucer but on one of those "primitive" French entertainers famous for their fascination with the lower body parts. Perhaps they assumed that no Dutch writer was clever enough to invent such a plot, but instead must have been merely copying something from French. Or perhaps they assumed that Chaucer, despite his having had a wife from Hainault and a patron born in Ghent, and despite the likelihood that in his various diplomatic or commercial functions he would have had dealings with the nearby Low Countries, just across the channel from Dover, never learned enough Middle Dutch to read the tale.

[3] "Chaucer's 'Milleres Tale,' " *Modern Language Review* 7 (1912): 145–48. Barnouw admitted that "no trace" of a French fabliau of the *Miller's Tale* type had ever been found. Barnouw's opinion was picked up by Stith Thompson, who presented the antecedents to the *Miller's Tale* in the original 1941 *Sources and Analogues.* Thompson notes that "the argument for a lost French fabliau as Chaucer's immediate source is strengthened by the presence of a fourteenth-century fabliau in Flemish." See Stith Thompson, "The *Miller's Tale,*" in *Sources and Analogues of Chaucer's Canterbury Tales,* ed. W. F. Bryan and Germaine Dempster (Chicago: University of Chicago Press, 1941), 106. For my chapter on the *Miller's Tale,* see *Sources and Analogues of the Canterbury Tales,* vol. 2, ed. Robert M. Correale and Mary Hamel (Woodbridge, Suffolk: D. S. Brewer, 2005), 249–75.

We cannot know now why scholars have chosen to bypass the analogue that we have in order to imagine a source that we do not have. I would like to think, however, that if they had had access to the terminology that I suggest above, they would have been more careful to distinguishing among the various analogues and to describe them, and that my words of caution about when to posit a lost source would have made them more reluctant to drag the red herring of such a possibility across the trail of those who sought to discover what was most original in the *Miller's Tale.* And I would like to think that they might even agree with me that we should read *Heile van Beersele* as a hard analogue with near-source status when we seek to discover what is most distinctively Chaucerian in the *Miller's Tale.* In any case, I suggest that, at least until some real evidence is discovered, we forget about that "lost" French source.

From Snickers to Laughter: Believable Comedy in Chaucer's *Miller's Tale*

[Having established in my chapter on the *Miller's Tale* for the new *Sources and Analogues of the Canterbury Tales* that the Middle Dutch *Heile van Beersele* was the most likely source for Chaucer's tale of John, Alisoun, Nicholas, and Absolon, I welcomed the chance to show how Chaucer, while building on the Heile story, also distanced himself from it. Both tales are funny, I argued, but Chaucer's is believably funny. Unlike the plot of the Heile story, the plot of the *Miller's Tale* is sufficiently realistic that we can almost imagine it actually happening to us or to people we know. Its characters behave much more like real people than do the sketchy one-dimensional characters in *Heile van Beersele*. While we snicker at the exaggerated comic actions of the people in the Middle Dutch tale, we laugh at those in the Middle English one because they sound a lot like you and me. "From Snickers to Laughter" first appeared in *Medieval English Comedy*, ed. Sandra M. Hordis and Paul Hardwick (Turnhout, Belgium: Brepols, 2007), 195–208.]

The closest we will probably ever have to Chaucer's source for the *Miller's Tale* is the Middle Dutch tale *Heile van Beersele.* Of the various analogues, it is the only one old enough that Chaucer could have been familiar with it. Also, it is in a language that Chaucer probably knew and is from a region that Chaucer had visited and with which he had family, business, and other ties. There are, furthermore, many parallels in plot and phrasing that make a connection almost inevitable.[1]

A comparison of *Heile van Beersele* with the *Miller's Tale* shows that while both tales are funny, Chaucer's tale is far more believably funny than the Middle Dutch tale. Time after time, Chaucer shows that he wanted to make his story more realistic than his source was. In this essay, however, I will generally use the term "believable" rather than the term "realistic" because the term "Chaucerian realism" is so fraught with multiple meanings that to use it is to invite confusion.[2] There may have been a number of reasons for that greater believability, but I propose that one of them was that Chaucer wanted his audience to feel that the characters were not just made-up people in an unlikely anecdote, or cartoon characters in a frame, but more like folks who act within the realm of imaginable human action. Indeed, it is almost as if Chaucer wanted his audience to be able to imagine the actions of the story as taking place on a stage with live actors performing the actions before our eyes. The plot is, of course, still pretty outlandish, but at least the people in Chaucer's little comedy act within the realm of human possibility.

[1] I present the full argument for the connection between the two tales in the chapter on the *Miller's Tale* in *Sources and Analogues of the Canterbury Tales,* ed. Robert M. Correale and Mary Hamel (Woodbridge, Suffolk: D. S. Brewer, 2005), volume 2, pp. 249–75. All of my quotations are taken from the edition of *Heile van Beersele* in that volume. The translations, though based on the version given there, reflect at times an alternative phrasing. My quotations from the *Miller's Tale* are taken from the first fragment of the *Canterbury Tales* in the *Riverside Chaucer*, 3rd edn., ed. Larry D. Benson (Boston: Houghton Mifflin, 1987).

[2] In his *Chaucerian Realism* (Cambridge: D. S. Brewer, 1994), Robert Myles identifies some of the kinds of realism that philosophical and semiological semanticists talk about: foundational realism, epistemological realism, ethical realism, semiotic and linguistic realism, intentional realism, psychological realism, Cratylic realism, scholastic realism, and so on (see pp. 1–2 of his book for some preliminary definitions). In this chapter by "realism" I mean something much simpler: that the actions of the characters would have been recognized as plausible by readers, who would be more likely to say, "yeah, that is sort of outlandish, but I can almost believe it," rather than, "hey, no way would people I know do that." My thinking here is in line with that of Dieter Mehl, who speaks in *Geoffrey Chaucer: An Introduction to His Narrative Poetry*

The increased believability of Chaucer's version of the tale alters the nature of the comedy. It is one thing to laugh at the words and actions of characters whom we cannot quite believe in. It is something different to laugh at—and sometimes with—people who seem to be more like ones we know, people who are more nearly like ourselves. I do understand, of course, that we can know little about the responses of audiences to tales told or read six centuries ago, and I shall not attempt to speculate in any detail about the quality of the laughter that Middle Dutch audiences would have given to the story of Heile and her customers, or about the different quality of the laughter English audiences would have given to the story of Alisoun and her suitors. I do, however, invite readers of my comparisons below to assess the nature of their own responses to scenes that seem to be made-up or cartoon-like, as opposed to their responses to scenes that seem far more likely actually to have happened to actual in-the-flesh people.

Dating from the second half of the fourteenth century, the Middle Dutch *Heile van Beersele* is a short fabliau-like tale of ninety-five octosyllabic couplets. It is about an Antwerp prostitute who makes appointments on the same evening with three customers, a miller named Willem, an unnamed priest, and a blacksmith named Hughe. The humor of the piece lies mostly in the fact that the three appointments that are intended to follow each other begin to bump into each other. While the miller is still with Heile, the priest comes a-knocking. Heile hides the miller in a hanging trough, then lets the priest in. After the priest has satisfied himself sexually, he preaches a little sermon about a coming flood, a sermon that the miller up in the trough hears. When the third visitor, the blacksmith, knocks for his turn with Heile, the busy lady tries to send him away, but he begs for at least a kiss. Heile persuades the priest to let the smith kiss his buttocks. Afterwards the angry smith rushes home to his forge and

(Cambridge: Cambridge University Press, 1986) of "the precise details of observed every day life" in the *Miller's Tale*. We get, Mehl says, "a sense of watching a more familiar world, a world that does not demand abstract reflection but only an immediate human fellow-feeling" (175).

returns with a hot poker that he then uses to scorch the butt of the priest. The priest's cry for "Water, water" signals to the miller that the predicted flood has come. He cuts the rope holding up his trough and comes crashing down, breaking an arm and a leg.

The nine examples I give below show Chaucer transforming the unlikely fictional materials of *Heile van Beersele* into more likely fictional materials. I do not pause after each one to say, "Gee, isn't that funny?" I do, however, invite readers to consider whether in making his own tale more believable, Chaucer transformed an audience's snickering at the outlandish plots and characters in the Middle Dutch tale into something more like genuine amusement.

Tale of a tub

Heile happens to have hanging from the beams in her house a large trough. We do not learn ahead of time that it is there, and the only explanation we get of why it is there is Heile's to her first customer, Willem, on the arrival of her second customer, the priest. The explanation is that it sometimes comes in handy:

> Heile seide, "daer boven hangt .i. bac,
> Dies ic hier voermaels ghemac
> Hadde te menegen stonden."
>
> (67–69)
>
> Heile said, "up there hangs a trough that I have found convenient here on many previous occasions."]

We are left to imagine in what ways it may have been "convenient" to her in the past—presumably to hide other clients who did not want to be discovered in the arms of a prostitute. And because the Middle Dutch author does not say, we are left to imagine how Willem manages to climb into the tub. We are not told how high the tub hangs, though we are presumably to imagine that it is pretty high off the floor, because Willem later breaks his arm and leg when he falls from it. Are we to imagine him initially climbing into the tub by standing on a high table, or shinnying up a rope, or climbing a ladder? In fact, we do not know because the author does not tell us.

Chaucer leaves far less for us to be puzzled at. We know why the three tubs are hanging from the beams—because at Nicholas's direction, foolish old John collects them, provisions them, and suspends them from the beams. And we know how the three characters get into the tubs—by means of ladders that, following Nicholas's instructions, John has built. We "see" the old carpenter hanging the tubs and provisioning them, see him using the ladder he has built to climb into it. Is it funny? Well, yes. I find no humor in the fact that a tub hangs in Heile's bedroom and that a man somehow gets into it. I find great humor in old John's feverishly acquiring the tubs, hanging them, provisioning them, building ladders for them, and finally, exhausted, climbing a ladder into his private little Noah's ark.

Counting the times

The Middle Dutch author tells us that the priest makes love with Heile three times before the third lover, Hughe the smith, arrives:

> Heile dede den pape te ghemake
> Ende alsi die wiekewake
> Driewerf . . . .
>
> (75–77)
>
> [Heile made the priest happy, and they made love three times . . . .]

Some readers or hearers may find the priest's stamina impressive, but I find it just puzzling. We are not told that priest is a randy teenager in the prime of his youth. Whatever his sexual recovery time, it would eat up a lot of the evening for him to perform three times, even with the skilled professional that we imagine Heile to be. More puzzling is why Heile, who knows that she has one client hanging in the trough above and another hanging around outside waiting his turn, would let the priest proceed at such a leisurely pace. We can perhaps imagine an explanation—that she is afraid of him, for example, or that she needs his priestly blessing, or that she does not want him to summon her to the ecclesiastical courts, or that he offers her more money—but in fact the text offers no such explanation. Three times is not impossible, but little is gained, except perhaps a snicker, by giving him an exaggerated number of "wiekewakes" with so unprofessional a prostitute.

By being less specific Chaucer makes the sexual activity of Alisoun and Nicholas more credible:

> And thus lith Alisoun and Nicholas,
> In bisynesse of myrthe and of solas,
> Til that the belle of laudes gan to rynge,
> And freres in the chauncel gonne synge.
> (3653–56)

We presume that the two young lovers, finally united in bed, are an active pair, but Chaucer does not strain our credulity by specifying precisely how often they make love.[3] The humor comes not in the number of times the randy-handy Nicholas makes love with Alisoun, but in the success of his clever plan to fool old John and bed his wife. Of course, there is more humor coming, as we come to see that the too-too-solid flesh of young Nicholas is soon to pay the price for his cleverness.

Preaching a sermon

After he makes love three times with Heile, the priest preaches her a little mini-sermon:

> Ghinc die pape liggen ghewaghen
> Uter ewangelien menech woert.

[3] By not mentioning the number here, Chaucer is consistent with his technique elsewhere. In three of the four most likely sources for the *Reeve's Tale* (conveniently gathered together and translated in volume 1 of *Sources and Analogues of the Canterbury Tales*), the first lover brags that he has made love to the young woman six or seven times. Chaucer tells us only that Aleyn and Malyne "were aton" (4197). To be sure, Aleyn later brags that he has "swyved" Malyne "thries" (see lines 4265–66), but the context suggests that the number is probably the result of a bragging college boy exaggerating his prowess to a chum. There is no bragging in *Heile van Beersele*, where the number is stated by the narrator as a simple fact.

> Oec soe seidi dit bat voert,
> Dat die tijt noch soude comen
> Dat God die werelt soude doemen,
> Beide met watre ende met viere;
> Ende dat soude wesen sciere
> Dat al die werelt verdrinken soude,
> Grote ende clene, jonge ende oude.
> (78–86)
>
> [Then the priest quoted many words from the scriptures. He also said that the time would soon come when God would destroy the world with water and fire, drowning everyone in the world, great and small, young and old.]

The priest's motivation here is not clear. Why, after making love with a prostitute, would the priest preach such a sermon? Perhaps we can imagine a plausible reason—for example, that he feels guilty about his sinful lust and so warns both himself and Heile that they should get right with God before death takes them—but in fact the Middle Dutch author gives no such explanation, and the priest's sermon remains a puzzling anomaly.

Chaucer's Nicholas makes a somewhat similar prediction about a coming flood that will drown all the world, but he does so not after he has sex with Alisoun, but before. Indeed, his goal is to make it possible for him to have sex with Alisoun, not somehow to atone for his having had it already. Nicholas's prediction to the foolish John that a second Noah's flood is coming is part of an elaborate plan to convince Alisoun that he is cleverer than John and to get rid of John so that he can spend a joyous night in bed with Alisoun: "For this was his desir and hire also" (3407). Nicholas's plan, of course, is outlandish and, on the face of it, so improbable that it can never work. It does work, however, because Chaucer has made John precisely the sort of funny old fool who would believe the prediction. He is foolish enough to imagine that he can cage his wife, even as he allows into the cage a randy young college boy. He is foolish enough not to imagine that his wife could be attracted to Nicholas or indeed to Absolon, who one night serenades his wife outside their bedroom window. He is foolish enough to imagine that God could select him to be a second Noah, even though God had made a covenant with Noah never to send another such flood. We believe the forecast flood in neither tale. In Chaucer's tale, however, we accept it as a funny ruse that works precisely because its intended fictional audience, old John, is foolish enough to swallow it, hook, line, and trickster.

Rejecting a suitor

Heile is a prostitute in need of money who does what prostitutes in need of money sometimes have to do: makes appointments with three different men spaced far enough apart that she can make a good night's wage by pleasuring them all. That part seems logical enough. What is strange, however, is that an experienced professional would not have spaced the appointments farther apart so that the men's visits would not overlap, or that she would not have kept better track of the time so that she could have sent one on his satisfied way before the next came knocking. A reader's puzzlement at the Middle Dutch story is even more pronounced when Heile rejects Hughe the smith, her third appointment. Hughe is, after all, both a neighbour and a customer who would have been good for additional business in the coming weeks and months. Instead of apologizing to him or whispering that she is busy and asking him to return later that night or another time, Heile cruelly spurns him. When he asks for at least a kiss, she tells the priest to humiliate him:

> "Ay, here, laet cussen desen knape
> U achterste inde, hi sal wanen wel
> Dat ict ben ende niemen el;
> Sone saeghdi boerde nie so goet."
>
> (110–13)

> ["Ah, sir, let this fellow kiss your behind, and he will surely think that it is I and no one else. You've never seen such a good jest."]

We might imagine, if we want to, that Heile is exhausted after her four sexual encounters (one with the miller and three with the priest) and is therefore motivated to spurn a fifth, but in fact the text offers no justification for such an imagining. Besides, surely we have reason to doubt that a prostitute-for-hire, even if she were weary, would insult a paying customer. No, the plot requires the buttocks-kissing so that the smith will be angry enough to go fetch the hot iron, but no actual prostitute could afford to treat her appointed clients so outrageously. It is just bad business.

Chaucer makes the whole scene more believable by making Alisoun a wife rather than a prostitute. Frustrated by a marriage to a man perhaps thrice her age, she arranges to take one lover, not three. The overlapping of the lovers in the *Miller's Tale* happens only because the uninvited Absolon insists on coming by. The first "suitor," her husband John, belongs there, since it is his home, and he is properly aloft snoring away. Alisoun rebuffs and insults her third suitor, Absolon with a cruel jest because she does not like him and because she has a lover she likes better. Absolon has no appointment with her and is not welcome. When he will not take no as her answer but begs instead for a kiss, she is for that reason motivated to play her nasty trick on him. She behaves just as a frisky young wife, in bed with her lover, would react to the foolish other suitor who begs for a kiss. Rather than being puzzled about why Heile insults a paying customer she had invited to visit her, we are free to be amused at the obscenely clever way Alisoun quite justifiably punishes a suitor she quite rightly spurns. Puzzling, no. Funny, yes.

Listening in a tub

The Antwerp priest in the Middle Dutch tale does not know that he has an auditor other than Heile when he preaches his illogical little sermon, but Willem, sitting in the trough above, overhears the priest's sermon:

> Dit hoerde Willem daer hi sat
> Boven hoge in ghenen bac,

Ende peinsde het mochte wel waer wesen
Sidermeer dat papen lesen,
Ende dewangelie gheeft getughe.
(87–91)

[Willem heard this from where he sat high above in the trough and thought it might well be true, since priests read the gospels, and the gospels bore witness to it.]

Immediately, however, there is a problem: if Willem is close enough to the bedroom that he can hear the priest's sermon, how is it that he has apparently not also heard the sounds, however muffled, of the priest's triple-encounter with Heile, and how is it that, immediately after he hears the sermon that is not intended for his ears, he apparently does not also hear the conversation between Heile and Hughe? If he had heard it, and had heard Heile telling the priest to let the smith kiss his buttocks, why does Willem know so little about what goes on down there that he does not realize, a few minutes later, that there really is no flood? He has, after all, been awake the whole time, has heard no thunder, seen no lightning, observed no patter of rain on the roof over his head. His assumption that the predicted flood has come makes no sense whatever.

Chaucer's tub-scene is more believable. After his hard day's work of acquiring, provisioning, hanging, and laddering the three tubs, poor old John is exhausted. Almost immediately he falls asleep:

The dede sleep, for wery bisynesse,
Fil on this carpenter right, as I gesse,
Aboute corfew-tyme, or litel moore.
(3643–45)

Old John does not hear Absolon's or Nicholas's conversations with Alisoun because he is dead asleep the whole time. He sleeps nervously "Awaitynge on the reyn, if he it heere" (3642). The next thing he hears in his slumber is the "thonder-dent" (3807) of a fart and then Nicholas's cry, "Water! Water!" (3815). He groggily assumes from the thunderclap and from the cry for water that the flood has come. It turns out to be a wrong assumption, but Chaucer, unlike the Middle Dutch author, has set things up in such a way that we accept that assumption as believable. Rather than be puzzled at or merely snicker at Willem's strange actions, we laugh at the foolish John's absurd and well-deserved fall.

Penetrating I

When Hughe kisses the priest's bottom, he does so with such zeal and force that his nose penetrates the priest's anus:

> Ende Huge waende that Heile ware
> End custe spapen ers al dare
> Met soe heten sinne,
> Dat sine nese vloech daer inne,
> Soe dat die smet sonder waen
> Harde well waende sijn gevaen
> Gelijc der mese inder cloven.
>
> (117–23)

> [And Hughe thought it was Heile and kissed the priest's arse right there with such hot desire that his nose shot inside, so that the smith undoubtedly thought that he was caught like a titmouse in a trap.]

That may be good slapstick comedy, but it is not believable. We all know that the human sphincter would not permit the penetration of even the most Pinocchio-like human nose. And as for the bird with his beak in a trap, can we really, except in a cartoon sequence, imagine such a thing as the result of a human kiss?

Chaucer eliminated the impossible nose-penetration:

> And Absolon, hym fil no bet ne wers,
> But with his mouth he kiste hir naked ers
> Ful savourly, er he were war of this.
>
> (3733–35)

The penetration in the Middle Dutch story we cannot believe; "savourly" in the English story we can. The "savourly" is, for

Absolon, a believable detail. His mouth has "icched al this longe day" (3682) and at night he has dreamed that "I was at a feeste" (3684). At the window he tells Alisoun that he yearns for her "as dooth a lamb after the tete" (3704). It is not strange at all that a young man who so consistently associates love with eating should kiss his beloved "ful savourly."

Getting the hot iron

Deeply insulted by his misdirected kiss, Hughe angrily rushes home to his smithy and heats up a hot iron:

> Hi liep thuus alse die was erre;
> Hine woende van daer niet verre.
> Een groet yser nam hi gereet
> Ende staect int vier ende maket heet
> Soe dat gloyde wel ter cure.
> (131–35)
>
> [He ran home as if he were mad. He lived not far from there. He immediately took a big iron, stuck it into the fire and made it so hot that it glowed, just the way he wanted it to.]

On the one hand it seems both logical and economical for a blacksmith in need of a hot iron to run home and fetch one. On the other, we might perhaps assume, though we are not told, that he had let his hearth go cold at the end of the day in anticipation of his visit to Heile, so his returning home to heat up the hearth again would have taken some time—perhaps enough time for his rage to cool enough that he would approach the fateful window the second time more cautiously.

Chaucer changed that by having Absolon visit a friend, Gerveys, who already has his smithy up and running, with a hot coulter already there in the forge—"that hoote kultour in the chymenee heere" (3776). He can then, after a very brief conversation with Gerveys, grab the coulter "by the colde stele" of the handle (3785) and rush back with it. In the heat of his anger he knocks again at the window, never thinking that the woman he intends to punish may be cleverer than he, never anticipating that the buttock he scorches may be that of a man rather than of the woman he has come to loathe. Rushing back he applies his instrument of revenge effectively enough, but does so in such a way that he is punished again, this time with a blinding fart in the face. Hughe the smith is not punished a second time. There is no need for him to be punished even the first time because he has done no wrong. Absolon, however, deserves not only the first punishment but the second as well, since he is a vow-breaking fraud of a parish clerk who presses his suit on a clever woman who has twice rejected him. Chaucer carefully sets the smithy-scene up so that Gerveys has the hot coulter ready, thus permitting Absolon to act quickly and without considering the possible consequences, thereby hilariously bringing on his own second and much-deserved punishment.

Penetrating II

When the priest puts his buttocks out the window to receive a second kiss, Hughe strikes while his iron is hot:

> Ende die smet stac onghelet
> Tgheloyende yser in den ers.
> (146–47)
>
> [And the smith immediately stuck the red-hot iron into his arse.]

While it may be funny to have the priest sodomized twice, once by Hughe's nose and once by Hughe's hot iron, the second sodomizing is as contrived as the first. It is, after all, pitch dark, the human anus is a narrow target, and Hughe has no hint about where to aim his hot iron, unless we are to assume that he is aided by its own red glow.

Chaucer treats the second window scene more believably. For one thing, the weapon is a coulter, the broad plow-knife designed to cut the earth vertically before the plowshare cuts it horizontally and turns it over. It is just the sort of implement that a blacksmith would be likely to have heating up in his hearth in the very early dawn of a spring morning, prior to sharpening it for the Oxford farmer who would use it that day.[4] For another thing, since it is not yet dawn, Absolon's aim cannot be so precise. He has, after all, only the sound of the fart to guide him—the fart itself being a believable human response to a man like Absolon. Hughe, we recall, had no clue about where to aim. Even if the early dawn light were beginning to bring the outlined forms out of the darkness, Chaucer tells us that Absolon has been blinded by the fart:

> This Nicholas anon leet fle a fart
> As greet as it had been a thonder-dent,
> That with the strook he was almoost yblent.
> (3806–08)

Striking blindly, the angry Absolon hits Nicholas not in the anus, even if he had been aiming for that specific part of the anatomy, but "amydde the ers" (3810). And, given the flattened breadth of the plow coulter, it seems appropriate that "hende" Nicholas receives not a puncture wound but, rather, a hilariously funny and appropriate buttocks-burn "an hande-brede aboute" (3811).[5]

Falling into a cesspit

The priest in *Heile van Beersele* is double-punished. First, he has his anus scorched by a cauterizing hot iron wielded by Hughe the blacksmith. His shout "Water, water" leads Willem to cut the rope[6] suspending his tub, and Willem's crashing down so surprises the

[4] J. A. W. Bennett tells us in *Chaucer at Oxford and at Cambridge* (Oxford: Clarendon Press, 1974) that "blacksmiths customarily worked at night to early morning—the best time to repair gear or 'tip' ploughshares that were needed on the morrow" (41).

[5] I cannot agree with the strain of criticism that sees Absolon's act as sodomitic. See, for example, Edmund Reiss, "Daun Gerveys in the *Miller's Tale*," *Papers on Language and Literature* 6 (1970), 123, and Roy Peter Clark, "Christmas Games in the *Miller's Tale*," *Studies in Short Fiction* 13 (1976): "The 'kultour' is a phallus-shaped weapon. . . . Absolon's thrusting of the hot iron up Nicholas's rear is an act of symbolic buggery" (283). There is no penetration in the *Miller's Tale.*

[6] A minor change in the direction of believability in the *Miller's Tale is* that Nicholas has John provide the tubs with "an ax to smyte the corde atwo" (3569), and that John at the appropriate

priest that he thinks the devil has come. The fearful priest rushes into the corner, where he receives his second punishment by falling into a cesspit:

> Die pape scoet in een winkel
> Ende waende dat die duvel ware;
> In enen vulen putte viel hi dare,
> Alsoe alsmen mi doet weten
> Quam hi thuus all besceten
> Ende sinen ers al verbrant.
> (172–77)
>
> [The priest ran into a corner, thinking [Willem] was the devil, and fell into a foul pit, as I have been told, and then went home all beshitten and with his arse branded.]

Chaucer makes a significant change in moving the cleric from the inside of the house, where he is in the Middle Dutch tale, to the outside. Absolon is not yet a full-fledged priest, of course, but this sensor-swinging parish clerk apparently aspires to be one. In any event, he is the referent of the anticlerical theme so characteristic of the fabliaux. By moving the clerical figure outside and putting Nicholas inside, Chaucer switched the scheme of punishment. Still wanting the priest to receive a double-punishment, Chaucer replaces one scatological element for another—and more logical—one. How logical is it, after all, to find a "vulen putte" (174) inside the house? Certainly we are not told in advance that one is there, and there is no mention of the reek or vermin that must have been associated with such a foul pit. Perhaps we are to assume, rather, that the pit is outside in a corner of the garden, but in fact the Middle Dutch poet says no such thing. The plot needs a cesspit, so the author provides it. We snicker when we see the priest tumble into it, but we have

time uses it: "And with his ax he smoot the corde atwo" (3820). Willem is not said to have any cutting instrument in the trough with him, but manages in his panic to produce a knife from somewhere: "Sijn mes hi gegrepe / Ende sneet ontwee den repe" (161–62) [He gripped his knife and cut the rope].

no reason to believe such a tumble because the author has not explained it. It seems to be a puzzling afterthought to a puzzling tale.

Chaucer makes no mention of the sanitary facilities associated with John's house in the *Miller's Tale*.[7] His plot, of course, requires no such site, so there is no reason for him to have mentioned it. Chaucer does, however, provide a double-punishment for the cleric Absolon. The first is the foul arse-kiss, the second is the foul fart. Both of these are logical enough given the details of characterization that Chaucer gives to the fair Alisoun who presents her buttocks for Absolon to kiss, and to the raunchy Nicholas, who produces the fart. Both of these punishments, given the preparation Chaucer has given them, are entirely logical and entirely funny in the context of the story Chaucer has so elaborately set up.

Chaucer's *Miller's Tale,* then, is far more believable than *Heile van Beersele.* It is so believable that some readers have even assumed that the story is based somehow on "real life."[8] My purpose here is not to prove that Chaucer's version of the story of the multiple lovers is superior to the Middle Dutch one. Most modern readers will of course prefer the *Miller's Tale* to *Heile van Beersele.* It has a more fully developed plot and more fleshed-out characters. And it supports a more consistently developed set of themes by punishing

[7] Little is known about the typical location of latrines in or around medieval houses. For a hint about what is known, see Georges Duby, ed., A *History of Private Life,* volume II, *Revelations of the Medieval World* (Cambridge: Harvard University Press, 1988), especially 460, 463–64.

[8] For example, see Robert A. Pratt, in "Was Robyn the Miller's Youth Misspent?" *Modern Language Notes* 59 (1944): 47–49, and Charles Long, "The Miller's True Story," *Interpretations* 6 (1974): 7–16. Long thinks that the events of the *Miller's Tale* actually took place "on a dark night, some twenty years ago in the home of John from Osenay, that is of Osewold" (8–9). Long discusses some of the changes that I discuss here, but reaches quite a different set of conclusions: "Chaucer intends for the story to be biographical or even autobiographical. . . . The Miller . . . had observed the events in his youth" (9). According to Long, although Robyn was himself off in London with Gille on the fateful Monday night in question, he "could easily have satisfied his curiosity by gleaning the varying tidbits of information from the stories of neighbors

the self-deceiving foolishness of old John, the prideful randiness of young Nicholas, and, especially, the self-serving religious pretensions of clerkly Absolon. *Heile van Beersele is* quite different from the *Miller's Tale.* It is much shorter—only a fifth the length of Chaucer's—and is by genre an anecdote that does not pretend to believable development of anything. It is a smirk-inspiring story about the troubles that three men make for themselves when they associate with a prostitute who has a bad sense of timing. We cannot help but be amused when three sexual encounters meant to be sequential turn out to be simultaneous. The Middle Dutch tale does what it sets out to do, and does it all with admirable economy. That economy, however, comes at the expense of verisimilitude. The characters are not believable, nor are they meant to be. Their actions could not really have happened, and we are not meant to think that they could really have happened.

In Chaucer's *Miller's Tale*, as in *Heile van Beersele*, we readers are aware always that we are dealing with fiction, not actual life. In reading the *Miller's Tale*, however, far more than in reading *Heile van Beersele*, we imagine the events as happening to human beings. Unlike the Middle Dutch author, clever though he was in telling a funny anecdote, Chaucer made a series of narrative moves that help us to believe that the events of the story might actually have happened to people whose behavior is in basic accord with human nature. Instead of scratching our heads in puzzlement at the strange actions

or from Nicholas and Alison as well. The Miller's story, then, is almost certainly based on an episode in his life, and Robyn the Miller is Old John's young apprentice, also named Robyn, who would have been a near 'eye witness' of the Nicholas-Alison-John triangle" (10). Long's argument is variously flawed. He never explains why a future miller would have apprenticed himself to a carpenter, for example, and the name and age of Osewald the Reeve do not sort well with those of old John or with the twenty-years-past events of the tale. Long's argument is even more tenuous when he surmises that John has long since separated from Alison and married "a new young wife," while Alison is currently the Wife of Bath on the pilgrimage to Canterbury. My own reasoning requires no such house of cards. A useful counter-reading to the Pratt-Long kind of "realism" is that of Charles A. Owen, Jr., "One Robyn or Two," *Modern Language Notes* 67 (1952): 336–38.

of the strange people in *Heile van Beersele*, we readers of the much more believable *Miller's Tale* can react with amusement at the human comedy that unfolds before us.

Perhaps in dwelling so long on the differences between the Middle Dutch tale and the Middle English one that Chaucer derived from it, I shall be thought to be doing just what Chaucer asked us to NOT to do, that is to make "ernest of game" (3186). On the contrary, I want to emphasize far more the "game" of the tale than its earnestness. In Middle English, the word "game" meant not only "playfulness," but also "play" in the sense of a piece of drama. One of the key differences between the *Miller's Tale* and what came before it is that Chaucer was, by means of dialogue and setting and imaginable human action, moving British fiction in the direction of drama. If I may return for a moment to the cartoon analogy, *Heile van Beersele* is like a comic strip. It is a series of static frames that, together, tell a story. The people have short speeches in the bubbles above their heads, but they are essentially frozen in place, immobile, in each rigid frame. We do not expect verisimilitude when we read a cartoon strip or comic book. Cartoons are, by definition, funny, but their humor derives more from situation than from logical action or psychologically complex motivation or truth to life. The *Miller's Tale,* on the other hand, is like a stage play with real actors. They move around in fluid frames. They speak more. They are played by human actors who are doing, for the most part, the kinds of things that people do. Because the actors are alive, their actions seem more believable and more motivated. We find out how and why the props got there and we come closer to understanding the human motivation of the actors. I cannot, of course, press these analogies too far, but if I am right, then one of the central changes Chaucer made was to transform the cartoon-anecdote that lets us respond by saying, "My, those characters sure did funny things," into the kind of dramatic action that lets us respond, rather, "My, those funny characters are a lot like you and me."

Where's the Point?: Punctuating Chaucer's *Canterbury Tales*

[When Emerson Brown died—way too early—two of his friends decided to put together a collection of essays in his honor. I submitted this piece on punctuating Chaucer. It was a topic Emerson had published on. He was one of the first scholars to remind us that virtually none of the punctuation in modern editions of Chaucer's works is Chaucerian at all. Rather, it is added by modern editors of his works. And Brown was one of the first to remind us that, since punctuation changes meaning, when modern editors make mistakes in inserting punctuation, they fundamentally alter Chaucer's poetry. In my essay I propose seven alternatives to the punctuation provided in the *Riverside Chaucer*, the standard scholarly edition. The last three, from the *Miller's Tale*, invite student discussion. "Where's the Point" originally appeared in "*Seyd in forme and reverence*"*: Essays on Chaucer and Chaucerians in Memory of Emerson Brown, Jr.,* ed. T. L. Burton and John F. Plummer (Adelaide, Australia, and Provo, UT: Chaucer Studio Press, 2005), 193–203.]

An essay on punctuating Chaucer is appropriate in a volume honoring Emerson Brown, Jr., whose essay on a possible error in punctuation in the *Knight's Tale*[1] got many Chaucerians thinking about

[1] "The *Knight's Tale*, 2639: Guilt by Punctuation," *Chaucer Review* 21 (1986): 133–41. Following Brown's lead, others have suggested repunctuating or even unpunctuating Chaucer.

challenging the pointing done by powerful editors. It always comes as a surprise to my Chaucer students to learn that six hundred years ago Chaucer did not know, and did not use, punctuation marks as we know them now. The many manuscripts of Chaucer's verse give us columns of verse with no periods, commas, question marks, exclamation marks, semicolons, colons, dashes, apostrophes, or consistent paragraph markers. To be sure, there is an occasional raised point that we have come to call a "punctus," and that punctus may be related in some way to the modern period, but there are few puncti in the manuscripts, and those we do find rarely appear where we would put periods. There are lots of virgules, or slash marks [/], in the manuscripts. In most lines we find at least one virgule, in some two. These may be the ancestors of the modern comma, since the virgules sometimes seem to mark a caesura or pause in the line. They almost never come at the end of the line, however, even when we would require a comma there. There are also in the manuscripts some paragraph markers [¶]. These serve as a kind of punctuation mark, and some of those are at places where we might indent for paragraphs. The punctus, the virgule, and the paragraph marker, however, are inconsistently used. That they vary in use from manuscript to manuscript suggests that at least some of them are scribal rather than Chaucerian marks. We do not have a single document that we *know* was from Chaucer's own hand. To the extent that we have any punctuation at all in the surviving manuscripts, then, the punctus, the virgule, and the paragraph marker are the only marks we find, and those were quite possibly put there by a scribe rather than by Chaucer.

See, for example, Howell Chickering's "Unpunctuating Chaucer," *Chaucer Review* 25 (1990): 96–109, and D. Thomas Hanks, Jr., Arminda Kamphausen, and James Wheeler, "Circling Back in Chaucer's *Canterbury Tales*: On Punctuation, Misreading, and Reader Response," *Chaucer Yearbook* 3 (1996): 35–53. Few earlier studies challenged the standard punctuation of modern editions. A notable exception is Albert E. Hartung's "Inappropriate Pointing in the *Canon's Yeoman's Tale*, G 1236–1239," *PMLA* 77 (1962): 508–09.

Where, then, does the punctuation in modern editions, using marks that Chaucer had never heard of, come from? The answer is simple enough: the punctuation comes from modern editors of Chaucer, most of whom take their lead from earlier editors of Chaucer, dating back as far as Thynne's sixteenth-century and Speght's seventeenth-century editions. Indeed, one of the most important services that a modern editor performs is to insert the kind of punctuation and paragraphing that will help modern readers, most of them college students, read Chaucer with comparative ease. These modern editors perform an important function, of course, because we teachers want to do all we can to help students understand and take delight in Chaucerian plots, characterization, humor, meaning, and subtlety. Still, modern editors sometimes get the punctuation wrong, and in doing so they mislead or confuse modern readers.

In this essay I present four examples that show the possible errors of modern editors' ways and the importance of a critical reading of all modern punctuation. Of these four, two are from the *Knight's Tale,* one from the *Franklin's Tale,* and one from the *Shipman's Tale.* I close with a challenge to Chaucerians and their students to rethink the standard punctuation of three sets of lines in the *Miller's Tale.* All arguments for one punctuation rather than another should be based not on what punctuation Chaucer used, but on how modern punctuation serves best to bring out the meaning that Chaucer most likely intended and would have presumably made clear through intonation, emphasis, and pause in an oral reading of his works.[2] Even to guess what Chaucer had in mind, we need to understand the context of any passages we discuss.

[2] I am skeptical of the view that students should be asked to read Chaucer in texts with no modern punctuation. It may be that any decision about punctuation can obscure a possible ambiguity, but surely in reading his texts aloud Chaucer would have indicated what his primary meanings were. The job of modern editors is to provide punctuation that will help students understand texts as Chaucer most likely wanted them to be understood. Scholars, of course, can profitably use unpunctuated texts.

Emily speaks to Diana

Just before the tournament in the *Knight's Tale,* Emily prays to Diana, the chaste goddess of virginity, asking that she not have to marry either of the young knights who want to take her virginity in marriage. In the *Riverside* her lines to Diana read thus:

> "Syn thou art mayde and kepere of us alle,
> My maydenhede thou kepe and wel conserve,
> And whil I lyve, a mayde I wol thee serve."
> (I 2328–30)

I propose an alternative punctuation by moving the comma in the third of those lines two words to the right.

> *Proposed*:
> "Syn thou art mayde and kepere of us alle,
> My maydenhede thou kepe and wel conserve,
> And whil I lyve a mayde, I wol thee serve."
> (I 2328–30)

In the *Riverside* punctuation, Emily promises, in exchange for Diana's protecting her maidenhead, to serve Diana as a maiden as long as she lives: "And as long as I live, I will serve you as a maiden." In my reading, Emily promises, in exchange for Diana's protecting her maidenhead, to serve Diana as long as she is a virgin: "And so long as I live as a maiden, I will serve you."

The changed punctuation changes the meaning of the word "while." According to the *Riverside* punctuation, "while" means "as long as." According to the punctuation I propose, "while" means "so long as." If he were reading the text out loud, Chaucer would have made his meaning clear by pausing either after "live" or "maid." The manuscripts themselves can offer no help since there were no commas in the line. It is purely a matter of deciding which reading makes the most sense. For me the alternative reading makes more sense. Why would Emily promise that as long as she gets to keep her maidenhead she will serve Diana as a maiden? Those who serve Diana are, by definition, maidens, so little is gained by Emily's stipulating that she will serve Diana as a maiden. It makes more sense for Emily to promise to serve Diana *if* she remains a maiden: "And so long as I live as a maiden, I will serve you." Not only is that a more realistic promise, since she promises to serve Diana only so long as she remains a maiden, but it also carries with it an implied request for Diana's protection not just this once, but on into the future, as well: "I will serve you only if you help me to continue to live as a maiden." I prefer this reading, also, because it gives Emily a bit more personality. There may, after all, be implied in her promise not merely a plea for Diana's continued protection, but also a veiled threat, as well: "If you do not offer me protection from the unchaste desires of these men, Diana, I will no longer serve you."

Saturn speaks to Venus

There is great rejoicing when Arcite wins the tournament near the end of the *Knight's Tale.* The people celebrate noisily to honor Arcite's winning in combat the hand of the fair Emily. Palamon, of course, is disappointed and confused. Venus herself is also upset at the outcome, since she had promised Palamon that he would get Emily. Venus, weeping and distraught, takes her case directly to her father Saturn. The mighty Saturn hears her, but tells her to hold her peace because she will have her way yet. Here is the passage in the *Riverside Chaucer*:

> Saturnus seyde, "Doghter, hoold thy pees!
> Mars hath his wille, his knyght hath all his boone,
> And, by myn heed, thow shalt been esed soone."
> The trompours, with the loude mynstralcie,
> The heraudes, that ful loude yelle and crie,
> Been in hire wele for joye of daun Arcite.
> But herkneth me, and stynteth noyse a lite,
> Which a myracle ther bifel anon.
>
> (I 2668–75)

The main problem with the *Riverside* punctuation is that in the next to last line above, "me" must refer to the narrator, the Knight himself. "Listen to me," says the Knight, "and stop your noise." To whom is the Knight speaking here? The only possible answer, in the *Riverside*, is the other twenty-odd pilgrims, who have presumably been making a lot of noise. Chaucer never tells us, however, that the other pilgrims have been noisy, and indeed they have nothing to be noisy about. Why would the pilgrims noisily cheer Arcite's success in battle? If they don't react to anything else in the tale, why would they react here, even if they were on Arcite's side, which they probably would not have been?[3] And even if they did react noisily, it seems distinctly out of character for the pilgrim Knight to tell them to shush up and "herkneth me." He is, after all, a polite and gentle sort of chap unlikely to speak villainously to others:

> And though that he were worthy, he was wys,
> And of his port as meeke as is a mayde.
> He nevere yet no vileynye ne sayde
> In al his lyf unto no maner wight.
> He was a verray, parfit gentil knyght.[4]
>
> (I 68–72)

But if we take the close-quotation mark from the end of line I 2870 and move it to the end of I 2874, then Saturn becomes the speaker of the lines, which he addresses still to his distraught daughter Venus.

> *Proposed*:
> Saturnus seyde, "Doghter, hoold thy pees.
> Mars hath his wille. His knyght hath all his boone.

[3] Chaucer, after all, changed the events of Boccaccio's *Teseide* to make Palamon the one who deserves Emily by seeing her first, praying more wisely, and being a hero defeated not by a horse bite but by a gang of twenty.

[4] Once we begin to question the standard punctuation, it is difficult not to meddle with it. These lines, for example, might be repunctuated thus, though in this case the difference in actual meaning is minimal:

> And though that he were worthy, he was wys.
> And, of his port as meeke as is a mayde,
> He nevere yet no vileynye ne sayde
> In al his lyf, unto no maner wight.
> He was a verray, parfit, gentil knyght.
>
> (I 68–72)

> And, by myn heed, thow shalt been esed soone.
> The trompours, with the loude mynstralcie,
> The heraudes, that ful loude yelle and crie,
> Been in hire wele for joye of daun Arcite.
> But herkneth me, and stynteth noyse a lite."
> Which a myracle ther bifel anon.
> (I 2668–75)

In my punctuation, Saturn speaks seven lines to Venus, not three, and in doing so makes it quite clear who the "me" of the seventh line is. It is not a belligerent Knight telling his fellow pilgrims to be quiet and listen to him, but a kindly Saturn telling his distraught and weeping daughter to do so, because he knows that the joyous trumpeters and musicians down there proclaiming Arcite's victory will soon stop their celebrating when a big surprise comes. It would be perfectly in character for Saturn, the wisest and most powerful of the planetary gods, to show a bit of firm impatience with his weeping daughter as he reassures her that she will get her way in the end.

My punctuation not only gets rid of the confusing equation of "me" with the Knight and of the Knight's curious admonition to his fellow pilgrims to be quiet, but has the additional advantage of lending a nice balance to Saturn's speech to his daughter. It starts with his telling her to hold her peace, and ends with his telling her to be quiet.[5] In my punctuation, the final line in the passage makes sense as the first line of the Knight's transition to the next section after Saturn's speech ends: "What a miracle comes next," he says. The "miracle" he refers to is that Saturn sends a fury from hell to frighten the victorious

[5] I have made some other changes, also, by removing the exclamation mark at the end of line 2668, thus making Saturn less harsh and more loving, by removing what we now call a comma splice in line 2669, by moving the paragraph indent at line 2671, making the seven lines one unbroken speech, and putting it before line 2675. Teachers might want to debate with students these smaller changes—and others they might want to suggest. Incidentally, I am aware that it may be unusual for Saturn to use the plural "herkneth" and "stynteth" in this line to speak in the imperative to his daughter, but I am not sure Chaucer would have been such a stickler for the finer points of grammar.

Arcite's horse, which then rears back and kills Arcite. The miracle of the fury brings an end to Venus's grief and lets her make good on her promise to Palamon.

Aurelius speaks to Dorigen

Near the end of the *Franklin's Tale,* the young lover Aurelius, upon learning from Dorigen that her husband Arveragus has sent his wife to keep her promise, feels pity for Dorigen, respect for Arveragus, and shame for his own selfish actions. He decides to follow Arveragus's lead and do the right thing. His speech to Dorigen ends thus in the *Riverside*:

> "I yow relesse, madame, into youre hond
> Quyt every serement and every bond
> That ye han maad to me as heerbiforn,
> Sith thilke tyme which that ye were born.
> My trouthe I plighte, I shal yow never repreve
> Of no biheste, and heere I take my leve,
> As of the treweste and the beste wyf
> That evere yet I knew in al my lyf.
> But every wyf be war of hire biheeste!
> On Dorigen remembreth, atte leeste.
> Thus kan a squier doon a gentil dede
> As wel as kan a knyght, withouten drede."
> (V 1533–44)

It is a moving speech that Aurelius makes, but the last four lines of it are not his to deliver. A modern editor has through punctuation misascribed them to him. Those last four lines make no sense in his mouth. Why would the lovesick Aurelius, having made a decision to give up the object of his love just when she is within his reach, warn other wives to beware of making promises like hers? It makes no sense for him to be thinking of other wives at all. Why would he in one breath praise her for being the "treweste and the beste wyf" he has ever known (V 1539), and in the next breath exhort other wives not to make promises like the one she made to him? If he did want to make such a statement, why would he make it in a speech to her as the sole listener rather than to other wives? And even if he wanted to make such a speech to her, why would he tell other wives to "be war of *hire* biheeste" rather than to "be war of *youre* biheeste"?

There are other problems with having Aurelius deliver those four lines. The most obvious problem is that the *Riverside* has him praise himself by saying, "Thus kan a squier doon a gentil dede" (V 1543). Such self-praise is out of character for a young man who has just learned the most important lesson and made the defining decision of his young life. Surely we are to admire his humility and wisdom and good judgment here, not watch him pat himself on the back for being every bit as noble as a knight.

Those four lines, however, are entirely appropriate in the mouth of the Franklin, the teller of the story. He has, after all, been critical of Dorigen before—critical of her impatience with the rocks and of her complaining nature—so it would be entirely appropriate for him to use her here as an example to other wives of the disastrous consequences that come from making rash promises to would-be lovers. Similarly, this Franklin, who is impatient with his own son and wishes that he would "comune with any gentil wight / Where he myghte lerne gentillesse aright" (V 693–94), would be eager to point out in his tale that young men can learn proper behavior by paying attention to the good examples of knights: "Thus kan a squier doon a gentil dede / As wel as kan a knyght" (V 1543–44). I would, then, render the passage differently. A careful reader will notice that in the following repunctuation of the passage, I have made a few more changes in pointing, though none as significant as moving the closing quotation mark four lines forward.

> *Proposed*:
> "I yow relesse, madame, into youre hond,
> Quyt every serement and every bond
> That ye han maad to me as heerbiforn
> Sith thilke tyme which that ye were born.
> My trouthe I plighte, I shal yow never repreve

Of no biheste. And heere I take my leve
As of the treweste and the beste wyf
That evere yet I knew in al my lyf."
    But every wyf be war of hire biheeste—
On Dorigen remembreth, atte leeste.
Thus kan a squier doon a gentil dede
As wel as kan a knyght, withouten drede.
(V 1533–44)

In my reading, the Franklin takes gentle issue with one of his own characters. Aurelius takes his leave of the truest and best wife he has ever known, but the Franklin offers a closing caution to all wives to beware of making foolish promises like Dorigen's and to all young men to learn from the example of gentle knights.

Daun John speaks to the wife of Saint Denis

At the beginning of the garden scene in the *Shipman's Tale,* the wife of the merchant of Saint Denis comes up to daun John and speaks to him. The lines run thus in the *Riverside*:

"O deere cosyn myn, daun John," she sayde,
"What eyleth yow so rathe for to ryse?"
    "Nece," quod he, "it oghte ynough suffise
Fyve houres for to slepe upon a nyght,

. . . . .

But deere nece, why be ye so pale?
I trowe, certes, that oure goode man
Hath yow laboured sith the nyght bigan
That yow were nede to resten hastily."
(VII 98–101, 106–9)[6]

[6] For the sake of simplicity, I have removed from consideration the monk's four-line statement to the wife about how tired old wedded men, who lie cowering like hound-harassed rabbits in a furrow, need more sleep than the five hours. That passage does not affect my argument.

Every modern edition agrees in punctuating the lines thus, or very nearly thus.[7] The sense of the passage, then, is, " 'Oh my dear cousin, sir John,' she said. 'What ails you that you rise so early?' 'Niece,' he replied, 'five hours of sleep at night is sufficient. . . . But, dear niece, why are you so pale? I'll bet your husband has been keeping you busy in bed since the night began!' " Three problems, however, immediately surface with this reading. First, why would the wife be surprised at finding the monk out saying his devotions early in the morning? Monks, after all, are required to get up early to say their devotions, so there is nothing for her to be puzzled about. Second, why does she ask him what ails him? The monk is not ailing at all, and the rest of the garden scene shows him to be healthy and relaxed. Third, how are we to make sense of the monk's answering her question about what ails him by saying that five hours is enough sleep? We are presumably to read the monk's reply as self-righteous bragging about how few hours of sleep pious monks need, because sleep takes away from their good works and their prayerful service to Jesus, but in fact he never does answer what ails him, and her question remains as puzzling as his non-answer.

[7] Both the Hengwrt and the Ellesmere scribes have seemed to suggest through paragraph markers that line 100 should start a new speech with the word "Nece." Modern editors, perhaps having seen that marker, may well have assumed that the mark was Chaucer's own and punctuated the passage accordingly. I suggest, however, that the positioning of the paragraph markers may well have been a scribal error that later editors picked up on. The Hengwrt MS has thirty-seven such markers in the *Shipman's Tale,* while the Ellesmere has thirty-six. But only thirty of those appear in the same places in the two versions. The Hengwrt has seven paragraph markers that the Ellesmere does not have, and the Ellesmere has six that the Hengwrt does not have. If, as most scholars now assume, the same scribe copied both the Hengwrt and the Ellesmere, it is interesting that he felt free to place the paragraph markers in somewhat different places in the two manuscripts. For example, while the Hengwrt has a marker at the start of line 98, with the wife's speech, the Ellesmere does not. We need not, then, be controlled in our reading by scribal paragraphing in the manuscripts.

I propose an alternative punctuation, and thus an alternative reading of the lines. My reading is accomplished by altering the punctuation slightly, ending the wife's speech in the first line (98) and giving the second line to the monk.

Proposed:
"O deere cosyn myn, daun John," she sayde.
"What eyleth yow so rathe for to ryse,
Nece?" quod he. "It oghte ynough suffise
Fyve houres for to slepe upon a nyght,

. . . . .

But deere nece, why be ye so pale?
I trowe, certes, that oure goode man
Hath yow laboured sith the nyght bigan
That yow were nede to resten hastily."
(VII 98–101, 106–9)

By changing only the punctuation, I have removed the three problems with the standard reading. In my alternative reading, the wife says only six words, presumably with a sad sigh: "Oh my dear cousin, sir John." The distress in that short speech signals to the monk that something is troubling her, and *he* then speaks the next line, asking what ails *her* that she is up so early.[8] Changing the punctuation gets rid of the first problem—why the wife asks him why he is up early—because in my alternative reading *he* asks *her* the question. While it is perfectly usual for a monk to be up early saying his morning devotions, it might well be unusual for *her* to be up so early unless

[8] The closest analogue to the *Shipman's Tale*, Boccaccio's *Decameron* 8.1, cannot guide us here, since in it there is no garden meeting and no conversation between Ambruogia and Gulfardo, the German soldier who wants to become her lover. In the thirteenth-century Old French tale *Aloul,* however, a lustful clergyman and a distraught wife meet early in the morning in an orchard. In a situation curiously parallel to the garden scene in the *Shipman's Tale,* the clergyman opens the conversation by asking the pretty wife why she is up so early (see line 69). *Aloul* is conveniently translated by John DuVal in *Fabliaux, Fair and Foul* (Binghamton: MRTS, 1992), 107–29.

something is wrong. Changing the punctuation also gets rid of the second problem—why the *wife* asks the *monk* what ails him when nothing does ail him. Rather, in my alternative reading, the *monk* asks the *wife* why she is ailing—a reasonable question since she is "ailing." Not only is she pale, but we soon discover that she is unhappy with her marital condition. Later lines reveal that she is distraught about her debts and the alleged failings of her husband: his stinginess, his incapacity in bed, and so on—the "thynges sixe" of lines VII 174–77. These are ailments enough for the wife of the merchant of St. Denis. As for the third problem—why in reply to her question about what ails him daun John says that five hours is enough sleep—that problem disappears also with my alternative punctuation. The monk's response makes sense as a response to *his* question about what ails *her.* He says, in effect, "What ails you that you are up so early? Five hours ought to be enough sleep, but you look awfully pale. I'll bet I know: your husband kept you working all night in bed! That's why you did not get five hours of sleep and look so pale."

I emphasize here that I have not changed the words or the word order at all, but only the editorially-inserted punctuation. That is, I propose not an emendation to what Chaucer wrote, but only an alteration in the punctuation that modern editors have supplied.

Does it make any difference, since readers have been making what they thought was perfectly good sense of the passage for some six centuries? I think so. By altering the punctuation we have not only made the passage more logical, but we have also corrected the characterization of the monk. Instead of listening to her question about what ails him, daun John takes the lead by asking her a question, and in so doing shows at least the appearance of concern for her: "What is ailing you, dear niece? Has your husband been working you too hard in bed all night?" His question, then, is less an expression of concern than an invitation to her to talk about her sex life—and she immediately does: "Nay, cosyn myn, it stant nat so with me" (VII 114). His question and his own hinted answer are therefore his sleazy moves towards seduction. By altering the punctuation, we have also altered the characterization of the wife. No longer asking the monk a meaningless question about what ails him when nothing does, she stops short with a self-pitying address and lets *him* inquire what ails *her.* Her opening words, then, are the lament of a woman in distress, a plea for help. Instead of asking a question that shows her concern for his welfare, she draws attention to her own sad condition.

My interest in repunctuating Chaucer is in part a pedagogical one. It is less that I want the rest of the world to punctuate Chaucer my way than that I want to encourage teachers to discuss with their students the importance of proper punctuation in general and the proper punctuation of Chaucerian texts in particular. We all know that punctuation alters meaning, but not all students quite understand that. I close by suggesting three alternatives to the standard punctuation of one of the Chaucerian tales that our students enjoy the most, the *Miller's Tale.* I have reasons for proposing the three repunctuations, but I do not state them here, thinking that perhaps teachers might like to invite students to argue the punctuation out and reach their own conclusions. In fact, if I were re-editing the *Miller's Tale,* I would adopt only two of the three alternative punctuations that I propose here. My purpose here is not to insist that the standard punctuation be changed, but to encourage teachers and students to argue for or against that standard punctuation, and in doing so learn that punctuation does matter.

Alisoun speaks to Nicholas

When Nicholas grabs Alisoun and commands that she give him her love, the startled Alisoun springs like a colt and twists out of his grip. Here is the *Riverside* passage:

> And seyde, "I wol nat kisse thee, by my fey!
> Why, lat be!" quod she. "Lat be, Nicholas,
> Or I wol crie 'out, harrow' and 'allas'!
> Do wey youre handes, for youre curteisye!"
> (I 3284–87)

I propose an alternative punctuation that includes the last line as part of what she threatens to cry out.

Proposed:
And seyde, "I wol nat kisse thee, by my fey.
Why, lat be," quod she, "lat be, Nicholas,
Or I wol crie out, 'harrow, and allas,
Do wey youre handes, for youre curteisye!' "
(I 3284–87)

Alisoun speaks to John

Part of Absolon's attempt to seduce the fair Alisoun in the *Miller's Tale* is his two-line song to her outside her bedroom window. Here is the *Riverside* reading:

He syngeth in his voys gentil and smal,
"Now, deere lady, if thy wille be,
I praye yow that ye wole rewe on me."
(I 3360–62)

Sleeping next to Alisoun, John hears the song and speaks to his wife about it:

"What! Alison! Herestow nat Absolon,
That chaunteth thus under oure boures wal?"
(I 3366–67)

In the *Riverside* punctuation, Alisoun replies with one line:

"Yis, God woot, John, I heere it every deel."
(I 3369)

I propose that we give her a second line by moving the closing quotation mark to the end of the next line, so that the whole passage reads differently.

Proposed:
He syngeth in his voys gentil and smal,
"Now, deere lady, if thy wille be,
I praye yow that ye wole rewe on me,"
Ful wel acordaunt to his gyternynge.
This carpenter awook and herde him synge
And spak unto his wyf and seyde anon,

"What, Alison, herestow nat Absolon
That chaunteth thus under oure boures wal?"
And she answerde her housbonde therwithal,
"Yis, God woot, John, I heere it every deel.
This passeth forth. What wol ye bet than weel?"
(I 3360–70)

Nicholas speaks to John

When he gives his prediction to John about what will happen the night of the flood, Nicholas talks about what to do with the axe once the waters rise. Again, I give the *Riverside* version first:

"And breke an hole an heigh, upon the gable,
Unto the gardyn-ward, over the stable,
That we may frely passen forth oure way,
Whan that the grete shour is goon away.
Thanne shaltou swymme as myrie, I undertake,
As dooth the white doke after hire drake."
(I 3571–76)

I propose that we change the comma to a period at the end of I 3573 and remove the period at the end of I 3574.

Proposed:
"And breke an hole an heigh, upon the gable,
Unto the gardyn-ward, over the stable,
That we may frely passen forth oure way.
Whan that the grete shour is goon away
Thanne shaltou swymme as myrie, I undertake,
As dooth the white doke after hire drake."
(I 3571–76)

The pedagogy of punctuation

My larger point is not that I am right in punctuating these passages in particular ways, but that we should as teachers of Chaucer be aware that modern editors can misguide both us and our students. There is pedagogical usefulness in letting our students know that the punctuation in modern editions is not Chaucerian and in giving modern students some unpunctuated Chaucerian lines and letting them come up with, and argue for, their own punctuation of those lines. I can think of no better way to end than by quoting Emerson Brown: "I am not prepared to advocate removing punctuation from classroom texts, but we might at least think about the problem and experiment some. Let's see how well our students can cope with passages transcribed from the manuscripts. They may surprise us" (139). And they may also come to see, perhaps for the first time, that in their own sentences as well as Chaucer's, punctuation absolutely affects meaning. One misplaced comma or quotation mark can make all the difference. I think Emerson would have agreed that that is an important point.

Transformations in Gower's *Tale of Florent* and Chaucer's *Wife of Bath's Tale*

[John Gower was Chaucer's contemporary and friend. In his *Confessio Amantis* (Confessions of a Lover), Gower tells a close analogue to Chaucer's more famous *Wife of Bath's Tale*. (For arguments about which of the two versions came first, see my article on owl similes on pp. 105–15 below.) The *Tale of Florent* is a fine narrative, but it is usually read merely as evidence that Chaucer's version of the same story was better. In this article I challenge the usual judgment about the superiority of Chaucer's version by showing that the two storylines are not the same at all: each served quite different thematic purposes. To give just one example, Gower's tale sets out to reward a near-perfect knight for his obedience to his ugly old wife, while Chaucer's sets out to have an ugly old wife teach obedience to a deeply flawed knight. In this republication of the article I change the term "hag" to "old woman," having been reminded by my friend Lorraine K. Stock that neither Chaucer nor Gower refers to her as a "hag." "Transformations" first appeared in *Chaucer and Gower: Difference, Mutuality, Exchange*, ed. R. F. Yeager, Number 51 (1991), 100–14.]

Comparisons of Chaucer's *Wife of Bath's Tale* with Gower's *Tale of Florent* tend to leap immediately to evaluation. Which tale, scholars ask, is better? The answer is almost always the same—that Chaucer's tale is better.[1] It is livelier and more realistic. It more interestingly reflects the complex personality and conflicting desires of its garrulous fictional teller. It demonstrates a more logical connection between the knight's crime of rape and the knight's punishment on his wedding night—a kind of rape-in-reverse in which a woman attempts to force an unwilling man have sex with her. It shows a better motivation for

[1] G. H. Maynadier set the tone for much of the subsequent comparisons between the *Tale of Florent* and the *Wife of Bath's Tale*: "From an artistic point of view, Chaucer's story is . . . superior to Gower's" *(The Wife of Bath's Tale: Its Sources and Analogues* [London: David Nutt, 1901], 137). Bartlett J. Whiting, similarly, found Chaucer's *Wife of Bath's Tale* superior to its analogues: "Despite the varying merits of the other documents, no better proof of Chaucer's overwhelming literary power and artistry is to be found than in a comparison of the Wife's Tale with its analogues" *(Sources and Analogues of Chaucer's Canterbury Tales,* ed. W. F. Bryan and Germaine Dempster [University of Chicago Press, 1941], 224). Whiting did not defend his view, but others did so after him. Francis G. Townsend, for example, in comparing the knights in the *Wife of Bath's Tale* and *Tale of Florent*, finds "neither logic nor consistency in Gower's characterization" of Florent ("Chaucer's Nameless Knight," *Modern Language Review* 49 [1954]: 2).

Typical of more recent critics is John Hurt Fisher, who believes that Chaucer's *Wife of Bath's Tale* was based on Gower's *Tale of Florent.* Fisher says that Chaucer's "conscious alterations" of Gower's tale were "designed to improve the pace and structure of the story"; a comparison of the two "answering scenes" is "all to Chaucer's advantage" and shows that Chaucer's is "more dramatic" (*John Gower: Moral Philosopher and Friend of Chaucer* [New York University Press, 1964], 296–97). Fisher finds only one passage in which Gower's telling is "more vivid" (298)—the description of the old woman. Others have commented on Gower's vivid description of the old woman. In discussing the passage, for example, Theodore Silverstein remarks that "if Gower's poetic line seldom reaches the richness of his friend's, his skill with larger device can sometimes be as deadly sure" ("The Wife of Bath and the Rhetoric of Enchantment," *Modern Philology* 58 [1961]: 167). Note, however, the characteristic adverbs—"seldom," "sometimes"—that undercut the compliment.

Although Derek Pearsall finds that "by any conventional standards, Gower's realization of the story is much superior to Chaucer's," he concludes that Chaucer's superiority demands that we not apply conventional standards. Gower's is a more "primitive" version than that of Chaucer, who is "working on a different level altogether from Gower." He concludes that "Gower, by any but these, the very highest standards, is an uncommonly fine narrative poet" ("Gower's Narrative Art," *PMLA* 81 [1966]: 483–84). Like most critwho compare the two writers, Pearsall uses Gower's Florent story as a foil to Chaucer's. Although he has some kind things to say about Gower's handling of the story, in the end he denigrates it by saying that "the truest measure of Chaucer's greatness, however, is in his treatment of a story analogous to Gower's tale of Florent" (*Gower and Lydgate* [Harlow: Longmans, Green, 1969], 21).

the queen's sending him on a quest to discover what women desire than does Gower's tale, in which Florent has not been guilty of imposing his will on a woman. Its chief character, the knight-rapist, undergoes a more dramatic change. The choice it offers to the knight is more complex, involving as it does not merely beauty but also morality. And so on.

There have been a few lonely—and generally unenthusiastic—defenders of the *Tale of Florent*[2] but if Gower's tale is read at all these days, it is read by and large as a measure against which to show how superior Chaucer's is. In this paper I propose to take another approach: to focus on Gower's *Tale of Florent* as a poem with its own unique logic and narrative beauty, using Chaucer's quite different tale as a means of highlighting not the superiority, but the different purposes of Gower's.

More recently Olga C. M. Fischer, having completed a stylistic comparison of the two tales, concludes that the *Wife of Bath's Tale* "shows a higher proportion of suspense and drama, vividness and intensity" ("Gower's *Tale of Florent* and Chaucer's *Wife of Bath's Tale:* A Stylistic Comparison," *English Studies* 66 [1985]: 216). Here is Fischer's conclusion, surely a classic case of damning with faint praise: "Thus, even though we may think of Gower's poetry as dull—I would prefer to call it soothing, harmonious—especially when compared with the sprightliness and raciness of Chaucer's verse, this 'dullness' has a function in the *Confessio Amantis*" (225).

[2] The defenses of Gower tend to be shorter and more apologetic. For example, Henry Seidel Canby offers this backhanded compliment to Gower's *Tale of Florent* as compared with Chaucer's *Wife of Bath's Tale:* "Lacking all the satire, most of the humor, and much of the beauty, Gower's poem is better narrative" *(The Short Story in English* [New York: Henry Holt, 1926], 65). Canby's statement leaves us to wonder how, if Gower's tale has no satire, little humor, and less beauty, how it can be "better narrative."

Peter Nicholson is more judicious: "Gower's version differs in a great many particulars, but it is just as well suited for its purpose, as a lesson for Amans, as Chaucer's version is suited to its teller" ("The 'Confession' in Gower's *Confessio Amantis,*" *Studia Neophilologica* 58 [1986]: 198). Alexandra Hennessey Olsen points out that "a comparison of the *Wife of Bath's Tale* and the tale of Florent on the level of linguistic and literary artistry indicates that both poets provide examples of medieval poetic artistry although they differ from one another" (*"Between Ernest and Game": The Literary Artistry of the Confessio Amantis* [New York: Peter Lang, 1989], 99). And most recently R. F. Yeager reminds us that we should hesitate to make fast or facile comparisons: "The intentions of the narrators concerned—Alison of Bath and Genius—are wholly dissimilar, and should render impossible any simple preference" (*John Gower's Poetic: The Search for a New Arion* [Cambridge: D. S. Brewer, 1990], 138).

On the surface the two tales are quite similar. In both a young knight is given a chance to save his life by going on a quest to find out what women desire. Both knights learn from an old woman that the answer is that women desire sovereignty. In exchange for the answer, both knights must marry the old women, who then present their reluctant husbands with a choice. Both knights wisely let their wives choose and are rewarded with a lovely young bride. Despite these surface similarities, however, the two tales have fundamentally different purposes. One way of describing the different purposes is to say that Gower has Genius tell the *Tale of Florent* as a means of transforming Amans, a character *outside* the tale, into a man worthy of a good woman's love, while Chaucer, on the other hand, has Alice tell the *Wife of Bath's Tale* to illustrate how a lusty young knight *inside* the tale is transformed into a man worthy of a good woman's love. Another way is to say that Gower's tale demonstrates how a cautious and near-perfect knight *does* behave in a dangerous and hostile situation, whereas Chaucer's tale shows how an impulsive and most imperfect knight *learns how to* behave in a far less threatening situation.

These differences can best be explained not by saying that one teller is better than the other, but by saying that two fine poets had quite different purposes in composing their tales. Let us consider how some of the smaller differences between the two stories derive from those larger differences in purpose.

The knight

In Gower's *Tale of Florent,* the knight Florent, the nephew of the emperor, is a "worthi knyht" (1408)[3] of the noblest character:

> He was a man that mochel myhte,
> Of armes he was desirous,

[3] All quotations from Gower are from volume 1 of G. C. Macaulay's edition of *The English Works of John Gower* (Oxford University Press, 1901). I generally refer to the *Tale of Florent* as Gower's rather than Genius's, just as I refer to the *Wife of Bath's Tale* as Chaucer's.

Chivalerous and amorous.
(1412–14)

Florent does not make mistakes. As we shall see in various incidents below, Florent is wise, kind, helpful, considerate, and, of course, obedient. If he seems at times a bit too good to be true, we must remember that Gower designed the tale in such a way that Florent was a positive example for Amans.

Chaucer's tale, of course, is quite different. The young knight is ignoble. A mere "lusty bacheler" (III 883),[4] he is noble neither in character nor by means of blood ties to the ruler. Shallow, thoughtless, and impulsive, he is just the sort of person who needs to be taught some lessons in nobility in the course of the tale.

The crime

The "crime" that Florent commits, if it can be considered a crime at all, is one befitting a noble knight. One day while he is seeking adventures in the lowlands, he is taken prisoner and carried off to a castle. In defending himself he kills Branchus, the son a local captain. We are told little about the circumstances of the fight, but we can safely assume that Florent was in the right, or at least that he comported himself in a proper manner. Even his enemies, after all, know his reputation for "worthinesse / Of knyhthod and of gentilesse" (1435–36).

Chaucer's knight, on the other hand, is guilty of the most ignoble of crimes, rape. Andreas Capellanus notwithstanding,[5] no

[4] All quotations from Chaucer are from Larry D. Benson, ed., *The Riverside Chaucer,* 3rd edn. (Boston: Houghton Mifflin, 1987).

[5] In Book One, Chapter 9, of the *Art of Courtly Love,* Andreas suggests that it is all right for a knight to take by force a peasant woman. The tone of that statement, of course, is suspect. In any case the Wife of Bath would not—at least openly—agree with Andreas that men should use force against women. For a useful discussion of medieval attitudes toward rape in literary works, see Kathryn Gravdal, "Camouflaging Rape: The Rhetoric of Sexual Violence in the Medieval Pastourelle," *Romanic Review* 76 (1985): 361–73.

knight of true virtue or nobility would think of forcing his will on a defenseless woman. This knight has lessons to learn about nobility. By the end of the tale, he learns them. Far from beginning the tale full of "gentilesse," he has to learn by listening to the woman's "pillow lecture" what it entails.

The quest-setter

The parents of the slain Branchus want to put the captured Florent to death immediately, but they are afraid to do so because he is related to the emperor. Uncertain what to do, they listen to the advice of the ancient grandmother of Branchus. She devises a scheme that she thinks will mean certain death to Florent, yet leave Branchus's family unscathed and unpunished. Her plan is that the family *appear* to give Florent a chance to save his life by sending him off on what will turn out to be an impossible quest, yet insist that he promise to return and accept death if he fails to find the answer to a certain question:

> "And over this thou schalt ek swere,
> That if thou of the sothe faile,
> Ther schal non other thing availe,
> That thou ne schalt thi deth receive."
>
> (1462–65)

The object of the plan is to make their execution of Florent *appear* legal by having Florent concur in the bargain, fail in the quest, and return to their custody having agreed in advance to his own death.

The person who sends the knight on his quest in Chaucer is also a woman. Guinevere, however, does not desire to kill the knight. Had she wanted the knight dead, she would not have intervened at all, but would have let the law of the land take its course:

> That dampned was this knyght for to be deed,
> By cours of lawe, and sholde han lost his heed—
> Paraventure swich was the statut tho.
>
> (III 891–93)

Rather than let him die for his crime, the queen begs Arthur to let him live: "So longe preyeden the kyng of grace / Til he his lyf hym graunted" (III 895–96). Far from wanting the knight dead, as Branchus's grandmother had, she wants him to live. Far from trying to trick him into a bad-faith bargain that will end in his death, she seems to want this erring knight to learn a lesson and thus the right to live. Even in sending the knight on his quest, as we shall see, she sets the knight up for success and life, not for failure and death.

The quest

Branchus's grandmother sets Florent the impossible task of discovering what it is that "alle wommen most desire" (1481). I call particular attention to Gower's repeated use of the word "alle" (cf. ll. 1502, 1608, 1660). Florent must learn not merely what women desire, but what *all* women desire. To make sure that he does not have much time to pursue his near-impossible quest, she gives him his freedom for a short period of time—not specified, but perhaps as little as a day or two[6]—and lets him return to the emperor's court to seek advice and counsel on the question of what all women desire. Once Florent is there, the emperor calls in the wise people in the land for counsel. Some say one thing, some say another, but they cannot agree:

> But such a thing in special,
> Which to hem all in general
> Is most plesant, and most desired
> Above alle othre and most conspired,
> Such o thing conne they noght finde.
> (1501–05)

[6] It is typical for critics interested primarily in Chaucer to read Gower's tale with less than exacting care. Derek Pearsall says of Florent that "if he does not provide the right answer within a twelve-month he will forfeit his life" (*The Canterbury Tales* [London: Allen and Unwin, 1985], 87). The grandmother makes no such stipulation. She sets a time and date for Florent's return (see ll. 1368, 1486), but we never learn how much time Florent is given. That it is much shorter than a year seems to be indicated by the fact that Florent has time only for one brief visit to his uncle's court, and then must return.

In the end, having requested that his uncle make no attempt to avenge it, Florent heads back for his appointment with death.

Chaucer's knight has an easier task. He has only to find what "what thyng is it that wommen moost desiren" (III 905; see also 921, 985, 1007, 1033). In repeated references to the quest, Chaucer never states the quest in terms of "all" women. The knight need not find the *one* answer that *all* woman will agree on, but merely general agreement on what women desire or love most. This distinction is important, but has been overlooked in previous criticism of the tale. Indeed, Guinevere never even says that the knight must return with the correct answer, but merely "an answerer suffisent in this mateere" (III 910). Furthermore, she gives the knight a full year of unlimited travel to find out the answer. Chaucer's ignoble knight, like Florent, fails, but he fails at an easier task after having had more time to complete it.

The surety

Florent, who is "worthi . . . and wys" (1472), can be trusted to keep his promise to return. He had, after all given "his oth" (1487). Noble chap that he is, he would rather die than break it:

> This knyht had levere forto dye
> Than breke his trowthe and forto lye
> In place ther as he was swore.
>
> (1511–13)

The grandmother knows that she can trust him and demands no token or surety other than his own word.

Guinevere, on the other hand, knows that her convict knight is not a man to be trusted. She demands "suretee"—apparently some sort of bond or special guarantee: " 'And suretee wol I han, er that thou pace, / Thy body for to yelden in this place' " (III 911–12). In the end he returns home with heavy heart. Chaucer does not say that he returns because he has given his word and would sooner die than break it. Chaucer says, rather, that he comes back simply because he has no choice: "But hoom he gooth; he myghte nat sojourne; / The day was come that homward moste he tourne" (III 987–88). And notice that it is to "hoom" that he returns, not—like Florent—to the camp of an enemy bent on putting him to death.

The old woman in the forest

On his way back, Florent sees an ugly old woman sitting under a tree. When she calls to him he turns his horse aside and goes to her. She tells him that unless he receives better counsel than he has had previously, he is sure to die. He asks for her counsel. She asks what her reward will be. He tells her she may have whatever she asks. She says she wants him to marry her: " 'I wol have thi trowthe in honde / That thou schalt be myn housebonde' " (1559–60). At first Florent refuses, saying that such a union cannot be. She reminds him that the alternative is sure death. Florent offers her land—park land, rental land, plow land—but she refuses. He considers the alternative, death, and finally agrees that, if her answer is the one that saves him, he will marry her. She then gives him the answer.

Chaucer's forest scene is quite different. The knight is initially confronted not with an ugly old woman, but with more than twenty-four dancing ladies.[7] They do not call to him, but of his own volition he rides over to them, only to find in their place a foul old woman. We should note, of course, that he goes to her out of lust for the dancing ladies, not—like Florent—out of kindness to help an old lady. She asks him what he seeks. He tells her that he wants to find out what women most desire and offers to reward her if she can tell him. She agrees to do so if he will promise to give her, after he has won his life, the very next thing that she asks of him. Impulsive still as he was in

[7] Chaucer's addition of the twenty-four-plus dancing ladies has received little commentary. Much of what it has received has been off the mark. D. S. Brewer, for example, sees Chaucer's refusal to explain the mystery of the dancers as still further evidence of Chaucer's superiority to the literal-minded Gower: "In [Chaucer's] poem there is, too, a genuine mysteriousness and freshness in the glimpse of the fairy ladies dancing 'under a forest side.' They disappear when the anxious knight approaches, and he finds only the old woman. Chaucer does not attempt, as Gower does, to go into the details of the enchantment; he knows when to leave well alone" (*Chaucer*, 3rd edn. [London: Longmans, 1973], 141). For another example of a misdirected

raping the maiden, the knight immediately agrees, never pausing to consider what her request might be. Having secured his promise, she whispers to him the correct answer.

The return

Florent rides out of the woods alone, leaving the woman to await his return. Confident that this near-perfect knight will return to keep his promise to marry her, she feels no need to accompany him. It may be, also, that she knows that it would be dangerous for her to enter enemy country to face the wrath of Branchus's grandmother. In any case, Florent returns alone, despairing of his chances of finding further joy in this world:

> He goth him forth with hevy chiere,
> As he that not in what manere
> He mai this worldes joie atteigne.
> (1619–21)

He knows that he must either die or unite himself with "th'unsemlieste" (1625) woman in the world.

The old woman in Chaucer's tale, apparently not trusting the knight to keep his promise and knowing that she has little to fear in Guinevere's court, comes along with her husband-to-be. The knight, unlike Florent, thinks he has little reason to despair. After all, he has his answer and he expects to get his freedom. Why should he not believe that he can take to heart the old woman's suggestion

interpretation, see Eric D. Brown's Jungian analysis of the tale: "The knight's vision of the dancing women is not difficult to explain psychologically. . . . The figures may be regarded as projections from the knight's psyche" ("Symbols of Transformation: A Specific Archetypal Examination of the *Wife of Bath's Tale*," *Chaucer Review* 12 [1978]: 212). A much simpler explanation is possible. Because the knight in Chaucer's story, unlike Florent, is not gracious enough to help an old woman simply because she needs help, Chaucer had to invent something more sexually attractive to bring him into the presence of the ugly old woman. Given his character and propensity for raping young women, the dancing ladies would have been quite enough to attract him. It is interesting, of course, that the old woman seems to have transformed herself into the dancing ladies to attract this knight, just as she later transforms herself into a lovely young woman to reward him for yielding to her the sovereignty.

that he should "be glad and have no fere" (III 1022) on his return to Guinevere's court?

The answer

Florent gives the grandmother every answer he can think of, but none satisfies her. Finally—and reluctantly, because he knows the price he will have to pay—he tells her the answer that the old woman had given him: that women desire to "be soverein of mannes love" (1609). The grandmother is furious that some traitorous woman had told Florent the secret that women had, apparently, agreed to conceal from men:

> Sche seide: "Ha, treson! Wo thee be,
> That hath thus told the privite,
> Which alle wommen most desire!
> I wolde that thou were afire!"
>
> (1659–61)

Note, once again, the adjective "all." The secret is one that every woman knows is true. To betray the secret is so serious that the grandmother would condemn the betrayer to the flames. Florent has won his life, but—noble fellow that he is—he must now carry out his promise to marry the old woman from the forest.

The knight in the *Wife of Bath's Tale* does not fiddle around giving other answers. Confident and ever impulsive, he seems to fear neither the punishment of death if he is wrong nor the reward he must give to the woman if her answer is right. He comes out directly with correct answer: that women desire "to have sovereynetee / As wel over hir housbond as hir love" (III 1038–39). The answer, although it specifically includes husbands among those over whom women desire to have sovereignty, is essentially the same as Florent's, but the reception it receives is much friendlier. We must remember that Guinevere had wanted the knight to live, not to die, that she had wanted him to succeed in his quest. Indeed, we suspect that she would have been satisfied with almost any answer, provided the knight gave it in a polite manner. He does give it politely. He addresses the queen as "my lige lady" (III 1037). After he gives his answer he tells her, "I am heer at youre wille" (III 1042). It may be that the women of Guinevere's court are more impressed with his manner than with his answer. In any case, it is interesting that neither the queen nor any other woman in court proclaims the answer he gives to be correct. Rather, they simply do not contradict it and give the knight his life:

> In al the court ne was ther wyf, ne mayde,
> Ne wydwe that contraried that he sayde,
> But seyden he was worthy han his lyf.
> (III 1043–45)

The answer is "suffisant" and the knight thinks he is free. But the old woman has come along with him and jumps up to announce that she had given the knight the answer in exchange for the next thing she would ask of him. She announces immediately, in the presence of Guinevere and the ladies of the court, that she requests that he marry her. Surprised at her request, the knight asks her to take all of his goods, but to let his body go. The old woman, however, will have none of his goods, and the knight has, finally, no choice but to marry her. He has been trapped by his own impulsiveness.

The marriage

True to his word, Florent returns to keep his promise to marry the ugly old woman. His doing so is not easy. The old woman is described in horrid detail (fifteen lines); Florent's misery is described almost as graphically (twenty lines). Florent takes his bride-to-be home by night so that no one will see them (seventeen lines). He tells his friends why he must marry this ugly woman and has some women in his castle try to clean her up and dress her up (twenty-two lines), but to no avail; she looks, if anything, even uglier when they are finished. After the bride and unhappy bridegroom are married they go naked to bed, and Florent turns away from his bride (thirty-six lines). Throughout, we are impressed not only with the care that Gower paid to these scenes, but with Florent's nobility. Had he been a more selfish, less honorable man, he could have escaped this terrible fate. He is, however, a knight, and knights keep their word: "He wolde algate his trowthe holde, / As every knyht therto is holde" (1715–16). Florent has given his word, and "for pure gentilesse" (1721) he keeps it.

The Chaucerian version of these scenes is much abbreviated. We are told in a mere fifteen lines that the knight and the old woman are married and go to bed. We are reminded not of the knight's gentility—he learns that, later, from her pillow lecture—but of his lack of choice: "The ende is this, that he / Constreyned was, he nedes moste hire wedde" (III 1070–71). He marries her not out of nobility or because his conscience tells him to keep his promise, but because he is "constrained." We know little about his thoughts or his feelings, and we are told almost nothing of the ugliness of his bride or the failure of any attempts to make her less ugly. Having no alternative to marrying her, he marries her.

The choice

When his bride asks him to turn toward her, Florent, "as it were a man in trance" (1800), obeys and finds at his side a lovely young woman of eighteen. He reaches out to pull her toward him, but she restrains him, telling him that he must make a choice:

> He mot on of tuo thinges chese:
> Wher he wol have hire such on nyht,
> Or elles upon daies lyht,
> For he schal noght have bothe tuo.
>
> (1810–13)

Florent hesitates, torn between two choices. He wants her young and lovely at night when he can enjoy her sexual favors, but his behavior in bringing his bride home at night so no one will see her, as well as his efforts to pretty her up for the wedding, show that he would also like her to be lovely when others see her. In the end, he gives her the choice:

> "I not what ansuere I schal yive;
> Bot evere whil that I may live,
> I wol that ye be my maistresse.

> For I can noght miselve gesse
> Which is the beste."
>
> (1823–27)

Now that it is clear that she has the mastery in their relationship—" 'ye have mad me soverein' " (1834)—she rewards him by being young and beautiful both day and night.

Chaucer's version of the choice is somewhat different. To begin with, it is preceded by more than a hundred lines of pillow lecture about the nature of gentility and the advantages of poverty, old age, and ugliness. It is worth noting that whereas Gower spends more than a hundred lines describing the events leading up to the confrontation in bed of the ugly old woman with her gentle husband, Chaucer spends that many lines describing the events that happen after the confrontation in bed. Gower devotes the space to demonstrating Florent's nobility in honoring his distasteful promise. Chaucer devotes the space to educating the foolish knight so that he will know how to be a more "gentil" man. In the end, the old woman in the *Wife of Bath's Tale* offers her husband a choice:

> "To han me foul and old til that I deye,
> And be to yow a trewe, humble wyf,
> And nevere yow displese in all my lyf,
> Or elles ye wol han me yong and fair,
> And take youre aventure of the repair
> That shal be to youre hous by cause of me,
> Or in some oother place, may wel be."
>
> (III 1220–26)

The choice she offers is more complex. It involves a choice not merely of public or private beauty, but of ugliness combined with the fidelity that comes with it, or of beauty combined with the potential infidelity that comes with it. The knight is uncertain how to choose. Having learned his lessons from his new old wife, however, he nobly offers the choice to his wife. Having gotten the mastery from him—" 'I may chese and governe as me lest' " (III 1237)—she rewards him with both beauty and fidelity. The knight in the *Wife of Bath's Tale* is rewarded for having learned the nobility that lets him offer his wife the choice. Florent, we have seen, already knew it.

The disenchantment

We learn at the very end why the old woman had wanted to marry and offer choices to Florent. She is really the princess of Sicily, but her evil stepmother had bewitched her and transformed her into an ugly old woman. The only way the princess can break her evil stepmother's enchantment is by winning

> The love and sovereinete
> Of what knyht that in his degre
> Alle othre passeth of good name.
> (1847–49)

She is condemned to be old and ugly always unless she can find a man of fine reputation who is noble enough both to love her and to yield his sovereignty to her. Who else but a near-perfect knight like Florent can save her from such a life? That he is the one is proved by the fact that he yields the sovereignty and falls in love with her: " 'The dede proeveth it is so' " (1851).

The imperfect knight in the *Wife of Bath's Tale* plays no role in the transformation of an enchanted princess, for of course in Chaucer there is no enchanted princess. Rather, the old woman can apparently change herself at will, using whatever shape she wants to attract, to repulse, to reward, and to educate any man. It seems likely that she had transformed herself before, when she appeared as twenty-four-plus dancing ladies to attract the lusty knight, then re-transformed herself into an old woman in the forest. She does not need the knight to effect her transformation now into a woman of youth and beauty. Rather, *he* needs *her* to effect his transformation from a "lusti bacheler" into a more sensitive, more generous, and more noble knight.

Different purposes

If Gower's *Tale of Florent* seems more static than Chaucer's *Wife of Bath's Tale,* we must remember that the two tales are quite different in conception and purpose. We might even say that Gower's tale is a straightforward romance in which a noble knight fights another knight, undertakes a dangerous quest, and finally saves a woman in distress. Chaucer's tale, on the other hand, can be seen as almost a feminist parody of the traditional romance: in it an imperfect knight fights no battle, undertakes a friendly quest, and in the end is saved by some women who pity his distress. Parody or not, Chaucer's tale is a story about how a young man learns a measure of nobility by making impulsive mistakes and by coming into contact with two women—a courtly queen and a forest queen—who save his life, teach him to respect the desires of women, show him that it is wiser to seek counsel than act impulsively, and transform him into a knight who has earned the right to a lifetime of "parfit joye" (III 1258). The transformation of this man from a foolish knight-rapist into a wise knight-husband is a dramatic one indeed, and it has deservedly captured the imagination of generations of readers.

The transformation that takes place in Gower's *Tale of Florent* is less dramatic for two reasons. First, the plot requires that Florent be, from the beginning, a near-perfect exemplar of knightly virtues. He must not be transformed by the events in the tale, because his reputation for near-perfect virtue is required to bring about the transformation of another character. In the *Tale of Florent,* we recall, the plot turns on the need of a princess to transform herself by breaking the spell her evil stepmother had cast upon her. In order for her to accomplish that transformation, she must find a noble man of fine repute who will gallantly allow her to be sovereign. The foolish and impulsive "bacheler" of Chaucer's story is unthinkable in such a role.

I began this paper with a list of reasons why most critics say that Chaucer's version is "better" than Gower's. If I wanted to, I might close with a list of arguments for preferring Gower's. I might argue, for example, that unlike Chaucer's tale Gower's does not leave a raped maiden stranded and forgotten in the opening pages of the tale. I might argue that in Chaucer's story a convicted rapist is sent off unattended to interview lots of women, a danger to women not present in Gower's. I might argue that unlike Chaucer's tale Gower's rewards with sexual bliss not a sex-driven rapist but a man whose consistent nobility shows that he is deserving of such a reward. I might argue the inconsistency in Chaucer's old wife's willingness to transform herself into a lovely young wife immediately after her pillow lecture arguing that just the opposite sort of mate is what a man should seek.[8]

If I wanted to, I might argue that unlike Chaucer's tale, the *Tale of Florent* provides a clear motivation to the old woman to accost the young knight in the forest: because by doing so she can break the spell placed upon her. I might argue that Florent's indecisiveness when faced with the choice offered to him at the end is carefully prepared for by his earlier indecisiveness, while that of Chaucer's impulsive bridegroom is quite out of character for him. I might argue that in Gower's tale the enchantment of the princess explains why and how an ugly old bride can be transformed through disenchantment into a lovely young bride, whereas Chaucer's merely posits, without explanation, a shape-shifting woman.[9] I might argue that there is a

[8] Others have noticed such problems in Chaucer's story. Derek Pearsall, for example, speaks of "a flow of meaning which is not completely in accord with the doctrine it purports to exemplify" (*The Canterbury Tales*, 90). And I am grateful to Susan K. Hagen for showing me a pre-publication copy of her "The Wife of Bath: Chaucer's Inchoate Experiment in Feminist Hermeneutics" (in the Medieval Institute's *Rebels and Rivals: The Contestive Spirit of the Canterbury Tales*). Hagen talks about the unsatisfying ending of the tale and suggests that if the Wife of Bath had really believed her own doctrine, there would have been no need for the old wife to change into anything more than she was.

[9] Douglas J. Wurtele points out that "in the Wife of Bath's version no explanation is given either for the re-transformation into beauty or for the original transformation into ugliness. Everything remains irrational, arguably more mysterious and not less so and, consequently, less and not more realistic than a supernatural event for which a rational explanation is given" ("Chaucer's Wife of Bath and Her Distorted Arthurian Motifs" (*Arthurian Interpretations* 2 [1987]: 57).

basic illogicality to Chaucer's tale: if the old woman is really a shape-shifter, then she had the power to make herself attractive to any man she wanted, and would not need to bother with the foolish "bacheler." I might point out another illogicality: that if the old woman is really so eager to establish her sovereignty over the knight, why is she so eager to yield that sovereignty to him in marriage by agreeing to be his servant: "And she obeyed hym in every thyng / That myghte doon hym plesance or likyng" (III 1255–56)?[10]

Such arguments, of course, are as simplistic as arguments that Chaucer's tale is better. I have no desire to make these kinds of arguments more persuasive. My point here is not to argue that one tale is better than another. Rather, it is to urge scholars to consider each tale in the light of its own purposes. Genius, the fictional teller of Gower's *Tale of Florent,* wants to demonstrate to Amans, his fictional listener, how a near-perfect knight is rewarded for his obedience in matters of love. The Wife of Bath, the fictional teller of Chaucer's tale, wants to demonstrate to her fellow pilgrims how a queen and an old wife can educate an ignorant young man and make him worthy of the love of a woman. Genius sets out to show that the magic of obedience can transform a spellbound old woman into a spellbinding princess. The Wife of Bath sets out to show that the magic of obedience can transform a quite foolish knight into a quite acceptable husband.

Those different purposes transform the same basic story into two quite different stories. Rather than trying to determine which one is superior to the other, why can we not pause to enjoy the skill with which two brilliant medieval writers managed to accomplish their own distinctive and worthy purposes? Rather than viewing literature as a

[10] Kemp Malone extends this illogicality to the relationship between the tale and the teller: "It is all the more striking, then, to find in the Wife of Bath's tale (as distinguished from her prologue) that the lady, after winning complete sovereignty over the hero, yields it up to him in marriage and becomes an obedient wife. This way of behaving most emphatically does not agree with the Wife of Bath's views on wedded bliss, as set forth in her prologue and repeated in her epilogue" ("*The Wife of Bath's Tale,*" *Modern Language Review* 57 [1962]: 483).

race in which we readers have to determine which runner won, why can we not be content to praise each runner for doing his personal best? Can we not be content to stand in awe of two very fine writers who both managed, six centuries ago, to bend similar fictional elements into two such distinctive works of art?

Chaucer's Wife of Bath's "foot-mantel" and Her "hipes large"

[I loved researching and writing this article. Could I really, after all these years, identify what a "foot-mantel" is? Most editors and translators—myself included—had misread it as an apron or outer skirt of some sort. Mostly by analyzing the Ellesmere illustration of the Wife of Bath, however, I was able to argue for its being a set of roomy leggings designed to be pulled up over Alisoun's shoes and dress to protect her from road dirt while she was on horseback. I also loved presenting an early draft of the paper at a medieval conference. At the end of my fifteen-minute presentation, I jumped up onto the flimsy table and pulled a newly-sewn replica of a medieval "foot-mantel" out of a brown paper bag and stepped into it. An even more exciting corollary of my argument was my suggestion that the Wife of Bath does not have large hips after all, but rather that she merely has the "foot-mantel" pulled up largely or loosely about her hips. "Chaucer's Wife of Bath's 'foot-mantel' " was originally published in *Chaucer Review* 34 (2000): 388–97.]

Every Chaucerian is familiar with the description of the Wife of Bath in the *General Prologue* to the *Canterbury Tales*: her gap teeth, her wimple, her hat, her five husbands, her heavy coverchiefs, her red hose, her matching red face, her deafness, her wandering by the way, her spurs, her remedies of love, her apron-like riding skirt, her large hips. Alisoun's "hipes large" have been a particular focus of Chaucerian readers and scholars since they seem to tell us, by implication, that she is an imposing woman with the size and commanding presence both to browbeat her older husbands and to hold her own in marital battle with her younger ones. My purpose in this paper is to offer a reinterpretation of line A 472, in which Chaucer describes the "foot-mantel aboute hir hipes large." Let us read the lines in context (all bold-face emphasis in this and other quotations is, of course, added):

> Upon an amblere esily she sat,
> Ywympled wel, and on hir heed an hat
> As brood as is a bokeler or a targe;
> **A foot-mantel aboute hir hipes large,**
> And on hir feet a paire of spores sharpe.
> (A 469–73)

Editors, translators, and scholars almost unanimously agree on the meaning of line 472: the Wife of Bath wears a protective outer skirt about her large hips. I challenge that reading on two counts: I do not believe that the "foot-mantel" is a skirt, and I think it quite possible that we are wrong to read the Wife of Bath as having large hips.

Perhaps I should start with a reminder that editors almost all hyphenate Chaucer's words "foot" and "mantel." I have no particular argument with that practice, since it seems that a single garment is referred to, but we should perhaps not totally lose sight of the fact that in none of the manuscripts is the word hyphenated. Skeat glossed "foot-mantel" as a "foot-cloth, 'safe-guard' to cover the skirt."[1]

[1] Walter W. Skeat, *The Complete Works of Geoffrey Chaucer* (Oxford: Clarendon Press, 1894), vol. 6, 101. I am grateful to Jeanne Krochalis for calling to my attention the *Middle English Dictionary's* 1344 reference to the word "foteclothes" in a passage on Edward III's wardrobe accounts. The word there appears to mean something like slippers or socks—a garment to enclose or cover the feet. That reference lends oblique support to my notion, explained below, that another foot-compound word, "foot-mantel," refers to a garment pulled up over the feet to the hips. A useful review of the problems associated with the term "foot-mantel" can be found in the note to line 472 in Malcolm Andrew's *A Variorum Edition of the Works of Geoffrey Chaucer*, vol. 2: The General Prologue, Part One-B, Explanatory Notes (Norman, OK: University of

Skeat also referred to Tyrwhitt, "who supposes this to be a sort of *riding-petticoat,* such as is now used by market-women."[2] Benson's *Riverside* edition glosses the term to mean an "apron-like overskirt."[3] Other editors gloss the word to mean "a protective outer skirt,"[4] "an outer, protective skirt,"[5] an "outer skirt to protect her gown as she

Oklahoma Press, 1993), 426–27. Andrew refers to Urry's 1721 gloss of the foot-mantle as "a woman's Riding-coat, coming down to the feet," It does not seem that we are to think of the foot-mantle as a long coat, however, since the Ellesmere illustration, discussed below, shows her wearing no such coat. Laura F. Hodges, in her excellent article on the costume of the Wife of Bath, has little to say about the foot-mantle except that, following Strutt (see next note), it may be a kind of petticoat and indicates little more than that Alisoun is an "experienced traveler" ("The Wife of Bath's Costumes: Reading the Subtexts," *Chaucer Review* 27 [1993]: 367).

[2] Skeat's reference to Tyrwhitt comes in volume 5: 45. Thomas Tyrwhitt's "*riding-petticoat*" note appears in his 1778 edition, which I checked in vol. 5: 94, of the 1830 edition published in London by William Pickering. Tyrwhitt's suggestion that the foot mantle is a kind of petticoat, presumably to be worn under the main dress, seems problematical since there would be little point in wearing such an undergarment while riding astride on horse-back. There would be more reason to wear an outer garment of some sort. Apparently Joseph Strutt drew from Tyrwhitt for his rather non-specific definition of Alisoun's foot-mantle as "a species of petticoat tied about her hips. A garment of the same kind is used to this day by the farmers' wives and market women, when they ride on horseback, to keep their gowns clean. The foot-mantle, even in the Poet's time, seems to have been a vulgar habit; for the prioress riding in the same company had a spruce *cloak,* which answered the same purpose" (*A Complete View of the Dress and Habits of the People of England,* first published in 1842 [London, rpt. 1970], 2: 267. Less specific is Robert D. French in his edition, where he glosses the word as simply "worn over the skirt when riding" in *Chaucer's Canterbury Tales* (New York: Appleton-Century, 1948), 14.

[3] *The Riverside Chaucer,* 3rd edition, ed. Larry D. Benson (Boston: Houghton Mifflin, 1987), 30; see also 819, where the on-page gloss is expanded to "apparently an apronlike overskirt, as illustrated in the Ellesmere drawing." The Ellesmere, of course, does not illustrate a garment that can be called "apronlike." All quotations from Chaucer are from this edition. F. N. Robinson, in the first and the second editions of what is now called the *Riverside Chaucer,* glossed "foot mantel" in this way: "*A foot-mantel,* which ordinarily meant 'saddle-cloth,' here seems to be an outer skirt": *Chaucer's Complete Works* (Boston, 1933), 765, and *The Works of Geoffrey Chaucer* (Boston, 1957), 663. Robinson does not tell us where he got his notion that the term "ordinarily" meant "saddle-cloth."

[4] John H. Fisher, *The Complete Poetry and Prose of Geoffrey Chaucer* (New York: Thomson Learning, 1977), 18.

[5] Francis King and Bruce Steele, *Selections from Geoffrey Chaucer's The Canterbury Tales* (Melbourne: F. W. Cheshire, 1969), 35.

rode along,"[6] a "short riding skirt,"[7] an "outer skirt,"[8] an "apron-like skirt,"[9] or simply "an apron."[10]

Joining the editors and glossators are the modern English translators. Although one translator, curiously, translates "foot-mantel" as a "saddleblanket"[11] and another as a "rug,"[12] almost all translators render it for modern readers as "an outer skirt,"[13] a "riding skirt,"[14] an "over-skirt,"[15] a "protective skirt,"[16] or just a plain "skirt."[17]

[6] Gloria Cigman, *The Wife of Bath's Prologue and Tale and the Clerk's Prologue and Tale from The Canterbury Tales* (New York: Holmes and Meier, 1976), 32.

[7] John S. P. Tatlock and Percy MacKaye, *The Modern Reader's Chaucer* (New York, 1912), 8.

[8] A. C. Cawley, *Geoffrey Chaucer: Canterbury Tales* (London, 1958), 15; William Frost, *The Age of Chaucer,* 2nd ed. (Englewood Cliffs, NJ, 1961), 44; Daniel Cook, *The Canterbury Tales of Geoffrey Chaucer* (Garden City, NJ, 1961), 472; Robert A. Pratt, *The Tales of Canterbury Complete* (Boston, 1974), 16; V. A. Kolve and Glending Olson, *The Canterbury Tales* (New York, 1988), 15. That this is the most frequent gloss is no doubt traceable to Robinson's note in both his editions (see my note 3 above).

[9] Albert C. Baugh, *Chaucer's Major Poetry* (New York, 1963), 249.

[10] Peter G. Beidler, *The Wife of Bath* (Boston, 1996), 43. Like many modern editors and translators, I was too eager to accept the authority of the on-page Benson *Riverside* gloss of the word as "apron-like" (31).

[11] James J. Donohue, *Chaucer's Canterbury Tales Complete* (Dubuque, IA, 1979), 13. Donohue is apparently following Robinson's undocumented suggestion (see note 3 above) that the word "ordinarily meant 'saddle-cloth.' "

[12] J. U. Nicholson, *Canterbury Tales* (Garden City, NJ, 1934), 15.

[13] David Wright, *The Canterbury Tales* (New York, 1964), 11.

[14] E. T. Donaldson, ed., *Chaucer's Poetry,* 2nd edn. (New York, 1975), 21; R. M. Lumiansky, *The Canterbury Tales of Geoffrey Chaucer* (New York, 1960), 10; David Wright, *The Canterbury Tales* (Oxford, 1985), 13.

[15] Michael Alexander, *The Canterbury Tales: The First Fragment* (London, 1996), 28.

[16] Vincent F. Hooper, *Chaucer's Canterbury Tales* (Selected)*: An Interlinear Translation* (Woodbury, NY, 1970), 30.

[17] Theodore Morrison, *The Portable Chaucer* (New York, 1949), 65. He renders the line as "A skirt swathed up her hips, and they were large." It is not clear where he finds the verb "swathed up" or what it means.

Some translators keep the word "mantle,"[18] assuming apparently that modern readers will know what a "mantle" is. If modern readers do recognize the word, or if they look it up in a modern English dictionary, they will imagine that the Wife of Bath is wearing some sort of long cape or cloak, since the translators who translate "foot-mantel" as "mantle" silently delete the prefix "foot-." That deletion suggests the modern world's failure to understand what a foot-mantle is.

The *OED* and the *MED* are both hampered by the rarity of the term, since, indeed, Chaucer's only use of "foot-mantel" is apparently the first recorded written use of the term, and apparently the last one for more than a hundred years. The composer of the *OED* reference calls the term "obscure" and speculates that it may be "an over-garment worn by women when riding, to protect their dress" (s.v. "footmantle"). The term "over-garment" suggests that it is, like an apron or skirt or cape, to be pulled down over the dress. The *MED* refers to the foot-mantle as, vaguely, "a garment reaching down to the feet" (s.v. "footmantle").[19]

[18] Frank Ernest Hill, *The Canterbury Tales* (New York, 1935), 12; Ronald L. Ecker and Eugene J. Crook, *The Canterbury Tales* (Palatka, FL, 1993), 13; Nevill Coghill, *The Canterbury Tales* (London, 1951), 32 (Coghill, curiously, adds an adjective to make it a "flowing mantle that concealed / Large hips"). A. Kent and Constance Hieatt translate the word as "footmantle"—scarcely a translation, of course, since they offer no gloss; see their *The Canterbury Tales by Geoffrey Chaucer* (New York, 1982), 23. Chaucer tells us that the wives of the guildsmen go to church feasts wearing "a mantel roialliche ybore" (A 378). The early editor Speght, in his 1602 edition, explains that parishioners came to some church events in their mantles: "Hither came the wiues in comely manner, and they which were of the better sort, had their mantles carried with them, as well for show, as to keepe them from cold at the table. These mantles also many did vse in the Church at the morrow Masses and other times" quoted from the note to line 377 in Andrew's *Variorum Edition,* 337.

[19] Norman Davis, et al., follow the *Middle English Dictionary* by referring to the foot-mantle as "a protective garment reaching to the feet," *A Chaucer Glossary* (Oxford, 1979), 59, but make no effort to say what kind of garment it is. Scholars occasionally refer, in passing, to what they suppose the foot-mantle is. Muriel Bowden, for example, in *A Commentary on the General*

I suggest, on the contrary, that the foot-mantle is just what the words suggest that it is: a kind of early mantle or covering, akin to modern riding chaps or, more exactly, since it was probably a one-piece garment, a set of loose leggings. It would have been worn by women in the days before women wore pants, and it would have provided warmth to their lower extremities and protection for their shoes, hose, and dresses from the mud, splashes, horse sweat, and excrement that must have been a regular part of horseback travel on unpaved medieval roads and pathways. The prefix "foot-" suggests that the garment is pulled up over the feet and legs from the bottom rather than pulled down over or wrapped around the shoulders or hips. The garment would have been donned just before a woman climbed onto her horse, perhaps from a stile or raised platform. Once she was on the horse it would have been held in place by the saddle or perhaps by a belt or suspender of some sort.

Such a foot-mantle would have been particularly necessary for a woman of even minimal modesty wearing skirts while riding astride,[20] as the Wife of Bath was. It seems clear enough that she was riding astride, since wearing spurs would have been both useless and dangerous for a woman riding side-saddle. The description of Alisoun in the *General Prologue* tells us with some precision that this cloth-maker of beside Bath was elegantly dressed for pilgrimage. Surely she would have wanted to protect from the mess of a medieval pilgrimage

Prologue to the Canterbury Tales (New York, 1948), 217, tells us that Alisoun is "careful enough to wear a protective outer skirt"; Kemp Malone tells us that she "wore a foot-mantle to shield her clothes against the mud cast by the horses' hoofs as they rode along," *Chapters on Chaucer* (Baltimore, 1951), 203; and R. M. Lumiansky tells us that she wears "a cloth to protect her skirt from dust and mud," *Of Sondry Folk* (Austin, 1955), 120. None of them attempts to describe the garment, however. Surely, to judge by the Ellesmere illustration, we are speaking of a sewn garment, not a "cloth."

[20] For evidence that fourteenth-century women often rode astride, see J. J. Jusserand, trans. Lucy Toulmin Smith, *English Wayfaring Life in the Middle Ages* (New York, 1925), 103: "Women were accustomed to riding almost as much as men, and when they had to travel they usually did it on horseback. A peculiarity of their horsemanship, which we have seen becoming again the fashion after a lapse of five centuries, was that they habitually rode astride."

not only her dress but also her "hosen . . . of fyn scarlet reed" (A 456) and her shoes "ful moyste and newe" (A 457)—two articles of clothing not depicted in the famous Ellesmere portrait of Alisoun because the artist concealed them both behind a blue garment. Let us consider that portrait in more detail.

The Ellesmere manuscript illustration clearly shows that the Wife of Bath is riding astride:

The Ellesmere portrait of the Wife of Bath, reproduced from EL 26 C9 f. 72r by permission of the Huntington Library, San Marino, California.

This fine illustration, almost certainly composed within ten years of Chaucer's death, shows us with rare precision just what a foot-mantle is—that coarse blue garment, apparently pulled up over Alisoun's feet and legs and worn loosely around her hips. I am puzzled about why virtually all of us have ignored this evidence in the past. The Ellesmere illustration shows us no apron or skirt or petticoat or cloak, but some thing more like a pair of loose leggings that would have had to be pulled on from below, with the spurs either attached to it permanently or, more likely, fitted on afterwards. I am aware that the Ellesmere portraits, which after all come not in the *General Prologue* but at the start of the various tales, cannot always be counted on to reflect accurately the words of the description in the *General Prologue,* but in this case we may well be justified in seeing in the portrait a pictorial gloss of the word "foot-mantel."[21]

I turn now to the second part of my discussion of line 472, "a foot-mantel aboute hir hipes large." There is such remarkable unanimity in the reading of those "hipes large" that virtually no editors bother to gloss the phrase at all. A look at the translations

[21] Two important articles on the Ellesmere portraits fail to discuss in any detail the foot-mantle of the Wife of Bath. Martin Stevens, in "The Ellesmere Miniatures as Illustrations of Chaucer's *Canterbury Tales*" (*Studies in Iconography* 7/8 [1981–82]: 113–34), speaks of "the fidelity with which the illustrators reproduced both the palpable features and the abstract impressions rendered by Chaucer in his portraits" (120), but mentions by way of illustration only Alisoun's spurs. Richard K. Emmerson, in "Text and Image in the Ellesmere Portraits of the Tale-Tellers" (*The Ellesmere Chaucer: Essays in Interpretation,* ed. Martin Stevens and Daniel Woodward [San Marino, CA, and Tokyo, 1997, 143–70]), gives in his appendix (160) a more detailed analysis of the Wife of Bath's portrait. He lists Alisoun's foot-mantle as a "*textual detail pictured*" in the portrait, though he does not attempt to define the term. Curiously, however, he lists as a "*textual detail pictured but not mentioned in, or disregarding, text*" what he calls a "blue overskirt"—as if the blue garment covering the lower half of Alisoun's body is something the artist invented, as it were, out of whole cloth, with no reference to the text. Perhaps I should take issue with Emmerson's statement that the artist gives "no hint of the Wife of Bath's trade" (148). That may be, but on the other hand her fine clothing and apparel may suggest that this clothmaker might have sewn her own travel apparel, and perhaps even designed and sewn the very foot-mantle we speak of. All of this, of course, is speculation—both on Emmerson's part and on my own.

into modern English shows the extent of the unanimity. In the translations I have seen, the adjective "large" is variously translated as showing that Alisoun's hips are "large," "ample," "broad," "great," and "enormous."[22] I suggest, however, that a word that virtually all editors, scholars, and translators have taken to be the adjective "large" is perhaps really the adverb "largely" or, more accurately, "loosely."[23] If I am right, then the line in question tells us not that the Wife of Bath wears a foot-mantle about her large hips, but that she wears a foot-mantle pulled up loosely around her hips—again, just as she does with that blue garment in the Ellesmere illustration.

Middle English adverbs could of course be formed by adding an "-e" to the adjectival form, unless the adjective already ended in "-e," in which case the adjective and adverb were identical. Thus, the adjective "large" and the adverb "large" would in Middle English have been identical. A glance at the *OED* and the *MED* shows that both list more adjectival uses for "large," but also shows clearly that in some contexts the word was an adverb meaning something like "amply," "fully," "abundantly," "generously."[24] The Middle English word "large" is usually an adjective in Chaucer, as in Diomede's "tonge large" *(Troilus and Criseyde*, V, 804) and the Nun's Priest's "large breest" (B^2 4646). Chaucer undeniably does upon occasion, however, use the word "large" as an adverb, as in Chaucer's own protestation

[22] The following gloss "hipes large" as "large hips": Coghill, 32, Lumiansky, 10, Hooper, 30; both Nicholson, 15, and Hill, 12, translate "hipes large" as "buttocks large"; Donohue, 13, Ecker and Crook, 13, and Hieatt and Hieatt, 23, translate "hipes large" as "ample hips"; Tatlock and MacKaye, 8, translate it as "broad hips"; and Wright translates it variously as "great hips" (1964, 11) and "enormous hips" (1985, 13).

[23] Interestingly, Michael Alexander glosses the word "large" as "loose (that is, the skirt)," 28. He still reads "large" as an adjective, however, since he thinks it modifies the foot-mantle, or what he glosses as an "over-skirt."

[24] See *Old English Dictionary,* s.v. "large" B, and *Middle English Dictionary,* s.v. "large" adv. The *MED* gives a line from Lydgate in which "large" was used as both parts of speech in close conjunction: "Þat he were tauȝt bettre to gouerne His large tonge . . . As doth he þis þat spoken haþ so large" (6.b). The first "large" is an adjective modifying "tonge," the second an adverb modifying "spoken."

that he must tell us precisely what he has been told, no matter how freely the teller speaks:

> Whoso shal telle a tale after a man,
> He moot reherce as ny as evere he kan
> Everich a word, if it be in his charge,
> Al speke he never so rudeliche and large.
> (A 731–34)

The word "large" in that passage clearly functions as an adverb modifying the verb "speke" and meaning "freely" or "without restraint."[25] I suggest that we consider the possibility that in line A 472 the word "large" is an adverb.

I understand why scholars—myself among them—have not before now considered this possibility. Perhaps most important, the word "large" can in modern English normally only be an adjective,[26] so we have not thought to consider that it may be in Middle English a different part of speech. A second reason is that to read "large" as an adjective modifying "hipes" seems to offer a nice parallel in the following line with the adjective "sharpe" as an adjective modifying "spurs." A third reason is that in this line there is no clear verb for an adverb "large" to modify. Chaucer, however, constrained by the need to write in iambic couplets, sometimes left out or implied certain words. Let's look at the lines again, with three implied instances of an absent verb added in brackets:

> Upon an amblere esily she sat,
> Ywympled wel, and on hir heed [she wore] an hat
> As brood as is a bokeler or a targe;

[25] In some passages it is not clear which part of speech Chaucer has in mind. When we are told, for example, that Absolon's hair "strouted as a fanne large and brode" (A 3315, with the editorial comma after "fanne" omitted), Chaucer could mean either that Absolon's hair flairs out like a large, broad fan (adjective), or that it flairs out freely and broadly like a fan (adverb). My own preference is for the adverbial usage, though most translators take "large" here as an adjective.

[26] There are a few unusual or antiquated holdovers of the use of "large" as an adverb: "The message was writ large," for example, and "My, you're living large!"

[She wore] A foot-mantel about hir hipes large,
And on hir feet [she wore] a paire of spores sharpe.
(A 469–73)

In these augmented lines, we can imagine that the foot-mantle was worn or draped "largely" about Alisoun's hips, as in the Ellesmere illustration. Considering that Alisoun was riding her horse astride, her dress under the foot-mantle must have been pushed up around her hips inside the upper part of the foot-mantle. If that is so, the largeness "aboute hir hipes" would have been caused by the bunched-up dress around her hips, not by the breadth of the hips themselves.

Chaucer knew how to tell his audience that a woman has large hips. He tells us, for example, that Malyne of the *Reeve's Tale* has "buttokes brode" (A 3975), and that White in the *Book of the Duchess* has hips that are "of good brede" (*BD* 956).[27] I hasten to note that in neither of these cases is the breadth of a woman's hips necessarily anything more than an indication of her beauty or attractiveness. My point here is merely that in neither case does Chaucer speak of the "largeness" of her hips or buttocks, but of their "breadth."

It is instructive that in the lines that provide the immediate environment for line 472, Chaucer is describing Alisoun's clothing, not her body. He tells us about her wimple, her hat, her foot-mantle, her spurs. Indeed, in the whole *General Prologue* description of Alisoun, Chaucer seems much less interested in Alisoun's body than in her fine apparel: her coverchiefs, her hose, her shoes, her hat, her wimple, her spurs, her foot-mantle. Chaucer seems not much

[27] Chaucer's selection of the word "broad" to suggest the size of a woman's hips is reflected elsewhere in Middle English. For example, the Gawain-poet in line 967 describes Morgan le Fay in this way, here with clear implications of unattractiveness: "Hir body watz schort and kik, / Hir buttokez balz and brode," quoted from Malcolm Andrew, Ronald Waldron, and Clifford Peterson in *The Complete Works of the Pearl Poet* (Berkeley, 1993), 252. Interestingly, we find in neither Chaucer's *Wife of Bath's Tale* nor Gower's *Tale of Florent* any description of the old woman's hips. In *The Wedding of Sir Gawain and Dame Ragnell* the old woman's hips are not mentioned, though we are told that her cheeks are as "syde as wemens hyppes" (line 236), quoted from the edition in Thomas J. Garbáty's *Medieval English Literature* (Lexington, 1984), 424. Garbáty glosses "syde" as "broad."

interested in her physical body, for he tells us only of her face, perhaps because it was the only part of her body that he as fellow traveler could see. We know that she has a bold, fair, red face and gap teeth, but that is all we know of her physical body. Why would he suddenly, out of the blue, describe the size of her hips as the only description of her body below her face—particularly since those hips are covered and he could not see them? Reading "large" as an adverb describing the way her foot-mantle was draped loosely around her hips rather than as an adjective describing the size of her hips keeps the focus on what Chaucer can see—her clothes.

Perhaps I should apologize for focusing on the size of Alisoun's hips. I do feel embarrassed by seeming to essentialize her physicality by focusing on a part of her body. I do so only, however, to suggest that Chaucer himself may *not* have invited us to think about the size of Alisoun's hips, but to think, rather, about the way a certain protective garment is draped about them.

Does it matter whether Alisoun has large hips or not? Actually, it can make considerable difference in the way we interpret the owner of those hips. As early as 1926 Walter Clyde Curry did a "scientific" analysis of the Wife of Bath's physical characteristics and concluded that "her large hips indicate excessive virility."[28] In 1968 Trudy Drucker did a medical analysis of Alisoun and argued that her large hips, in conjunction with some other features, help us to diagnose her condition: "Her 'reed of hewe' complexion, 'hipes large,' florid personality, and middle age are compatible with the mild chronic hypertension that is found in overnourished matrons of agreeable disposition."[29]

In 1975 Kevin S. Kiernan, speaking of Alisoun's "obesity" and her "massive girth," concluded that the reason Alisoun's person is not described more fully is that she is "too big and too unenticing to

[28] *Chaucer and the Mediaeval Sciences* (Oxford, 1926; revised and enlarged 1960), 108.

[29] "Some Medical Allusions in the *Canterbury Tales*," *New York State Journal of Medicine* 68 (1968): 445.

describe in detail."[30] In 1986 Robert O. Payne described the Wife of Bath as being "middle aged, travel-worn, and sprung in the hip"[31]—whatever that means. In 1993 Catherine S. Cox suggested that Alisoun is a textual construct by a male author, and that Chaucer constructs her as eating and drinking too much: "It is therefore quite fitting that the Wife should be initially described as having 'hipes large' (I.472), as having excessive flesh or girth, for she apparently fails to respect any boundary or limit of consumption."[32] There is no question, of course, that Alisoun is a male construct, but it may be that, since the only evidence of her overeating and excessive flesh is her "hipes large," Chaucer does not give her those particular constructions.

If so many interpretations can come from reading "large" as an adjective describing Alisoun's hips, then we should stop to question whether the word really is an adjective. I don't know that I have proved that it is an adverb, but I hope that scholars will henceforth at least pause to reflect on the possibility that Chaucer may in line 472 tell us nothing about the size of Alisoun's hips. It is tempting to suggest that Chaucer may be deliberately ambiguous here, coyly leaving his readers in suspension as to whether "large" is an adjective or an adverb, or both, though my own view is that we should consider the evidence and decide. My hermeneutic preference is that Chaucer tells us of the Wife of Bath's hips only that she has a pair of medieval riding leggings pulled up loosely or "largely" about them.

Recalling that the possible adjectival reading of "large" as modifying "hipes" is the only indication Chaucer gives us about the size of Alisoun's physical body, we also need to rethink the physical stature of the Wife of Bath. Most of us have imagined her as a big, strong woman who is fully capable of defending herself in the rough-

[30] "The Art of the Descending Catalogue, and a Fresh Look at Alisoun," *Chaucer Review* 10 (1975): 13.

[31] *Geoffrey Chaucer,* 2nd ed. (Boston, 1986), 120.

[32] "Holy Erotica and the Virgin Word: Promiscuous Glossing in the Wife of Bath's Prologue," *Exemplaria* 5 (1993): 217.

and-tumble arenas of medieval business, pilgrimage, and marriage. If those imaginings are not necessarily supported by Chaucer's text, we should reconsider her possible physical vulnerablity to her husbands. It may not be appropriate to speak of Jankyn's domestic abuse of his wife, but if it is, surely she is in some sense his victim if we trust her comment about the pain in her "ribbes al by rewe" (D 506) and about her having been "beten for a book" (D 712). Perhaps we should imagine her not as a weighty woman who can hold her own against any man, but as a woman who is perhaps smaller and more vulnerable. If we do, we can also imagine her as having a particular empathy with the maiden of her tale who has her maidenhood taken "by verray force"(D 888) by an impulsive knight.

The Owl Similes in the *Tale of Florent* and the *Wife of Bath's Tale*

[My interest in the relationship between John Gower's *Tale of Florent* and Geoffrey Chaucer's *Wife of Bath's Tale* continued even after I had published my "Transformations" article (pp. 72–90 above). I found myself drawn time and again to the fact that both authors had used the striking image of a man hiding like an owl after he marries an ugly old bride. How were the two images related, which came first, and in which tale was the owl simile most appropriate? I answer those questions in this article, which appears here for the first time.]

Chaucerians down through the decades have been eager to credit Chaucer with being the first to see the literary potential in Nicholas Trevet's "historical" account in the Anglo-Norman *Chronicles* of the travels and trials of Constance. We have been all too willing to follow Edward A. Block[1] when he magisterially announced that, while Chaucer knew Gower's *Tale of Constance* from the *Confessio Amantis*, Gower provided only some forty words that Chaucer did not find in Trevet, Chaucer's main source for the *Man of Law's Tale*. We Chaucerians simply did not want to let our favorite author seem to rely for his inspiration on the work of Gower, an English contemporary who was generally viewed as artistically inferior to the more brilliant

[1] "Originality, Controlling Purpose, and Craftsmanship in Chaucer's *Man of Law's Tale*," *PMLA* 68 (1953): 572–616.

Chaucer. But we have altered our views. Thanks to the careful work of scholars like Peter Nicholson,[2] Chaucerians now almost universally agree that in writing his tale of the travels and trials of Constance, Chaucer relied primarily on the work of his friend Gower.

We have, however, been far more reluctant to accept Chaucer's having learned the basic plot of his wonderful *Wife of Bath's Tale* from John Gower's *Tale of Florent*. We are willing to let Chaucer learn what most of us take to be one of his lesser tales from Gower, but not the brilliant Arthurian tale of a knight sent on a quest to find out what women most desire. Many scholars think that Chaucer and Gower must have shared a common source, now lost.[3] Many other scholars, rightly troubled that no such source has ever actually come to light but unable to find what they consider to be reliable evidence one way

[2] "Not only does it appear that Gower was Chaucer's most important model, but that it was Gower's tale rather than Trivet's that Chaucer chose to retell" ("Chaucer Borrows from Gower: The Sources of the *Man of Law's Tale*" in *Chaucer and Gower: Difference, Mutuality, Exchange*, ed. R. F. Yeager [Victoria, British Columbia: English Literary Studies, 1991], 85–99 at 86). Nicholson uses similar language at the end of "The *Man of Law's Tale*: What Chaucer Really Owed to Gower," *Chaucer Review* 26 (1991): 153–74, at 171. Because of Nicholson's work, Robert M. Correale can say in the introduction to his chapter on the *Man of Law's Tale* in the new *Sources and Analogues* that "though there has been some difference of opinion about which one of the English poems preceded the other, the consensus is that Gower wrote first and Chaucer borrowed from him" (*Sources and Analogues of the Canterbury Tales*, volume 2, ed. Robert M. Correale and Mary Hamel [Woodbridge, Suffolk: Boydell and Brewer, 2005], 277–350, at 284).

[3] See, for example, G. H. Maynadier, *The Wife of Bath's Tale: Its Sources and Analogues* (London: David Nutt, 1901), 137: "even if his story was suggested by Gower's, Chaucer in all likelihood knew some different version—a version distinct enough to warrant our virtual agreement with Mr. Clouston and Dr. Skeat, that 'there seems [...] no good reason' for supposing Chaucer to have borrowed from Gower." Sigmund Eisner announces in *A Tale of Wonder: A Source Study of the Wife of Bath's Tale* (Wexford, Ireland; John English, 1957), 65, that Chaucer's and Gower's "loathly lady tales are so similar that a common source may be presumed"—and he goes on to give a synopsis of what such a common source might have looked like. Following Eisner, Christine Ryan Hilary in her Textual Notes to the *Wife of Bath's Tale* in the influential *Riverside Chaucer*, 3rd edition, ed. Larry D. Benson (Boston: Houghton Mifflin, 1987), 872–74, at 872, reports that the "particular form [of the story] that Chaucer used, that in which the disenchantment is connected with the theme of sovereignty, apparently originated in Ireland." Although many scholars now question the existence of such a "lost source," it persists in some quarters. Susan Carter, for example, announces that "Scholarly opinion is that all extant

or the other, conclude that we simply cannot know. Most recently and influentially, noting that the *Confessio Amantis* was first published in 1390, John Withrington and P. J. C. Field, the editors of the chapter on the *Wife of Bath's Tale* in the new *Sources and Analogues*, raise the question of priority only to dismiss it as unworthy of speculation: "not enough is known about Chaucer and Gower for it to be worthwhile speculating as to which of the two texts was written first, let alone whether they were indebted to each other or had a common source."[4] There is, of course, something to be said for such a view. In her generally sensible recent article on "Dating Chaucer," Kathryn L. Lynch reminds us of the massive uncertainty inherent in virtually all attempts to assign dates to any of Chaucer's works. She closes with a plea for "a moratorium on dating Chaucer."[5]

Two recent scholars, both publishing in 2007, the same year as Lynch's article, argue that Gower's *Tale of Florent* must have been the direct source for Chaucer's *Wife of Bath's Tale*. B. W. Lindeboom writes that "When one [...] considers that the two tales

works which use the Loathly Lady motif have evolved from earlier oral forms, probably Celtic, pagan, and certainly irretrievable" ("A Hymenation of Hags," in *The English Loathly Lady Tales: Boundaries, Traditions, Motifs*, ed. S. Elizabeth Passmore and Susan Carter [Kalamazoo, MI: Medieval Institute Publications, 2007]), 83–99, at 94n6, and , at 95n23, "It is generally accepted that Gower and Chaucer probably shared the same source but that this is unknown," R. F. Yeager also speculates about a common, probably Arthurian, lost source: "That Gower, like Chaucer and the various anonymous authors of the 'Loathly Lady group,' came upon the narrative details which he remodeled into his tale for the *Confessio* in an as-yet undiscovered romance seems the best guess" ("The Politics of *Strengthe* and *Vois* in Gower's Loathly Lady Tale" in *The English Loathly Lady Tales: Boundaries, Traditions, Motifs*, ed. S. Elizabeth Passmore and Susan Carter [Kalamazoo, MI: Medieval Institute Publications, 2007]), 42–82, at 49]. For my skepticism about placing much faith in the supposed existence, let alone the supposed nature, of purportedly "lost" sources, see "New Terminology for Sources and Analogues: Or, Let's Forget the Lost French Source for the *Miller's Tale*," *Studies in the Age of Chaucer* 28 (2006): 225–30, reprinted pages 29–36 above.

[4] From their introduction to the chapter on the *Wife of Bath's Tale* in *Sources and Analogues of the Canterbury Tales*, volume 2, ed. Robert M. Correale and Mary Hamel (Woodbridge, Suffolk: Boydell and Brewer, 2005), 405–48, at 407.

[5] *Chaucer Review* 42 (2007): 1–22, at 17.

are incontrovertibly one another's closest analogues in place, time, and substance, it really seems rather perverse to deny Chaucer's debt to Gower."[6] And Russell Peck announces that in his view, "Gower, drawing upon folk narratives, put together the basic narrative as we know it" and that the *Tale of Florent* "functioned as the primary literary source" for the *Wife of Bath's Tale*.[7] Both scholars note that the two men were friends, that they knew each other's work, and that Gower's tale almost certainly was composed and available before Chaucer's. On the basis of my own study of the owl similes in the two tales, I endorse the conclusions of Lindeboom and Peck that Gower's tale both preceded and influenced Chaucer's.[8]

It seems obvious enough that since an owl simile is not a necessary feature in a tale about a knight who is sent on a journey to discover what women desire, its appearance in both versions of the tale is strong evidence that the two tales are connected. Rather than gnaw further on the question of priority, I take it as sufficiently demonstrated that the *Tale of Florent* was the chief literary source of the *Wife of Bath's Tale*. In this paper, rather, I seek to show that Gower and Chaucer make quite different uses of the owl similes in their tales and that the simile is more organically integrated by Gower than by Chaucer.

In Gower's tale, where Florent's offense is that he kills, apparently in fair combat, an enemy knight named Branchus, Florent

[6] "*Venus' Owne Clerk: Chaucer's Debt to the Confessio Amantis* (Amsterdam: Rodopi, 2007), 195.

[7] "Folklore and Powerful Women in Gower's *Tale of Florent*" in *The English Loathly Lady Tales: Boundaries, Traditions, Motifs*, ed. S. Elizabeth Passmore and Susan Carter (Kalamazoo, MI: Medieval Institute Publications, 2007, 100–45, at 100).

[8] I am not the first to note the importance of the two owl similes in discussing source relationships. Hilary states in her *Riverside* notes that "Chaucer knew and probably echoes Gower's version" (872). Peck states that "the owl who flies by night is a trope that Chaucer picks up from Gower" (138n70). Withrington and Field are less eager to take a stand on influence: "Given that *The Wife of Bath's Tale* is generally thought to have been written in the early to mid 1390s it is possible that the two texts [Chaucer's and Gower's] were actually contemporaneous:

is captured and would have been executed except that Branchus's family fears that Florent's powerful uncle, the emperor,[9] will in retaliation punish them. To avoid that punishment, Branchus's diabolical grandmother devises a plan to get Florent to agree to bargain his life on an impossible quest. She reasons that when he fails, as he must, she can put him to death and claim that he had agreed to a sacrifice of his own life. The owl simile in the *Tale of Florent* comes shortly after Florent has given Branchus's grandmother the correct answer: that all women most desire to be "soverein of mannes love" (*TF* 214). In exchange for that correct answer, Florent has made another pledge, this one to the loathly old woman who gives him the answer: that if her answer saves his life, he will marry her. He does not try to avoid keeping this promise, but he does want his marriage to such a foul old woman to be kept secret. Because of the plot Gower has devised, Florent is able to keep the secret for a while, because no one yet knows about his agreement to marry the old woman. She trusts him both to go off alone to give his answer and to keep his pledge to return to make her his wife. She does not travel with Florent to the

both, in fact, make striking use of the owl's supposed reluctance to be seen abroad in daytime as a metaphor for the heroes' reluctance to be seen abroad with their Loathly Ladies" (407). As will be evident below, I call into question Withrington and Field's assertion that the reference to owls in both tales shows the two "heroes' reluctance to be seen abroad with their Loathly Ladies." That description somewhat fits Gower's Florent, but does not fit Chaucer's rapist knight, who has already been seen with his bride. For a longer comparison of the two versions of the loathly-lady tale, see my "Transformations in Gower's *Tale of Florent* and Chaucer's *Wife of Bath's Tale*," in *Chaucer and Gower: Difference, Mutuality, Exchange*, ed. R. F. Yeager, in English Literary Studies: University of Victoria Monograph Series, No. 51 (1991): 100–14, reprinted pages 72–90 above.

[9] The Latin marginal rubric to the *Tale of Florent* identifies him as Emperor Claudius, who was the emperor of Rome from A.D. 41 to 54. It is interesting that, like Gower, who sets his tale in "daies olde" (*TF* 12), Chaucer puts his version of the tale far back in "th'old dayes of the king Arthour [...] many hundred yeres ago" (*WB* 857, 863). Unlike Florent, however, Chaucer puts the setting closer to home in Arthur's England, not in "th'empire" of Rome (*TF* 87). My quotations from the *Tale of Florent* are to the edition in *Sources and Analogues*, volume 2, 410–19, from the *Wife of Bath's Tale* to my edition in *The Wife of Bath* (Boston: Bedford Books of St. Martin's Press, 1996), 73–85.

appointed meeting with Branchus's grandmother. Florent, ashamed to be seen with his ugly fiancee, is so eager to keep the secret that he returns, owl-like,[10] to his own castle with his rag-clad bride-to-be:

In ragges, as sche was totore,
He set hire on his hors tofore
And forth he takth his weie softe;
No wonder thogh he siketh ofte,
But as an oule fleth by nyhte
Out of alle othre briddes syhte,
Right so this knyht on daies brode
In clos him hield, and schop his rode
On nyhtes time, til the tyde
That he cam there he wolde abide.
(*TF* 329–37)

Florent can keep the secret of his impending marriage by traveling at night because no one, either in the enemy camp or among Florent's

[10] It is not clear precisely what significance Gower may have assigned to owls. Looking at medieval bestiaries, where owls generally represent the Jews who turn away from the light of Christ's godliness, is not helpful here. See, for example, *A Medieval Book of Brass: The Second Family Bestiary*, ed. and trans. Willene Clark (Woodbridge, Suffolk: Boydell Press, 2006), 178, and *The Bestiary*, trans. T. H. White (New York: Putnam, 1960), 133–34. It may well be that Gower learned the tradition that owls fly by night and hide by day from the thirteenth-century debate poem, *The Owl and the Nightingale*, where the nightingale more than once criticizes the owl for her devious ways. The owl, of course, defends herself and her night-flying. Interesting, but not directly relevant to this study, is the anonymous fifteenth-century *Weddyng of Syr Gawen and Dame Ragnell*. Dame Ragnel, the foul old woman in the tale, in her own voice uses an owl metaphor as a means of pleading to King Arthur her right to a mate. King Arthur has expressed his reluctance to let Gawain marry so ugly a woman. Her argument to Arthur is that just as the ugly owl has a right to a mate, so she does, however ugly she is: "No force, Syr King, though I be foull, / Choyse for a make hath an owll" (*WSG* 309–10 [see also lines 315–16], quoted from the Withrington and Field edition in *Sources and Analogues*, 420–41). The owl comparison is used here to describe the old woman, not the knight as in the other two tales, and describes physical appearance, not behavior, as it does in Gower and Chaucer. The unknown author probably knew both Gower's and Chaucer's versions of the tale, as well as *The Owl and the Nightingale*, where the nightingale criticizes the owl for her ugliness.

friends, yet knows anything about his relationship with the old woman, her having revealed the answer, or his agreement to marry her. By traveling quietly at night, he can get her to his home undetected:

> And prively withoute noise
> He bringeth this foule grete coise
> To his castell in such a wise
> That noman myhte hire schappe avise.
>
> (*TF* 338–42)

Note that he wants no one—"noman"—to know about the bodily "schappe" of his traveling companion. The longer he can keep it a secret, the longer he will be protected from the shame that will surely come his way when the secret is out.

The acute sense of shame that makes the owl simile in Gower's *Tale of Florent* work so well is very much built into Florent's character. Florent is a man who cares, almost too much, about his public reputation. Indeed, one of the very first facts we learn about Florent is that he cares deeply about "the fame of worldes speche" (*TF* 20). His concern about his worldly reputation motivates many of his actions in the story, including his entering hostile territory at the start of the tale, where he kills Branchus and is captured. His concern about what other people think of him, then, sets up the whole plot.

Florent's concern about being seen with an ugly fiancé or being known as her fiancé or husband is evident from the first. When he learns that he will probably lose his life unless he promises to make the loathly old woman his wife, he reasons it out and decides that because she is already old and may not live long, he will soon be rid of her. Meanwhile, he thinks, he can banish her to some far-off island where no one will know she exists:

> That sche was of so greet an age,
> That sche may live bot a while
> And thoghte put hire in an ile,
> Wher that noman hire scholde knowe,
> Til sche with deth were overthrowe.
>
> (*TF* 181–85)

Already it is other men's knowledge of his connection to her that worries him most. Having reasoned out a plan that will conceal her on an island, where "noman" will know of her, he accepts the foul old woman's proposal.

When it turns out that the old woman's answer is the correct one, Florent's life is saved but his problems begin anew because he is said specifically to dread being made ashamed: "he, which alle schame dradde" (*TF* 273). When he does get the old woman back to his castle, Florent takes her not into the great hall, but directly into "the chambre" (*TF* 342), which I take to be the bedroom, a place of privacy. Then, with all apparent secrecy, he summons into "prive conseil" (*TF* 343) there a few of the men he trusts most and tells them of his plight. Then, also with apparent secrecy, he sends the "prive wommen" (*TF* 348) to bathe, comb, and dress his bride-to-be. The order of the day is concealment—concealment by location and concealment by array. When they cannot comb or cut the old woman's unruly hair, her handlers stuff it into a cap of some sort in an attempt to conceal it from sight. Her locks are "hid so craftelich aboute, / That noman myhte sen hem oute" (*TF* 360–61). For Florent, it is all a question of hiding his wife—by banishment to an island, by cover of night, by closed doors, by clothing—so that "noman" can see how he has aligned himself with so ugly a bride. Significantly, the two are wedded not in the daytime, as was typical for a wedding, but "in the nyht" (*TF* 366).

It is also significant that the bride, after her transformation into a lovely bit of eighteen-year-old eye candy, gives him the choice that will be, given his character, the most difficult for Florent: whether to have her so at night, when only he can see her, or by day, when others can. The confused Florent, torn by the choice of having a young and lovely bed-partner visible at night only to him or having her so when other men can *see* that she is young and lovely, throws in the towel and lets his bride decide. He has been so fully described as hating shame and desiring the admiration of other men, that we accept his anguished relinquishment of the choice as the best way out of his quandary.

The owl simile in Gower, then, which likens Florent on his trip home to a nocturnal bird that flies out only "by nyhte / Out of alle othre briddes syhte" (*TF* 332–33), grows out of Florent's character as Gower has consistently shown it to us: a man "which alle schame dradde" (*TF* 273).

Before we move to Chaucer's portrayal of the knight, we should notice that the loathly old woman in Gower's tale would have had her own reason for not wanting to accompany Florent to his appointed interview with Branchus's grandmother: that she wants to protect herself from that woman's anger. Branchus's grandmother is, indeed, angry. She would have burned the one who gave away the answer, had she known who had thus treasonously betrayed women:

> And whan that this matrone herde
> The manere how this knyht ansuerde,
> Sche seide: "Ha treson! wo thee be,
> That hast thus told the privite
> Which alle wommen most desire!
> I wolde that thou were afire!"
>
> (*TF* 262–67)

Fearing for her life, the loathly old woman wants no one to know either that she gave Florent the answer or that he in exchange had promised to marry her. It is usually assumed that Florent wants to travel by night, like an owl, only because he is ashamed to be seen in public with his fiancé. It may also be that he wants to protect the identity of his informant by not being seen in public with her. Because he has heard Branchus's grandmother's threat, Florent would know that his bride-to-be was in danger. The issue has no bearing on the *Wife of Bath's Tale* since no one in Arthur's court is upset that the loathly old woman, present at court, has revealed the answer. Surely Arthur's queen, who had initially saved the knight from beheading, would have no reason to incinerate the woman who gave him the life-saving answer.

That brings us to Chaucer's portrayal of the rapist knight. The situation in Chaucer's tale is similar in broad outline to the one in

Gower's, but the details are quite different. Never once is Arthur's impulsive knight said to be concerned about his worldly fame or his reputation among others. If he were worried about what others thought of him, of course, he would presumably not have attacked a defenseless maiden in the first place, especially in a land where that offense was punishable by death. When he is described at all he is described as "lusty" (*WB* 882), "manly" (1036), and, especially, "sorweful" and full of "wo" (913, 986, 1079, 1082, 1083, 1228). He is sorrowful about the impossible quest he is assigned and full of woe about the upsetting liaison he has been tricked into making with the old woman.

Even if he wanted to, Arthur's knight could not keep his connection to the old woman a secret since she has accompanied him to the queen's court, tells everyone that she gave him the answer, and announces publicly that she expects him to marry her: " 'Before the court thanne preye I thee, sir knight,' / Quod she, 'that thou me take unto thy wif' " (*WB* 1054–55). Take her to wife he does, but he marries her "privily" (*WB* 1080) and there was "ne feeste at all" (1078). Even so, everyone knows who he has married. There is, then, no point in his trying to conceal his bride or his marriage to her by traveling at night. We should also recall that because, unlike Florent, he is already at home, he has no distant castle to take his wife to and no journey during which to hide her during the daylight hours.

When Chaucer's knight is offered a choice, it is not whether to have his wife fair when others see her during the day or at night when only he can see her. His choice, that is, is not between shame and lust. Rather, his choice is to have his wife fair and therefore perhaps not faithful to him, or ugly and therefore faithful. In other words, his choice is between beauty and fidelity. Neither choice has any direct or obvious bearing on the knight's reputation. Why would it, since he is not concerned about his reputation?

Chaucer's knight's hiding like an owl, then, has nothing to do with concealing either his bride or his marriage, since everyone in court has seen the former and been told about the latter. Rather, the sorrowful young man hides like an owl for no other apparent reason than that he wants to avoid having to look at his ugly bride between his morning wedding and the approaching night when he must pay his marital debt to her:

> There nas but hevinesse and muche sorwe,
> For prively he wedded her on morwe.
> And all day after hidde him as an owle,
> So wo was him, his wif looked so foule.
>
> (*WB* 1079–82)

He is hiding *himself* from the sight of his bride, not *his bride* from the sight of others. He hides like an owl not because he is ashamed to be seen with her but because he cannot stand to look at her.

Because we are not told precisely where he hides like an owl, we are left to imagine anything we want to imagine—in a closet, in the woods, in a stable, wherever. The only thing we can be sure of is that he does not, like Florent, hide *with* her to avoid others' seeing them together, but *from* her to avoid having to look at her. Florent wants to conceal his bride; the rapist knight wants to conceal himself.

The owl simile, then, works wonderfully in the *Tale of Florent* because it reinforces Florent's carefully established desire to protect his reputation by concealing his wife. Because Chaucer changes the story line, the owl simile works quite differently. Chaucer apparently liked Gower's image of a knight hiding like an owl during the day, but had to adapt it to its new setting. It works less well in Chaucer because the rapist knight hides like an owl not from other men, but from his wife. Owls by nature hide during the day to avoid being seen; they do not hide during the day to avoid having to look at their wives.

The Price of Sex in Chaucer's *Shipman's Tale*

[The crafty wife of the merchant of Saint Denis tells the monk daun John, a family friend, that she needs to borrow 100 francs to pay off certain debts she has incurred by buying clothing. The monk says he will lend her the money, then in turn secretly borrows 100 francs from her husband. He later gives it to the wife in exchange for a night of sex with her. I set out to come up with a rough U.S. dollar equivalent of the 100 francs, hoping to find out at least in broad terms whether the wife of Saint Denis sells her sexual favors cheap or dear. Because I hoped to publish my essay in a special festschrift issue of the *Chaucer Review* honoring my friend and medieval colleague Albert E. Hartung, I started my search with a query to him. He had no idea at that time why I was asking and was surprised to see my topic when the essay appeared in volume 31 (1996): 5–17.]

One of the advantages of having been for years a colleague of Al Hartung is that I could ask him all sorts of questions—about teaching, about this strange profession of ours, about how to raise children, about *The Manual of the Writings in Middle English,* about Chaucer. I have not availed myself of that advantage often enough over the years, but one day in the early 1990s I asked Al if he knew how much 100 French francs might have been worth in Chaucer's time. He answered that it was worth a night of pleasure with the wife of the merchant of Saint Denis, but knew that was not the answer

I was searching for. I told him that one of my students had asked me during my class on the *Shipman's Tale.* Al suggested that I start by reading the section on money in the still-useful introduction to Manly's outdated and bowdlerized edition of the *Canterbury Tales.* That started me on a search that was to go on for several years and culminates in a paper that I herewith dedicate to the man who pointed the first direction for my search.

A quick visit to the library revealed that Manly's discussion was too general for my purposes, but it served as a useful warning that whatever figure I came up with for the 100 francs would be, at best, imprecise:

> Many attempts have been made to establish a multiple for converting money of ancient times into their modern equivalents in purchasing power. It is obviously a very difficult task—in the strict sense of the word an impossible one—for the relative values of money and commodities varied from year to year in ancient times as they do now, and varied still more from century to century. English scholars of the nineteenth century arrived at the conclusion that for working purposes the money of the fourteenth century could be roughly translated into nineteenth century English money by multiplying by fifteen. If this is true, there can be little doubt that, considering the rise in wages and prices and the consequent depreciation in the value of money in the twentieth century, it would be necessary to multiply fourteenth century money by thirty to ascertain its present [1928] purchasing value. Americans would have to apply a further multiple to change English pounds into American dollars. This may be roughly taken as five. Undoubtedly the results attained by this process will in some cases seem absurd.[1]

[1] John M. Manly, *Canterbury Tales* (New York, 1928), 65. For a more recent and more fully informed discussion of the complexities of international exchange in medieval times,

Perhaps because he did not want to seem absurd, Manly ventured no guess as to the modern-day value of the 100 medieval French francs in Chaucer's *Shipman's Tale.*

By the time I got back from reading Manly's introduction, I had an e-mail message waiting for me from Al Hartung:

> Pete: The new *Riverside Chaucer* notes a franc as equivalent to a demi-noble. A demi-noble is 60 grains; at .002 ounces per grain, that equals .12 ounces in one franc. 100 francs equals 12 ounces of gold 24 carat fine. At my quoted 1982 price (the last I have readily available) of $343 per ounce 24 carat fine, this would come to $4116. Although I can't believe the Shipman's wife would have the gall to expect over four thousand dollars for a night in bed, my strong suspicion is that she does get a lot of money (note that the monk in the tale tells the merchant that he is going to use the loan to buy "beasts" to "store" a property owned by his monastery; certainly he needs a goodly sum). But I also strongly suspect that this illustrates the difficulty, if not impossibility, of ever determining such equivalents with any accuracy. But obviously she has a good opinion of herself, and it won't cost the monk a farthing in the long run (although he may experience a certain degree of fatigue).[2]

I decided to see what else I could find out about currency equivalents. I discovered great variety in scholarly efforts to

see Alison Hanham, *The Celys and Their World: An English Merchant Family of the Fifteenth Century* (Cambridge, England, 1985), especially Chapter 2, "Monetary Matters," 164–202. Hanham does not discuss the French franc, since her interest is mostly in the English wool trade with the Low Countries, and she is mostly dealing with trading practices a century after Chaucer, but the material is fascinating. Given minting and exchange procedures, it is amazing that international trading was even possible.

[2] Al Hartung apparently got his information about the grain weight of the deminoble from the chart on page 64 in Manly's edition. I must express my gratitude not only to Al, but also to the other scholars whose letters to me I quote, with their permission, in this article. I am also grateful to Erik Hertog, Carol A. Everest, and Derek S. Brewer for helping me to make connections with some of these scholars, and to Thomas Hanks for a helpful reading of the manuscript.

determine the modern equivalent of the £10 that for a time was Chaucer's annual salary. J. Logie Robertson, for example, in 1902 estimated that Chaucer's pay was "worth at least £400 a year in our money"[3]—perhaps $2000 in U.S. currency at the time. Edwin Johnson Howard and Gordon Donley Wilson estimated in 1947 that £10 pounds was worth "about $1,500."[4] Sheila Delany in 1975 put it at "probably close to $25,000 today."[5] A note in the *Riverside Chaucer* on the value of 100 French francs suggests that it was worth around 15 pounds sterling in Chaucer's time.[6] If that note is correct, then a simple multiplication by 1.5 to expand the £10 sterling to £15 suggests that Roberston, Howard and Wilson, and Delany might have estimated the 100 francs would be worth around $3000, $2250, and $37,500, respectively.

A hasty review of what others have said about the 100 francs in the *Shipman's Tale* revealed that, while the various economic and financial dealings in the *Shipman's Tale* have come under repeated scrutiny,[7] almost no one tries to estimate directly the modern value of the 100 francs. Surely the neglect of so simple a question is not caused by the fact that no one thinks the question very important. If

[3] *The Select Chaucer* (Edinburgh, 1902), xix.

[4] *The Canterbury Tales of Geoffrey Chaucer* (New York, 1947), 24.

[5] "Sexual Economics, Chaucer's Wife of Bath, and *The Book of Margery Kempe*," *Minnesota Review* 5 (1975): 105.

[6] The *Riverside Chaucer*, ed. Larry D. Benson (Boston, 1987), 912. All quotations from Chaucer are from Fragment VII (Group B²) in this edition. The full note to "an hundred francs" in line 181 is: "About £15 sterling, a considerable sum. The 'franc a cheval' was first issued in 1360, and established itself as a common French gold coin in Chaucer's lifetime, valued at approximately half an English noble (i.e., 3s 4d)." The notes to the *Shipman's Tale* were written by John A. Burrow and V. J. Scattergood. If they are right about the £15 sterling, then it is interesting that the price of sex in the *Shipman's Tale* is just about the same as the £16 that Edward III paid to ransom Chaucer himself after his capture in France in 1360. See Martin M. Crow and Clair C. Olson, *Chaucer Life-Records* (Austin, 1966), 23–28.

[7] See, for example: Kenneth S. Cahn, "Chaucer's Merchants and the Foreign Exchange: An Introduction to Medieval Finance," *Studies in the Age of Chaucer* 2 (1980): 81–119; Gerhard Joseph, "Chaucer's Coinage: Foreign Exchange and the Puns of the *Shipman's Tale*," *Chaucer*

the wife sells herself for almost nothing, then her complaints about her husband's stinginess seem justified, she becomes the sympathetic victim, driven to polite prostitution to keep clothes on her back, and he becomes the tight-fisted villain of the story. If the wife of Saint Denis sells herself for a lot of money because she wants to pay off a large debt for expensive clothes, that makes her the extravagant spendthrift who wastes her husband's money on fancy clothes.

Those few scholars who discuss the value of the 100 francs do so only in the most general terms, and even among those there is little agreement. In the notes to his translation of the *Canterbury Tales,* for example, Nevill Coghill tells us that the 100 francs is a "trifling" amount,[8] and Hazel Sullivan tells us that it is "a small sum, compared to the hospitality [the monk] was receiving."[9] On the other hand, John A. Burrow and V. J. Scattergood tell us that 100 francs is "a considerable sum."[10] In discussing the related question of whether the wife of Saint Denis is justified in calling her husband stingy, A. H. Silverman speaks of his "lack of generosity" and his "niggardliness,"[11] while Murray Copland and, more recently, Carol F.

Review 17 (1982–83): 341–57; Thomas Hahn, "Money, Sexuality, Wordplay, and Context in the *Shipman's Tale*," in Julian N. Wasserman and Robert J. Blanch, *Chaucer in the Eighties* (Syracuse, 1986), 235–49; William F. Woods, "A Professional Thyng: The Wife as Merchant's Apprentice in the *Shipman's Tale*," *Chaucer Review* 24 (1989): 139–49; Lee Patterson, *Chaucer and the Subject of History* (Madison, 1991), 349–65; Wight Martindale, Jr., "Chaucer's Merchants: A Trade-based Speculation on Their Activities," *Chaucer Review* 26 (1992): 309–16.

[8] In the notes to his Penguin translation (1951) of the *Canterbury Tales,* Nevill Coghill refers to the 100 francs the monk owes the merchant as a "trifling debt" (515 in the 1977 reprinting).

[9] "A Chaucerian Puzzle," in *A Chaucerian Puzzle and Other Medieval Essays,* ed. Natalie Grimes Lawrence and Jack A. Reynolds (Coral Gables, 1961), 33.

[10] See note 6 above. Some other scholars appear to assume that the amount of money is large rather than small. Paul Stephen Schneider, for example in " 'Taillynge Ynough': The Function of Money in the *Shipman's Tale*," *Chaucer Review* 11 (1997), hints that it may be a lot of money when he says that the wife's need for clothes is "excessive" and her spending "extravagant" (202–03).

[11] "Sex and Money in Chaucer's *Shipman's Tale*," *Philological Quarterly* 32 (1953): 331. Other commentators on the *Shipman's Tale* use language that suggests that they probably think of the 100 francs as a small sum. For example, George R. Keiser, in "Language and Meaning in the *Shipman's*

Heffernan find the husband to be "generous."[12] Well, is the 100 francs a "trifling" or "considerable" amount? Is it worth $4,000 in modern U. S. dollars or $40,000? Is the husband of Saint Denis "niggardly" or "generous" in lending 100 francs to his friend?

Internal evidence

Surely Coghill and Sullivan are wrong to suggest that the 100 francs was a small amount of money. The narrative seems to require that the 100 francs be a lot of money. The introductory lines, for example, usually taken as evidence that Chaucer originally wrote this tale for the Wife of Bath, suggest that women spend *large* amounts on clothes:

> The sely housbonde, algate he moot paye,
> He moot us clothe, and he moot us arraye.
>
> . . . . .
>
> And if that he noght may, par aventure,
> Or ellis list no swich dispence endure,
> But thynketh it is wasted and ylost,
> Thanne moot another payen for oure cost,
> Or lene us gold, and that is perilous.
>
> (B² 1201–02, 1205–09)

After that opening, it would make no sense for the wifely prostitute[13] in the story to spend only a trifling amount on clothes, or to tell the monk that if she does not repay it she will surely die:

Tale," *Chaucer Review* 12 (1978), speaking of the merchant's "My gold is youres" speech to the monk in line 1474, tells us that "although this speech has been seen as an indication of the merchant's generosity, it may simply indicate that he too is given to extravagant language" (154).

[12] Murray Copland, "The *Shipman's Tale*: Chaucer and Boccaccio," *Medium Ævum* 35 (1966): 18; Carol F. Heffernan, "Chaucer's *Shipman's Tale* and Boccaccio's *Decameron*, 8.1: Retelling a Story," in *Courtly Literature: Culture and Context,* ed. Keith Busby and Erik Kooper (Amsterdam, 1990), 264.

[13] Because she does not sell sex to large numbers of men or to the general public, it is perhaps inaccurate to speak of the wife of St. Denis as a "prostitute" at all. Several hints, however, suggest that

> "A Sonday next I moste nedes paye
> An hundred frankes, or ellis I am lorn.
> . . . . .
> Lene me this somme, or ellis moot I deye."
> (B² 1370–71, 1376)

Nor does it make sense for the monk to have to borrow anything but a large amount from a wealthy merchant. If it were only a little cash he needed to pay for sex with an ordinary prostitute,[14] the monk would not have needed to go to all the trouble—and risk—of borrowing it from his friend "that riche was" (B² 1192).

The husband's apparent generosity in lending the monk the 100 francs makes sense only if a large amount is at stake:

> "My gold is youres, whan that it yow leste,
> And nat oonly my gold, but my chaffare.
> Take what yow list; God shilde that ye spare."
> (B² 1474–76)

For the amount to be small would be for the merchant to be saying to his friend, in effect: "What's mine is yours—my gold, my goods, everything. Spare nothing. Go ahead, take a couple of bucks."

The wife's terms of repayment in the bedroom are consistent with the fact that 100 francs is a large amount of money: "Score

Chaucer wanted us to think of her as akin to the sisterhood. She sells sex, after all, not only to the monk, but also to her husband. And it is interesting to note that French prostitutes were known to want to dress in fancy clothes. For studies of prostitution in Chaucer's time, see Jacques Rossiaud, *Medieval Prostitution,* trans. from the Italian by Lydia G. Cochrane (Oxford, 1988), and Leah Lydia Otis, *Prostitution in Medieval Society* (Chicago, 1985).

[14] There is little specific information about the cost for the services of prostitutes. Prostitutes in Dijon a century or so after Chaucer typically charged quite a small sum, at least in comparison with the wife of St. Denis: "Fees were one *blanc* the *esbattement,* a sum equivalent to what a woman could earn in half a day's work in the vineyards. They could expect from three to six times that when they agreed to spend the night with a 'young son' " (Rossiaud, 34–35). In private correspondence, Peter Spufford informs me that the silver blanc, a coin first issued in 1385, was worth 1/24th of a franc. For 100 francs, then, a man might have enjoyed 2400 sessions with a licensed prostitute, or sex every night for six and a half years, with no Sundays taken off for rest. In times of famine or other economic hardship, of course, the price would have fluctuated

it upon my taille, / And I shal paye as soone as ever I may" (B^2 1606–07). The wife's long-term repayment plan for her 100-franc debt makes narrative sense only if the 100 francs is an amount of money so large that she could not repay it quickly from the medieval equivalent of a hoard of pin money.

Three small bits of internal evidence in the *Shipman's Tale* are consistent with a high rather than a low estimate for the value of the 100 francs. The first is that the wife tells her husband that she has spent the money "on myn array . . . for youre honour" (B^2 1608, 1611). The narrator has told us that these clothes are paid for in "gold" (B^2 1209). That they are expensive enough to bring "honour" to her husband suggests that they are probably stylish and elegant. No one who visits any big-city boutique today can come away doubting that it would be easy to spend thousands on fancy dresses designed to show off the status of a woman—and her husband.

The second bit of evidence is that the monk, who makes purchases for the monastery farms, tells his friend the merchant that he needs the 100 francs to buy "certein beestes" (B^2 1462) to stock one of the monastic farms.[15] It must have been clear to Chaucer's audience that by stating his needs in that way the monk was obliquely calling the wife an animal, but to the merchant no such meaning comes through. The monk does not specify the number or kind of beasts he has in mind, but buying farm or ranch animals today can be an expensive proposition. A single cow or beef steer, not pedigreed, can cost easily between $500 and $1,000.

downward. Rossiaud reports that a chronicler in Metz noted that during the severe food shortages of 1419 "you could have four women for the price of an egg" (70).

[15] It is not clear, of course, precisely what kinds of "beestes" the monk was thinking of; the *MED* suggests that these are large farm animals. In F. R. P. Akehurst's translation of *The "Coutumes de Beauvaisis" of Philippe de Beaumanoir* (Philadelphia, 1992), 150, we find this definition of the term, at least as it applied to wills: "If a testator leaves all his animals [*bestes*] without further specification, and he had a flock [*Tout*] of sheep, you should understand that that is what he left. And nevertheless because of the general nature of the term, we believe the legatee would take everything which is called an animal [*beste*]: horses, cows, pigs, and other animals, if he had them."

The third bit of evidence is the size of the husband's profit as a result of his own financial transactions in the tale. The husband travels from Saint Denis to Bruges "to byen there a porcioun of ware" (B^2 1246); then back to Saint Denis; then immediately to nearby Paris, where "nedes moste he make a chevyssaunce" (B^2 1519) so that he can pay back a large loan to certain Lombard moneylenders; and then, after stopping to visit his friend the monk, back to Saint Denis. He comes home delighted with his transactions because he is now "riche and cleerly out of dette" (B^2 1566), having earned "a thousand frankes aboven al his costage" (B^2 1562). That profit is so large[16] that he comes home sufficiently elated that hearing that his wife has spent the equivalent of ten per cent of it on clothing does not trouble him. "Murie as a papejay" (B^2 1559), he is sufficiently randy that the prospect of getting paid back in bed apparently seems rather appealing. If the logic of the story requires that a thousand-franc profit from complicated transactions in two of the financial capitals in Europe be large, then surely we can imagine that ten per cent of that amount is also a comfortable sum. We should recall that the merchant is aware of the importance of appearing prosperous (see B^2 1420, 1479). Having made a fine killing in the medieval international money market, he must have been pleased to have his wife show off his success with some expensive clothes purchased and worn for his own "honour."

Economic evidence

The evidence from within the tale, then, suggests in a general way that the 100 francs is a substantial amount of money. In trying to find a more definite estimate of the value of 100 francs, I discovered why others had not gone far up this crooked trail before me. To

[16] Thomas Hahn suggests that the merchant makes a 7% profit on the transaction, but "estimated on an annual basis this is a return of eighty-four percent" (238)—ample reason for the merchant to be cheerful at the success of his venture.

make even a guess requires a knowledge of medieval economics, exchange rates, and international trade practices that few literature professors—and, indeed, few historians—can pretend to. I decided that I needed to "network." I started close to home by calling Jon Innes, my friend in the economics department at Lehigh University. "Is there any way," I asked him, "to estimate how much 100 French francs in 1385 might be worth today? I mean, is there any way to apply some sort of exchange rate and inflation rate to that figure and give it to me in 1990s U.S. dollars?"

"Well," he said, "you might use a variation on the 'basket of groceries' approach. You figure out somehow how much 100 francs would buy back then, from market lists or price indices or whatever you can find, and then estimate how much it would take to buy those same groceries today. That's pretty tricky, though. Let me work on it and see what I can come up with." What he came up with was a figure of around $9000 for the 100 francs. Jon Innes sent me this note:

> I arrived at my estimate with the aid of two sources. I used H. A. Miskimin, *Money, Prices, and Foreign Exchange in Fourteenth-Century France* (New Haven: Yale University Press, 1963) to convert the franc to an equivalent number of British pounds (pound Tower). I used E. H. Phelps Brown and S. V. Hopkins, "Seven Centuries of the Prices of Consumables, Compared with Builders' Wage-rates," *Economica* (November 1956, 296–314) for a price index up through 1954. Then I converted pounds to dollars and applied inflation rates to bring the 1954 value up to a more reasonable recent estimate. But my assumptions were heroic, and I have zero faith in my calculations. Surely that is too high a figure for the kind of service the wife offers.

I wrote to James Murray, a history professor at the University of Cincinnati. His approach was to try to figure out the value of 100 francs by computing not an equivalent cost of goods, but an equivalent value in labor. By computing in francs the average daily wage of laborers in Paris in the late fourteenth century, Jim Murray concluded that a skilled carpenter would earn one franc for ten days' work. To earn 100 francs, a carpenter would have worked, then, around 1,000 days. Jim Murray did not give me a dollar value, perhaps because he knew it would seem enormously high:

> First the disclaimer: it is always difficult to fix a value to old coinages and currencies. The essential book is Peter Spufford's *Handbook of Medieval Exchange* (London, 1986).
>
> The franc Chaucer refers to is almost certainly the *franc a cheval* issued by the French crown between 1360 and 1385. This was a gold coin containing 3.82 grams of fine gold and was circulated widely in France and the Low Countries. Its book value, that is, its value in money of account, was either 20s. tournois or 16s. parisis. I should explain that the livre tournois and livre parisis were the two monies of account in fourteenth-century France, that is units of value unattached to any circulating coin, so that a coin like the franc had both bullion content and value as money of account. I don't want to drag you any further into the fascinating muck and mire of medieval coinage, but suffice it to say that one franc equalled one livre tournois, or 16s. parisis.
>
> Now to assess the value or buying power of 16 or 20s. in 1385: this, again, is difficult, but to simplify a bit, the average wage of a skilled laborer in Paris after 1360 was about 1s. 6d. to 2s. parisis per day; the wage of an unskilled laborer was precisely half that. Thus, one *franc a cheval* would be earned by a skilled laborer in ten days. So you can see that 100 francs was a huge sum to the average Frenchman in 1385, equal to at least 1,000 workdays for a skilled workman, and if a year contained c. 240 workdays, this was more than four years' earnings.

I did a quick calculation myself. If today we pay a carpenter $10 per hour—not a union carpenter, of course, and not even a very good carpenter—that comes to $80 for an eight-hour day. For 1000 eight-hour days, that brings the value of 100 francs to $80,000—not a lot for 1,000 hours—some four years—of work by a skilled carpenter, but generous indeed for one night with another man's wife.

I followed up the reference to Peter Spufford's 1986 *Handbook of Medieval Exchange* as essential to his calculations. I did not know Peter Spufford, but I bought a copy of his book. It had lots of charts and tables, but I did not know how to read them. I wrote to Spufford at Queens College, Cambridge, to explain my problem. Could he, I asked, come up with a figure for the 100 francs in 1990s pounds or dollars?

Peter Spufford kindly replied to my letter. He used his tables to come up with a fourteenth-century British equivalent of £18 for the 100 francs, then applied a price index to get a rough equivalent for the modern world. The figure he came up with was around $15,000 in 1990s U.S. money:

> The calculation you want is a little tedious. In 1385 the franc was again the livre tournois (20s.) so that 100 francs was 100 livres tournois. At that date the Florentine florin was worth 16s. 8d. tournois, so that 100 livres was worth 120 florins. At the same time the florin was worth 3s. sterling, so that 120 florins was worth £18. In other words for Chaucer the 100 francs he wrote about was worth £18 sterling. That comes from my exchange rate volume.
>
> Now to the problem of what it was worth, and here we have the methodological problem of how to translate across great periods of time, especially crossing from the preindustrial world to the industrial world. One way of doing it is to compare units of consumables, as was done with the Phelps Brown and Hopkins index. In this their unit of consumables was indexed at 108 in the 1380s and at 3,825 when they stopped in 1954. Following the same line of argument and using a modern cost-of-living index would make £18 in the 1380s able to pay for around £8500 worth of ordinary goods in 1992. This is slightly dubious, but does give some idea of the order of magnitude. Using a modern exchange rate this comes out at around $15,000.

> What is clear is that this is a perfectly suitable sum for a successful international merchant to be in a position to lend. What is not clear is whether Chaucer is being humourous or satirical in making the merchant's wife sell herself for this sum. She was certainly not making herself cheap!
>
> I hope that this is some use, but take care how you use it.

I wrote to Richard Unger, of the history department at the University of British Columbia, and explained what I was looking for. He talked with some of his friends and did a series of calculations. Like Jim Murray's, they were based in part on the conversion rates from Spufford's *Handbook*:

> Here is the best I can do on the question of the 100 francs. The *franc a cheval* (which I believe showed the king of France on horseback) was introduced by the king of France on 5 December 1360. It was a gold coin, of very high quality (i.e., 24 carat gold) and equal in value to one livre tournois. It was 3.88 grams of gold by weight. In England one ounce Troy of gold was the same as 321.7 pence. That being the case, one penny was .0967 grams of fine gold. Alternatively there were approximately 40 English pence to a franc.
>
> So the price of 100 francs was equal to 4,000 pence. What would 4,000 pence buy around 1380? You could buy 500 gallons of wine. It was equal to the annual rent of eight or nine shops close to Cheapside, the most expensive street in London, each shop having a floor area of about 60 square feet, and would have rooms on the two floors above. That amount of money would also buy around 1,000 pounds of copper wire, 50 swords, 250,000 chestnuts, or 111 pounds of basil. In sum, the figure is high but not outlandish. These are well-off individuals who deal in big sums.
>
> For all this you have to thank Angela Redish and Robert Allen of the Department of Economics at the University of British Columbia, and Derek Keene of the Centre for Metropolitan History at the University of London. The

> conversion to English shillings of silver is based on Albert Feavearyear, *The Pound Sterling: A History of English Money* (Oxford: Clarendon, 1963), 439.

It is interesting to speculate on the dollar equivalents of some of the commodities Unger mentions. If 100 francs would have bought around 500 gallons of wine in Chaucer's time, I might note that at some supermarkets today I can buy a minimally decent gallon of domestic table wine for around $10. One does not speak of the bouquet of such wine, but the cost for 500 such gallons would be somewhere around $5,000, plus tax. I leave it to others to estimate the value of a quarter-million chestnuts. I don't even like them.

Which of these figures is correct? Does the wife sell herself for $4,000 or $9,000 or $15,000 or $80,000? The variation in the figures suggests, once again, that there is no exactness to this business of determining price equivalents across the centuries, and surely none of the estimates is "correct" in any exact sense. And we must note the caution given by Kenneth S. Cahn about the geographical fluctuations of all international exchange rates:

> Both exchanges—that is, sterlings changed to shield and shields changed back into sterling—were done at the current and fluctuating exchange rates. But what determined the current rates in the Middle Ages? In one sense, the rates were much as they are today; they fluctuated daily and usually stayed within a certain range of value. In another sense, however, they were quite different from the modern exchange rates. Since the invention of the cablegram, the exchange rate of a particular money is virtually identical at home and abroad at any given moment. During the Middle Ages, and indeed well beyond that period, the value of a given money tended to diminish rather rapidly with the increase of its distance (or time) from home. Thus, on a given day, the sterling was usually worth most in England and somewhat less on the continent. Similarly, the *sheelde* was worth 24 to 27 English sterlings at the money market at its home in Flanders,

> while that same shield was only worth between 23 and 26 sterlings in the English money market.[17]

Even if we could speak with any degree of accuracy about the value of 100 French francs in Chaucer's time, we must take into account where one was doing the exchanging. Add to the geographical distance the temporal distance of 600 years, and the uncertainty is even more pronounced. Perhaps we are wisest not to try to think of the 100 francs in terms of a specific amount of money, but simply a large, round number, something like the 1000 pounds of the *Franklin's Tale*. One thing seems clear, though: 100 francs in Chaucer's time was a substantial amount of money—certainly a great deal to pay for a single night of lust with another man's wife.

Comparative literary evidence

Can we put the 100 francs into a literary context? Boccaccio's *Decameron* 8.1 is the mostly likely source for Chaucer's *Shipman's Tale*.[18] In this analogue the wife sells herself for 200 gold florins. This paper is not the place to attempt a detailed conversion of the 200 Florentine florins. As I have already shown, all such attempts are in any case based on questionable assumptions and yield conflicting results. In private correspondence, however, Peter Spufford suggests that in Chaucer's time 200 florins was worth something more than 150 French francs. That makes the price of sex in the Italian stories at least a couple of thousands of U.S. dollars more than the amount we find in Chaucer. Assuming that a Continental traveler and customs official would have known something about international exchange rates, and

[17] Cahn, 88.

[18] Most scholars now think it unlikely that Chaucer could have known Sercambi's "Of Avarice and Lust" in his *Novelle*. It is, however, derived from the *Decameron* version and the amount charged—200 gold florins—is the same. The *Decameron* is available in several translations. "Of Avarice and Lust" may be found in translation in *The Literary Context of Chaucer's Fabliaux*, ed. Larry D. Benson and Theodore M. Andersson (Indianapolis, 1971), 313–19. The "lost French source" that some earlier scholars posited is fortunately rarely spoken of today.

that an avid reader of Italian might have known either the *Decameron* or the *Novelle,* it may well be that Chaucer somewhat reduced the amount that the wife charges for her sexual services. If so, perhaps he wanted to make the amount seem less outlandish. Chaucer always had an eye out to realism, and it may be that he wanted the price of sex in the *Shipman's Tale* to seem large, but not so large that a money-conscious merchant would be frightfully concerned about losing it, or outraged at exchanging it for a series of sexual favors from his wife. This latter exchange, of course, does not appear in either Italian analogue, where the wife, caught out in her trick, is expected to return the 200 florins to her husband in cash, not services.

In a recent letter, Peter Spufford informs me that 200 florins would have been an exorbitant price indeed for what the wife of Boccaccio's merchant of Milan offers the soldier in exchange for it. In that time with 200 florins the soldier could have purchased three young love slaves:

> These slave girls would also expect to be used for other domestic duties, as well. Slavery was not legalised in Florence until the 1360's, but by the end of the century Circassian slave girls, aged between 15 and 25, were easily purchasable for 45 or 50 florins (although one particularly handsome fifteen-year-old cost as much as 65 florins, but this was still only a third of the fee in the *Decameron* version of the story). Many well-to-do households had slave girls, and the bastard children that they gave their owners were frequently brought up in the household along with the legitimate ones. In the next century, one of Cosimo de Medici's became an abbot.[19]

By the time I found all this out, of course, the student who asked the original question had long since graduated, surely having forgotten that she ever asked the question. But the question was a good one, and it will be asked again. What have we learned? First,

[19] From Iris Origo, "The Domestic Enemy: The Eastern Slaves in Tuscany in the Fourteenth and Fifteenth Centuries," *Speculum* 30 (1955): 336–37.

we have learned that it is impossible to derive an exact or accurate modern equivalent for the 100 francs.

Second, we have learned that scholars like Nevill Coghill and Hazel Sullivan were surely wrong to suggest that 100 francs is a "trifling" or a "small" amount. It was, almost any way we figure it, a large amount of money, measuring well into the medieval equivalent of thousands of modern dollars. I suggest that a quite conservative $5,000 be considered a specific lower limit to the value of that amount in 1990s U. S. dollars, but that we recognize that 100 francs was probably worth considerably more.

Third, we have learned that the merchant of Saint Denis is, if somewhat greedy and gullible, generous both to his false friend and to his high-spending wife. Far from being a neglectful cheapskate, he is the most generous of the three people who touch his 100 francs.

Fourth, we have learned that the wife in the *Shipman's Tale* has an exalted opinion of her own worth. To think she is worth so much as a sexual partner suggests that she is guilty not only of avarice and lechery, but of pride, as well.

And, fifth, we have learned that, while Chaucer was wise enough to see that the story of deception, falseness, and infidelity works only if the price the wife of Saint Denis puts on her sexual services is high, he was also wise enough not to make that figure outlandishly high. While a $5000-minimum price for sex in the *Shipman's Tale* seems at first blush outrageous, in comparison to what Boccaccio did with a similar plot, the price of sex in Chaucer's *Shipman's Tale* seems downright conservative.

Teaching Chaucer as Drama: The Garden Scene in the *Shipman's Tale*

[What most unites Chaucerians is the classroom experience of teaching the amazing works of Geoffrey Chaucer, yet it has been almost impossible to find a forum for discussing, let alone publishing, our ideas about teaching his language and his works. In this essay I described my practice in having my undergraduate students act in readers'-theater-like skits taken from selected scenes in the *Canterbury Tales*. The prime example I used in the article is from the *Shipman's Tale*—the wonderful garden scene in which the merchant's sexy wife propositions the sleazy monk. (For other pedagogical articles, see my "Chaucer and the Trots: What to Do about Those Modern English Translations," *Chaucer Review* 19 (1985): 290–301, and "Low-Tech Chaucer: An Experimental Iambic Pentameter Creative Project," *Exercise Exchange* 46 (2000): 16–20.) "Teaching Chaucer as Drama" first appeared in *Exemplaria* 8 (1996): 485–93.]

When I say that it is useful to "teach Chaucer as drama" I must hasten to say first what I do *not* mean by that phrase. I do *not* mean that we should teach the "dramatic theory" as made almost famous by George Lyman Kittredge,[1] made almost absurd by Robert M.

[1] G. L. Kittredge, *Chaucer and His Poetry* (Cambridge: Harvard University Press, 1915). Kittredge suggested that the various tales should be seen as dramatic soliloquies by their fictional tellers, rather as if Chaucer were Shakespeare (155): "The Pilgrims do not exist for

Lumiansky,[2] and made almost obsolete by C. David Benson[3]—and made almost upside-down by H. Marshall Leicester, Jr.[4] That is, I do not mean that we should urge on students the necessity of interpreting every tale through the real or supposed biography or psychology of its fictional teller.

Nor do I mean that we should teach "Chaucer aloud" in the sense that Betsy Bowden means that term[5] and that Alan T. Gaylord challenged by saying that it should not be "allowed."[6] That is, I do not mean that we should get a series of well-known Chaucerians to read a series of passages in an effort to see how such readers inflect the text and inflict on us their own interpretations.

Nor do I mean that we should teach "Chaucerian theatricality" in the rather specialized and postmodern sense discussed by John M.

the sake of the stories, but *vice versa.* Structurally regarded, the stories are merely long speeches expressing, directly or indirectly, the characters of the several persons. They are more or less comparable, in this regard, to the soliloquies of Hamlet or Iago or Macbeth."

[2] R. Lumiansky, *"Of sondry folk": The Dramatic Principle in the Canterbury Tales* (Austin: University of Texas Press, 1955). Lumiansky urged us to read the tales as sources of information about the various Canterbury pilgrims.

[3] C. David Benson, *Chaucer's Drama of Style: Poetic Variety and Contrast in the Canterbury Tales* (Chapel Hill: University of North Carolina Press, 1986). Benson showed the limitations of the dramatic theory and argued instead for a variety of contrasting poetic voices or "styles" in the *Canterbury Tales.*

[4] H. M. Leicester, Jr., *The Disenchanted Self: Representing the Subject in the Canterbury Tales* (Berkeley: University of California Press, 1990). Influenced by the deconstructive approaches of Jacques Derrida, Leicester says that the pilgrims do not create the texts that they speak on the road to Canterbury. Rather, the texts, by virtue of being spoken, create the pilgrims.

[5] Betsy Bowden, *Chaucer Aloud: The Varieties of Textual Interpretation* (Philadelphia: University of Pennsylvania Press, 1987). Bowden made recordings of thirty-odd Chaucerians reading selected passages from Chaucer and showed how their methods of reading the passages indicated certain assumptions they were making about how Chaucer expected us to interpret them.

[6] Alan T. Gaylord, "Reading Chaucer: What's Allowed in 'Aloud'?" *Chaucer Yearbook* 1 (1992): 87–109. Gaylord argued that the "primary and ultimate" audience for Chaucer's poetry was not a listener but a solitary reader.

Ganim.[7] That is, I do not mean that we should teach the Canterbury stories as carnivalesque expressions by pilgrims suddenly freed from the social constraints normally placed on them.

Nor do I mean by "teaching Chaucer as drama" that we should force our students to listen to the tapes of "performed readings" that Paul Thomas and Tom Burton of the Chaucer Studio[8] are now making available to teachers. That is, I do not mean that we should have our students listen to other people doing oral dramatizations of the various tales.

I reject none of these approaches. Indeed when I teach Chaucer as drama I sometimes find myself brushing up against several of them, and doing so with pleasure. It is simply that they are not what I mean when I say that it is useful to "teach Chaucer as drama." I mean, rather, that it is useful from a pedagogical standpoint to involve our students in small readers' theater productions of scenes from Chaucer. I began experimenting with such skits in my own Chaucer classroom several years ago, and now they are a regular feature of my undergraduate classroom teaching of Chaucer.

I got started doing these skits because I take seriously my teaching of Chaucerian Middle English. Indeed, for many years now the first two or three full weeks of my fourteen-week semester have been taken up with teaching Chaucer's language. I have worked up a series of exercises designed to acquaint students with pronouncing Chaucerian Middle English, understanding it, and learning the basics

[7] John M. Ganim, *Chaucerian Theatricality* (Princeton: Princeton University Press, 1990). Ganim connects Chaucer with a sense of "carnival" as discussed by Bahktin, and sees in the *Canterbury Tales* "an interplay among the author's voice, his fictional characters, and his immediate audience" (5).

[8] In these recordings different professors of medieval literature read parts of the tale. For the *Friar's Tale*, for example, one reader would be the Friar's narrative voice, another would be the yeoman, another the summoner in the tale, and so on. Of the Canterbury stories, the tales of the Knight, the Miller, the Reeve, the Friar, the Summoner, the Franklin, the Merchant, the Prioress, the Nun's Priest, the Shipman, and the Wife of Bath are currently available from Paul R. Thomas of the Department of English at Brigham Young University.

of its grammar and diction. In the third week I have every student come individually to my office for a twenty-minute conference; they recite from memory six lines of their own choosing from the *General Prologue* and then read aloud to me some lines from the *Knight's Tale*. From that tale they must read to me one set of lines they know about in advance and can work up, and another set I select for them to read from the tale cold, with no practice. For reasons I have not quite figured out, some of the students do better on the piece they have not had a chance to study in advance.

Along the way I have my students write and turn in a couple of passages in Modern English iambic pentameter rhyming couplets. I put them through that agony because I find that one of the most serious impediments to effective readings of Chaucer's verse is that many students simply do not know what an iamb is or what it means to string five of them into a line. The rhyming is easy for them; the iambic pentameter is not.

In any case, these exercises and the individual oral performance in my office have most of my students reading Middle English pretty well after the first three weeks. Then we shift away from these linguistic and prosodic matters and set to work on our discussion of the literary qualities of the tales themselves. It is that shifting away that began to trouble me, and that got me started in teaching Chaucer as drama.

I love teaching Chaucer, and I am always amazed that after two or three weeks most of my students are quite competent readers of Middle English, a few of them able to match me. But I noticed that, after those three weeks, my students' language skills often seemed to decline, if only because, in the press of reading all those tales silently, they were slipping into a more Modern English way of reading the lines. In order to encourage my students to keep their Middle English reading skills alive after their one-on-one sessions in my office, I have begun the practice of selecting from the tale of the day a scene or two for oral reading in class.

For the first such scene, I have come to encourage a couple of my best readers to "volunteer." Curiously, they are eager to do so, proud of their new-found skill, and pleased that I tell them how good they are. The volunteers come to my office the day before their performance and we read through the scene together. I help them with their pronunciation and make sure they have understood their characters, and then we do simple blocking. The next day the students read their parts in front of the class, bow to the polite applause of their classmates, and beam when I tell the rest of the class how well they did.

After that I send around a sign-up sheet asking for others who would like to volunteer to take part in a skit later in the term. Typically around two-thirds of the students do volunteer. The ones who do not are either ashamed—often with some justification—of their ability to read Middle English, or just plain shy. Sometimes students whose Middle English is not well polished want to volunteer, either to improve their pronunciation or just because they want to be part of the fun. I am realistic enough to know that those who do volunteer do so in part because they know that some portion of their final grade assesses the quality and spirit of their class participation, but mostly it seems they just think it looks like fun. And it is.

The volunteers always come together in my office at some time the day before they perform so that they have a chance to meet one another, practice their lines, and learn the routine. They then have time that evening or the next day before class to review their lines so they can be less halting in front of their peers.

Sometimes, if the scene lends itself to simple actions, we experiment with the simplest of stage movements—entering, exiting, kneeling. More complicated stuff is hampered by the fact that the performers all have scripts in their hands. (Incidentally, I find that it works best if I prepare for each performer an enlarged Xerox copy of the lines in the scene, with his or her lines highlighted in yellow. That frees them from having to drag the book up to the front of the room and makes it far less likely that they will lose their places during their performance.) Sometimes we have a simple prop: a wooden sword, a stuffed animal, a pail of water, a Bible. Sometimes a character will wear a black sheet over her shoulders to show that she is a friar or a monk. If the scene calls for a tree or a window we sometimes draw them on the blackboard.

After the scene is performed I sometimes want to comment on or ask questions about the scene. Indeed, I now find myself selecting for dramatization scenes that I *want* to comment on, or that may clarify certain puzzling points or raise interesting issues. By now these little skits—rarely more than a hundred lines—are a regular feature of my teaching. I now "do" some eight or ten scenes from the *Canterbury Tales* in my course, depending in large part on how many volunteers I have. Sometimes I read a part myself, but usually I don't. The simple play-acting my students do has become one of my most useful pedagogical devices.

It is time for an example. One of my own favorite scenes is the wonderfully dramatic garden scene in Chaucer's *Shipman's Tale,* the scene in which the monk, daun John, and the wife of the merchant of Saint Denis meet and arrange their little liaison. Lines 1279, where daun John rises and walks in the garden to say his "thynges," to 1393, where he grabs the wife by the flanks and kisses her, make a wonderfully dramatic scene. Before my student narrator, monk, and wife do their thing in front of their classmates, I like to read the class, from the first story of the eighth day of Boccaccio's *Decameron*, the passage parallel to Chaucer's garden scene in the *Shipman's Tale.* This tale may have been Chaucer's source for the *Shipman's Tale*; certainly it is one of the closest analogues. *Decameron* 8.1 is about a German soldier who visits Milan and falls in love with the wife of a wealthy Milanese merchant. In Boccaccio's version of the events that Chaucer was later to place in the garden scene, we find this brief narrative account (my translation):

> One day the soldier sent the merchant's wife a messenger imploring her to reward his devotion and assuring her that he would do whatever she might ask of him. After much hesitation, the lady made up her mind and sent word to him that she would comply with his request on two conditions: first, he must never tell anyone about it and, second, since he

> was well off and she wanted to buy something for herself, he was to give her two hundred gold florins, and then she would be at his service.

After I read that section from the *Decameron*, my students perform the parallel passage in the *Shipman's Tale*, the scene in which the monk and the wife of the merchant of Saint Denis meet in the garden. It is a wonderful scene in Chaucer. As the monk says his prayers in the dawn garden, the wife comes to him. In the conversational interplay between them the wife says she would confess her troubles but does not want to cast aspersions on the monk's cousin, and the monk disclaims cousinship to encourage her to confess her unhappiness. The wife then complains about her husband's stinginess and asks for the loan of a hundred francs, in exchange for whatever services the monk wants. The scene ends with Daun John grabbing the merchant's wife by the flanks and kissing her. Incidentally, one of the decisions that needs to be made about performing the garden scene is whether to have the monk actually kiss the wife and grab her by the haunches. Different groups come up with different decisions. One group arranged to drop a sheet in front of the two as the narrator reads those lines; another merely mimed the actions, without physical contact. Making such decisions, of course, is part of the fun.

After my students' brief performance of the scene, I reread the parallel Boccaccio passage and ask them to compare the two. Here are some of the responses I hope to elicit from my class. Usually I am not disappointed, but sometimes my students need a little teacherly encouragement and guidance:

Chaucer gives us a longer scene. If we actually add up the words in the two passages, Chaucer's passage is ten times as long as Boccaccio's. I ask my students what Chaucer does that takes so much time, indeed that makes the garden scene a full quarter of the total length of the *Shipman's Tale.*

Chaucer dramatizes the scene. Whereas Boccaccio has the soldier and the merchant's wife arrange their affair by means of messages sent through a third party, Chaucer gives us a face-to-face meeting between the two in which the would-be lovers negotiate their affair directly. There are not only the delightful conversation itself, but also entrances and exits and movement and shaking of heads and grabbing and kissing. I ask my students to tell me more about the kissing.

Chaucer gives us two kiss-events. There is no kissing, no physical contact at all, in the parallel scene in Boccaccio, whereas Chaucer gives us not one, but two kiss sequences. The first is innocent enough, perhaps, the familial kiss of cousins. The second, however, is quite different, where Daun John lustily catches the wife by the flanks and embraces her hard and kisses her often. I ask my students to tell me how Chaucer prepares for the dramatic difference in the two kissing incidents, how the conversations lead us to see that the first garden kiss is far different from the second.

Chaucer gives us dialogue. Whereas Boccaccio had reported messages and arrangements, Chaucer has the two principals talk. Whereas the narrator does all of the talking in Boccaccio, in Chaucer the narrator does only seventeen percent of the talking in the hundred and fifteen lines of the garden scene, leaving the rest, or eighty-three percent, to the direct reporting of the speeches of the monk and the wife. I ask my students who does more of the talking, the monk or the wife?

Chaucer increases the role of the wife. In the dialogue, the wife has almost twice as many lines (fifty-three percent of the total one hundred and fifteen lines) as the monk (with only thirty percent). And whereas in Boccaccio, the soldier had been very much the aggressor in the affair, propositioning the wife, in Chaucer the situation is quite different. In the garden scene the wife comes to the monk and salutes him; she complains of her husband's sexuality and his stinginess; she says she needs a hundred francs and that if Daun John can lend them to her, she will not fail to express her thanks in whatever "service" he likes. I ask my students whether the monk is totally innocent in the affair.

Chaucer darkens the role of the lover. Whereas in Boccaccio the soldier had been a good man acting the proper role of the courtly lover who is properly indignant when the wife he admires is so base as to ask for money for her sexual services, in Chaucer Daun John is rather more sleazy. He is, for one thing, a monk who has taken vows of celibacy, not an adventurous soldier for whom an attraction to another man's pretty wife seems entirely appropriate. But Daun John also too quickly renounces his cousinhood to his friend the merchant of Saint Denis, tells his friend's wife that he has loved her especially, "aboven alle wommen," and at the end of the scene grabs her by the flanks and kisses her hard and repeatedly.

Well, there is more that my students and I can talk about in the important garden scene in the *Shipman's Tale*: the setting (why a garden rather than, say, a parlor?); the maid child (who is she and where is she for the kissing scenes?); the "thynges sixe" that the wife says all wives need (why does her husband seem to measure up so well in giving them to her?); the tree (does that suggest that this scene is meant to parallel the Garden of Eden?); and so on. We can also discuss the way my students portrayed a certain character by asking questions like "Would you have played the monk in that way?" I hasten to admit that my performing students are far more worried about their pronunciation than their acting, but inevitably the student-performers present a certain character when they read the words of a Chaucer's monk or lady, even if they do so fumblingly. My point is that my students, having just seen the scene portrayed in class, are ready to discuss such detailed questions with me, and with each other. Certainly they are far readier than they would be if I had to rely on a single and hasty reading they had done in their rooms the night before—if at all.

I close by mentioning five advantages of doing little skits or dramatic enactments in our classes. First, doing these skits reinforces the sounds of Chaucerian Middle English for our students. I find that students who are not comfortable with their Middle English are more willing to "practice it" in a group with their peers in a dramatic setting than they are if I ask them to read a certain passage solo, and without practice, out loud in class. I find, also, that students can hear the difference between a good reader, one who reads with expression and feeling, and one who reads without really comprehending the meaning of her or his lines. They can tell good from less good, and in the hearing are learning what to do when their time comes.

Second, I find that being in a skit sometimes breaks the ice for them, and that after they have been on stage for a few minutes they are afterwards more willing to contribute to the discussion. The skits seem to bring me closer to my students and my students closer to each other. By having short rehearsals in my office the day before we do a scene in class, I not only get to know my students better as individuals, but also introduce them to one another. We tend to forget that most of our students are strangers to one another.

Third, doing the short dramatic enactments focuses students' attention on Chaucer's text. Those who volunteer will have read a certain scene, or at least the words of a certain character, several times before coming to class, and we all know that no students even begin to understand Chaucer until they have reread him. But putting certain key scenes before an audience makes those students, too, readier to discuss what happens in the scene than they would otherwise be. Instead of relying on a clouded and hasty private reading the night before, my students can build on what they have just heard and seen in class. The skits do wonders for discussion.

Fourth, students in the '90s are naturally attuned to the dramatic possibilities in Chaucer's fiction because they have been raised on a fare of television rather than reading. They feel very much at home taking part in and being audience to the dramatic scenes in Chaucer's fiction. The skits help them to "visualize" the story in ways that are more familiar to them.

Fifth, and most important, by making dramatic presentations of certain scenes in Chaucer we are emphasizing one of the key features of Chaucer's fiction—its drama, its theatricality. Chaucer never wrote a play, but there is no question that he knew about medieval drama. The *Miller's Tale*—with its reference to the Miller's Pilate-like voice, to Absolon's playing Herod upon the high scaffold, and to the troubles that Noah had getting his wife into the ship—offers evidence of that knowledge, as does the detail that the Wife of Bath liked to go to miracle plays. I am convinced that Chaucer's fiction was influenced by the drama of his time and that Chaucer introduced into fiction techniques of drama—scene development, actor movement, characterization, dialogue—that were virtually unknown in fiction before him. I have found that it is easy to make skits of Chaucer because he has given us the characters and the settings and the dialogue that are the very stuff of drama. Far from merely pandering to the television-trained tastes of contemporary students, then, I insist that by introducing dramatic performances into our Chaucer classrooms we are helping our students to see not only why Chaucer's fiction has survived when much other medieval fiction has not, but also why it is accurate to suggest that Chaucer influenced the dramatists—most fundamentally Shakespeare—who came after him. Chaucer wrote great poetry, yes. Chaucer wrote great fiction, yes. But he also wrote great drama; more accurately, he wrote some of the most dramatic poetic fiction the world has ever known. Surely it is part of our jobs as teachers of Chaucer in the '90s to find ways to acquaint our students with that fact. What better way is there than, by having our students perform in brief skits, to "teach Chaucer as drama"?

Contrasting Masculinities in the *Shipman's Tale*: Monk, Merchant, and Wife

[In the second half of the twentieth century feminist approaches to literature laid for themselves a solid foundation, and since then strong and beautiful edifices have been built on that foundation. The success of these approaches has suggested that more subtle approaches to the nuanced varieties of masculinity might be in order. In the May 1996 program at the International Congress on Medieval Studies at Kalamazoo, I noticed that eight or ten of the Chaucer papers dealt with males and manhood in Chaucer's works. I decided to try to put together a collection of these papers, to be augmented by other invited essays. Behold, soon we had available a book of original essays on Chaucerian masculinities. My own contribution to the volume attempts to show how slippery the term *masculine* can be as it applies to the three central characters in the *Shipman's Tale*—one of whom, indeed, is a woman. I try to show, especially, how Chaucer made some dramatic shifts in adapting to the Wife of Bath Boccaccio's tale of lust, betrayal, and greed. "Contrasting Masculinities in the *Shipman's Tale*" first appeared in *Masculinities in Chaucer: Approaches to Maleness in the Canterbury Tales and Troilus and Criseyde*, ed. Peter G. Beidler (Woodbridge, Suffolk: D. S. Brewer, 1998), 131–42.]

The term "masculine" can refer to a nest of negative qualities often associated with being male: brutality, self-aggrandizement, sexual irresponsibility, selfishness, inability to feel or express emotion, inconstancy. It can also refer to a host of positive qualities: self-reliance, leadership, generosity, loyalty, sexual performance, responsibility for one's family, independence, good business sense. In the two central male characters in the *Shipman's Tale*, Chaucer gives us contrasting masculinities, the negative aspects of masculinity being associated with the monk of Paris, the more positive aspects being associated with the merchant of Saint Denis. Throughout my discussion of the contrasting masculinities in the *Shipman's Tale*, I shall compare Chaucer's tale of the lover's gift regained with its closest analogue and most likely source, the first tale of the eighth day of Boccaccio's *Decameron*. I shall have much to say about the important differences in treatment of the male characters in these two tales, but will close with a brief suggestion that the *Shipman's Tale*, originally written for the Wife of Bath, shows us a wife who, while remaining undeniably and gloriously a woman, demonstrates traits that were in Chaucer's time usually associated more with men than with women.

The *Shipman's Tale* has not received the scholarly attention that Chaucer's other fabliaux have received. What scholarship there has been has generally focused on one of four problems: what the tale reveals about medieval business practices;[1] how it reflects religious

[1] Closely related to the mercantile quality of the tale is its punning. The following are some of the studies that deal with mercantile issues and puns: Albert H. Silverman, "Sex and Money in Chaucer's *Shipman's Tale*," *Philological Quarterly* 32 (1953): 329–36; Paul Stephen Schneider, " 'Taillynge Ynough': The Function of Money in the *Shipman's Tale*," *Chaucer Review* 11 (1977): 201–09; Kenneth S. Cahn, "Chaucer's Merchants and the Foreign Exchange: An Introduction to Medieval Finance," *Studies in the Age of Chaucer* 2 (1980): 81–119; Lorraine Kochanske Stock, "The Meaning of *Chevyssaunce*: Complicated Word Play in Chaucer's *Shipman's Tale*," *Studies in Short Fiction* 18 (1981): 245–49; Gerhard Joseph, "Chaucer's Coinage: Foreign Exchange and the Puns of the *Shipman's Tale*," *Chaucer Review* 17 (1983): 341–57; Thomas Hahn, "Money, Sexuality, Wordplay and Context in the *Shipman's Tale*," in *Chaucer in the Eighties*, ed. Julian N. Wasserman and Robert J. Blanch (Syracuse: Syracuse University Press, 1986), 235–49; and Wight Martindale, Jr., "Chaucer's Merchants: A Trade-Based Speculation on Their Activities," *Chaucer Review* 26 (1992): 309–16.

symbolism;[2] its relationship to its antecedents;[3] and its possible early assignment to the Wife of Bath rather than the Shipman.[4] In most studies the monk is seen as clever but immoral, the husband as overly preoccupied with his business and not sufficiently attentive to his wife, and the wife as either a greedy prostitute or a neglected wife justified in complaining about her husband. Few scholars have touched on the issue of masculinity as it is portrayed in the tale, except to note that the merchant is inadequately manly. But let us first consider his cuckolder, daun John.

The monk of Paris

Daun John's behavior and motives are in direct contrast to those of Gulfardo, his counterpart in *Decameron* 8.1, written at least thirty

[2] See, for example, Theresa Coletti, "The Meeting at the Gate: Comic Hagiography and Symbol in the *Shipman's* Tale," *Studies in Iconography* 3 (1977): 47–56, and "The *Mulier Fortis* and Chaucer's *Shipman's Tale*," *Chaucer Review* 15 (1981): 236–49; Gail McMurray Gibson, "Resurrection as Dramatic Icon in the *Shipman's Tale*," in *Signs and Symbols in Chaucer's Poetry*, ed. John P. Hermann and John J. Burke, Jr. (Tuscaloosa, AL: University of Alabama Press, 1981), 102–12; Lorraine Kochanske Stock, "The Reenacted Fall in Chaucer's *Shipman's Tale*," *Studies in Iconography* 7–8 (1981–82): 135–45; and R. H. Winnick, "Luke 12 and Chaucer's *Shipman's Tale*," *Chaucer Review* 30 (1995): 164–90.

[3] See, for example, Murray Copland, "The *Shipman's Tale*: Chaucer and Boccaccio," *Medium Ævum* 35 (1966): 11–28; Michael W. McClintock, "Games and the Players of Games: Old French Fabliaux and the *Shipman's Tale*," *Chaucer Review* 5 (1970): 112–36; Richard Guerin, "The *Shipman's Tale*: The Italian Analogues," *English Studies* 52 (1971): 412–19; V. J. Scattergood, "The Originality of the *Shipman's Tale*," *Chaucer Review* 11 (1977): 210–31; Lorraine Kochanske Stock, "La Vieille and the Merchant's Wife in Chaucer's *Shipman's Tale*," *Southern Humanities Review* 16 (1982): 333–39; Joerg O. Fichte, "Chaucer's *Shipman's Tale* within the Context of the French Fabliaux Tradition," in *Chaucer's Frame Tales: The Physical and the Metaphysical*, ed. Joerg O. Fichte (Tubingen: Narr, 1987), 51–66; and Carol F. Heffernan, "Chaucer's *Shipman's Tale* and Boccaccio's *Decameron* 8.1: Retelling a Story," in *Courtly Literature: Culture and Context*, ed. Keith Busby and Erik Kooper (Amsterdam: John Benjamins, 1990), 262–70.

[4] See, for example, Richard F. Jones, "A Conjecture on the Wife of Bath's Prologue," *Journal of English and Germanic Philology* 24 (1925): 512–47; Robert A. Pratt, "The Development of the Wife of Bath," in *Studies in Medieval Literature*, ed. MacEdward Leach (Philadelphia: University of Pennsylvania Press, 1961), 45–79; and William W. Lawrence, "Chaucer's *Shipman's Tale*," *Speculum* 33 (1958): 56–68.

years before Chaucer wrote the *Shipman's Tale*.[5] Here is a summary of the key actions of Boccaccio's version of the story of a man who borrows from a merchant enough money to pay for sexual services from the merchant's wife:

> *Decameron* 8.1. Gulfardo, a brave German soldier in Milan, is known for his trustworthiness in repaying loans. He falls in love with Ambruogia, the wife of a wealthy merchant named Guasparruolo, with whom he is on friendly terms. One day Gulfardo sends Ambruogia a message expressing his love, requesting her to reward his devotion to her, and affirming that he will do whatever she might ask of him. The lady considers his request, then tells Gulfardo that she will grant it, but only if he will give her 200 gold florins so that she can buy something for herself. Gulfardo is disillusioned that the woman he had come to love could cheapen that love by being so rapaciously greedy, and his love turns to hatred. He vows to punish her. After sending Ambruogia word that he will give her the money, Gulfardo goes to Ambruogia's husband and asks for a loan of 200 florins, at the usual rate of interest, for a certain business transaction. The husband readily agrees and gives him the money on the spot. Not long after, when her husband is off in Genoa on business, Ambruogia summons Gulfardo. He comes and, in the presence of a witness, gives

[5] This is not the place to argue the importance of *Decameron* 8.1 as the most likely source for Chaucer's tale. Readers who want to pursue the point can read my essay, "Just Say Yes, Chaucer Knew the *Decameron*: or, Bringing the *Shipman's Tale* out of Limbo" following this essay, pp. 161–90. Giovanni Sercambi's *novelle* "De avaritia et lussuria" ("Of Avarice and Lust") is sometimes considered to be a contending source for the *Shipman's Tale*, but there is growing evidence that the book that contained it—which is based unquestionably on the *Decameron*—would not have been available to Chaucer in time for it to have influenced the composition of this tale. The text and a modern English translation are conveniently available in Larry D. Benson and Theodore Andersson, eds., *The Literary Context of Chaucer's Fabliaux* (Indianapolis: Bobbs-Merrill, 1971), 312–19. The notion that Chaucer's real source was a lost French fabliau is widely disregarded now. My quotations from Chaucer are from the *Riverside Chaucer*, ed. Larry D. Benson, 3rd edn. (Boston: Houghton Mifflin, 1987).

> her the 200 florins with the request that she should return them to her husband. So that the witness will not guess that the money is anything but a business matter, Ambruogia agrees, then pours the gold onto the table and counts it. She hides the money and takes Gulfardo to her bedroom. They make love that day and many others before her husband returns. As soon as the merchant gets back from Genoa, Gulfardo goes to him with the witness and reports, in the presence of the wife, that he had not needed the money after all and had given it to his wife to return to him. Since there was a witness to the transaction, Ambruogia says that, yes, she had received the money, but had forgotten to tell her husband about it. The husband agrees to strike the loan from the books, and the wife gives him the 200 florins.

That summary of a two-page story does not reveal the extent to which Gulfardo, the German soldier, is held up for admiration. Neifile, the fictional teller, explicitly announces that she tells this tale not to criticize the male lover for his behavior but, on the contrary, to praise him for his clever way of punishing Ambruogia. Gulfardo is a brave soldier who is loyal to those who employ him, always pays his debts, is discreet, and is capable of true and lofty love. There is not a hint of irony in any of this praise. After she has completed her tale, Neifile again explicitly praises the wise Gulfardo for punishing the rapacious and depraved Ambruogia by finding a way to enjoy her sexual favors at no cost.

The narrator of the *Shipman's Tale* also praises the male lover, but the praise is laced with irony. Daun John is said to be "a fair man" (VII 25) and "so fair of face" (28), but handsomeness seems a curiously unnecessary, even harmful, quality in a monk. He is said to be "noble" (62) and "a man of heigh prudence" (64), but his actions in the story—cheating both the woman he says he loves and his life-long friend—surely suggest, at least in retrospect, that such praise is spoken with more than a hint of sarcasm.

Chaucer fundamentally reorients his version of the tale. Far from portraying daun John as a good person whose courtly love for a woman justifies his propositioning her and whose sense of outrage at her mercenary character justifies his tricking her, Chaucer portrays him as a sleazy opportunist who himself deserves to be punished, a man whose masculinity is almost entirely negative. Indeed, what Neifile sees as the positive masculinity of Gulfardo throws into appropriate contrast what the narrator of the *Shipman's Tale* sees as the negative masculinity of daun John. Gulfardo is a brave and reliable bachelor eligible for love. Daun John is a monk whose vows of chastity ought to make him ineligible for love. By making the lover a vow-breaking ecclesiast who takes advantage of his professional position to seduce wives, Chaucer drops him to a level with Absolon. Gulfardo genuinely falls in love with a married woman and then discreetly asks his lady for her favors. Daun John merely lusts after another man's wife. His subsequent professions of love are both indiscreet and insincere.

Although Gulfardo is said to be on friendly terms with the merchant of Milan, the two men come not merely from different cities but from different nations. Their friendship is business-based, so far as we can tell, deriving from Gulfardo's having borrowed from Guasparruolo and having repaid all of his past loans on time. Daun John, on the other hand, is a life-long friend of the merchant of Saint Denis, with whom he had grown up in the same village. In proposing a liaison with Guasparruolo's wife, Gulfardo proposes to cuckold a business associate. In proposing a liaison with his best friend's wife, daun John proposes to betray a lifelong friendship. Gulfardo is no kinsman to the man whose wife he loves. Daun John, on the other hand, claims to be a "cousin" to his friend—that is, until it is convenient to his lustful purposes to make hasty and unequivocal denial of that cousinship: "He is na moore cosyn unto me / Than is this leef that hangeth on the tree!" (149–50). Gulfardo has only a business connection with the merchant of Milan. Daun John, on the other hand, has actually sworn vows of brotherhood with the merchant of Saint Denis. His wickedness is more infamous because he cuckolds, without a moment's hesitation, not only his best friend and cousin, but the man whose interests he has sworn to support and protect always.

Why do the two male lovers negotiate sex with another man's wife? Gulfardo does so because he is in love. Daun John does so because he wants sex. How do the two male lovers introduce the question of sex? Gulfardo does it by sending Ambruogia a message expressing his love. Daun John does it directly, in a quasi-public garden scene and in the presence of a "mayde child" (95). He jests that the wife of Saint Denis must be tired from her husband's having "laboured" (108) her all night long. He promises to keep secret anything she confesses to him. He raises the question of love by telling his friend's wife that he has loved her "specially / Aboven alle women" (153–54). And daun John, in an action that has no counterpart in Boccaccio, grabs the wife: "he caughte hire by the flankes, / And hire embraceth hard, and kiste hire ofte" (202–03). This aggressive sexuality is very much Chaucer's addition to the character of daun John. The point here is not only that daun John's initiating the question of sex is more direct than Gulfardo's, but that for a monk to have any part at all in such talk, let alone fondling his friend's wife, is unambiguously wrong. As a monk he should have a higher love in the forefront of his consciousness than sexual love-making with his best friend's wife.

Daun John's masculinity, then, is loveless, sex-based, disloyal, self-centered, fraudulent, opportunistic, and immoral in the extreme. His immorality is based not just on his shabby treatment of both his best friend and his lover, but on the fact that, as a monk, he ought to stand above the kinds of actions he participates in. He ought, rather than engage in sexual activity himself, to caution others against the dire consequences of such rampantly destructive masculinity.

The merchant of Saint Denis

It is easy enough to see the merchant of Saint Denis in a negative light. This husband of a beautiful and demanding wife seems so preoccupied with his counting house and business dealings that he ignores his wife and so invites his own cuckolding. He seems too foolish to see that his best friend is his worst deceiver. His own wife, who ought to know, suggests that he is lacking in most or all of the "thynges sixe" (174) that women want in husbands. In doing so she gives expression to her own list of ideal masculine qualities:

> "They wolde that hir housbondes sholde be
> Hardy, and wise, and riche, and therto free,
> And buxom unto his wyf, and fressh abedde."
> (175–77)

I am particularly interested in the wife's two central complaints about her husband—that he is neither "free" with his money nor "fressh abedde"—though I shall have a bit to say also about his wisdom and the extent to which he measures up to the wife's other requirements.

The portrayal of the merchant of Saint Denis seems flatly to contradict his wife's claim that he is not free with his money. When the monk asks for 100 francs, his response is unhesitating: "My gold is youres, whan that it yow leste, / And nat oonly my gold, but my chaffare" (284–85). Unlike Guasparruolo, he does not charge his friend interest. In some ways, ironically, the merchant is the least mercenary of the three characters. Certainly he is the most generous. He specifically invites his friend to come to Saint Denis for a visit; he spends time with him; he provides good meals for him; he lends him as much money as the monk asks for and offers more; he does not charge interest; he does not ask his friend to return it when he visits him in Paris—even though he has gone to Paris specifically to raise money to cover certain expenses he has incurred.

The husband's generosity to his wife is more problematical. Before he leaves for Bruges, he appears to make full provision for his wife's household needs: "Of silver in thy purs shaltow nat faille" (248)—a statement that seems to contradict his wife's assertion to the monk that her husband is niggardly. The matter is complicated, of course, by the wife's motive of gaining sympathy from daun John so that he will give her a lot of money. In view of that goal, she can scarcely be expected not to tell the monk that her husband is stingy. The matter is complicated also by the husband's pompous-sounding lecture to her about the important work that merchants do and his exhortation to her to "kepe oure good" (243). Besides, it may be that his perception of how much silver is enough for a thrifty household may be quite different from hers. Still, the merchant's apparent generosity to both his friend and his wife reinforces in at least general ways the narrator's statement in the opening description of him that the merchant of Saint Denis is known for his "largesse" (22). That that generosity extends to his wife is evident enough in the final scene, where he allows his wife to keep the 100 francs. More precisely, he agrees to let her pay him back with sexual services—a sexual debt that she owed him already by virtue of being his wife.

One of the most strikingly original features of Chaucer's *Shipman's Tale* is that the merchant is masculinized—that he is given a phallus and allowed to use it. This feature of the story is simply not present in the *Decameron* version. In that brief tale the merchant is married, yes, but Boccaccio's tale gives no evidence whatever about Guasparruolo's sex life. His wife cheats on him, to be sure, but there is no hint that she does so because of any real or imagined sexual inadequacy on his part. She never complains about his lack of manhood in the marital bed. Ambruogia's motivation for granting sex to another man is entirely greed: she sleeps with Gulfardo not because she wants more sex, but because she wants more money. There is no husband-wife sex scene in *Decameron* 8.1. Boccaccio has essentially neutered the husband. His sexuality, or lack of it, is simply not an issue.

The husband's sexuality is very much an issue in Chaucer's version of the story. The wife of the merchant of Saint Denis seizes the initiative in the garden with her response to daun John's blushing suggestion that her husband has "laboured" (108) her all night:

> "Nay, cosyn myn, it stant nat so with me;
> For, by that God that yaf me soule and lyf,
> In al the reawme of France is ther no wyf
> That lasse lust hath to that sory pley."
>
> (114–17)

After she has assurances of the monk's secrecy and his lustful feelings for her, she hints again at her husband's sexual inadequacy, but refuses to go into detail:

"Myn housbonde is to me the worste man
That evere was sith that the world bigan.
But sith I am a wyf, it sit nat me
To tellen no wight of our privetee,
Neither abedde ne in noon oother place;
God shilde I sholde it tellen, for his grace!"
(161–66)

Although she does not describe her husband's sexual inadequacies, she hints at them so broadly that daun John cannot—and does not—mistake her meaning. He apparently believes her.

We readers are permitted to believe her also—until the final scene. There the husband performs so tirelessly in bed that even his wife can find nothing to complain about except perhaps that he is entirely too "fressh abedde":

And al that nyght in myrthe they bisette
For he was riche and cleerly out of dette.
Whan it was day, this marchant gan embrace
His wyf al newe, and kiste hire on hir face,
And up he gooth and maketh it ful tough.
"Namoore," quod she, "by God, ye have ynough!"
And wantownly agayn with hym she pleyde.
(375–61)

It is perhaps easy to question the sexuality of a merchant whose interest in sex is said to be particularly keen after his successful business trip when he is "riche and cleerly out of dette." I caution, however, against reading those lines as evidence that when he is not rich, or that when his debts trouble him, the merchant is inadequate sexually. Rather than saying, "Hey, this fellow can succeed sexually only after he has succeeded financially," I prefer to say, "Like most of us, he feels particularly eager for sex after a day in which things have gone well. Surely he is not always so demanding of sexual services as he is after his financial success in Paris, but that does not mean that the rest of the time he has no energy for sexual activity."

It is noteworthy that Chaucer devotes far more space to the sex scene between the wife and her husband than between the wife and her lover. I have made a rough comparison of the number of lines Boccaccio and Chaucer devote to the sex between the wife and her lover. Boccaccio devotes some 25% of his tale to the soldier-wife sex in the *Decameron*. Chaucer reduces that to only 4%. Indeed, the 4% is an exaggeration. All Chaucer really tells us about their sexual encounter is a single and most general line: "In myrthe al nyght a bisy lyf they lede" (318). On the other hand, Chaucer devotes 14% of his version of the tale to the sex scene between the merchant and his wife. In that scene Chaucer not only gives us the generic "And al that nyght in myrthe they bisette" (375), but also devotes some fifteen lines (376–81, 413–17, 422–26) to their sexual relations. Chaucer was clearly far more interested in portraying the merchant's nocturnal activities with his wife than the monk's. Indeed, it is notable that in one of Chaucer's two most explicit descriptions of sexual intercourse—the other being the pear-tree encounter between Damian and May in the *Merchant's Tale*—he celebrates the joy of marital sex.

In any case, the merchant's sexuality is shown in the closing bedroom scene to be such that we are led to infer that his wife's earlier innuendos about his inadequacies were fiction. Unlike the merchant in the *Decameron* version, Chaucer's merchant gets to prove his sexual manhood in that final scene. I must emphasize again that the final bedroom scene in which the merchant proves his sexual masculinity is entirely Chaucer's addition to the tale. It has no counterpart in *Decameron* 8.1. Chaucer appears to have used this scene to clear the merchant of the two main charges his wife had earlier leveled against him: that he is ungenerous and that he is not "fressh abedde." By showing the merchant both sexually active in bed with his wife and generously willing to accept the terms of her offer to pay him back with her sexual favors, Chaucer seriously undermines her earlier accusation that her husband is stingy with money and inadequate in bed.

Before moving to my discussion of the wife I want to discuss the wisdom of the merchant. There is some reason to doubt that wisdom.

The merchant appears, after all, too foolish to see what is so obvious to the rest of us, that his best friend is a fraud capable of the ultimate in disloyalty. And he appears too foolish to see that his wife sleeps around behind his back. The opening lines of the *Shipman's Tale* may hint that the husband's reputation for wisdom is based more on his ability to accumulate wealth than to use common sense: "A marchant whilom dwelled at Seint-Denys, / That riche was, for which men helde hym wys" (1–2). On the other hand, the merchant may show his greatest wisdom in not inquiring too closely about the sexual dealings of his best friend and his own wife. Let me explain what I mean.

The *Shipman's Tale*, like *Decameron* 8.1, was almost certainly meant to be assigned to a female teller. The Wife of Bath is the only possible candidate on the road to Canterbury. Indeed, the tale fits her well enough. It is, after all, about marriage and infidelity, two interests of Alisoun of Bath. It is about a woman who uses her wits to seduce another man for her own financial gain, a woman who, quite unlike the unfortunate Ambruogia, is able by her cleverness both to convince her husband of her innocence and to keep the money. The telltale female pronouns near the start of the tale are entirely suitable to her:

> The sely housbonde, algate he moot paye,
> He moot us clothe, and he moot us arraye
>
> . . . . .
>
> And if that he noght may, par aventure,
> Or ellis list no swich dispense endure,
> But thynketh it is wasted and ylost,
> Thanne moot another payen for oure cost.
>
> (11–12, 15–18)

Despite those words, the tale is generally assigned to the Shipman, but that appears to have been a late and unintegrated assignment.[6] The

[6] There have been several attempts to explain how or why the Shipman seems to speak in female pronouns, and so to question the evidence that the Wife of Bath was the original teller of the *Shipman's Tale*. See, for example, Frederick Tupper, "The Bearings of the Shipman's Prologue," *Journal of English and Germanic Philology* 33 (1934): 352–72; Robert L. Chapman,

pronouns and the tale, on the other hand, are entirely appropriate to Alisoun of Bath. Indeed, the merchant of Saint Denis comes across as a showcase husband, to judge by the Wife of Bath's own criteria. Not the least of his virtues is that he is trusting, wise enough not to inquire overmuch about his wife's activities. From a lusty woman's point of view, he has the wisdom appropriate to husbands, a wisdom that does not bother about where one's wife bestows her sexual favors so long as she keeps her husband happy in bed. Alisoun puts it this way in her long diatribe to her old husbands:

> Of alle men yblessed moot he be,
> The wise astrologien, Daun Ptholome,
> That seith this proverbe in his Almageste:
> "Of alle men his wysdom is the hyeste
> That reckketh nevere who had the world in honde."
> By this proverbe thou shalt understonde,
> Have thou ynogh, what thar thee recche or care
> How myrily that othere folkes fare?
> For, certeyn, olde dotard, by your leve,
> Ye shul have queynte right ynogh at eve.
> He is to greet a nygard that wolde werne
> A man to lighte a candle at his lanterne;
> He shal have never the lasse light, pardee.
> Have thou ynogh, thee thar nat pleyne thee.
> (III 323–36)

To be sure, such "wysdom" (III 326) can make a husband a cuckold, but the Wife of Bath seems to want to suggest that cuckoldry hurts no one unless the husband finds out about it. Some husbands deserve

"The Shipman's Tale Was Meant for the Shipman," *Modern Language Notes* 71 (1956): 4–5; and Hazel Sullivan, "A Chaucerian Puzzle," in *A Chaucerian Puzzle and Other Medieval Essays*, ed. Natalie Grimes Lawrence and Jack A. Reynolds (Coral Gables: University of Miami Press, 1961), 1–46. The widest opinion, however, and my own, is that the pronouns do indicate a female teller, and that this person can only have been the Wife of Bath. See William W. Lawrence, "The Wife of Bath and the Shipman," *Modern Language Notes* 71 (1957): 87–88.

to be cuckolded because of their sexual inadequacies—John in the *Miller's Tale*, perhaps, and January in the *Merchant's Tale*. The merchant of Saint Denis, however, is apparently not one of them. Indeed, Chaucer's having given us the "mayde child" (VIII 95)—presumably his daughter—may be read as evidence of the merchant's sexual potency, just as Chaucer's having given us the bedroom scene may be read as evidence of his satisfactory sexual performance. Neither the child nor the sex scene appears in the *Decameron* version.

In dealing with the two men in the *Shipman's Tale*, in any case, Chaucer has given us, if not his own, then the Wife of Bath's contrasting opinions about masculinity. He has greatly debased the lover by having the young monk demonstrate the most negative masculine qualities: disloyalty, dishonesty, sexual immorality, selfishness. Incapable of a love that transcends sexual desire, he uses the wife of Saint Denis, then abandons her. Chaucer takes the most attractive character in Boccaccio's *Decameron* 8.1, and transforms him into the least attractive character in the *Shipman's Tale*. If what daun John shows us is masculine behavior, Chaucer seems to be saying, then we want no part of it.

Chaucer has, on the other hand, enhanced the character of the merchant-husband, a relatively insignificant personage in *Decameron* 8.1. Chaucer has endowed the merchant with a set of positive masculine qualities: he has good business sense combined with a generosity of spirit. He comes across as a near-ideal husband—at least from the Wife of Bath's point of view. What more could such wives want in a husband than a man sufficiently careful in business to provide a comfortable and safe home for his family, secure enough in his manhood not to be suspicious of her, sexually active enough to satisfy her in bed, generous enough to let her keep the money a debtor had repaid to him?

Chaucer, then, has retold an old story but given it a new twist. Despite his wife's petulant allegations to the contrary, the merchant seems to provide his wife with the "thynges sixe" (174) she says wives want: he is (1) "hardy" and (2) "wise" enough, at least to judge from his bold and successful business dealings; he is (3) "rich" and, so far as we can tell, (4) "therto free"; although he sometimes preaches his wife a small sermon—apparently well-deserved—on thriftiness and solvency, he seems (5) "buxom" enough to her, letting her have great freedom in her dealings with others and indulging her penchant for spending money on fancy clothes; and, as we have seen, he is remarkably (6) "fressh abedde." Some wives might desire in a husband a man who might also be her friend and intellectual companion, but those are not qualities that either the Wife of Bath or the wife of Saint Denis list as desirable qualities in a husband. Hardy, wise, rich, generous, obedient, fresh in bed — surely if any man is a good enough husband to deserve the sexual rewards bestowed on him in that final scene in the *Shipman's Tale*, the merchant of Saint Denis is. If any husband is masculine enough to take advantage of the sexual activity she offers, he is.

The wife of Saint Denis

Even in a paper about masculine qualities shown in the *Shipman's Tale*, we must speak more of the wife of the merchant of Saint Denis. In the monk and the merchant, Chaucer offers contrasting simplifications of masculinity. The monk's corrupt masculinity is redeemed by no virtues. The merchant's brighter masculinity is balanced somewhat by his sometimes pompous and patronizing preoccupation with his financial dealings, but he has no apparent outright vices. Curiously, the character who shows the most interesting and balanced mixture of positive and negative qualities associated with these men is not a man at all.

Like the monk, the wife of the merchant of Saint Denis is unfaithful, aggressively self-centered, and mercenary, but she is, like her husband, likeable, clever, aggressive, resourceful, and apparently able to keep a spouse happy in bed. If Chaucer makes the monk more evil in adapting *Decameron* 8.1, to his own narrative design, and if he makes the husband more sympathetic, surely he makes the wife more complex. There is no question that she is far more attractive than Ambruogia, her shallow, greedy, and not-very-bright counterpart in the

Decameron. Neifile holds Ambruogia up as an example of a woman who deserves to be punished for cheapening love by putting a price tag on it. The wife of Saint Denis also puts a price tag on her love, but she is never punished for the deed. Indeed, we are more likely to admire her for her cleverness than to castigate her for her immorality.

The wife is, after all, in charge all the way through the *Shipman's Tale*. Unlike the passive Ambruogia, who is propositioned by Gulfardo, the wife of Saint Denis actively takes her case to daun John by coming to him in the garden, complaining about her husband, asking for a loan of 100 francs, and suggesting Sunday for the day of delivery. Whereas in the *Decameron* tale the wife had been in the position of responding to the aggressive advances of Gulfardo, in the *Shipman's Tale* the wife's aggressive advances to daun John put him in the secondary role of responding to her advances. In exchange for the money she gives the monk only one night in bed, not several, as does Ambruogia. Her crowning achievement, of course, comes in the final bedroom scene. In that scene the wife is confronted in bed by her husband with the embarrassing accusation that she had not told him about daun John's returning to her the 100-franc loan. At the parallel moment in *Decameron* 8.1, Ambruogia lamely reports that she had forgotten to tell her husband about the transaction, then returns the money to him. The wife of Saint Denis, on the other hand—"nat afered nor affrayed, / But boldely" (400–01)—admits that, yes, she had received certain money from the monk, but she had assumed it was a gift in repayment for all the hospitality he had received so often at the merchant's house, and she reports that she had spent the money on clothes for her husband's honor. Furthermore, she offers to repay the money in services: "Ye shal my joly body have to wedde; / By God, I wol nat paye yow but abedde!" (423–24). While we may be troubled by the commercialization of sex—and the jokes about scoring the financial debt upon the wife's "taille" (416)—we can but admire the moxie of the wife of the merchant of Saint Denis.

The Italian tale is told precisely to castigate greedy and unfaithful wives. Neifile sets up her tale by saying that any woman who sells her virtue for monetary gain ought to be burnt alive. A woman who yields her virtue for love, Neifile explains, is easily forgiven, but not one who yields it for money. After Neifile's story in the *Decameron*, the others in the company applaud Gulfardo's tricking of the greedy Ambruogia. At the end of the *Shipman's Tale*, however, there is no castigation of the wife of Saint Denis. Rather, the Host warns his fellow travelers to "draweth no monkes moore unto your in" (442). Boccaccio wants his readers to dislike Ambruogia and admire her soldier-lover. Chaucer and the Wife of Bath, by contrast, seem to want readers to admire the wife of Saint Denis and dislike her monk-lover. In the process of bringing about that fundamental change in the story, Chaucer has given the wife of Saint Denis an engaging mix of qualities often associated with men.

The wife of Saint Denis is without doubt a woman. She is aware of her sexuality as a woman. She knows that as a woman she has very little she can trade on except her sexuality. And she uses that female sexuality to bring about most of the key actions in the tale. So strong and important are her feminine qualities that we cannot use the term "masculine" to describe either her character or her actions. It is interesting to note, however, that the Wife of Bath gives the wife of Saint Denis a full measure of the qualities sometimes associated with successful men in the Middle Ages—leadership, independence, sexual aggressiveness, cleverness, self-assurance, articulateness, and an ability to do successful business. Through the force of their own personalities, both the Wife of Bath and the wife of Saint Denis transform traits often seen in medieval times as masculine into traits that seem both appropriate to and admirable in a woman. For traditionally masculine traits to be associated in a positive way with women is common in the twentieth century. In the fourteenth century it was no less than revolutionary.

Just Say Yes, Chaucer Knew the *Decameron*: Or, Bringing the *Shipman's Tale* Out of Limbo

[One of the most important questions still to be answered definitively is whether or not Chaucer knew Boccaccio's *Decameron*, the wonderful collection of a hundred tales, some of them remarkably similar to ones that Chaucer later put into the *Canterbury Tales*. Almost a half-century ago I wrote my master's thesis (never published) arguing that Chaucer must have known the *Decameron*. At that time I was virtually alone in my conviction, but I later published several articles—some of them included in this volume—arguing that one or another of Chaucer's tales was almost certainly influenced by its counterpart in the *Decameron*. In this essay I try to identify the reasons why so many scholars have been so reluctant to accept the likelihood of Chaucer's knowledge of Boccaccio's collection. I argue that their reasons are specious. I celebrate here the growing tide of modern scholars who are willing to accept what ought to have been obvious all along. I argue specifically that accepting Chaucer's almost certain acquaintanceship with the *Decameron* has the desirable side effect of anchoring the *Shipman's Tale* to the "hard analogue" that is its most likely source—the first tale of the eighth day. "Just Say Yes" first appeared in *The Decameron and the Canterbury Tales: New Essays on an Old Question*, ed. Leonard Michael Koff and Brenda Deen Schildgen (Teaneck, NJ: Fairleigh Dickinson University Press, 2000), 25–46.]

Chaucer's knowledge of Boccaccio's *Decameron* is one of the most vexing issues for scholars who seek to understand Chaucer's originality in the *Canterbury Tales.* This essay is an effort to show why I believe scholars should act on the assumption that Chaucer knew the *Decameron.* My argument will sound rather old-fashioned to scholars of the new historicist, deconstructive, and psychoanalytic persuasions, but my goal here is to review the opinions of other scholars and to sort out the strong from the weak arguments. In the course of this paper, I shall give a brief review of the opinions of others who have considered Chaucer's knowledge of the *Decameron*, discuss the double standard that scholars have applied when attempting to grant source status to Boccaccio's *Decameron*, analyze the reasons why scholars have been unusually reluctant to accept the evidence that Chaucer read the *Decameron*, and try to make a useful distinction between the terms *source*, *hard analogue*, and *soft analogue.* To ground my arguments, I will reconsider the likelihood that the first tale of the eighth day of the *Decameron* was Chaucer's primary source for the *Shipman's Tale.*

The pendulum swings

The scholarly pendulum with respect to Chaucer and the *Decameron* has swung back and forth over the decades. At first, the weight of scholarly opinion was that, yes, of course, Chaucer *must* have known the *Decameron*. After all, we knew that Chaucer had traveled to Italy on at least two, and quite possibly three, separate occasions. We knew that he could have met Boccaccio in Italy and could read Italian with ease. We knew that he had read and used as source material other important works of Boccaccio—the *Filostrato* and the *Teseida,* for example. We knew that the *Decameron* was the most lively collection of framed tales before Chaucer's *Canterbury Tales.* We knew that the

Decameron provided parallels with the character of the Pardoner,[1] with the plague background to the *Pardoner's Tale*,[2] and with the intrusions, apologies, links, and language of the *Canterbury Tales*. More importantly, we knew that the *Decameron* contained parallels with some half-dozen of the tales in Chaucer's masterpiece: those of the Miller, the Reeve, the Merchant, the Franklin, the Clerk, and the Shipman. The evidence was clear, the conclusion obvious: Chaucer knew and was influenced by the *Decameron*.

That opinion held sway until 1916, when Hubertis M. Cummings published his dissertation on Chaucer's indebtedness to Boccaccio.[3] Rejecting the arguments and the evidence of earlier scholars, such as Pio Rajna (1903)[4] and Lorenz Morsbach (1910),[5] Cummings said that Chaucer almost certainly did *not* know the *Decameron*. Cummings's arguments seemed to be buttressed by Willard Farnham (1924),[6] who argued that because there is no evidence that the *Decameron* had existed in England before the fifteenth century, Chaucer could scarcely have had a copy there and so could scarcely have been directly influenced by it. The arguments of Cummings and Farnham have been reiterated by many scholars—for example, in a book by Herbert

[1] For a recent discussion of parallels with the Pardoner, see John M. Ganim, "Chaucer, Boccaccio, and the Anxiety of Popularity," *Assays: Critical Approaches to Medieval and Renaissance Texts* 4 (1987): 54–57.

[2] For a discussion of the plague background, see my "The Plague and Chaucer's Pardoner," in this volume, pp. 286–301.

[3] Hubertis M. Cummings, *The Indebtedness of Chaucer's Works to the Italian Works of Boccaccio* (Cincinnati, OH: *University of Cincinnati Studies* 10, 1916).

[4] Pio Rajna, "Le origini della novella narrata del 'Frankeleyn' nei *Canterbury Tales* del Chaucer," *Romania* 32 (1903): 204–67.

[5] Lorenz Morsbach, "Chaucers Plan der *Canterbury Tales* und Boccaccios *Decamerone*," *Englische Studien* 42 (1910): 43–52.

[6] Willard Farnham, "England's Discovery of the *Decameron*," *PMLA* 39 (1924): 123–39.

G. Wright[7] and in articles by Svetko Tedeschi[8] and Edmund Reiss.[9] The Cummings-Farnham-Wright-Tedeschi-Reiss argument generally carried the day until the late 1970s when the pendulum began to swing back. That swing culminates both in this volume and in the new *Sources and Analogues.*[10]

[7] Herbert G. Wright, *Boccaccio in England from Chaucer to Tennyson* (London: Athlone Press, 1957). Wright says little about Chaucer and the *Decameron* but merely concludes that "there is no convincing internal evidence that Chaucer had read any of the tales or that the framework for his *Canterbury Tales* was suggested by that of the *Decameron.* If there are such strong reasons against Chaucer's acquaintance with the *Decameron* . . ." (114). This last statement is a puzzling premise because Wright gives no "strong reasons."

[8] Svetko Tedeschi, "Some Recent Opinions about the Possible Influence of Boccaccio's *Decameron* on Chaucer's *Canterbury Tales,*" *Studia Romanica* 33–36 (1973–74): 849–72. Tedeschi's article is primarily a refutation of Richard Guerin's unpublished 1966 dissertation ("*The Canterbury Tales*" *and* "*Il Decamerone*" [Ph.D. diss., University of Colorado, 1966]). Guerin had argued in favor of Chaucer's knowledge of the *Decameron.* Tedeschi's refutations are unconvincing. Typical is his conclusion: "Boccaccio's *Decameron* comprises 100 stories and Chaucer allegedly knew or imitated only 6 or 7 of them. What about the other 93? We have no traces of them in the *Canterbury Tales.* So it seems very probable that he knew none of the *Decameron's* stories at all" (872).

[9] Edmund Reiss, "Boccaccio in English Culture of the Fourteenth and Fifteenth Centuries," in *Il Boccaccio nella cultura inglese e anglo-americana*, edited by Giuseppe Galigani (Florence: Olschki, 1974), 15–26.

[10] *Sources and Analogues of the Canterbury Tales,* ed. Robert Correale and Mary Hamel (Woodbridge, Suffolk: D. S. Brewer, vol. 1, 2002, vol. 2, 2005). Several prominent scholars now speak as if the *Decameron* was, of course, known to Chaucer. See, for example, David Wallace, *Giovanni Boccaccio: Decameron.* Landmarks of World Literature (Cambridge: Cambridge University Press, 1991): "The most significant witness to the *Decameron's* influence in England is Chaucer's *Canterbury Tales*" (111), and Derek Pearsall, *The Life of Geoffrey Chaucer: A Critical Biography* (Oxford: Blackwell, 1992): "There had been many story collections before, and some with a narrative frame, but the only one that decisively influenced Chaucer was Boccaccio's *Decameron*" (240). Helen Cooper, in "*Sources and Analogues of Chaucer's Canterbury Tales*: Reviewing the Work" (*SAC* 19 [1997]), presents a strong case on pp. 192–99 for Chaucer's knowledge of the *Decameron.* Speaking of the framework for Chaucer's collection of tales, she points out that "very few works offer any detailed resemblance, and of those that do, the *Decameron* is by far the closest, to the point where deliberate imitation becomes more likely than mere coincidence" (192).

The double standard

Why have so many scholars been so reluctant to grant the strong possibility that Chaucer knew and was influenced by the wonderful collection of Italian tales called the *Decameron*? Surely it is not merely that Chaucer may never have met Boccaccio; Chaucer probably met few if any of the writers from whom he borrowed, Petrarch and Gower being the two most likely exceptions. Surely it is not merely that no copy of the *Decameron* has been found in England dating from the fourteenth century; contemporary copies of few of Chaucer's acknowledged sources have been found in England either. Surely it is not merely that had he known the *Decameron* he would certainly have borrowed more from it; we make no such arguments about other works Chaucer is assumed to have consulted. Surely it is not merely that he does not acknowledge in the *Canterbury Tales* that he borrowed from the *Decameron*; he acknowledges his real sources almost nowhere. Rather, scholars seem to want to insist on a higher standard of proof for Chaucer's knowledge of the *Decameron* than they do for other Chaucerian sources. There is no "proof" that Chaucer knew the Italian *Novellino* version of the pear-tree story or the French *Le meunier et les .II. clers* or the Middle Dutch *Heile van Beersele* or Trevet's *Life of Constance* or Gower's *Tale of Florent.* Still, no serious scholars who want to know what is most uniquely Chaucerian about the *Merchant's Tale*, the *Miller's Tale*, the *Reeve's Tale*, the *Man of Law's Tale*, or the *Wife of Bath's Tale* will refuse to look at those analogues or refuse to treat them as if they were likely Chaucerian sources. Why, then, should scholars refuse to look at the *Decameron* just because there is no incontrovertible proof that Chaucer knew it? Why, for this one possible source, will skeptics be convinced by nothing less than a signed copy of the book, or a will leaving Chaucer's copy of it to Lewis, or a letter from Chaucer to Cecilia saying how much he enjoyed borrowing her copy of the *Decameron*?

Let me suggest three reasons why scholars have been reluctant to face up to the evidence for Chaucer's knowledge of the *Decameron.* The first is what might be called patriotism or nationalism. Just as some English scholars have been reluctant to admit that there was an Old Dutch source for *Everyman,* and just as some American scholars like to deny or ignore the influences of British literature on an emerging national American literature, so some scholars have been reluctant to acknowledge that Boccaccio's masterpiece may have had a considerable influence on Chaucer's masterpiece. Tatlock (1913) put it this way almost ninety years ago:

> As to the *Decameron,* no evidence has ever yet been found either to prove or to disprove clearly that Chaucer knew it, for the obvious arguments *pro* are well offset by other arguments *con.* There has been a marked disposition on the part of English and American writers to believe that he did not, and on the part of Continental writers (not only Italian but German and French also) to believe that he did. This influence of patriotism is suggestive of the lack of evidence.[11]

Some Chaucerians have seemed unusually reluctant to accept the notion that Chaucer was merely "the English Boccaccio." In his 1974 article, Reiss tells us that, "although it used to be popular to consider Chaucer the English Boccaccio, such a view, as we may now see, is both misleading and wrong."[12] Reiss's term, "the English Boccaccio," suggests that for him to admit that Chaucer probably knew the *Decameron* would be to admit that Chaucer was merely an imitator

[11] John S. P. Tatlock, "Boccaccio and the Plan of Chaucer's *Canterbury Tales,*" *Anglia* 37 (1913): 69.

[12] Reiss, "Boccaccio in English Culture," 21. See also Tedeschi, "Some Recent Opinions": "Chaucer's genius . . . was not shaped by that of Boccaccio—at least as regards his *Canterbury Tales.* And as his way was not that of Boccaccio—he would have followed it even without him" (872). Donald R. Howard, in *Chaucer and the Medieval World* (London: Weidenfeld and Nicholson, 1987), noticed this kind of misguided effort to defend Chaucer's "genius": "'We must,' one author concluded, 'continue to doubt the English poet's knowledge even of the existing person of the Italian writer'—and then tipped his hand: 'The English poet served no apprenticeship to the Italian. He never became a literary disciple to him. He did not weakly imitate him as a master.' For years this was the accepted opinion. Chaucer's greatness would be diminished if Boccaccio were more than one of many negligible influences" (281).

of or footnote to Boccaccio, rather than a native-born English genius. Janet Levarie Smarr, on the other hand, means no disrespect when she writes that "in some sense Chaucer is the English Boccaccio after all."[13] Surely contemporary scholars can rise above issues of national genius. To help us do so, I suggest that we not use the term "the English Boccaccio" at all, since it seems to draw *unnecessary* attention to the issue of nationalism. We do not, after all, refer to Shakespeare either as the "English Plutarch" because he was influenced by a Greek historian or as the "Renaissance Chaucer" because he learned from Chaucer and retold several of his stories.

A second reason for scholarly reluctance to consider the evidence for Chaucer's knowledge of the *Decameron* is the notion that for Chaucer to have learned even part of his amazing artistry from another artist—of whatever nationality—somehow diminishes Chaucer's greatness by making him a mere imitator or pupil. After discussing the reluctance of scholars to accept Chaucer's obvious use of Boccaccio's *Filostrato* as a source for *Troilus and Criseyde*, Donald Howard puts the problem with the *Decameron* with remarkable succinctness: "Anything that seemed to cast aspersions on Chaucer's originality met, and to a large extent still does, with massive resistance: if we *must* admit that he used the *Filostrato*, we will in retaliation deny that he even knew the *Decameron.*"[14] Even if in some respects the great Boccaccio did show Chaucer a new range of possibilities for writing in a vernacular language and did give him certain ideas for story lines, surely that fact increases rather than diminishes Chaucer's own greatness. Chaucer was clever enough to know good vernacular writing when he saw it, English enough to want to share some of that writing with his countrymen in their own language, and inventive enough to transform that writing into distinctively Chaucerian tales.

[13] Janet Levarie Smarr, "Mercury in the Garden: Mythographical Methods in the *Merchant's Tale* and *Decameron* VII, 9," in *The Mythographic Art*, edited by Jane Chance (Gainesville: University of Florida Press, 1990), 199.

[14] Howard, *Chaucer and the Medieval World*, 261.

Chaucer learned from Boccaccio, but quickly established his own territory on the literary landscape—his own standards and goals.

A third reason for the reluctance of some scholars to admit that Chaucer read and was influenced by the *Decameron*, is that Boccaccio was known, because of the *Decameron*, as an immoral writer. His work was undeniably popular in Italy, and it was soon translated into French, Latin, Spanish, German, Dutch, and finally English. Boccaccio himself was aware that his book was seen to be inappropriate to certain readers. As David Wallace puts it: "In 1373, just two years before his death, Boccaccio wrote in humorous vein to his friend Mainardo Cavalcanti, advising him to keep the *Decameron* away from the female members of his household. It is clear that by this time the *Decameron* already enjoyed immense popularity and was moving around the European trade routes with the merchant classes who figure so prominently in its pages."[15] Even in Italy, however, it earned a reputation for immorality such that several early editions were seriously expurgated, as were virtually all of the translations. The *Decameron* was placed on the Roman Catholic Index in 1563, but that banning probably increased the demand for the book. Certainly, it inspired a number of expurgated editions in Italy, the most widely read being Salviati's edition of 1582. Salviati's version made sweeping changes, not merely in the explicit sexuality of the original, but also in removing virtually every Roman Catholic monk, friar, and nun whom Boccaccio had shown in a morally compromising light. The Salviati edition is of some importance to the reception of the *Decameron* in England, since the first English translator, possibly John Florio, relied heavily on this edition.[16]

So widespread was the conviction that Boccaccio's *Decameron* was a dangerously subversive document that it may be that Chaucer

[15] Wallace, *Giovanni Boccaccio: Decameron*, 108–9.

[16] For more information about the early reception of the *Decameron*, see Herbert Wright's monograph, *The First English Translation of the Decameron*, Essays and Studies on English Language and Literature 13 (1953). For a more general and lighthearted study, see the introduction to *The Decameron*, trans. G. H. McWilliam, 2nd edition (London: Penguin, 1995).

himself was reluctant to have his name associated with the "immoral" Boccaccio's. More to the point for my present argument is that modern scholars may also be reluctant to admit that Chaucer might have been influenced by a writer of such reputation. Again, such reasoning seems misguided. Even if we are reluctant to have Chaucer painted with the same brush that blackened Boccaccio's reputation, surely such reluctance must not be permitted to obscure the evidence of influence. Chaucer certainly would have found much to imitate in Boccaccio's criticism of corrupt clergymen, and as for Boccaccio's sexual and scatological explicitness, surely Chaucer would have enjoyed most of it at the same time that he gave his own distinctive twist to sexuality and scatology in the *Canterbury Tales*.

Whatever the several reasons for scholarly reluctance to take seriously the evidence suggesting Chaucer's knowledge of and use of the *Decameron*, the result has been a double standard for many of those who wish to consider the *Canterbury Tales* in relationship to its most revealing analogues. While we have considered as near sources many other analogues that have turned up, for authentic analogues in the *Decameron*, we demand virtually incontrovertible proof in advance that Chaucer knew this work. Fortunately, however, the pendulum is shifting back to a more reasonable and balanced view.

McGrady's argument

An important push on the pendulum was given by Donald McGrady in an excellent 1977 article.[17] McGrady's analysis and his sixty-eight footnotes provide an accurate and generally reliable account of the state of scholarship up to around 1975. Although I cannot completely review that scholarship here, I do want to review McGrady's arguments rebutting Cummings and Farnham, two of the early doubters of Chaucer's knowledge of the *Decameron*. I take up McGrady's refutation of Cummings first:

[17] Donald McGrady, "Chaucer and the *Decameron* Reconsidered," *Chaucer Review* 12 (1977): 1–26.

1. Cummings's five-page discussion of the question of whether the *Decameron* influenced the *Canterbury Tales* is slender and cursory, in no sense a probing or convincing piece of work.
2. Cummings treats as mere coincidences the similarities of Chaucer's and Boccaccio's "apologies" to readers for telling ribald tales and the appearance in both of the metaphoric comparison of an old man with a leek—both have a white head and a green tail.
3. Cummings treats the possible *Decameron* influence on only two of Chaucer's tales, those of the Clerk and the Franklin, and that possible influence he discusses in no depth. He ignores similarities that have been obvious—and telling—to other scholars, not only in the tales of these two pilgrims, but in those of four more as well.
4. Cummings treats as evidence for his view the notion that Chaucer would surely, had he known the *Decameron*, have made wider use of it. Because he did not, he must, therefore, not have known it at all.

McGrady reaches this conclusion: "Cummings did not analyze carefully the *Decameron* in order to carry out his five-page study, but rather seems to have applied *a priori* ideas to the problem. In view of these deficiencies in Cummings's method, it is somewhat surprising that his work continues to be cited as a standard authority."[18]

McGrady is even more harsh with Farnham's arguments that Chaucer could scarcely have known the *Decameron* because copies of it were not generally available in the fourteenth century. Here are his major points:

1. Farnham's notion that Boccaccio was deeply ashamed of the "wicked" *Decameron* and tried to suppress it has been shown by recent biographers to be a fiction; indeed, we have a holograph manuscript of the hundred tales that shows that Boccaccio was

[18] Ibid., 4.

working on the *Decameron* as late as 1370–72, twenty years after he finished the first copy and not long before his death in 1375.

2. Farnham's notion that the *Decameron* had little popularity or influence in Italy or other European nations has been shown by later scholarship to be false. It influenced several storytellers in Italy in the fourteenth century, and copies or records of copies show that the *Decameron* was also available in France, Spain, Germany, and the Low Countries during Chaucer's lifetime.
3. Although Farnham is right that no copies or records of copies of the *Decameron* have been found in England in Chaucer's time, that fact carries no more weight as evidence that it did not exist there than does the absence of surviving fourteenth-century copies of the *Canterbury Tales* prove that there were none. Indeed, the very absence of fourteenth-century copies of both works may attest to their popularity rather than to their lack of popularity, since they were perhaps "read hard" and "used up" by consumers rather than placed safely away on bookshelves.
4. Farnham's assertion that Chaucer "might well have missed" seeing a copy of the *Decameron* during his trips to Italy is easily refuted. Moreover, Florentine merchants of the sort that Chaucer would have dealt with regularly in London might well have known Boccaccio's work and sold or traded Chaucer a copy of their townsman's book.[19]

McGrady reaches this conclusion about Farnham's work: "Thus, although Farnham's approach contrasts with Cummings's (and at the same time complements it), since it deals exclusively with factors

[19] McGrady's argument has been buttressed by a more recent study of Wendy Childs, "Anglo-Italian Contacts in the Fourteenth Century," in *Chaucer and the Italian Trecento*, edited by Piero Boitani (Cambridge: Cambridge University Press, 1983), 65–87. Childs discusses in detail the many and varied contacts Chaucer might well have had, even in London, with Italian merchants, bankers, military people, doctors, religious people, and pilgrims. She concludes that as a London man of affairs in the second half of the fourteenth century, Chaucer "would have been surrounded by Italians" (67) and that "once his curiosity in things Italian had been aroused it would have been very easy for him to sustain his interest in London" (75).

outside the texts of the *Decameron* and the *Canterbury Tales*, it shares the same weaknesses, and is therefore just as easily demolished."[20]

McGrady's weaknesses: memorial borrowing

Excellent as his article is, however, McGrady is more effective in demolishing the arguments of those who oppose the notion that Chaucer knew and was influenced by the *Decameron* than he is in establishing his own view about the relationship between Chaucer and the *Decameron.* That view is quite definite: that Chaucer had a copy of the *Decameron* with him in London while he worked on the *Canterbury Tales*, that he consulted it at will, and that he wove materials from it into various Canterbury stories. While it is quite possible, perhaps even likely, that Chaucer had a copy in England and consulted it, McGrady has not proved that he did, any more than Cummings and Farnham proved that he did not. McGrady's conviction that he has "furnished persuasive evidence of the direct indebtedness of the English storyteller to the Italian"[21] casts unnecessary doubt on the possibility that Chaucer had read the *Decameron* earlier, perhaps on one of his trips to Italy. Had he done so, Chaucer might well have remembered and incorporated certain features into his own collection of tales.

McGrady specifically discredits this notion of "memorial borrowing"—the notion that Chaucer might have read the *Decameron* at some earlier time and then, when he came to write tales of his own, remembered certain details or motifs and incorporated them into his own work. The problem with this memorial borrowing, McGrady tells us, is that we find parallels between the *Decameron* and the *Canterbury Tales* so specific that such long-distance memories can scarcely account for them: "The types of details echoed by Chaucer from the *Decameron* are not at all likely to have

[20] McGrady, "Chaucer and the *Decameron* Reconsidered," 5.

[21] Ibid., 14.

remained in his recollection over a period of one or two decades."[22] It is difficult, of course, for us to say just what kinds of details Chaucer might remember, but it is perhaps not wise to sell short the memorial capacity of a man whose knowledge was so eclectic, whose intelligence was so great, and whose reading was so wide. Furthermore, many of the kinds of "borrowings" that have been adduced are precisely those that Chaucer might well have remembered much later.

McGrady, of course, can be forgiven for having made his statements about Chaucer's memory before Mary Carruthers's important 1990 study of the role of memory in the Middle Ages.[23] While we now no longer are much impressed with men and women who have good memories—"all they can do is memorize things"—and while techniques for remembering or memorizing texts are no longer cultivated in our schools, the situation was much different in prebook medieval Europe, where a strong memory was both cultivated and admired, especially in literary performers. Carruthers's argument is long, technical, and persuasive. It bears careful reading in connection with the question of Chaucer's possible recollection of books he may have read much earlier. I shall quote here only Carruthers's translation of Petrarch's anecdote in his *Rerum memorandarum libri* about his friend's amazing ability to remember quite specific details of events long since past:

> It was enough for him to have seen or heard something once, he never forgot; nor did he recollect only according to *res,* but by means of the words and time and place where he had first learned it. Often we spent entire days or long nights in talking: there was no one I would rather listen to; for even after the passage of many years, if the same things were spoken of, and

[22] Ibid., 13.

[23] Mary J. Carruthers, *The Book of Memory: A Study of Memory in Medieval Culture* (Cambridge: Cambridge University Press, 1990).

> if I were to say much more or less or say something different, at once he would gently remind me of this and moreover correct the word in question; and when I wondered and asked just how he could have remembered it, he recalled not only the time during which he would have heard it from me, but under what shady tree, by what river-bank, along what sea shore, on the top of what hill (for I had walked long distances with him along the coasts), I recognized each particular.[24]

We cannot assume, of course, that Chaucer's memory was as keen as Petrarch's friend's, but neither should we assume that Chaucer would have been incapable of remembering either the broad outlines of the *Decameron* read some years earlier or some of the more minute details. In any case, surely Carruthers's book lends support to Donald Howard's speculation: "The *Decameron* versions cannot be shown through verbal parallels to be Chaucer's sources; still, Chaucer could have heard or read them in Italy and remembered the stories without having a text before him as he wrote."[25]

Remembering the *Decameron*

What are some of the features that Chaucer might have remembered from the *Decameron*? It has long been noted that there are certain broad similarities between the "plan" or "frame" of the *Decameron* and that of the *Canterbury Tales.* Morsbach (1910) pointed out, for example, that in each, the stories are told by members of an established company of travelers, that the company met by chance, that the stories are connected by links in which the actions of the company are described, and that one of the storytellers acts as director. Later, Tatlock (1913) showed that there were additional similarities—that the telling of tales lasted more than one day and that each speaker was to narrate more than one story. These general similarities might well have stayed in Chaucer's memory long after he had read the

[24] Ibid., 61.

[25] Howard, *Chaucer and the Medieval World*, 274.

Decameron. I hasten to add, of course, that most of these features were also available in other collections of tales that Chaucer could have known: Boccaccio's *Filocolo* and *Ameto,* for example. A feature that Chaucer could have found in none of these other sources—that each teller was to tell more than one tale—is of sufficient importance that it seems entirely possible that Chaucer remembered it when he came to design his own framed collection. Certainly, he need not have had a copy of the *Decameron* in his hands to have been influenced by such a broad feature.

Other features, too, can be found in the plans of both works. It is interesting to note, for example, that we find in both collections certain thematic groupings of tales, that the tellers in both works are seeking to escape sickness—physical sickness in the *Decameron*, spiritual sickness in the *Canterbury Tales*—and that members of the traveling group respond to each other's tales. It may also be significant that both sets of tales are said to offer both entertainment and morality. See, for example, Boccaccio's statement in his prologue that readers "will be able to derive, not only pleasure from the entertaining matters set forth . . . but also some useful advice."[26] That passage bears useful comparison with the Host's stipulation in the General Prologue that the best tales are those that demonstrate "best sentence and moost solaas" (*Riverside*, I 798).

Then, too, there is the matter of the authorial "apologies" for the ribald tales. In the author's conclusion at the end of the *Decameron*, as part of a long defense of tales that some will find improper, Boccaccio tells us that certain readers may perhaps wish that he had left some out: "Saranno similmente di quelle che diranno qui esserne alcune che, non essendoci, sarebbe stato assai meglio. Concedasi: ma io non poteva né doveva scrivere se non le raccontate, e per ciò esse che le dissero le dovevan dir belle, e io l'avrei scritte belle" (*Conclusione dell' autore*) [I could only transcribe the stories as they were actually told, which means that if the ladies who told them had told them

[26] McWilliam, *Decameron*, 47.

better, I should have written them better (McWilliam 800)]. Boccaccio goes on to say that he has provided little summaries at the start of each tale so that "Tuttavia chi va tra queste leggendo, lasci star quelle che pungono, e quelle che dilettano legga" (*Conclusione dell' autore*) [Anyone perusing these tales is free to ignore the ones that give offense, and read only those that are pleasing (801)]. These lines, of course, bear a striking resemblance to Chaucer's words in the prologue to the *Miller's Tale*, where he tells us that he must recount

> Hir tales alle, be they bettre or werse,
> Or elles falsen som of my mateere.
> And therfore, whoso list it nat yheere,
> Turne over the leef and chese another tale;
> For he shal fynde ynowe, grete and smale,
> Of storial thyng that toucheth gentillesse,
> And eek moralitee and hoolynesse.
> (I 3174–80)

It is noteworthy that Chaucer used the characters of the tellers as revealed in the General Prologue and the links as warnings of salacious story materials, whereas Boccaccio used introductory plot summaries of the stories themselves, but the similarities are nonetheless impressive. My point here is not that the parallels prove that Chaucer must have known the *Decameron*, though nothing quite like them is known to exist before Boccaccio and Chaucer used such "apologies." It is, rather, that if indeed Chaucer had read the *Decameron* passage, he might well have recalled some years later the Boccaccian "apology" for offensive tales, the denial of an author's culpability for churlish tales, and the invitation to readers to browse for better ones.

Chaucer might also have picked up from Boccaccio the old-man-as-leek parallel. In the introduction to the fourth day of the *Decameron*, Boccaccio tells us that he has heard complaints from readers who are shocked to learn that so old a man as he is telling such spicy tales: "E quegli che contro alla mia età parlando vanno, mostra mal che conoscano che, perché il porro abbia il capo bianco, che la coda sia verde" (*Decameron 4. Introduzione*) [As for those who keep harping on about my age, they are clearly unaware of the fact that although the leek's head is white, it has a green tail (288)]. Chaucer's Reeve, just before he tells a bitter and ribald tale, explains that for white-headed old men like him it is natural to speak sharply:

> "For in oure wyl ther sticketh evere a nayl,
> To have an hoor head and a grene tayl,
> As hath a leek; for thogh oure myght be goon,
> Oure wyl desireth folie evere in oon.
> For whan we may nat doon, than wol we speke."
> (I 3877–81)

The comparison of an old man to a leek is sometimes said to be "proverbial,"[27] but in fact, Boccaccio gives us the first recorded use of the "proverb," and his use of it, reinforced by Chaucer's, may well have begun a usage that later became proverbial. In any case, my central point here is that if Chaucer had read the old-man-as-leek metaphor in the *Decameron*, the image is bold enough that he might have remembered it later.

I have been dealing here with only one small aspect of McGrady's argument—that the similarities we see between the *Decameron* and the *Canterbury Tales* cannot readily be explained as the result of "memorial borrowing" and that, therefore, Chaucer must have had a copy of Boccaccio's collection of tales before him as he wrote. My purpose is not to prove McGrady wrong; rather, it is to suggest that there is insufficient evidence to conclude that the kinds of details we are talking about imply that Chaucer owned a copy and used it in England. I think it quite possible that he did. I do not, however, want to see the question of *whether* Chaucer knew the *Decameron* clouded by rigid claims about exactly *how* Chaucer knew the *Decameron*. We have strong evidence that he knew it; I am reluctant to weaken that general argument by insisting on precisely how he knew it.

[27] McGrady, "Chaucer and the *Decameron* Reconsidered," 17n11.

McGrady's weaknesses: the *Miller's Tale*

It appears that McGrady was eager to convince his readers that Chaucer must have had a copy of the *Decameron* before him when he wrote because he wanted to buttress his own argument about the origins of the *Miller's Tale*: that the chief source for Chaucer's *Miller's Tale* was the *Decameron*. To make that point stick, however, McGrady relies on a series of parallels that he thinks are convincing only if Chaucer had a copy of the *Decameron* before him as he wrote, only if he could consult the Italian work directly as he wove various Boccaccian motifs together. McGrady finds in the *Decameron* not just one tale as the source of the tale of John, Alisoun, Nicholas, and Absolon, but several tales providing motifs that Chaucer used. Specifically, McGrady suggests that Chaucer wove together motifs from three tales: from *Decameron* 8.7, where a woman makes love with one man while another, less favored one waits outside in the snow and later punishes the woman; from *Decameron* 3.4, where a monk dupes an old husband into accepting a scheme for salvation while he frolics in bed with the man's young wife; and from *Decameron* 7.4, where an adulterous wife escapes the censure of her neighbors by cleverly making them think her husband is a drunken brute.

Most troubling about McGrady's thesis on the source for the *Miller's Tale* is that it all but ignores the fourteenth-century Middle Dutch analogue about Heile of Beersele that is closer to the *Miller's Tale* than any of the three tales in the *Decameron*, or than McGrady's suggested Chaucerian tapestry of them. Somewhat less troubling is that, once we begin to see Chaucer as weaving together motifs from several different *Decameron* tales, it is difficult to know where to stop. In writing the *Miller's Tale*, for example, Chaucer might have woven ideas not only from the three tales that McGrady cites, but also from at least three more: from *Decameron* 3.8, where a clever abbot tricks a foolish yeoman by making him think he is in purgatory for guarding his wife too closely and then has sex with the yeoman's wife; from *Decameron* 7.2, where a clever woman hides her lover in an empty wine barrel when her husband comes home unexpectedly; and from *Decameron* 7.6, where a clever wife accepts one lover, is bothered by a second but unwanted one, and then devises a cunning plan to explain to her husband why she has two men in her home.

My point is not to discredit McGrady's central thesis that Chaucer knew and was influenced by the *Decameron*, but to urge caution in insisting that Chaucer must have had the *Decameron* in front of him as he wrote, or that it was necessarily the key source for the *Miller's Tale.* Scholars are generally on more secure ground if they claim that Chaucer augmented other sources with material gleaned or remembered from a reading of the *Decameron*. If McGrady had been less eager to prove the primary importance of the *Decameron* in Chaucer studies, or that Chaucer had a copy before him as he wrote, he might have been more successful in convincing others to take seriously Boccaccio's hundred tales as potential sources for some of what we find in the *Canterbury Tales.*

I must skip over the evidence that McGrady brings to bear from a discussion of the other tales. Suffice it to say that he is able to demonstrate that certain tales in the *Decameron* might well have provided Chaucer with a number of features that he could have learned in no other known contemporary analogues. McGrady discusses, however briefly, *Decameron* 10.5 as source for the *Franklin's Tale*; *Decameron* 9.6 as source for the *Reeve's Tale*; *Decameron* 8.1 as source for the *Shipman's Tale*; *Decameron* 7.9 and 2.10 as sources for the *Merchant's Tale*; and *Decameron* 10.10 as source for the *Clerk's Tale.* I have had more to say elsewhere about the *Decameron* as source for the *Merchant's Tale*[28] and the *Reeve's Tale*,[29] and I will also discuss it below as source for the *Shipman's Tale.*

[28] See my 1973 article "Chaucer's *Merchant's Tale* and the *Decameron*" reprinted below, pp. 240–60.

[29] Peter G. Beidler, "Chaucer's *Reeve's Tale*, Boccaccio's *Decameron* IX, 6, and Two 'Soft' German Analogues," *Chaucer Review* 28 (1994): 237–51.

McGrady's weaknesses: artistic independence

Before moving to a discussion of the connections between the *Decameron* and Chaucer's *Shipman's Tale*, I must take gentle issue with a third point of McGrady's: that Chaucer wanted to assert his independence from Boccaccio by seeking less artistic sources than those he found in the *Decameron*. In making this suggestion, McGrady is attempting to answer the question that has troubled scholars for decades: why, if he knew the *Decameron*, did Chaucer make so little use of it? Cummings, we recall, raised this question as part of his proof that Chaucer could not have known the *Decameron*: "If Chaucer had known the *Decameron* and had it at his disposal, he would surely have availed himself of its splendid store of *novelle* to enrich the collection of his *Canterbury Tales*."[30] Because saw almost no evidence of direct borrowing, he dismissed the little evidence he did see because he could not imagine that Chaucer, had he known the *Decameron,* would not have borrowed from it far more heavily.

McGrady raises the matter in a somewhat different way: "The question then arises why Chaucer generally took only minor details from the *Decameron*, while imitating it so frequently." McGrady's question is a good one, but his answer, like that of Cummings before him, is less than satisfying: "Had he followed the *Decameron* in each of the passages in question, no less than six of Chaucer's twenty-two complete tales—plus portions of the cornice [i.e., the frame] and other bits—would have derived from a solitary source. Quite conceivably, such a dependence upon a single work might have appeared unseemly to the poet and his contemporaries. . . . Had Chaucer imitated the *Decameron* more closely, his reputation as an original poet would doubtless have suffered."[31] It is difficult enough to know why Chaucer *did* do something; it is almost impossible to know why he did *not* do something.

[30] Cummings, *Indebtedness of Chaucer's Works*, 180.

[31] McGrady, "Chaucer and the *Decameron* Reconsidered," 15.

If Chaucer had complete and long-term access to the *Decameron*, one can imagine all sorts of reasons why he did not retell more of its stories than he did: he may have had an incomplete version of the *Decameron*; he may have died before he had a chance to tell more of its stories (we must recall that he had envisioned some 120 tales); he may not have liked most of the tales Boccaccio told; he may have disapproved of the "low style" of many of the *Decameron* prose stories and wanted to establish a higher or different standard for vernacular English poetry, something closer to the more elevated style of Petrarch and Dante, both of whom he mentions favorably; he may have had trouble envisioning a pilgrim narrator for most of the *Decameron* tales; he may have been distressed with the immorality of Boccaccio's stories; and so on. Because there is no way to answer this question, we are ill-served by speculations that will only divide those who argue that Chaucer must have known and been influenced by the *Decameron.* Besides, we have here once again a double standard at work. We take the French *Le meunier et les .II. clers* as Chaucer's most likely source for the *Reeve's Tale* without inquiring why Chaucer did not use more stories from the same writer. Why should we not do so for Boccaccio's *Decameron*?

To return to McGrady's notion that Chaucer would have considered it "unseemly" to borrow from Boccaccio, I see little reason to think that he would have. Boccaccio was apparently Chaucer's favorite author. He borrowed more from him than from any other writer. Would he have worried about a damaged reputation for originality if he had borrowed more from the *Decameron*? I doubt it, the reputed immorality of Boccaccio and his hundred tales notwithstanding. Virtually everything Chaucer wrote had a narrative source, and Chaucer did not take even elementary precautions to conceal that he was retelling an old story. While he does not mention Boccaccio in the *Knight's Tale*, for example, which derives unquestionably from Boccaccio's *Teseida*, neither does he change the names of the characters to make it seem more "original." Similarly, in *Troilus and Criseyde*, which derives unquestionably from Boccaccio's *Filostrato*, Chaucer neither mentions Boccaccio nor makes any attempt to pretend to write a completely "original" story. Had Chaucer wanted to use far more of the *Decameron* than he did, he would presumably have employed a similar technique: picked the tales he liked, indicated in some of them something about "myn auctor," and cleverly adapted them to his own narrative, characterizing, and thematic ends.

We cannot help but wonder who McGrady was envisioning as the contemporary audience among whom Chaucer's "reputation as an original poet would doubtless have suffered." Such a statement suggests that Chaucer's audience knew the *Decameron* well enough to detect influence, but there is no evidence that they did. Besides, indications are that medieval audiences did not place a high premium on what we now think of as "originality." It was quite enough—indeed, it was preferable—to retell an old story, so long as one told it well. John Gower retold many old tales, and no one seems to have thought him or his art any less "original" for his having relied so heavily on, say, Ovid's *Metamorphoses.*

Rather than speculate on why Chaucer did not tell more of the stories he might have read in the *Decameron,* we would do better to try to establish which of the *Decameron* tales he is most likely to have known, to try to discover what evidence we have that Chaucer knew these, and then to ascertain what a comparison of Chaucer's tales with Boccaccio's shows us about the methods and skills of two writers.

Decameron 8.1 and the *Shipman's Tale*

John Webster Spargo, in one of the most puzzling but also most consequential critical responses to the relationship between Chaucer's *Shipman's Tale* and its possible sources, wrote in the original Bryan and Dempster *Sources and Analogues*: "In the absence of an authentic source, the likeliest thing that can be said is that, if we had one, it would probably be an Old French fabliau very similar to the *Shipman's Tale*, of which the atmosphere is all French. The closest analogue, *Decameron* 8.1, is reprinted here simply because it is that, not because it is Chaucer's source."[32] Few scholars now put much stock in a lost French *fabliau* since, apart from the existence of the *Shipman's Tale*, there is no evidence whatever that one ever existed. A notable exception is Tedeschi, who wonders why, if Chaucer had used an Italian source, "the action of the *Shipman's Tale* did not take place in Italy."[33] Notice, again, the double standard. No one questions why, if Chaucer knew the French *Le meunier et les .II. clers*, he did not give the *Reeve's Tale* a French setting. My own view is that, if Chaucer had based the *Shipman's Tale* on an Italian original, he would have been inventive enough to alter the geographical setting of the tale. Let us, in any case, consider Chaucer's knowledge of Boccaccio's *Decameron* 8.1, which Spargo himself admits is the closest analogue to the *Shipman's Tale* that we have.

Decameron 8.1 is a slender narrative—only a couple of pages long—about a German soldier who visits Milan and falls in love with the wife of a wealthy money-lending merchant. He sends the wife word of his love and his desire for her. The wife agrees to sleep with him only if he will give her two hundred gold florins. When he learns of her answer, the soldier becomes so enraged at her greed, at her putting a price on love, that he vows to teach her a lesson. He borrows the money from her husband and then, when the husband is out of town on business, gives it to the wife in the presence of one of his companions. Later, the soldier enjoys the wife's favors in bed. When the merchant returns, the soldier goes immediately with his companion to the merchant's home and tells the merchant, in the presence of his wife, that he had not needed the money after all and had returned it to her. Seeing the witness present, she, admits that she had received

[32] John Webster Spargo, "The *Shipman's Tale*" in *Sources and Analogues of Chaucer's Canterbury Tales*, edited by W. F. Bryan and Germaine Dempster (Chicago: University of Chicago Press, 1941), 439 (439–46).

[33] Tedeschi, "Some Recent Opinions," 863.

the money but says that she had forgotten to tell her husband. The merchant is satisfied and cancels the soldier's debt, and the wife returns the money to her husband.

Chaucer's *Shipman's Tale* is, of course, considerably different: it is much longer and has more dialogue; the setting is France, not Italy; the male lover is a monk, not a soldier; he does not become enraged at the wife's request for money; the wife asks for the money face to face rather than through an intermediary; she obliquely asks for money to repay a loan, rather than in blunt exchange for sexual services; she gets to keep the money or, rather, repays her husband in bed; and so on. Still, the *Decameron* version could well have provided Chaucer with the germ of the story. Certainly, there are a number of quite specific, and nonessential, similarities between Boccaccio's and Chaucer's stories. For example, the fictional narrator of the story is a woman, Neifile, recalling the almost universally acknowledged fact that what we now call the *Shipman's Tale* was originally written for the Wife of Bath. Furthermore, the lover is specifically said to be a friend of the merchant, whom he cuckolds and from whom he borrows the money, and the lover pledges secrecy to the wife.

These three features are not present in the only other extant analogue that Chaucer could conceivably have known, Sercambi's *novella, De avaritia et luzuria (Of Avarice and Lust).*[34] It is based on *Decameron* 8.1 and has some superficial resemblances to Chaucer's tale—most notably that the union of the lovers takes place on a Sunday.[35] More significant than such similarities are its differences

[34] Sercambi's tale is conveniently edited and translated in Larry D. Benson and Theodore M. Andersson, *The Literary Context of Chaucer's Fabliaux: Texts and Translations* (Indianapolis, IN: Bobbs-Merrill, 1971), 312–19. Sercambi's *Novelle* contains 155 tales. It is not clear to me why Nicholson refers to the analogue to the *Shipman's Tale* as number 32, while McGrady refers to it as number 31.

[35] Robert A. Pratt, "Chaucer's *Shipman's Tale* and Sercambi," *Modern Language Notes* 55 (1940): 142–45, called attention to this detail and certain others, such as that in both Sercambi and Chaucer the husband leaves the day after the loan is made, while in Boccaccio, he leaves a few days later.

from Chaucer's version. The teller, for example, is not one of the fictional travelers, but Sercambi himself, who narrates all of the tales in the *Novelle.* The wife in Sercambi's tale is specifically said to be a prostitute. Indeed, the soldier who propositions her is bold to do so in part because she has a reputation for selling her sexual services, and he wisely uses a go-between who has performed similar missions for previous clients. He specifically arranges with the merchant that if he does not need the borrowed money after all, he will return it to his wife. The lover's sexual encounter with the wife is described in almost grotesquely obscene detail, and he later gives the husband a gift of eels and a fish. In these and other respects Sercambi's version is different from both Chaucer's and Boccaccio's. That is, in neither the *Shipman's Tale* nor *Decameron* 8.1 is the teller the author himself. In neither is the wife a prostitute, does the lover arrange in advance to repay the money to the wife, is the lovemaking between the lover and wife presented in grotesque detail, or does the lover give aquatic gifts to the husband.

Despite the differences between Chaucer's and Sercambi's versions of the story, and despite the fact that no known version of Sercambi's *Novelle* were known to be extant anywhere until 1400—too late for Chaucer to have used it—some scholars have insisted that there was an earlier version, now lost, that Chaucer could have known. They say that this version, tentatively called the *Novelliero*, probably contained a story similar to the *Shipman's Tale* and that Chaucer could well have known that earlier version, now lost. Peter Nicholson, basing his findings in part on the work of Giovanni Sinicropi's edition of Sercambi's *Novelle*, demonstrated in 1976 that the supposed existence of the earlier *Novelliero* version of 1374 was based on a series of errors and assumptions. Nicholson also shows that, even if the *Novelliero* did exist, there is no assurance that it contained the same tales that were to appear in the 1400 *Novelle*: "Among the tales in the *Novelle* which could not have appeared in the *Novelliero* in its present form is number 32, the analogue of Chaucer's *Shipman's Tale*, for it is set in a city outside Tuscany." Nicholson shows that Sercambi would have had little leisure to write so long a work as the

Novelle until close to 1400, and "if that was so, then the possibility of his influence on Chaucer disappears altogether. . . . The *Novelliero* is therefore a historical chimera."[36]

Despite the lack of anything approaching definite evidence that a Sercambi work called the *Novelliero* ever existed or that, if it did exist it contained an analogue of the *Shipman's Tale*, some scholars have been reluctant to let it go. Indeed, Donald McGrady, even after having read Nicholson's work, cavalierly states that "another persuasive documentation of the indebtedness of Chaucer to Sercambi occurs in the *Shipman's Tale.* Although Sercambi had taken his *novella* 31 from *Decameron* 8.1, his version of the narrative, and not Boccaccio's, served as the principal model of the Shipman's story, while the influence of Boccaccio was limited to a few accessory circumstances."[37]

Even a scholar as astute as McGrady, who had earlier argued strongly that Chaucer owned a copy of the *Decameron* and had it with him in England as he wrote the *Canterbury Tales*, is reluctant to grant Boccaccio the primary status he deserves. We have, after all, an extant copy of a version of the narrative quite similar to the *Shipman's Tale*, old enough in its extant version that Chaucer could have known it. It is by the author from whom Chaucer borrowed more than he borrowed from any other writer. It was in a book that had circulated widely, especially along trade routes. We can see that it has several features that make it a more likely source for Chaucer's tale than Sercambi's. Why, then, are we so reluctant to say that Chaucer knew it? One of the purposes of this essay, of course, has been to suggest some of those reasons, and to attempt to refute them, to offer my enthusiastic support to the common sense words of Helen Cooper: "It strains credibility less to believe that Chaucer knew the *Decameron*, than to believe that the circumstantial evidence for

[36] Peter Nicholson, "The Two Versions of Sercambi's *Novelle*," *Italica* 53 (1976): 209, 211.

[37] McGrady, "Were Sercambi's Novelle Known from the Middle Ages On?" *Italica* 57 (1980): 5.

his knowledge of it is all mere coincidence, or that he found the inspiration for the *Canterbury Tales* in Boccaccio's uninspired imitators."[38] Another of this essay's purposes is to suggest that we adopt a more precise terminology when dealing with Chaucer's sources and analogues.

A new terminology

It may be that there is a basis for a wider agreement about Chaucer's knowledge of the *Decameron* than scholars have had in the past, an agreement based on a more refined terminology than we have been using. Part of the trouble is that we have, collectively, been sloppy in our use of the terms *source* and *analogue.* I suggest the following definitions for Chaucerians:

Source: a work that we are sure that Chaucer knew, either because of external evidence or because of the closeness of narrative or verbal parallels. Examples for the *Canterbury Tales* would be Boccaccio's *Teseida* (for the *Knight's Tale*), Trevet's *Life of Constance* (for the *Man of Law's Tale*), Renaud's *Livre de Mellibee et Prudence* (for the *Tale of Melibee*), and both Petrarch's second (1374) Latin translation of *Decameron* 10.10 and the anonymous French translation of Petrarch's first (1373) translation (for the *Clerk's Tale*). For some tales, of course, there is no known source, perhaps because it is now lost to us, or because Chaucer had no single narrative source, or because Chaucer so combined ideas from so many narratives that it is inaccurate to speak of a single "source" for the resulting work. Such tales include the *Cook's Tale*, the *Wife of Bath's Prologue*, the *Squire's Tale*, and the *Canon's Yeoman's Tale.* Some works, such as Jerome's letter *Adversus Jovinianum*, can be considered to be Chaucerian sources, even though they did not supply narrative materials for a whole Chaucerian work. A single Chaucerian work may be said to have two sources if both can be shown to have been known to Chaucer

[38] Helen Cooper, *The Structure of the Canterbury Tales* (London: Duckworth, 1983), 36.

and both can be shown to have contributed significant passages to or have specific verbal parallels with the Chaucerian work. The term *lost source* should be used with great caution to refer to an analogue that is known to have existed and that might have been known to Chaucer but that is no longer extant. No doubt Chaucer actually used several sources that have not come down to us. Until actual copies come to light, however, we should exercise the greatest caution in discussing what they may have contained or whether Chaucer may have known them.

Hard analogue: a work that would have been available to Chaucer and that bears certain striking resemblances, usually more narrative than verbal, to the Chaucerian work in question. A hard analogue can be said to have "near-source status" if it is old enough for Chaucer to have known it and if it gives closer parallels in plot or character than are available in other works Chaucer could have known, even if there are no or few specific language parallels. Examples would be the Flemish tale *Heile van Beersele* (for the *Miller's Tale*), the French *Le meunier et les .II. clers* (for the *Reeve's Tale*), Gower's *Tale of Florent* (for the *Wife of Bath's Tale*), the Italian *Novellino* version of the pear-tree story (for the *Merchant's Tale*), the French *Roman de Renart* (for the *Nun's Priest's Tale*), Boccaccio's *Decameron* 10.10 (for the *Clerk's Tale*), and Boccaccio's *Decameron* 8.1 (for the *Shipman's Tale*). Chaucer scholars must consider the hard analogues if they wish to analyze the stories that Chaucer may well have known so that they can see in what way Chaucer may have transformed his originals. These hard analogues may or may not have been sources for Chaucer, but in the absence of a more definite source, they are the best that we have, and we must not ignore them.

Soft analogue: a work that, either because of its date or because of the remoteness of its specific parallels with the Chaucerian narrative in question, Chaucer could scarcely have known. Examples would be Hans Sach's *The Smith in the Kneading Tub* (for the *Miller's Tale*), Rüdiger von Munre's *Irregang und Girregar* (for the *Reeve's Tale*), and Sercambi's *De avaritia et luzuria* (for the *Shipman's Tale*).

Chaucerians should be aware of the existence of soft analogues to Chaucerian tales but need to consult them only for general interest or when they reveal narrative parallels with Chaucer not available in either sources or hard analogues. Soft analogues may be later renditions of story elements that Chaucer might have known through an earlier redaction now lost to us, but Chaucerians should keep in mind that for most soft analogues there is at least as much chance that Chaucer influenced the analogue as that Chaucer was influenced by it, and that for many of them there was probably no connection with Chaucer at all.

Decameron 8.1 as hard analogue

Armed with a more precise vocabulary for speaking of Chaucer's possible sources, let us return to Spargo. I have no objection to Spargo's referring to "the absence of an authentic source," but I do object to the red herring of a lost French *fabliau* that has unnecessarily stood between the *Shipman's Tale* and *Decameron* 8.1. I propose the following as phrasing that most Chaucerians might agree with: We do not have a definite source for the *Shipman's Tale. Decameron* 8.1 is a hard analogue that Chaucer could quite easily have known. It tells the same basic story of a man who borrows from a merchant the money to pay for sex with the merchant's wife, and it shows a number of narrative, if not verbal, parallels with the *Shipman's Tale.* Sercambi's *De avaritia et luzuria*, which derives directly from the *Decameron* version, is a soft analogue. It probably appeared too late for Chaucer to have used it and, in any case, it is more distant from the *Shipman's Tale* in narrative conception than *Decameron* 8.1. It is remotely possible that Chaucer could have known a French *fabliau* version now lost to us, but we have no evidence that such *a fabliau* ever existed. In the absence of anything closer, scholars seeking to know the kind of story Chaucer might have transformed into the *Shipman's Tale* should on no account overlook *Decameron* 8.1.

If Chaucerians can agree on such a statement, then perhaps we are ready to take a new direction in scholarship on the *Shipman's*

Tale. Such voyages have been delayed by two problems. First, the *Shipman's Tale* has had no teller. With those troublesome female pronouns in the opening lines of what is now called the *Shipman's Tale*, the tale of the love triangle between a monk, a merchant, and a wife has seemed only remotely to be connected to the personality of any of the pilgrims. This is not the place to take up the problem of the relationship between this tale and its rival tellers, but I urge scholars to read the tale as the second tale of the Wife of Bath. I shall argue for that suggestion in another place. It has been my purpose in this essay to treat in some detail a second problem—that what we call the *Shipman's Tale* has seemed in the past to be sourceless, to have no trustworthy basis of comparison, no analogue that could give us a reliable place from which to measure Chaucer's originality in the tale. I urge scholars to consider the first tale of the eighth day of the *Decameron* as a hard analogue to the *Shipman's Tale*, an analogue with near-source status. Doing so can give us legitimate access at last to a tale that Chaucer had probably read at some point in his career, a tale with a similar plot and set of characters, a tale from which to measure the distance that Chaucer moved away from it.[39]

[39] In a recent book on Chaucer's knowledge of the *Decameron*, N. S. Thompson (*Chaucer, Boccaccio, and the Debate of Love* [Oxford: Clarendon, 1996]) presents new evidence to show that Chaucer knew the *Decameron*. The book details the general similarities between the two works and discusses the common attitudes and literary orientations shared by Chaucer and Boccaccio. Thompson remains, however, overly cautious about drawing conclusions from his evidence; he lets his readers weigh for themselves whether Chaucer knew the *Decameron*: "I have sought to explore, rather than to prove one side right or wrong in the debate about influence" (2). I welcome Thompson's book as an important contribution to what I consider to be the most important unresolved question about external influences on the *Canterbury Tales*, though I wish he had gone further than the conclusion that "there are stronger connections than have previously been thought" (313).

Chaucer's French Accent: Gardens and Sex-Talk in the *Shipman's Tale*

[Although I firmly resist the notion that there is a lost Old French version of the story of the lover's gift regained that served as Chaucer's source for the *Shipman's Tale*, I argue in this essay that while writing his version of the tale he encountered in *Decameron* 8.1, Chaucer was else influenced by what he learned by reading around in Old French fabliaux. I identify here in the fabliau *Aloul* a scene that could well have influenced the amazing garden scene in the *Shipman's Tale*. I also show, by reference to the language of several other fabliaux, that the monk daun John's talk of tired rabbits hiding in grassy furrows is a not-so-subtle sexual innuendo designed to let the wife of the merchant of Saint Denis know that he stands ready to pleasure her. "Chaucer's French Accent" first appeared in *Comic Provocations: Exposing the Corpus of Old French Fabliaux*, ed. Holly A. Crocker (New York: Palgrave, 2006), 149–61.]

It has sometimes been assumed that, because of its Parisian-area setting and its macaronic use of bits of the French language—"*Quy la?*"[1] (Who's there?)—Chaucer's *Shipman's Tale* must have had a French fabliau source, now lost to us. John Webster Spargo in his

[1] Fragment VII, line 214. This and all other quotations, cited hereafter parenthetically in the text, are taken from Larry D. Benson, ed., *The Riverside Chaucer*, 3rd edn. (Boston: Houghton Mifflin, 1987).

introductory note to the tale in the original *Sources and Analogues* gave that theory the weight of authority with this opening comment: "In the absence of an authentic source, the likeliest thing that can be said is that, if we had one, it would probably be an Old French fabliau very similar to the *Shipman's Tale*, of which the atmosphere is all French."[2] That theory, if not discredited or abandoned altogether, has generally been set aside as unhelpful to scholars who seek to understand the more English emphases of the tale of the merchant of Saint Denis, his clever wife, and his good friend the monk daun John. Writing in a time when the accepted view was that Chaucer had never read Boccaccio's *Decameron*, Spargo confidently declared that *Decameron* 8.1, while the closest analogue, was not the source of the *Shipman's Tale.* Many scholars, myself included, are now taking seriously the idea that Chaucer's primary source was indeed the first tale of the eighth day of the *Decameron.*[3]

While I agree that *Decameron* 8.1 was probably the primary source of the *Shipman's Tale*, in this paper I urge that we once again consider Chaucer's French accent in the tale. I do not suggest that we exhume the dead notion that Chaucer's source for the *Shipman's Tale* was a lost French fabliau. I do suggest, however, that certain elements in the garden scene in the *Shipman's Tale* point to the influence of several extant Old French fabliaux. The implications of my work

[2] *Sources and Analogues of Chaucer's Canterbury Tales,* ed. W. F. Bryan and Germaine Dempster (Chicago: University of Chicago Press, 1941; repr. Humanities Press, 1958), 439. Spargo's phrasing is echoed by Thomas D. Cooke in *The Old French and Chaucerian Fabliaux* (Columbia: University of Missouri Press, 1978): "The *Shipman's Tale* is very similar to the French fabliaux in its economy and symmetry. . . . [I]t comes closest in both style and content of all of Chaucer's fabliaux to the French" (171–72).

[3] I review the history of the relationship between the *Shipman's Tale* and *Decameron* 8.1, in "Just Say Yes, Chaucer Did Know the *Decameron*: Or, Bringing the *Shipman's Tale* Out of Limbo," reproduced in this volume, pp. 161–90. See John Scattergood, "The Shipman's Tale," *Sources and Analogues of the Canterburry Tales*, ed. Robert Correale and Mary Hamel (Woodbridge, Suffolk: D. S. Brewer, 2005), 2: 565–81. For a convenient translation, see Giovanni Boccaccio, *Decameron*, ed. and trans. G. H. McWilliam, 2nd ed. (New York: Penguin, 1995).

will be of most interest to Chaucer scholars, because I propose that Chaucer was probably influenced by French fabliaux even when he worked primarily from an Italian original. They will also be of interest to those who work primarily on the Old French fabliaux because I propose that French comic tales were not isolated texts that appealed only to contemporary audiences listening on specific occasions in one or two locations, but that they had a broader influence well past the time of their initial composition and delivery.

I focus here on two elements in the hundred-line garden scene in the *Shipman's Tale.* First, the meeting of a frustrated wife and a lecherous cleric in a garden-like setting sounds at times remarkably similar to a scene in the fabliau *Aloul* (3.14). Second, daun John's mention of a weary rabbit in his suggestive sex-talk to the wife in that garden picks up the flavor of animal euphemisms common in French fabliaux. These elements suggest that when Chaucer adapted the Italian story to French settings and characters, he might have been influenced by several pieces of French fabliaux. These pieces, taken together, contribute to our understanding of it and give it a French intonation or accent. In a sense, then, I am urging a different kind of support to Spargo's statement that in the *Shipman's Tale* the "atmosphere is all French," not just because the garden is in Saint Denis, a town near Paris, but also because it involves elements probably derived from the fabliaux.

The garden encounter in *Aloul*

At the start of the *Shipman's Tale* the wife and the monk meet while daun John says his morning devotions in the garden of the merchant of Saint Denis. That amazing hundred-line scene, in which the wife and the monk come together as relatives ("cousins") but part a few minutes later as promised lovers with an arrangement to meet for purposes of prepaid sexual pleasure, shows Chaucer at his most original. There is no parallel scene in *Decameron* 8.1, in which the two lovers, the German soldier Gulfardo and the proud Milanese wife Ambruogia, do not meet face-to-face, but rather use a letter-carrying go-between to negotiate the terms of his lust and her greed. Chaucer's garden scene is without question his most strikingly original addition to the story of the traditional fabliau love triangle—cuckolded husband, deceiving wife, lecherous cleric—but it bears a suggestive similarity to a scene in the Old French fabliau *Aloul.*

In the thirteenth-century *Aloul*, a story about a rich but miserly farmer named Aloul who marries a nobleman's daughter, the wife and her future lover meet in a natural outdoor setting. Because Aloul loves his money more than he loves his wife, however, he is less than generous with his cash:

> Alous estoit uns vilains riches,
> Mes mout estoit avers et ciches,
> Ne ja son vueil n'eüst jor bien:
> Deniers amoit seur toute rien,
> En ce metoit toute s'entente.
> (3.14.5–9)[4]
>
> [Aloul was rich. He earned his living
> by farming, but he wasn't giving:
> in no case would he spend his wealth,
> he loved his coins beyond all else
> and lavished on them all his care.]

Even though Aloul's wife has been faithful to him and he has no reason to suspect her of infidelity, he is irrationally jealous and never lets her go out without him, even to church. After two years, she is so angered and frustrated by his stinginess and his jealousy that she scarcely sleeps. She is ready to accept a lover just to spite him:

> A la dame forment desplest
> Quant ele premiers l'aperçoit,

[4] I am grateful to Nathaniel E. Dubin for giving me permission to quote from his to-be-published edition, with facing lively verse translations, of the Old French fabliaux that I refer to in this chapter. A somewhat different translation of *Aloul*, without the original French text, appears in *Fabliaux, Fair and Foul*, trans. John DuVal with introduction and notes by Raymond Eichman (Binghamton, NY: *Medieval and Renaissance Texts and Studies*, 1992), 107–29.

Lors dist que s'ele nel deçoit,
Se lieu en puet avoir & aise,
Dont sera ele mout mauvaise.
Ne puet dormir ne jor ne nuit:
Mout het Aloul et son deduit,
Ne set que face ne comment
Ele ait pris d'Aloul vengement,
Qui le mescroit a si grant tort.
(3.14.30–39)

[From when she first got the impression
of his mistrust she was aggrieved
and swore that he would be deceived
if she could find the place and time,
or else she wasn't worth a dime.
By day and night all sleep has fled,
she hates Aloul and hates his bed,
she doesn't know what she can do
to take revenge on Aloul, who
harbors suspicions without cause.]

One April morning this sleep-deprived and angry wife arises early and walks out into the orchard for a barefoot stroll on the dewy lawn. There she encounters the local priest, who lives in the house next door and is up early to take a morning stroll:

La dame s'est prise a lever,
Qui longuement avoit veillie;
Entree en est en son vergie,
Nus piez en va par la rousee,
D'une pelice ert afublee
Et un grant mantel ot deseure.
Et li prestres en icele eure
Estoit levez par matin.
Il erent si tres pres voisin
Entr'aus dues n'avoit c'une essele.
(3.14.48–57)

[The lady rose, and she got moving,
who'd long awake been lying there,
and went out to her orchard barefoot, walked across the dew-soaked lawn,
wearing the light cloak she's put on
and a large mantle over it.
The priest that day had also quit
his bed to take the morning air.
Their two houses were very near,
between them just some wooded land.]

A wall separates the two orchards. The priest begins the conversation from his side of the wall by asking what causes the wife to rise so early in the morning. The wife's reply introduces talk about the health benefits of the "dew" (which pretty clearly is meant to suggest semen) and the medicinal qualities of a certain "root" (by which the priest clearly means his penis):

—Sire, dist ele, la rousee
Est bone et saine en icest tans
Et est alegemenz mout granz,
Ce disent cil fusicien.
—Dame, dist ce cuit je bien,
Quar par matin fet bon lever.
Mes l'en se doit desjeüner
D'une herbe que je bien connois.
Vez le la, pres que je n'i vois;
Corte est et grosse la racine,
Mes mout est bone medecine:
N'estuet meillor a cors de fame.
(3.14.70–81)

["Father," the lady answered, "isn't
the dew both good and beneficial?
It lightens the heart something special,
so all the doctors say, they do."
"Lady," he said, "I think so too,
for rising early is a treat,

and for one's breakfast one should eat
an herb about which I could teach
you something. See—it's there in reach.
The root of it is thick and short,
but such good medicine that naught
is better for the health of women."]

Aloul's wife is immediately interested and invites the priest to come across the wall to show her this special herb-root. The priest, of course, is only too happy to come over and show her:

—Sire, metez outre vo jambe,
Pet la dame, vostre merci,
Si me moustrez se ele est ci.
—Dame, fet il, iluec encontre.
A tant a mise sa jambe outre,
Devant la dame est arestez.
"Dame, dist il, or vous seez,
Quar au cueillir i a mestrie."
Et la dame tout li otrie,
Qui n'i entent nule figure.
(3.14.82–91)

[The lady in her turn asks him in:
"Step over, Father, please, and show
me. Have we some? Where does it grow?"
"Right over there, lady." Then he
climbed across to her property
and came and stood in front of her.
"Lady," he said, "sit you down there,
for gathering it calls for skill."
The lady submits to his will,
quite ignorant of rhetoric.]

They have sex right there. Although the wife seems to resist, she also enjoys the encounter and immediately promises the priest that, if he will keep their affair secret, she will meet him often and make him wealthy in sexual pleasure:

—Sire, dist ele, cest afere
Gardez que soit celé mout bien,
Et je vous donrai tant du mien
Que toz jors mes serez mananz.
Foi que doi vous, bien a deus anz
Qu'Alous me dent en tel destrece,
Qu'ainc puis n'oi joie ne leece.
(3.14.108–114)

["Father," she answered him, "see to it
that what's occurred here stays unknown,
and I'll give you from what I own
so much that you'll be rich from now
on. For well-nigh two years, I vow,
Aloul's kept me in such distress
I've known no joy or happiness."]

She offers to please him and herself sexually because, after all, her husband makes her miserable.

There are obvious differences between the garden scene in the *Shipman's Tale* and the orchard scene in *Aloul.* Aloul is a farmer, not a merchant, for example, and he sleeps through his wife's encounter with the man who becomes her lover, rather than sequestering himself in his counting house. He is said to be jealous, unlike the merchant of Saint Denis, who is not. The lover is a priest, not a monk, and never claims to be a friend or cousin to the man he cuckolds. The wife of Saint Denis, unlike Aloul's wife, has gone into debt to buy clothing, and she charges the monk for the sexual pleasure she gives him. The site for their meeting is a garden, not an orchard, there is no wall that the monk has to scale, no sexual allegory of "dew" and "root," no sexual assignation on that site, and so on. And, of course, the story line in *Aloul* goes on in ways that have no relation to the events in the *Shipman's Tale.* The main story in *Aloul*—85 percent of the total narrative—is yet to come.

Despite these broad differences, the similarities are sufficiently specific that the orchard scene in *Aloul* might well have provided

Chaucer with the fundamental structure for the garden scene and some of the subsequent characterization in the *Shipman's Tale*: a dissatisfied wife receptive to the advances of a clerical suitor she chances to meet very early in the morning in an outdoor setting while her husband is otherwise occupied in the house; the husband's concern for making money (see *Shipman's Tale* VII 287–90); the greeting in which the cleric asks why the wife is up so early (VII 99); the wife's complaints about her husband's deficient sexuality and generosity (VII 114–17, 161–77); the cleric's conviction that he can help her (VII 125–30); the wife's agreement to provide sexual services to the cleric if he promises to agree to keep matters secret (VII 130–33); and the sleazy cleric's obscene sex-talk to the intended victim of his lust.

Daun John's fabliau sex-talk

Chaucer's monk speaks very much in the manner of the Old French fabliaux when he talks to his friend's wife about the nocturnal doings of husbands and wives. When they first meet in the outdoor setting, the priest in *Aloul* quickly asks the wife why she is up so early:

> "Dame, fet il bon jor aiez!
> Por qu'estes si matin levee?"
> (3.14.68–69).
>
> ["Lady, good day to you!' he said. 'Say, why are you so early risen?' "]

The priest's opening is nicely reflected in the monk's opening words to the wife of Saint Denis in Chaucer's story:

> "What eyleth yow so rathe for to ryse,
> Nece?" quod he.
> (VII 99–100).[5]

[5] I have argued elsewhere that the standard punctuation of these lines is wrong. All editors have placed the close-quotation mark at the end of line 99, thus giving the "why-are-you-up-so-early" line to the wife. I would, rather, place the quotation mark after the first word in line 100,

Daun John then launches immediately into what I am calling sex-talk:

> it oghte ynough suffise
> Fyve houres for to slepe upon a nyght,
> But it were for an old appalled wight,
> As been thise wedded men, that lye and dare
> As in a fourme sit a wery hare,
> Were al forstraught with houndes grete and smale.
> (VII 100–105)

These lines are interesting for several reasons. For one thing, the monk is the first to bring up the subject of what happens between a man and his wife in the bedroom. He says that five hours of sleep at night is plenty, except for an old wedded man who lies in bed motionless, like a tired rabbit cowering in a grassy burrow while hounds harass him just outside. The implication of the monk's reference to the sexual incapacity of married men is clear enough: the monk, single and fresh from a night's rest, would not be so like a weary rabbit. That the monk has some such meaning in mind seems clear enough from his immediately following reference to the husband's "labor" all night long, thus driving his wife out of her bed so she can get some rest:

> But deere nece, why be ye so pale?
> I trowe, certes, that oure goode man
> Hath yow laboured sith the nyght bigan
> That yow were nede to resten hastily.
> (VII 106–109)

The monk is so embarrassed by his talk of sexual laboring that he laughs and then blushes:

giving line 99 to the monk. A cleric, of course, was supposed to be up early making his morning devotions—daun John is saying "his thynges . . . ful curteisly" (VII 91)—so there would be no need for the wife to ask why he was up so early: the reason is obvious. It is the wife's early-morning visit to the garden that is unusual. For a more complete statement of my argument, see "Where's the Point?: Punctuating Chaucer's *Canterbury Tales*," reprinted in this volume, pp. 55–71.

> And with that word he lough ful murily,
> And of his owene thought he wax al reed.
> (VII 110–111)

Clearly, then, the monk has introduced sex-talk into his conversation with the wife. Seeing that she has got up early and is pale, he immediately jumps to the conclusion that her husband is either a cowering rabbit or that he overworks her sexually. That gives the wife a perfect opening to assure the monk that the latter is certainly not the case, and that she is the least sexually satisfied wife in "al the reawme of France" (VII 116).

I want to return to the image of the tired rabbit ("wery hare") cowering in the grassy hollow or burrow ("fourme").[6] The hare and the form, especially in the erotic context of a fabliau, might well have suggested to a Chaucerian audience that they should be taken as symbolic of the male and female genitals. Old French fabliaux regularly refer to the human genitals by not-very-veiled animal euphemisms. Though the explicit words *con* and *vit* were often used of the female and male genitals, other terms were used, particularly when educating supposedly naive or inexperienced women and men about sexual matters, or when an attempted seduction might prove more successful with a certain indirection of speech. A favorite among these euphemisms was the use of animals as genital identifiers.

There is, of course, nothing surprising in the use of animals to identify human sexual parts. We do it still in English: pussy, beaver, cock, lizard, one-eyed snake, and so on. There is no need here to give extended examples to show how the writers and speakers of Old French fabliaux used animal euphemism for the human genitalia, but a short survey will demonstrate just how widespread they are across

[6] It is not entirely clear exactly what this "fourme" in line 104 is. Some take it to be a rabbit warren, some a rabbit's hole or burrow, some a shallow gully or furrow or depression in the grass where the rabbit can hide. For my reading of the line any of these is acceptable. The *Middle English Dictionary*, ed. Hans Kuratn and Sherman M. Kuhn (Ann Arbor: University of Michigan Press, 1952–2001), vol. F.1, 770 calls it "the burrow or retreat (of a hare, etc.)."

the fabliaux. Perhaps the most literal example occurs in *La Sorisete des Estopes* (6.66), in which a stupid peasant has to be taught by his bride's mother what and where his wife's *con* is. On his mother-in-law's instructions, he believes that it is hidden in a basket of rags. On his way home with the basket of rags, a mouse escapes from the bundle of rags and runs off through the fields. He chases the creature, then pleadingly addresses it as his "sweet cunt." Others use the figurative potential of language for sexual humor. In *Porcelet* a young man and wife decide to have fun by giving pet names to their genitals (6.67). She names his "wheat," apparently because of its similarity in shape to a stalk of wheat and its use as a satisfying food for her, and hers "piggie" because it is never clean and because of its appetite.

In *Guillaume au Faucon* (8.93) the wife of a nobleman invents a private language to convince the young man who is literally dying for love of her that he may have her sexually after all. She tricks her husband into unwittingly giving Guillaume his "falcon," thus saving Guillaume's life by giving him a present of his wife's genitals. The lexical fun is compounded when we note that in French *faucon* is a pun on "false cunt." And in *La Damoisele qui ne pooit oïr parler de foutre* (4.26), which features a woman of refined sensibilities who will not allow her father to hire any workmen who use the word "fuck," the humor of the story derives from an enterprising young man's ability to seduce the young woman with an elaborate fiction involving animal euphemisms. By calling his penis his "horse," he eventually convinces the young woman to allow him access to her genitals, which she's called her "pasture" and her "spring." In *Cele qui fu foutue et desfoutue* an inexperienced young woman is led to think that a young man who has killed a bird offers to trade it to her for "a fuck" (4.30). Although the young man's penis is never directly called a crane (or heron), there is more than a hint of that association in the language he uses.[7]

[7] This tale has two manuscript traditions, which were considered separately until the *NRCF* combined them under one title, *Cele qui fu foutue et desfoutue* (4.30). Here I refer to the *NRCF's*

A famous example of an animal euphemism for the penis comes in *L'Esquiriel* (6.58), which involves the sexual initiation of a young woman whose mother has insisted that the literal name for penis, "vit," is indecent. As it turns out, the erotic potential of figurative language is even more potent, particularly that of animal euphemism. When the girl asks an approaching young man what he is holding there inside his pants, he tells her it is a squirrel and invites her to pet it. When the girl regrets that she ate the nuts she would have fed the squirrel, Robin assures her that it is not too late, and not long afterwards Robin's squirrel does scurry up to the nuts. One last example of the use of animals as is the improbable *Le Prestre et la Dame* (8.95), which is about a randy priest who bets a woman's tipsy husband a goose that he is strong enough to lift three people at once. As he is performing this feat of strength, the fabliau uses animal euphemisms to confirm the priest's sexual trickery. He puts his "ferret" (*fuiron*) into the designated place, which the author explains with his own pun about rabbits: "a coney gets lonely when it doesn't have a ferret in her nest" (8.95.139–41).[8] When he is finished the priest admits that he failed to lift the three bodies and promises to bring a fat goose around to the wife the next day. The priest hints that the fat goose is another euphemism for his ferret.

To return to Chaucer, the point is that when the monk in the *Shipman's Tale* speaks of a weary rabbit cowering in the form, he is by indirection speaking of a flaccid penis lying lifeless and inert in or beside a woman's vagina—too worn out, too frightened—to do

version I, which exists in five manuscripts (A, B, E, D, F), and is elsewhere referred to as *La Grue* (Joseph Bédier, *Les Fabliaux: Études de littérature populaire et d'histoire littéraire du moyen âge* [Paris: É. Champion, 1925)], no. 73; Per Nykrog, *Les Fabliaux: Étude d'histoire littéraire et stylistique médiévale* [Copenhagen: E. Munksgaard, 1957], no. 76. Version II in the *NRCF,* represented in one manuscript, is often called *Le Heron* (Nykrog, *Les Fabliaux,* no. 78). See Noomen, *NRCF*, volume 4, 153–55, for a discussion of these versions and the *NRCF's* decision to combine them under a standardized title.

[8] Translation mine. Dubin renders these lines as follows: "Their mood is bad, / Because these coneys feel depressed / When there's no ferret in their nest."

anything but lie there immobile. By using that metaphor of the rabbit-as-penis, the monk would have been connecting not only with the fabliau tradition of using animal euphemisms for the genitals, but also with a widespread tradition associating the rabbit with sexuality—or the failure of sexuality.

I am by no means the first to comment on the monk's reference to the weary hare cowering in a form.[9] Others have noted the generally sexual nature of hares. D. W. Robertson, Jr., for example, speaks of the iconography of the rabbit as "a small furry creature of Venus" and of the "play on words . . . possible in French involving *con* and *conin*"[10]—the latter being, as we have seen in *Le Prestre et la Dame*, a French word for hare. Robertson, however, makes no specific reference to Chaucer's use of the weary hare in the *Shipman's Tale.* Beryl Rowland has a whole chapter on the symbolism of the hare and finds many alternative readings of its "shifting symbolism": "Indicative of worldliness, timidity, lechery, physical exhaustion, ignorance of love, fortuitous love and sexual deviation, the [hare] provides striking illustrations of human frailty."[11] Her reading of the monk's comment in the *Shipman's Tale* is curious but perhaps not far from the mark: "By means of the expressive hunting image, conjuring up the picture of the timid husband, his ardour exhausted, quailing before his insatiable mate, he prepares the accommodating wife for the frank enquiry to follow."[12] Thomas W. Ross mentions the monk's

[9] I suspect a Chaucerian pun on both parts of the term "wery hare" (VII.104). The hare is both a rabbit and a penis. As a cowering rabbit the husband is said to be "wary"—i.e., vigilant, frightened, suspicious; and as a penis he is said to be "weary"—i.e., tired, worn out, weak, depleted.

[10] D. W. Robertson, Jr., *A Preface to Chaucer: Studies in Medieval Perspective* (Princeton: Princeton University Press, 1962), 113.

[11] Beryl Rowland, *Blind Beasts: Chaucer's Animal World* (Kent, OH: Kent State University Press, 1971), 102.

[12] Ibid., 94. On page 93 Rowland, with little explanation, refers to the monk as having "the good wife on the psychoanalyst's couch."

comparison of "the merchant to a hare that lies motionless in a rabbit warren, beset with hounds," but he immediately affirms confidently that "there is no connection with symbolic sexual hunting here."[13] On the basis of the French connections I have been exploring in this paper, I disagree with Ross, and suggest instead that Chaucer scholars need to look more at the larger corpus of fabliaux to gain a richer understanding of Chaucer's engagements with the form.

Although there has been little scholarly agreement about the meaning of the monk's reference to the weary rabbit cowering in a form, there is wide recognition of the association in the Middle Ages between rabbits and sexuality. Karl P. Wentersdorf gives a manuscript illustration showing a nude man embracing a rabbit larger than he is (see his figure 6), and speaks of lechery as "the vice primarily symbolized by the hare."[14] Medieval illustrations often show rabbits in close association with holes. For example, *The Hunting Book* of Gaston Phoebus shows a colorful illustration of a dozen rabbits either in or in close proximity to a series of burrows, with a text that reads, "The wild rabbit is of an idle and roving disposition, even though he spends the day cramped in his burrow. At dusk he goes in quest of his

[13] Thomas W. Ross, *Chaucer's Bawdy* (New York: E. P. Dutton, 1972), 102. Chaucer clearly knew of possible associations of hares with sexuality. In describing the Monk he says, "Of prikyng and of huntyng for the hare / Was al his lust" (I 191–92). In this context, of course, the hare would mostly be a euphemism for the female organ, not the male. The Friar says that, "thogh this Somonour wood were as an hare, / To telle his harlotrye I wol nat spare" (III 1327–28). In the *Knight's Tale* Theseus comments with amusement on the fact that Emily, the object of the hot passion of Arcite and Palamon, knows "namoore of al this hoote fare, / By God, than woot a cokkow or an hare" (I 1809–10). The connection of the cuckoo with sexual misconduct was well known, so associating it with hares in a romantic context is more than suggestive. We should remember that in the *Merchant's Tale*, another Chaucerian fabliau, Priapus is referred to as the "god of gardyns" (IV 2035). The fact that the monk's rabbit-remark takes place in a garden might in itself have suggested phallic associations. There was, of course, neither a rabbit nor a garden in *Decameron* 8.1.

[14] Karl P. Wentersdorf, "The Symbolic Significance of *Figurae Scatologicae* in Gothic Manuscripts" in *Word, Picture, and Spectacle*, ed. Clifford Davidson (Kalamazoo, MI: Medieval Institute Publications, 1984, 3 [1–19].

favorite herbs along with the rest of his clan or exercises himself in amorous pursuit of lady rabbits."[15]

It seems logical enough to conclude, in view of the fabliau use of animals to stand for the human genitals, and in view of the frequent references in the medieval period to the symbolism of the rabbit as a sexual symbol for the male or female organs, or for lechery in general, that the monk in the *Shipman's Tale* employs overt sex-talk when he compares the husband of the woman he desires to a "wery hare" who lies motionless in its "fourme" afraid to move because of the hunting dogs. He is really talking about a penis too limp and inactive to do a woman's genitals any good. The implication, of course, is that the monk's own rabbit is ready to rise up and show the merchant's wife's bunnie a ripping good time. He does not want to come right out and say that, but he clearly hopes that the wife of Saint Denis will take his meaning. She apparently does take his meaning, because she immediately after tells the monk that she has a miserable sex life:

> In al the reawme of France is ther no wyf
> That lasse lust hath to that sory pley.
>
> . . . . .
>
> Wherfore I thynke out of this land to wende,
> Or elles of myself to make an ende,
> So ful am I of drede and eek of care.
>
> (VII 116–17, 121–23)

Daun John is of course unctuously sympathetic to the lovely young wife, and a few minutes later she calls daun John "my deere love" (VII158), tells him of her need for a hundred francs, offers to give him in exchange whatever "plesance and service" (VII 191) he may desire, and then, a deal having been struck, lets him grab her "by the flankes,"

[15] Gaston Phoebus, *The Hunting Book,* Bibliothèque Nationale, MS français 616. The text is quoted from the reproduction by Miller Graphics (Fribourg, 1978), 24. See also folio 176v in the Luttrell Psalter, BL Additional MS 42129, conveniently available in Janet Backhouse, *Medieval Rural Life in the Luttrell Psalter* (Toronto: University of Toronto Press, 2000), plate 21.

embrace her "harde," and kiss her "ofte" (VII 202–203). She has apparently understood his euphemistic sex-talk well enough. Is there any reason why we should miss it?

If I am right in making the associations I have been urging, then there is a connection between the Old French fabliaux and the *Shipman's Tale* after all. The orchard scene in *Aloul* might have suggested to Chaucer certain motifs that he incorporated into the garden scene, and the Old French penchant for using animal euphemisms for the sexual parts may give us, as it apparently gave the wife of the merchant of Saint Denis, clues to the meaning of daun John's suggestive language about rabbits and burrows. Certainly there are no such animal euphemisms for the genitals in *Decameron* 8.1. Is it any wonder that the French monk blushed when he engaged in such sex-talk? And is there any reason that we, as readers of this tale about a woman who claims, with obvious hyperbole, to be the most sexually frustrated wife in the whole realm of France, should not hear Chaucer's French accent in the tale?

Medieval Children Witness their Mothers' Indiscretions: The Maid Child in Chaucer's *Shipman's Tale*

[Alone among tellers of the story of the lover's gift regained, Chaucer in the *Shipman's Tale* provides a direct, face-to-face negotiation for seduction between the wife and the lover. The central subject of this essay is the fact that present for that garden negotiation is a "maid child." I argue that this maid child is the daughter of the wife of the merchant of Saint Denis, not the serving maid that most scholars have taken her to be. Along the way to proposing that the wife of Saint Denis takes her young daughter along into the garden purposefully to educate her in the ways of a woman with a man, I consider two other medieval tales in which children witness their mothers' indiscretions. I show, finally, how the tale's having been originally written for the Wife of Bath supports my reading: surely Alisoun would have approved of a mother's teaching her young daughter how to negotiate her sexuality into a better life for herself. "Medieval Children Witness Their Mothers' Indiscretions" first appeared in *Chaucer Review* 44 (2009): 186–204.]

In this paper I discuss three medieval fabliaux in which young children witness their mothers' infidelities: a thirteenth-century French story in which a boy watches his mother make love to a priest;

a mid-fourteenth-century Italian one in which a boy is taken into the bedroom where his mother makes love to a friar; and, at greater length, a late-fourteenth-century English one in which a maid child witnesses her mother's offering of sexual pleasure to a monk in exchange for a loan of one hundred francs. Although the first two are in no sense sources for or even analogues to the Chaucerian third, the three tales share some features: an innocent child, a lecherous man of the church, a cuckolded husband/father, a clever wife/mother. Because each is written for a different set of literary purposes, the first two help us see what is distinctive in Chaucer's treatment of the situation in which a child is witness to her mother's indiscretion.

"The Man Who Kicked the Stone"

We have two extant versions of the very short thirteenth-century anonymous French fabliau called "The Man Who Kicked the Stone," in which a boy watches his mother make love to a priest. In the shorter version, which runs to sixty-two lines of octosyllabic couplets, a certain priest comes to the house of one of his parishioners. He is welcomed by the wife, whose husband is out working, and who has a young son at home with her. In the yard is a stone that they intend to make into a mortar. When the wife kicks the stone, the priest tells her to let it be:

> "Se la botez ne ça ne la,
> je cuit que je vos foutré ja."
> (46–49)
>
> ["Kick it a little or a lot
> and I will fuck you on the spot!"[1]]

[1] "De celui qui bota la pierre" is preserved in three manuscripts: B (Berne, Bibl. de la Bourgeoisie 354), K (Paris, Bibl. nationale fonds fr. 2173), and l (i.e., a lowercase "L," Cologny, Bodmer 113). I am grateful to N. E. Dubin for allowing me to use his prepublication edition and translation of the B version. The lines quoted here are 23–24. Subsequent references to the lines in the poem, included in parentheses, are to this version.

The wife is pleased with that prospect and again kicks the stone. With her consent, the priest picks her up and carries her to the bed, where they make love. The little boy sitting near the fire sees them and speaks quietly:

> "En moie foi," dist l'enfançon,
> "je cuit bien que issi fout l'on!"
> (37–38)
>
> ["I think," muttered the innocent,
> "when they say fuck, that that's what's meant."]

Not long afterwards the priest gets up and leaves, just before the boy's father, who has been out tilling the fields, comes home. The boy's father starts to move the stone, but his son stops him:

> L'enfens li dist: "Pere, ne faire!
> Se la boutez ne sa ne la,
> nostre prestres vos foutra ja
> sicom it fist ore ma mere."
> (46–49)
>
> [His son said, "Da, leave it alone!
> Move it a little or a lot,
> our priest will fuck you on the spot
> just like he did to Ma just now."]

The boy's father understands what his wife has been doing and takes his revenge later on—the timing and the method of the revenge are not specified. The story ends with a specific moral:

> Se l'enfançon n'eust veil
> lo prestre jöer a sa mere,
> il noel deïst pas a son pere.
> (60–62)
>
> [If the kid hadn't seen the priest
> and his mother having a lark,
> his dad would still be in the dark.]

The other version of "The Man Who Kicked the Stone," also in octosyllabic couplets, is almost twice as long (114 lines). The chief differences are in the characterization of the mother and the father. In the longer version, the mother, particularly, comes across as a coquette who is enamored of the priest and who makes the first moves to get him to make love to her, while the father comes across as a loving man who cares about his child and, instead of postponing his revenge, punishes his wife straightaway by dragging her by the hair, rolling her around, and stomping on her. The stated moral, however, is similar: Beware of little children because, like insane people, they hide nothing that they see.

A fundamental narrative illogicality mars "The Man Who Kicked the Stone." Why, for example, would the mother select a stone to kick in the first place, why is a stone in the house at all, and why would a priest seize on that particular action in his threat to have sex with her? In the short version, the stone is said to be a potential mortar-stone, which may let us imagine a pre-Freudian hint of a phallic pestle grinding in it, but nothing is made of that hint. The child is an attentive little rascal who hears the priest's threat to make love to his mother if she moves the stone. It is not clear whether he understands the nature or purpose of the activity that takes place in the bed, but he has somehow—we are not told how—learned the term for it and is later able to warn his father not to move the stone or he will be treated in a similar way.

While there may be a certain humor in all this illogicality, can we help but wonder at the mother's caring so little about the moral development of her son that she would so carelessly engage in sexual infidelities in his presence? In the medieval world of small houses and thin walls, of course, there would have been little of the privacy in sexual matters that we have grown accustomed to in a later age, but even so, the fornicating mother who is about to have illicit sex with a supposed pillar of the church could have asked the boy to go out to play in the yard. Then, however, he would not have seen what the plot requires him to see, and he could have given no warning when his father tries to move the stone.

Clearly, the point of the French fabliau is not really to condemn mothers for engaging in illicit sex with priests, nor really to condemn them for engaging in primal-scene activities in front of their young children. Rather, the point seems to be a merely practical warning to mothers: you may be caught and punished if you engage in sexual infidelities in the presence of your young children.

Boccaccio's *Decameron* 7.3

In the third tale of the seventh day of Boccaccio's *Decameron*, a man named Rinaldo lusts for Agnesa, the lovely wife of a rich but gullible husband. To gain easier access to Agnesa, Rinaldo persuades the husband to name him the godfather of the couple's soon-to-be-born child. When Agnesa resists his advances, Rinaldo decides to become a friar. At first Friar Rinaldo gives up some of his vices, but he soon returns to them and pays regular visits to Agnesa and her son. As both godfather and friar, Rinaldo easily persuades Agnesa to become his lover. On one of their trysts, the mother takes her son by the hand and leads him and Friar Rinaldo into her bedroom: "he and the lady, who was holding her little boy by the hand, made their way into her bedroom, locking the door behind them. And having settled down on a sofa, they began to have a merry time of it together."[2]

When they have twice made love, the husband comes home unexpectedly and knocks on the bedroom door. Agnesa leaps up and quickly gets dressed. She tells Friar Rinaldo to get dressed, listen to what she tells her husband, and act accordingly. Agnesa then, in feigned innocence, greets her husband. She tells him that their son had been stricken nearly to death by a terrible disease, but that Friar Rinaldo had come, had properly diagnosed the disease as an advanced case of worms in the boy's body that were about to attack his heart, and had cast a spell on the worms and killed them all. Friar Rinaldo hears all this as he dresses. He picks up the boy, cradles him in his arms, and comes forward to corroborate the story by claiming to have

[2] Trans. G. H. McWilliam, in Giovanni Boccaccio, *The Decameron,* 2nd edn. (London, 1995), 498.

with his special prayers cured the boy's disease and saved his life. The gullible husband is delighted to have his son alive and well, embraces the boy, repeatedly kisses him, and gratefully rewards Friar Rinaldo with a meal of fine wine and food.

The plot of this story is unlikely enough. Why, after all, would the wife this one time lead her son into the bedroom of her infidelity? That plot element seems designed only to fulfill the requirements of the theme for the seventh day. As king for day seven, Dioneo has called for stories about wives who—either to advance their love affairs or to preserve their own lives—play tricks on their husbands. This story, though not realistic, does fit the theme.

The story is unrealistic in other ways, as well. Is it really likely, after all, that a man who is frustrated in his desire to have sex with a pretty wife would become a friar just to improve his chances? That plot element serves mostly to give the teller the chance to complain at length about the evil corruption of worldly friars. As for the boy himself in *Decameron* 7.3, he is scarcely characterized. We do not know how old he is, though we might guess from the fact that he can walk and even run, and from the fact that he is easily cradled in the arms both of the friar and the husband, that he may be between two and five. If he watches his mother in her act of infidelity, we are not told that fact, nor are we told whether he understands what he has seen. The lad never speaks in the story, and he does not tell his father what his mother has been up to with his godfather. He is, in other words, scarcely a character at all. Rather, he serves a function in a story designed to show just how clever unfaithful wives can be in making excuses to explain to their gullible husbands why they are in the bedroom with men to whom they are not married. The reader's attention is focused not on the immorality of the boy's being present during one of his mother's sexual trysts, but on the pawn's role he plays in a tale that reveals his mother's cleverness at concealing her guilt, his father's foolishness in believing her absurd story, and his friar-godfather's inappropriate worldliness.

Chaucer's *Shipman's Tale*

In the *Shipman's Tale,* we recall, a Parisian monk named John comes to Saint Denis to visit his old friend, a merchant, and the merchant's lovely wife, both unnamed. Near the start of the tale the wife goes to the garden where daun John is saying his morning prayers and propositions him. It is easy to forget that present during that scene of sleazy seduction is a "mayde child" who comes into the garden with the wife of Saint Denis. The maid child is, so far as we can tell, a Chaucerian addition to this story of the lover's gift regained. In the first tale of the eighth day of Boccaccio's *Decameron*, the closest analogue we have to Chaucer's story and its most likely source, there is no garden scene at all and no child.[3] The three lines in which the maid child's presence is described, then, are original with Chaucer:

> A mayde child cam in hire compaignye,
> Which as hir list she may governe and gye,
> For yet under the yerde was the mayde.
> (VII 95–97)[4]

Those three lines are all we know of the maid child. She is presumably there through the whole garden scene, though she is never mentioned again. Since we are not told that she leaves, we are apparently to assume that this child witnesses the encounter between the wife and the monk—including the wife's seductive proposition to daun John and his grabbing the wife by the "flankes," his embracing her "harde," and his kissing her "ofte" (VII 202–3).

[3] In *Decameron* 8.1, the German soldier Gulfardo falls in love with a merchant's wife, sends her a message that he loves her, and asks her to be kind to him. She considers his message and, after thinking it over, sends a message back that she will be kind to him if he will give her a large sum of money. Chaucer handles the seduction sequence quite differently. He makes the lover not a foreign soldier but a monk who is a close friend of the family. Because daun John visits the merchant's home socially with considerable frequency, he knows his friend's wife and can without suspicion have a face-to-face meeting with her.

[4] This and other quotations from the *Canterbury Tales* are taken from the *Riverside Chaucer,* ed. Larry D. Benson, 3rd edn. (Boston: Houghton Mifflin, 1987).

Chaucer's treatment of a small child witnessing its mother's infidelity is different from that of both the French and the Italian authors. Chaucer's plot, for one thing, is more logical and realistic in that the actions of the various people arise from their characters, not merely from the needs of the plot or the need to work toward a moral. Chaucer builds on the people he creates, not merely on the events he wants to tie up in a certain way. The child in Chaucer's tale is a girl, not a boy. The story is more discreet in that the child does not witness her mother engaged in actual coitus with her lover, but merely observes her making arrangements for that coitus. In addition, the connection of Chaucer's tale with a fully characterized teller introduces a theme of the education of young children that does not appear in the earlier versions. To explore these and other issues, I take up four related questions: (1) what is a "mayde child"?; (2) how old is the "mayde child" in the *Shipman's Tale*?; (3) why does Chaucer put the maid child in the garden scene?; and (4) why does it matter that Chaucer originally wrote the *Shipman's Tale* for the Wife of Bath? Because Chaucer tells us so little about the maid child, our answers must be somewhat speculative, but in fact by adding the little girl in the garden, he invites such speculation about her role there.

What is a "mayde child"?

Some scholars have suggested that this maid child may be a female servant to the wife of Saint Denis.[5] The only evidence they usually offer involves quoting, out of context, lines that Sylvia L. Thrupp quotes from a fifteenth-century document about an arrangement that a merchant tailor made when he turned his business over to his son. The retiring tailor asks his son to provide, if requested, "an honest

[5] See, for example, the widely referenced explanatory note to lines VII 95–97 by J. A. Burrow and V. J. Scattergood in *The Riverside Chaucer*, 911: "Like other gentlewomen, merchants' wives sometimes had a girl to wait on them." The use of "other" seems to assume that the wife of the merchant of Saint Denis is a "gentlewoman," but she is not. She is of the merchant or middle class. See next note.

mayde chyld to wait upon my wife." We must, however, consider the quotation in the context that Thrupp provides. First, we should notice that Thrupp's quotation appears in the section of a chapter on the various "symbolic elements" by which medieval men and women demonstrated their prosperity—fancy clothes and furs, expensive jewelry, fine houses, and so on, including the ostentatious attendance of servants:

> Like a gentleman or a nobleman, a merchant considered it essential to his dignity and that of his wife be waited on. In order to demonstrate that they were in this happy position, the older people were accustomed to have a servant in attendance whenever they chose to go out. Among the demands made by a retired tailor on his son was that ". . . at all due tymes whan that I or my wyf walketh oute that my said sone shall late me have an honest man chyld to wayte upon me & an honest mayde chyld to wayte upon my wyf at his own propre coste yef we desire it:" The mercers, when they appeared on horseback at one of Edward IV's entries into the city, were each attended by "a clenly man or Childe," also mounted but dressed in black and russet instead of in red. Aldermen competed with each other in the number of attendants they brought to hold their gowns at civic ceremonies.[6]

In context, the "man chyld," the "maid chyld," and the "clenly . . . Childe" refer not to children at all but to adult servants who would in public appearances lend ostentatious dignity to someone who wanted to demonstrate his or her status. But that context does not fit the situation in the *Shipman's Tale.* We should remember that the wife of Saint Denis is not "walking out," as the bragging merchant wives in

[6] Sylvia L. Thrupp, *The Merchant Class of Medieval London* [1300–1500] (Chicago, 1948), 151 (ellipsis in original). Thrupp's notes, 149–51, give references to the documents she quotes. Note that the actual phrasing that Thrupp uses is "Like a gentleman or a nobleman, a merchant . . . ." Thrupp does not use the adjective "other." That adjective is mistakenly added by Burrow and Scattergood (see previous note).

Thrupp's citation do. Rather, she is strolling in her own private garden, where she needs no one to "wayte upon" her. Nor would she have any need to demonstrate her status to daun John, a repeated visitor to his friend's household who would have known pretty well how many servants there were, since he brought them gifts whenever he came:

> He noght forgat to yeve the leeste page
> In al that hous; but after hir degree,
> He yaf the lord, and sitthe al his meynee,
> Whan that he cam, som manere honest thyng.
> (VII 46–49)

The wife of Saint Denis could scarcely have fooled daun John with any show of ostentation by showing up with a servant pretending to serve her. More importantly, she would not have wanted to in the first place. After all, the merchant's wife's whole purpose in going into the garden is to appear poverty-stricken so that the monk will give her the hundred francs for clothing. The very last thing she would have wanted was to look prosperous by showing up with a serving maid who would appear to serve her. Besides, given the nature of her sex-business with the monk, the wife would scarcely have wanted any servants around to carry tales back to other servants or to her husband.

We should also note that the references to "mayde chyld" in Thrupp's quotation appear almost a century after Chaucer wrote the *Shipman's Tale.* The merchant tailor document is dated 1467, and Edward IV was king from 1461 to 1483. The meaning of the term "mayde child" may well have shifted by then away from the meaning it almost always had for Chaucer—a young person, not an adult servant.[7] The only other time he uses the term "a mayde child" is in the *Clerk's Tale*, in a context in which the term clearly refers to the young daughter of Griselda:

[7] The only possible exception is in the *Pardoner's Tale*, where one of the tavern rioters refers to the servant-lad as a child: "The child seith sooth" (VI 686). Even there, however, the meaning is ambiguous, since he is referred to earlier as a "knave" (VI 666) and a "boy" (VI 670). He is apparently quite young, in any case, and the word *child* is used in a context that suggests

> Nat longe tyme after that this Grisild
> Was wedded, she a doghter hath ybore,
> Al had hire levere have born a knave child;
> Glad was this markys and the folk therfore,
> For though *a mayde child* coome al bifore,
> She may unto a knave child atteyne
> By liklihede, syn she nys nat bareyne.
>
> (IV 442–48; italics added)

Line IV 446, as well as the immediate context of the phrase in the *Shipman's Tale*, suggests that the "mayde child" in the merchant's garden is the biological daughter of the wife of Saint Denis. In that context, the wife is said to have the power to "governe" and "gye" her and to keep her "under the yerde." A "yerde" was a whip that people used to discipline those in their care or under their authority. While a "yerde" was a physical rod or whip, the term seems to suggest in this context something more like "authority" or the right to correct with a view to improvement.[8] And while a wife might presumably have

"offspring" at least as much as "servant." Just before the taverner calls him a "child," the boy refers to having learned something from his mother, "my dame" (VI 684), and immediately after that the taverner—perhaps the boy's father?—reports that death has carried off "Bothe man and womman, child, and hyne, and page" (VI 688). In that line, the word "child" almost certainly refers to a young person in contrast to the immediately previous adult "man and womman." Susanna Fein helpfully suggests that the boy, as one of three truth-tellers in the tale, serves as an emblematic representative of youth: "The boy, taverner and old man derive from a familiar scheme for depicting man's times of life as three ages—Youth, Middle Age, and Age" ("Other Thought-Worlds," in Peter Brown, ed., *A Companion to Chaucer* [Oxford, 2000], 332–48, at 344). In other cases, at any rate, Chaucer usually uses the term *child* to refer to "offspring." I exclude, of course, the meaning of *child* as a noble young knight, as in the *Tale of Thopas*, VII 810, 817, etc. I should note, also, that the only meaning assigned to the term *maide child* in the *MED is* "female child" (s.v. *child*, item 13). The first meaning for *maid* in the *MED is* "an unmarried woman, usually young . . . a girl, a young girl." The third is "a maidservant, female attendant, lady in waiting." I am suggesting that the first meaning is appropriate in the context of the *Shipman's Tale*.

[8] The *MED*, s.v. *yerd* n. (2) gives as meaning 1a "a stick, pole, rod . . . a branch on a tree" and 1b "an instrument for inflicting pain or punishment; a club, cudgel . . . a flail or whip." There is no reason to think that the wife of Saint Denis beats her daughter. By contrast, the Parson

the power to whip a wayward servant, in this context the term seems more logically to refer to having the moral authority over her own child, whom she has the responsibility to "govern and gye." While it is possible that the woman in charge of a wealthy merchant household might have the power or the inclination to "guide" the maidservants in her house, would she be likely to use a whip or cudgel on them? On the other hand, she would surely have been expected to guide, and perhaps even hold the threat of a whip over, her own child. In any case, the notion of a mother's guiding her young is, as I will show below, important to the theme of the *Shipman's Tale.*

We should note that in the three lines we are considering, Chaucer uses the term "mayde" twice, once as an adjective and once as a noun. That is, he refers to the child not only as a "maid child" but also as "a maid." J. A. Burrow and V. J. Scattergood seem to assume that Chaucer in line VII 95 wrote "child maid" rather than "maid child," and that in line VII 97 the term *maid* refers to a "female servant" rather than to a "maiden." While the noun *maid* can refer to a servant girl, in Chaucer it almost never means that unless a pronoun

tells an anecdote about an impatient philosopher who brought a whip to punish a "child," his disciple. When the child saw the "yerde" he asked the philosopher what he was going to do with it. The philosopher said that he was going to "bete thee . . . for thy correccioun." The child then castigates the philosopher and says that "ye oghten first correcte youreself, that han lost al youre pacience for the gilt of a child." Realizing that the child is right about his impatience, the philosopher weeps, then gives the whip to the child and asks the child to correct him for that impatience (X 670–73). Several scholars see a bawdy pun in the reference in the *Shipman's Tale* to the "yerde," which can also mean "penis." Murray Copland, for example, says that the maid child "is governable ('under the yerde') only because she has not yet tasted the 'yerde' in the other sense" ("The *Shipman's Tale*: Chaucer and Boccaccio, *Medium Ævum* 35 [1966]: 11–28, at 22). Thomas W. Ross picks up on the idea by suggesting that perhaps "under the yerde" may mean that she is "too small for the 'yerde' (penis)"—a possibility that even he tells us is unlikely: "I doubt it" (*Chaucer's Bawdy* [New York, 1972], 240). Lee Patterson carries the pun even further by suggesting that there is double-punning, since "yerde" can refer both to "virgin" and to "penis," so that "the maid child thus invokes both an original innocence and the fact of its loss" (*Chaucer and the Subject of History* [Madison, 1991], 364–65). The so-called pun works here, however, only with unusual, and quite unnecessary, wrenching. The *MED* gives only as meaning 5 the possibility that *yerde* could mean "a penis . . . also, a foreskin, prepuce."

of possession precedes it, as in "our maid" or "her maid."[9] The noun *maid* used by itself is almost always a one-syllable synonym for *maiden* and refers to a girl or young woman before she has had sexual experience.

How old is the "mayde child" in Chaucer's tale?

We cannot be really precise about the age of the virginal maid child of Saint Denis, of course, because Chaucer is not more precise, but surely she is not a newborn. She is said, after all, to "come" into the garden with her mother, not be carried into it or pushed in a medieval pram of some sort. The fact that she is referred to as maid[en] suggests that Chaucer's audience may have thought of her as approaching the age of puberty and the possibility of sexual activity. She seems, then, to be not an infant but just what Chaucer calls her, a "child" For most medieval analysts, the age of seven marked the end of infancy and the start of childhood. In his *The Ages of Man*, Burrow discusses a number of medieval methods of dividing the various ages of "man" (usually meant, at least by implication, to include women, as well) into four, seven, or a dozen distinct "ages" or "seasons." Burrow translates thus the categorization of Hippocrates, an authority often consulted in medieval times: "In man's life there are seven seasons, which they call ages, little boy, boy, lad, young man, man, elderly man, old man. He is a little boy until he reaches seven years, the time of the shedding of his teeth; a boy until he reaches puberty, i.e. up to twice seven years." Burrow also translates from the eleventh-century *Elementarium Doctrinae Rudimentum*: "The first age of man, called infancy, lasts for seven years. The second age, called boyhood, lasts for another seven

[9] See, for example, the maid Gille in the *Miller's Tale*: "hir mayde" (I 3417) and "thy mayde" (I 3556). See also the maids referred to in the *Wife of Bath Prologue*: "hir owene mayde" (III 233) and "oure mayde" (III 241). The only exception I am aware of is in the *Franklin's Tale*, where Arveragus tells Dorigen to take "a squier and a mayde" with her to meet Aurelius (V 1487). The context makes clear that the maid is an adult servant. In none of these is the maid said to be a child.

up to fourteen. The third, extending two further sevens up to twenty-eight, is called adolescence."[10]

John McLaughlin has suggested, also, that seven is the age at which a young person ceases to be an infant and becomes a child, and twelve the age at which a female child becomes an adult.[11] If he is right, then our "mayde child" would be between seven and twelve. Splitting the difference, I am supposing—on admittedly tenuous evidence—that the maid child in the *Shipman's Tale* is perhaps around ten. She seems to me, in any event, younger than the age of Virginia, the more famous young maiden in the *Canterbury Tales*: "This mayde of age twelve yeer was and tweye" (VI 30). At fourteen, Virginia is the object of a man's lust. Because the monk in the *Shipman's Tale* lusts not for the maid child but for her mother, I am imagining the maid child in the garden as somewhat younger than that—old enough to be thought of as a maiden but young enough to be thought of as still a child—in short, a "mayde child."

Why does Chaucer put the maid child in the garden scene? Most scholars who write about the *Shipman's Tale* say nothing about the character or function of the maid child. Of those who do, there is little consistency of interpretation. Some, indeed, see her as a mistake,

[10] J. A. Burrow, *The Ages of Man: A Study in Medieval Writing and Thought* (Oxford, 1988), 38 and 85.

[11] I am in possession of a copy of a paper that Professor John McLaughlin, then of East Stroudsburg State University, gave orally at the Medieval Forum in Plymouth, New Hampshire, in April of 1997. The unpublished paper was entitled "Medieval Child Marriage: Abuse of Wardship?" The relevant quotation is: "By 'child' in this context is meant a male or female human being above the age of seven—for either gender—and below the age of fourteen for males, and twelve for females. This follows medieval canon law, in recognizing these as the limits of infancy and puberty, below which the infant could not give meaningful consent, and above which the person was no longer a child" (quoted with his kind permission). McLaughlin cites several authorities, of which these three are most relevant: Frances and Joseph Gies, *Marriage and the Family in the Middle Ages* (New York, 1987), 139–40; Christopher N. L. Brooke, *The Medieval Idea of Marriage* (Oxford, 1991), 137–38; and James A. Brundage, *Law, Sex, and Christian Society in Medieval Europe* (Chicago, 1987), 238.

an unrevised Chaucerian or scribal flaw.[12] Others see her as a kind of chaperon to the wife,[13] or as a sign of the merchant's ostentatious opulence,[14] or as proof of the merchant's virility,[15] or as a way of emphasizing, by contrast with her young innocence, the corruption

[12] Hazel Sullivan refers to the maid child as "useless cast" and sees her as evidence that a tampering scribe carelessly "patched" the three lines on the maid child in from a totally different story ("A Chaucerian Puzzle," in Natalie Grimes Lawrence and Jack A. Reynolds, eds., *A Chaucerian Puzzle and Other Medieval Essays* [Coral Gables, FL, 1961], 9). T. W. Craik thinks that the maid child, though she adds "piquancy to a situation which she is too young to understand . . . seems superfluous, for the mood of the meeting is clear without her, and at its end she has simply vanished" (*The Comic Tales of Chaucer* [New York, 1964], 56). Nevill Coghill calls her "a distracting irrelevance" ("Chaucer's Narrative Art in the *Canterbury Tales*" in Derek Brewer, ed., *Chaucer and Chaucerian: Critical Studies in Middle English Literature* [Tuscaloosa, AL: Alabama University Press, 1966], 114–27, at 126). Trevor Whittock finds that the three lines on the maid child may provide "the occasion for [the Physician's] outburst on the upbringing of children" near the start of the *Physician's Tale*: "The Physician would be offended by the notion of such a scheming woman as this being a guide and model to an innocent child" (*A Reading of the Canterbury Tales* [Cambridge, U.K., 1968], 195). Carol F. Heffernan, taking the child to be a "young maid servant," speculates that she is a non-functional "vestigial remnant of the extra character that Boccaccio includes in his plot: the witness present when the financial arrangements are concluded" ("Chaucer's *Shipman's Tale* and Boccaccio's *Decameron* 8.1: Retelling a Story" in Keith Busby and Erik Kooper, eds., *Courtly Literature: Culture and Context* [Amsterdam, 1990], 261–70, at 262).

[13] Craik calls her "a sort of innocent chaperon" (*The Comic Tales*, 56), a notion that Ross apparently picks up on by calling her a "little chaperon" (*Chaucer's Bawdy*, 240). It is difficult to see how the term applies in the *Shipman's Tale,* however, since a chaperon is usually an older person who supervises the behavior of younger people. It may be that the wife and monk *need* a chaperon, but the young girl does not *act* as one since the monk and wife behave in her presence with considerable freedom. If by "chaperon" we mean that her presence in the garden lends a measure of credibility or legitimacy to the wife's being there, I would find less objection. I can imagine the wife's replying, if questioned by the monk about what she is doing in the garden, something like, "Who, me? Oh, nothing. I just thought I'd take little Nellie for a stroll to look at the lovely flowers. We had no idea we'd find anyone else out so early. And what brings you here, cousin John?"

[14] V. J. Scattergood, taking the maid child to be the "personal servant" of the merchant's wife, finds that she appears in the story "simply as another dimension of the opulence of this particular merchant household" ("The Originality of the *Shipman's Tale*," *Chaucer Review* 11 [1977]: 210–31, at 213). I argue above that the wife of Saint Denis would absolutely not want at this point to appear opulent. On the contrary, she would want to appear to be the poverty-stricken victim of a niggardly husband, and thus in need of money from the monk.

of the wife and the monk,[16] or as a morally endangered witness to Chaucer's reenactment of the Fall of Man in the Garden of Eden.[17] Most recently, Karla Taylor sees the maid child as "presumably uncomprehending" of what really happens between the wife of Saint Denis and daun John in the garden: "she is present to stress the divide between a proper conversation, whose meaning is open to all, and the furtive exchange whose meaning is closed to her." Taylor sees her as "a child below the age of reason" and speaks of her "linguistic incomprehension." Taylor argues that the little girl may perhaps grasp

[15] For a discussion of other evidence of the husband's virility than the mere fact that he has fathered a child, see my "Contrasting Masculinities in the *Shipman's Tale*: Monk, Merchant, Wife," reprinted in this volume, pp. 144–60.

[16] Gail McMurray Gibson finds that the maid child "emphasizes the defiled innocence of the meeting and of its garden setting" ("Resurrection as Dramatic Icon in the *Shipman's Tale*," in John P. Hermann and John J. Burke Jr., eds., *Signs and Symbols in Chaucer's Poetry* [Tuscaloosa, AL: Alabama University Press, 1981], 102–12, at 109). In Gibson's exegetical reading, the child suggests the "Resurrection pattern as well, an allusion to 'the other Mary,' who in the Gospel and in the liturgical Easter dramas accompanied Mary Magdalen to Christ's sepulcher" (109). Surely, however, this last is too much freight of meaning for the young maiden, in this context, to bear. Patterson finds the maid child to be "an innocent foil to the sordid transactions to which she is a witness" (*Chaucer and the Subject of History*, 363). Copland suggests that "merely by reason of her sex, the girl is bound to follow in her mother's footsteps sooner or later" ("The *Shipman's Tale*," 22).

[17] Lorraine Kochanske Stock sees in the garden scene an iconographic replay of the temptation scene in the Garden of Eden, with "the monk as tempter, the wife as Eve, and the merchant as a hapless medieval Adam" ("The Reenacted Fall in Chaucer's *Shipman's Tale*," *Studies in Iconography* 7–8 [1981–82]: 135–45, at 143). I am skeptical of Stock's reading of the garden scene. The very presence of a child in the garden is strong evidence against it, since there was no such child in Eden. I am more impressed with Stock's notion that the *Roman de la Rose*, in which la Vieille serves as a guide to younger women, may have provided Chaucer with at least a rough parallel to "a young, innocent girl, who learns from the older woman—through lectures or through direct example—a variety of the tricks of the trade of love" ("La Vieille and the Merchant's Wife in Chaucer's *Shipman's Tale*," *Southern Humanities Review* 16 [1982]: 333–39, at 335). I should note, however, C. David Benson's suggestion that the language of the wife and the monk is sufficiently ambiguous that "the 'mayde child,' who apparently is a witness to the entire exchange . . . would have no reasons for suspicion" (*Chaucer's Drama of Style* [Chapel Hill, NC, 1986], 109). I am less interested in the maid child's suspicion of her mother than in her gaining worldly knowledge from her mother.

in a general way "the sexual meaning of the exchange, although I think this is open to debate. What is not debatable is the incapacity of the 'mayde child' to comprehend its illicitness, which emerges only from a verbal texture designed to hide it behind a facade of propriety."[18]

I remain unconvinced by these views of the character and function of the maid child. I propose, on the contrary, that the wife of Saint Denis takes her daughter with her to educate her—to teach her, to "guide" her—about how to get along in a world in which all decks are stacked against women and wives. It is a world in which most women are dependent on their fathers or their husbands for their economic viability, not to mention for their sexual activity.

Surely it is not just by chance that the wife encounters the monk daun John in the garden. He is, after all, a frequent visitor to her house, and she must know that she will find him alone there in the early morning saying his devotions (his "thynges," VII 91). Knowing that her husband is in his counting house, she goes "pryvely / Into the gardyn, there he walketh softe, / And hym saleweth, as she hath doon ofte" (VII 92–94). Surely she knows, since she has been there often, who she will find in the garden once again, and surely she knows before she goes this time the precise nature of her business with him.

Just as surely, she need not have taken her daughter with her. The plot requires no such daughter, and she plays no role as a witness. As for bringing her along because she has no daycare for her daughter, the merchant's household has a large retinue of hired staff. As we have

[18] Karla Taylor, "Social Aesthetics and the Emergence of Civic Discourse from the *Shipman's Tale* to *Melibee*," *Chaucer Review* 39 (2005): 298–322, at 305. I have no objection to Taylor's doubting that the maid child would have missed the subtle French-English sexual wordplay she finds in the garden scene (I missed it myself!). But the maid child could scarcely have missed the main thrust of the garden exchange, including her mother's complaints about her husband, her profession of love for the monk following his for her, her request for money in exchange for "pleasance and service" (VII 191), the agreement to meet again when the husband is out of town, the kisses, and the flanks-grab. The maid child's understanding of all that is the heart of the matter: she needs to be able to comprehend and learn from what she is observing.

seen, daun John is said to bring gifts to the merchant's large domestic staff ("al his meynee" [VII 48]). The wife in a wealthy merchant household with a large staff could surely have left her daughter with a servant during her short visit to the monk in the garden. But, no, she brings her maid child along with her.

And having brought her along, she is not said to send her daughter off to play alone while she conducts her illicit business with the monk. Nor is there any evidence that she whispers that business in her talk with the monk. On the contrary, and apparently with her daughter listening, the wife of Saint Denis gets down to business almost immediately by complaining of her husband's sexual neglect of her and of his general stinginess and inadequacy as a husband. Surely we are to think that she *wants* her daughter to observe her.

Why would the wife of Saint Denis want such a thing? I suggest that she wants to teach her daughter the ways a woman can get what she needs in the world. Scholars have focused on the immorality of the wife of Saint Denis, the fact that she sets such a negative example to her maid child by allowing her to witness her seductive ways. Those seductive ways include her overtly sexual deal-making, her allowing the monk to clutch her by the flanks, her hard embrace, and her kisses. If this young maiden needs a lesson in how to seduce a man, how to cheat on a husband, how to conceal and then pay off secret debts for fancy clothes, how to elicit sympathy by threatening suicide, surely she could have found no better teacher than her own mother. And her mother knows it. As her daughter approaches the age of sexual possibility and of marriage, the wife of Saint Denis apparently thinks—and why should she not?—that it is time to initiate her into the ways of a woman with a man.

I realize that my answer is somewhat speculative, and that the wife of Saint Denis never says to her maid child, "Watch me, my dear daughter, and you'll learn some valuable lessons that will help you when you get a little older." Indeed, we might wish that Chaucer had made clearer his reasons for inserting the three lines that are original in his version of the tale and for introducing into the garden a young girl who appears at first blush—or failure to blush—to play no function in the tale. I believe, however, that the motives of the wife in taking the child with her would have been clearer in the tale as it was originally presented and told by a different teller.

There is little reason why the Shipman would tell this tale of the lover's gift regained at all. The piratical sea-captain seems far removed from this domestic comedy of inland France. Why would this man, who presumably deals with merchants all the time in various seaports, care much about the illicit doings of merchants' wives in Saint Denis or the immorality of oversexed Parisian monks? Indeed, virtually all scholars agree that the tale of lechery in Saint Denis was not written for the Shipman at all, but rather almost certainly for the Wife of Bath.

Every reader of the *Shipman's Tale* has had to come to terms with the opening section in which the narrator of the tale uses personal pronouns that can refer only to a wife:

> The sely housbonde, algate he moot paye,
> He moot *us* clothe, and he moot us arraye,
> Al for his owene worshipe richely,
> In which array *we* daunce jolily.
>
> . . . . .
>
> Thanne moot another payen for *oure* cost,
> Or lene *us* gold, and that is perilous.
>
> (VII 11–14, 18–19; italics added)

While a few scholars have attempted to make sense of such lines as suitable to a male teller, they have failed, and the mass of scholars now accept the obvious: that the lines are unrevised evidence that what was later assigned to the Shipman was originally written for the Wife of Bath,[19] the only Canterbury pilgrim in whose mouth they

[19] See, for example, Frederick Tupper, "The Bearings of the Shipman's Prologue; *Journal of English and Germanic Philology* 33 (1934): 352–72; and Robert L. Chapman, "The *Shipman's Tale* Was Meant for the Shipman," *Modern Language Notes* 71 (1965): 4–5. William W. Lawrence's rejoinder to Chapman is still worth reading ("The Wife of Bath and the Shipman," *Modern Language Notes* 71 [1957]: 87–88). This is not the place for a thoroughgoing stylistic

make any sense. Previous scholars, however, have not reflected on the meaning of Chaucer's having added the maid child to a tale told by the Wife of Bath.

Why does it matter that Chaucer wrote the *Shipman's Tale* for the Wife of Bath?

To the Wife of Bath, herself initiated at age twelve into the business of marriage, it could not have seemed too early for a medieval merchant's wife to begin training her own young virginal daughter into the ways of women with their men. The Wife of Bath is, after all, very much on record about matters of concern to young virgins entering puberty. One of those matters, of course, is the whole question of virginity, a condition Alisoun of Bath would much rather talk about than have.

Indeed, far from being troubled that her young maid child may, before long, find it necessary to give up her virginity, the Wife of Bath would almost surely approve of her discovering as early as possible how to use her sexuality to her own economic and emotional advantage. After all, the Wife of Bath speaks of envying not Jesus or Saint Paul, who were virgins, but Solomon, who was refreshed with seven hundred wives and three hundred concubines. She speaks with envy not of being a virgin again but of being "refresshed half so ofte" (III 38) as Solomon.

We should remember that the Wife of Bath learned much practical wisdom from her own mother: "My dame taughte me that soutiltee" (III 576); "I folwed ay my dames loore" (III 583). Having learned so much about managing husbands and other men from her mother, how could she do anything but approve of the special training that the wife of Saint Denis was providing to her daughter during the

comparison of the language, theme, and tone of the *Shipman's Tale* with the prologue and tale of the Wife of Bath, but my own preliminary comparisons suggest that the manner in which the wife of Saint Denis tricks her husband and her husband's best friend into letting her have her way and her fine clothes sounds downright Alisounian.

garden scene? We have no evidence that Alisoun had any children of her own, but it is easy enough to imagine that if she had a daughter, she would want to teach her some of what her own mother had taught her. The Wife of Bath speaks often of how "wise" women behave: "A wys womman wol bisye hire evere in oon / To gete hire love" (III 209–10), "A wys wyf, if that she kan hir good, / Shal beren hym on honde the cow is wood" (III 231–32), and "This knoweth every womman that is wys" (III 524; see also III 224–30). How do women gain their wisdom? Certainly not by authority, for that comes entirely from clerks and other men who have no interest in letting women be wise. Rather, they gain wisdom through their own "experience" (III 1) and through instruction from other women of experience. Surely the Wife of Bath would have seen the presence of the maid child at the seduction scene in the garden not as a piece of immorality on the part of the girl's mother, but rather as among the most responsible lessons that a mother could give to a girl on the verge of, and perhaps already feeling the natural urges and curiosities of, puberty.

And what would those lessons have been? In the garden scene the maid child would have learned how to make a man take an interest in her; how to tread the delicate line between flirtation and serious seduction-planning; how to complain to a potential lover about her husband; how to pick up on signals of lecherous interest from a supposedly celibate cleric; how to gain a pledge of secrecy from a man; how to gain advantage by threatening suicide; how to get a man to risk for her a long friendship with his best friend; how to lead a man into giving her a hundred francs by offering him in exchange sexual "plesance and service" (VII 191). She would have learned about two kinds of kissing, at first in a cousinly manner (VII 141) and soon after in a lecherous (if not downright treacherous) manner (VII 203); she would have learned to recite a list of what *she* likes in a man—particularly generosity, obedience, and freshness "abedde" (VII 176–77); she would have learned that most men are slaves to their sex drives and that a woman can harness those drives for her own benefit; she would have learned that sex can for women be a barter commodity. The maid child would have learned, in short, that a woman can use her beauty, her youth, her sexuality, her boldness, her cleverness, and her words—particularly her bold and clever words—to get a man to give her whatever she wants or thinks she deserves.

To be sure, these are all lessons that a misogynist male might list as the typical wiles of evil women. There are, after all, some fairly broad antifeminist strokes in the *Shipman's Tale.* It is relevant here to consider a scene in Boccaccio's *The Corbaccio,* written in the mid-1350s. *The Corbaccio* (the word can be translated as "old crow" or "evil crow") is a dream-vision in which the narrator, spurned by the woman he thinks he loves, is visited by the ghost of that woman's former husband. This husband-spirit tells the narrator, in one of the most viciously and graphically misogynist treatises ever written, just how awful his former wife was, and that he is well shut of her. In one of his many antifeminist tirades, the spirit tells the narrator that, like his former wife, all women delight in jabbering on without any knowledge as if they know everything, and that they insist on teaching their nasty tricks to their own daughters. I give here a few sentences to suggest the tone of the passage before quoting the couple of sentences about what women teach their daughters:

> Women, even if they remain in church one morning just long enough to hear Mass, know how the firmament turns; how many stars there are in the sky and how big they are; what the course of the sun and the planets is; how thunder, lightning, hail, rainbows, and other things are created in the air; how the sea ebbs and flows, and how the land produces fruit. They know what is going on in India and Spain; how the homes of the Ethiopians are made, and where the source of the Nile is found; and whether crystal is generated in the north from ice or from something else; with whom their neighbor slept; by whom that other woman is pregnant and in what month she is to give birth; and how many lovers that other has, and who sent her the ring and who the belt; and how many eggs the neighbor's hen lays a year; and how many spindles she uses to spin an ounce of linen; and, in brief, they return fully informed about all that the Trojans or the Greeks or the Romans ever

> did. If they cannot find anyone else to lend them an ear, they chatter incessantly with the maid, the baker's wife, the green-grocer's wife, or the washerwoman, and become greatly put out if they are reproved for talking to any of them.
>
> It is true that from this so sudden and divinely inspired knowledge of theirs springs an excellent doctrine for their daughters. They teach them all how to rob their husbands, how to receive love letters and how to answer them, how to bring their lovers into the house, how to feign illness so that their husbands will leave the bed free for them, and many other evils. He who believes that any mother delights in having a daughter more honest or virtuous than herself is a fool.[20]

Whether or not Chaucer knew Boccaccio's *Corbaccio*, the two writers share an interest in the way mature women share the purposes and methods of sexual infidelities with their daughters. Chaucer's treatment of that theme in the *Shipman's Tale* is less openly satirical and critical of women than Boccaccio's, but that may be because the tale was originally written for a female teller who was less hostile to women than the deceased husband of the title character in *The Corbaccio.*

In the mouth of a medieval shipman, the merchant's wife's taking her young daughter with her into her garden of infidelity seems like the rankest irrelevance or irresponsibility. But from the mouth of the Wife of Bath, who is a professional at pleasing men and thus getting them to please her, lessons about how a woman can not only survive European patriarchy but also thrive in it were vital. And if a young daughter can learn those lessons at her mother's knee, so much the better. I do not insist that Chaucer wants us to approve of the pedagogical motives that must have led the wife of the merchant of Saint Denis to bring her maid child into the garden with her. But I do

[20] Trans. Anthony K. Cassell, in Giovanni Boccaccio, *The Corbaccio or The Labyrinth of Love*, 2nd edn. (Binghamton, NY, 1993), 30–31.

think that Chaucer wants us to think that the Wife of Bath would have lent her own tacit approval to those motives. A tale approving such motives is quite in character for such a woman. And if Alisoun would approve of the wife of Saint Denis's bringing her maid child into the garden of knowledge with her, perhaps some of her auditors would have seen in the tale reason to nod in approval of this clever wife who wants not only what is good for herself, but also what may be best for her daughter.

One final question: what are the implications of the word "govern" in VII 96: "Which as hir list she may governe and gye"? The word is usually taken to have something like its modern political meaning of *govern*: "to rule, to control, to manage," Sometimes govern does have such a meaning for Chaucer. Here, in conjunction with "gye" or guide, however, it may well mean something like "teach," as in the now almost-defunct term *governess*, "a teacher or tutor." We should notice that this meaning is suggested in the Physician's injunction to women who have the care of daughters of lords:

> And ye maistresses, in youre olde lyf,
> That lordes doghtres han in *governaunce,*
> Ne taketh of my wordes no displesaunce.
> Thenketh that ye been set in *governynges*
> Of lordes doghtres
>
> . . . . .
>
> therfore, for Cristes sake,
> To *teche* hem vertu looke that ye ne slake.
>
> . . . . .
>
> Ye fadres and ye moodres eek also,
> Though ye han children, be it oon or mo,
> Youre is the charge of al hir surveiaunce,
> Whil that they been under youre *governaunce.*
>
> (VI 72-76, 81-82, 93-96; italics added)

Of course, the Physician's ideas of what principles ought to be taught to the young maiden-daughters of lords are different from those that the wives of Saint Denis and of Bath would teach to the maiden-daughters of the merchant class, but it seems clear that for all three the meaning of *governing* in the context of raising young maidens was very close to "teaching."

Neither the Wife of Bath nor the wife of Saint Denis created the world in which they and other middle-class women had to function. But for both women, for a mother to teach her young daughter how to maneuver in that world is less base immorality than base necessity. The wife of Saint Denis is not corrupting her child but educating her, acting as her governess and guide. Unlike the unfaithful mothers of "The Man Who Kicked the Stone" and *Decameron* 7.3, who show no interest in giving moral or practical education to their sons, the wife of Saint Denis takes seriously her responsibility as a mother who needs to teach, by her own example, her vulnerable young daughter.

The Climax in the *Merchant's Tale*

[I am now somewhat embarrassed by this early article in which I brashly took on a scholar named Emerson Brown, Jr. In 1968, having just completed my dissertation on the *Merchant's Tale* and taken my Ph.D., I felt myself to be the world's authority on the tale of January, May, and Damian. Then in 1970 Emerson Brown's article appeared in the *Chaucer Review*. In it Brown argued that Damian does not achieve sexual climax with May in the pear tree. I shot off this refutation. I stand by my conclusions but wish I had adopted a more conciliatory tone. I later met Emerson Brown and was pleased to contribute an essay to a festschrift in his honor (see pp. 55–71 above). "The Climax in the *Merchant's Tale*" first appeared in *Chaucer Review* 6 (1971): 38–43.]

I find unconvincing the suggestion, made a year ago in these pages by Emerson Brown, Jr., that in the *Merchant's Tale* Damian "does not bring his arboreal activity with May to a completely satisfactory conclusion."[1] Brown, challenging the traditional interpretation of the final scene, believes that Damian is interrupted by January before he has achieved sexual climax in his lovemaking with May. Because

[1] "*Hortus Inconclusus*: The Significance of Priapus and Pyramus and Thisbe in the *Merchant's Tale,*" *Chaucer Review* 4 (1970): 34. Subsequent page references to Brown's article will be included within parentheses in the text. All quotations from Chaucer are cited from F. N. Robinson, ed., *The Works of Geoffrey Chaucer,* 2nd edn. (Boston: Houghton Mifflin, 1957).

Brown's arguments, based on two allusions within the tale, on Chaucer's changes from his sources, and on the Merchant's own supposed attitudes and personal background, lead him to a conclusion that seems to be out of step with Chaucer's emphases in the tale, I should like to discuss the validity of those arguments.

Brown argues that in alluding to Priapus (E 2034–37) Chaucer not only reinforces the carnal function of garden, but also calls attention to a specific parallelism between Priapus and Damian: just as Priapus was interrupted by the braying of Silenus's ass and frustrated in his attempt to sexually enjoy Lotis, so Damian, by implication, when interrupted by January, is frustrated in his attempt to complete the sex act with May. This use of allusion to clarify an inexplicit element of Chaucer's plot is at best inconclusive, at worst invalid and misleading. The reliability of the method as applied in individual cases must depend on the number and weight of the parallels between the creature alluded to and the person in the tale whose actions are allegedly clarified by the allusion. In the case under consideration the parallels are rather unimpressive. Damian and Priapus are both perhaps young (though Priapus is not universally depicted as young, and Chaucer makes no mention of his age), and both are lustful and quick to fall in love; but then, many would fit that description. On the other hand, Damian is different from Priapus in many ways. For one thing, he lacks (apparently) the phallic deity's major physical characteristic. For another, their situations are quite different. Priapus wished to ravish an unwilling maiden; Damian's May is neither a maiden nor unwilling—indeed, far from being raped, she herself arranges the arboreal meeting with Damian. Priapus's encounter takes place on the ground and at night, Damian's in a tree on a bright and clear morning. Priapus is discovered by many people before he even begins to sexually enjoy Lotis, and is laughed at by them; Damian is discovered by only *one* person, who does *not* laugh at him, and that *after* he has begun the sexual act with May. I wonder, then, whether it is accurate to refer to Damian as a man "whose circumstances parallel those of Priapus" (34), and whether it is acceptable to see Priapus's sexual frustration (a frustration not specifically referred to in the tale) as evidence for Damian's.

Brown finds additional support for his view of Damian's sexual frustration in Chaucer's allusion to Pyramus and Thisbe (E 2125–31). The most obvious reason for this allusion is the parallel it offers to May and Damian's efforts to foil January: when something keeps them apart, lovers will find a way to get together anyway. The allusion to Pyramus and Thisbe may also convey an implied contrast between the true love of the classical lovers and the adulterous lust of Damian and May. Brown, however, suggests further implications in the allusion: just as the careful plans of Pyramus and Thisbe are finally frustrated, so also are the careful plans of Damian and May, and Chaucer means to indicate by the allusion that Damian is interrupted before he can complete the act of copulation with May. Here again, however, the parallels seem to be insufficient to convey such implications. Pyramus is noble, Damian ignoble. Thisbe is pure, May impure. Thisbe is the victim of her father's, not her husband's, imprisonment. Her love, unlike May's lust, is never consummated, for she and her lover both die violently. Damian and May are different in character and situation from Pyramus and Thisbe, and act out their roles in a much different plot. There seems little reason to suppose that Chaucer's allusion conveys any special information about their sexual encounter.

A second argument that Brown advances in support of his view that Damian's copulation with May is interrupted concerns the length of time elapsing between the beginning of the intercourse and January's anguished interruption of it. The length of time is not specified, but it does appear to have been rather short. Brown is right to remind us that the "completion of the affair is by no means a foregone conclusion" (36). The apparent shortness of the available time, however, does not make the frustration of the affair a foregone conclusion either. After all, that "cursed monk, daun Constantyn" (E 1810), tells us that some men, those with "warm and dry organs," for example, "will be very lusty" and "will also have an excessive desire for intercourse and will finish quickly."[2] We know nothing, of course, about the condition of Damian's organs, and it is idle to speculate about his speed in lovemaking. My point is simply that we should not try to draw conclusions about his success or failure in the pear tree on the basis of the length of time he apparently spends in it with May.

At first glance Brown's study of the analogues to the *Merchant's Tale* seems to support his view, for he finds that Chaucer has shortened the time the lovers spend in the fruit tree before the interruption. In the analogues the supernatural interveners begin their conversation while the lovers are enjoying each other, and so the copulation is permitted to go on while they talk. Chaucer, however, has Pluto and Proserpina discuss the affair before the wife even climbs the tree. Then, later, when they actually view the outrage in the branches, they have already decided their course of action and can act immediately, without further talking. Now, it is quite true that Chaucer is unique in his pre-positioning of the divine conversation, and that as a result of this the time spent in the tree appears to have been shortened a bit from what it was in the "Class A" analogues.[3] We need not necessarily conclude, however, that Chaucer rearranged the events in the garden scene to frustrate Damian by giving him insufficient time to conclude

[2] The *De Coitu* has been conveniently translated by Paul Delany in *Chaucer Review* 4 (1970): 55–65. I quote from p. 58.

[3] I refer to Germaine Dempster's useful subdivision of the analogues in *Sources and Analogues of Chaucer's Canterbury Tales,* ed. W. F. Bryan and Germaine Dempster (New York: Humanities Press, 1941), 341–56. Brown compares Chaucer's tale only with the Class A analogues; in the Class B analogues, a version of which Chaucer might have known, or in an "optical illusion" story such as *Decameron* 7.9, which Chaucer might also have known, the time spent in the act of copulation is no longer than it is in Chaucer. In the Class B analogues, for example, there is no divine conversation at all. The husband hears noises in the tree over his head, correctly suspects foul play, and asks a deity to restore his sight so that he can make sure. The deity immediately does so.

his act with May. Perhaps he rearranged them, for example, so that the leisurely divine conversation, seven times longer in Chaucer than it is in any of the analogues, is much less intrusive than it would have been if Chaucer had allowed it to take place *during* the copulation itself. Or perhaps Chaucer's rearrangement was made to provide a dramatic irony absent from the analogues. Because in his version the conversation takes place before May climbs the tree, Chaucer's audience knows in advance that Damian and May will couple ("his owene man shal make hym cokewold" [E 2256]), that January will see them ("he shal have ayen his eyen syght" [E 2260]), and that May will talk her way out of her difficulty ("I shal yeven hire suffisant answere" [E 2266]). I am suggesting, then, that Chaucer may have rearranged the garden scene for larger and more artistic reasons than simply to deprive Damian of his moment of ecstasy.

Brown's third argument for Damian's final frustration is based on his interpretation of the fictional narrator's attitudes. The Merchant, Brown feels, is so bitter and enraged that he would not permit any of his characters to be successful: "given the bitterness the Merchant obviously feels towards all the parties involved in the tale he is telling, would he be likely to present the pear tree episode as ending successfully for anyone?" (37–38). Perhaps not, but arguments based on an interpretation of the feelings of the teller of a tale, rather than on direct evidence in the tale itself, can be accepted only with great caution.[4] Even, however, if we grant Brown the right to let the supposed attitudes of the Merchant influence his reading of the tale, and agree with what he feels to be the Merchant's "obvious" bitterness

[4] A number of scholars, indeed, believe that we have no right to read the tale as the "dramatic" performance of the Merchant, for the tale is really *Chaucer's*, and should be read and reacted to as such. See, for example, Bertrand H. Bronson, "Afterthoughts on the *Merchant's Tale*," *Studies in Philology* 58 (1961): 583–96; Robert M. Jordan, "The Non-Dramatic Disunity of the *Merchant's Tale*," *PMLA* 78 (1963): 293–99; and T. W. Craik, *The Comic Tales of Chaucer* (London: Methuen, 1964), 133–53.

toward all the characters in his tale (even toward Justinus?), does not the story itself refute Brown's contention that the Merchant would not let the pear-tree episode end successfully for anyone? Surely it ends successfully for May. She has her ready answer and she triumphs over her husband. She has lost nothing in the pear tree and has gained both the physical solace of her lover (with the implicit promise of many happy returns) and the increased gratitude and trust of her husband. If the Merchant will let the episode end so triumphantly for May, then why would he be reluctant to permit Damian his little success also?

Brown suggests that there may be a special reason for the Merchant's animosity toward Damian: "it would surely be inconsistent with his sustained bitterness and rage for the Merchant to have presented Januarie's 'hoomly foo' as succeeding in the game at which he himself, presumably, had failed" (36–37). We are to believe that the Merchant's own personality and background are such that he would take the events in his tale personally and would foist off his own frustrations onto his characters. Because the Merchant has been frustrated in his game of physical lovemaking, he will, like a jealous child who cannot have a piece of candy, frustrate his characters also. But what evidence is there that the Merchant has been frustrated in his personal attempts at lovemaking? We know that after two months of married life he is unhappy with marriage and that he considers his wife to be a cursed shrew, but we know nothing whatever about his sex life, and we have no reason to "presume" that he has proved a failure in the game of physical love. Such guesses and impressions about the character and personal experience of the Merchant can scarcely be said to carry much weight as evidence for Damian's failure to achieve a climax in the pear tree.

Are we left, then, with the traditional interpretation—that Damian *does* finish his act in the pear tree? Not quite. Brown's article is valuable in that it forces us to reexamine our assumptions about the climactic scene in the *Merchant's Tale.* Many of us, myself included, had too quickly accepted Milton Miller's suggestion, published twenty years ago, about January's heir.[5] Acting on the assumption that Damian did finish before he was interrupted, Miller suggested that he could have made May pregnant in the pear tree, with the resulting exquisite irony that January's goods would after all fall "in straunge hand" (E 1440). If we are cautious about accepting Brown's arguments that Damian did not achieve sexual climax, and so could not have impregnated May, we must be equally cautious about accepting arguments that he did finish and did impregnate her. Only Damian knows whether he finished, and he is not talking. How, then, can we pretend to know whether he did, any more than we can pretend to know, for example, what contraceptive precautions he or May might have taken?

The point is that there are some things Chaucer chose not to tell us about the characters in the *Merchant's Tale.* It seems logical to assume that he had good reasons for not telling us these things. I would suggest, for example, that he does not tell us precisely how finally successful Damian's coital encounter with May is because the degree of success is irrelevant to his chief purpose in the tale: to tell about January. The *Merchant's Tale* is the "tale of Januarie" (E 2417), not the tale of May, or the tale of Damian. What matters in that final scene is not whether May *really is* pregnant, but that January thinks she is. What matters is not whether Damian *technically* completes the act of intercourse, but that January is deservedly cuckolded, and that he himself witnesses that cuckolding. January's folly is that he sees what he wants to see, rather than what is actually before him. As critics, we must guard against sharing that folly.

[5] "The Heir in the *Merchant's Tale*," *Philological Quarterly* 29 (1950): 437–40. Miller's suggestion, of course, may still be valid as a strictly conditional one: *if* May really is pregnant by the end of the tale as January believes she is, the father of the child *may* be Damian rather than January.

Chaucer's *Merchant's Tale* and the *Decameron*

[The *Merchant's Tale* of the decrepit old January's marriage to the frisky young May is one of Chaucer's most original stories. Its originality lies not in Chaucer's having made it up out of his own raw imagination but in his having combined so many different sources into a tapestry so rich that it is, finally, not really like any of its many contributory threads. This article, derived in part from my doctoral dissertation on the relationship between the *Merchant's Tale* and its disgruntled teller, is the first of my publications in which I argue—rather too cautiously, perhaps—specifically for Chaucer's knowledge of Boccaccio's *Decameron*. Neither the story of Nicostrato and Lydia in *Decameron* 7.9 nor the story of Ricciardo and Bartolomea in *Decameron* 2.10 was mentioned, let alone printed, in the first (1941) *Sources and Analogues of Chaucer's Canterbury Tales*. I am pleased to note that both of them, in the original Italian and in English translation, are presented prominently in the second (2005) *Sources and Analogues*. "Chaucer's *Merchant's Tale* and the *Decameron*" first appeared in *Italica* 50 (1973): 266–84.]

Chaucerians have for many years wondered whether Chaucer may have been influenced by Boccaccio's *Decameron.* The evidence has not been strong enough to convince most of them that he was, and so negative arguments have largely prevailed: Chaucer could not have come across a copy of the *Decameron* in England; he never mentions the *Decameron* in any of his writings; he has not borrowed any of his own tales directly from the one hundred tales of Boccaccio. Counter arguments have been largely ignored: Chaucer might well have heard of the *Decameron*, since it was written by the man from whom he borrowed more than he borrowed from any other writer, and he might well have availed himself of a copy on one of his diplomatic journeys to Italy; Chaucer fails to mention many of his sources, such as Boccaccio's *Teseida*, his acknowledged source for the *Knight's Tale*, or Boccaccio's *Filostrato*, his source for *Troilus and Criseyde*, and so we should not attach any particular significance to his failure to mention Boccaccio's *Decameron*; while it is true that Chaucer did not borrow any complete tales directly from the *Decameron*, we do find evidence that he may have incorporated certain details from it into the *Canterbury Tales.* These details, found frequently as additions to or alterations of more primary sources, might well have been recalled from an earlier reading of the *Decameron.*

Evidence of borrowing

This is not the place for a review of all of the evidence for Chaucer's having borrowed from the *Decameron.* Instead I shall quote briefly from J. S. P. Tatlock and from the unpublished dissertation of Richard Stephen Guerin. Tatlock wrote near the end of a lifetime devoted to Chaucer studies:

> In view of his several months of sojourn and travel in Italy, including a visit to Florence, and in view of his taste for reading and inexhaustible curiosity, it is incredible that he had not heard of the *Decameron,* and indeed seen it. If he never bought a copy, that may have been because it was a very large and expensive book and he was not an affluent man. No one can doubt that it would have appealed to him. . . . As to proof of Chaucer's knowledge of it, undeniable direct borrowings there are none; but there are passages so similar as to suggest reminiscence, and both works contain some four times a similar or identical story. . . . An acceptable explanation of

> the resemblances to Boccaccio is that, having read his book in Italy, Chaucer remembered certain of its contents, and later came across other versions.[1]

Guerin, in whose study can be found most of the available evidence and relevant bibliographic information on the subject, concludes that the evidence strongly suggests

> the possibility that Chaucer read the Italian stories or at least some of them while he was in Italy, remembered parts of them, and that later while he was engaged in writing the *Canterbury Tales*, he employed a process of memorial borrowing for the purpose of adding interest and color to tales for which he almost invariably had other more direct sources.[2]

Guerin finds evidence of apparent borrowing in the *Miller's Tale*, the *Reeve's Tale*, the *Man of Law's Tale*, the *Wife of Bath's Prologue*, the *Clerk's Tale*, the *Franklin's Tale*, and the *Shipman's Tale.* He does not, however, consider the *Merchant's Tale.* Because I believe that one of the best cases for Chaucer's knowledge of the *Decameron* can be made from a consideration of its possible contributions to the tale of January and May, and because I believe that criticism of the *Merchant's Tale* has suffered from an unjustifiable refusal by scholars to consider the *Decameron* as a possible source, I shall present in this study the evidence for Chaucer's having been influenced by the Italian work when he wrote the *Merchant's Tale.* I shall suggest, specifically, that in Chaucer's tale we find echoes of *Decameron* 7.9 and *Decameron* 2.10.

Because the *Merchant's Tale* has a confusing array of sources and analogues, it may be useful here to review them briefly. It has become traditional to speak, at least with reference to its sources, of three parts of the *Merchant's Tale.* The first part, encompassing January's premarital deliberations and the advice he receives from

[1] Tatlock, *The Mind and Art of Chaucer* (1950; rpt. New York: Gordian Press, 1966), 90–91.

[2] Guerin, "The *Canterbury Tales* and *Il Decamerone*," Diss. Colorado 1966, 6.

his brothers, is almost surely based largely on Deschamps' *Miroir de Mariage.*[3] The second part, including the description of old January on his wedding night, is probably based largely on young Agapes' description of her old husband in Boccaccio's *Ameto*, and probably also has echoes of the *Elegiac Maximiani.*[4] The third part, including the deception of January in the garden, is based on one or more of the many versions of the so-called "pear-tree" deception story. Some years ago Germaine Dempster suggested a useful subdivision of the existing analogues to this third part of the tale.[5] They fall, she said, into two basic categories: (1) the blind husband and the fruit tree and (2) the optical illusion. In stories of the first group, of which no fewer than fourteen have been discovered, the blind husband, after his eyesight is restored by supernatural interveners, looks up and sees his wife with her lover in the tree above his head, and is subsequently convinced by her quick response that her purpose was to cure his

[3] Partially reprinted in *Sources and Analogues of Chaucer's Canterbury Tales*, ed. W. F. Bryan and Germaine Dempster (New York: Humanities Press, 1941), 333–39, and discussed by John C. McGalliard in "Chaucer's *Merchant's Tale* and Deschamps' *Miroir de Mariage*," *Philological Quarterly* 25 (1946): 193–220.

[4] The *Ameto* is partially reprinted in *Sources and Analogues*, 339–40, and discussed by J. S. P. Tatlock in "Boccaccio and the Plan of Chaucer's *Canterbury Tales*," *Anglia*, 37 (1913): 80–108. For the influence of Maximianus, see Albert E. Hartung, "The Non-Comic *Merchant's Tale*, Maximianus, and the Sources," *Mediaeval Studies*, 29 (1967): 1–25.

[5] "On the Source of the Deception Story in the *Merchant's Tale*," *Modern Philology* 34 (1936), 133–54. In this study, devoted mainly to defending her view that Chaucer knew a French fabliau version now lost to us, Germaine Dempster does devote a paragraph (153–54) to Chaucer's possible knowledge of *Decameron* 7.9. She does not definitely rule out the possibility that Chaucer may have known the story, and she does note several of the parallels I discuss below. Generally, however, she is not much impressed with the parallels, thinking, for example, that while Nicostrato, like January, is old, "January's sixty years are . . . much more likely to have been decided upon in connection with the opening episodes of the *Merchant's Tale*." And a few years later, when the time came to do the chapter on the *Merchant's Tale* in *Sources and Analogues*, she found space for a nineteenth-century Portuguese analogue about an old man, his daughter, and a cherry tree, but did not include the *Decameron* version which offers more parallels with Chaucer's version, and is old enough (finished around 1350) to have been known by him.

blindness.[6] In stories of the second group, the husband is not blind at all, but is simply tricked by his wife into believing that his witnessing of his wife's adultery is an optical illusion caused, in some versions, by an enchanted pear tree.[7]

Dempster felt that stories of the second, or optical illusion, group are not really analogues of the deception story in Chaucer's *Merchant's Tale*, because in these stories the husbands are not blind, are not aided by supernatural interveners, and do not witness an arboreal adultery. Most scholars have followed her lead and have rigorously excluded stories of the optical illusion type from consideration as possible sources for the *Merchant's Tale.* I have no objection to excluding most of the optical illusion stories, for most of them have little in common with Chaucer's tale. One of the tales in this group, however, may be an exception, and deserves more careful consideration than it has been given.

Decameron 7.9

In the ninth story of the seventh day of Boccaccio's *Decameron* a rich nobleman, Nicostrato, marries in his old age the young and beautiful Lidia. Lidia, unimpressed by her husband's attempts to

[6] Among the stories in this first group, and reproduced in *Sources and Analogues*, 341–56, are two Italian versions, two German versions, two Russian versions, two Latin versions, a Portuguese version, and a French version. In the last decade several more versions of this type have come to light: three Irish versions (see Karl P. Wentersdorf, "The Enchanted Pear Tree Motif in Irish Folklore," *Folklore* 77 [1966]: 21–30, and Charles A. Watkins, "Modern Irish Variants of the Enchanted Pear Tree," *Southern Folklore Quarterly* 30 [1966]: 202–13), and a Spanish version (see Wentersdorf, "A Spanish Analogue of the Pear-Tree Episode in the *Merchant's Tale*," *Modern Philology* 64 [1967]: 320–21). In addition to these fourteen versions, two "lost" versions of the type have been hypothesized (see Dempster, note 5 above, and Wentersdorf, "Chaucer's *Merchant's Tale* and Its Irish Analogues," *Studies in Philology* 43 [1966], 604–29).

[7] In other versions, such as the recent Irish optical illusion stories, the wife convinces her husband that he had seen double because of a certain food he had eaten or because it was a special day of the year, and so had mistakenly thought she was with a lover. See *Sources and Analogues*, 341, n. 1, for more information about the optical illusion stories.

satisfy her, falls in love with Pirro, one of her husband's skilled and trusted young servants. Determined to have him, she sends Lusca, her maidservant, to tell him of her love and her desires. Pirro, fearing that his loyalty to his master is being tested, refuses her advances. He finally agrees to satisfy her only after she has proved her sincerity by performing three deeds: she must kill her husband's favorite falcon before his eyes; she must send Pirro a lock of Nicostrato's beard; and she must send him one of Nicostrato's best teeth. Lidia determines to perform these deeds and, to prove to Pirro that old Nicostrato is not so wise and careful as Pirro fears he is, she also promises to lie with him before her husband's very eyes. After performing the three deeds to Pirro's satisfaction and allaying his suspicions, she makes arrangements with him for fulfilling her final promise. Pretending to be sick one day, Lidia asks Nicostrato and Pirro to carry her to the garden. They do so. Seeing the laden pear tree, she claims to have a strong desire for pears and asks Pirro to climb the tree for some. According to prearranged plan, he climbs the tree and while there he looks down and pretends to see Nicostrato making love to his wife. They, of course, deny that they are doing any such thing. Pirro climbs down and insists once more that he had seen them together from the tree. Nicostrato is amazed and, wondering if the pear tree is bewitched, climbs it himself. From the tree he looks down, sees his servant and his wife making love, and immediately denounces them. As he angrily climbs back down the tree, the lovers return to their original positions, and the old man sees them sitting as they were when he left them. They soon convince him that the bewitched tree had made him see what he thought he saw, and that they themselves are innocent.

This tale is not close enough in its broad narrative outlines to be considered the immediate source for the deception story in the *Merchant's Tale.* The Italian *Novellino* version[8] is more likely to

[8] The *Novellino* is the closest of the blind-husband analogues to the *Merchant's Tale*, and one of the very few old enough (ca. 1300) to have been known by Chaucer in its presently available

have been Chaucer's direct source. There are, however, a number of important elements common to Chaucer's story and the *Decameron* story that are not to be found in the *Novellino* or any of the other blind-husband analogues. These suggest that Chaucer may at some point have made himself familiar with the *Decameron* version and remembered it when he fashioned his own story.

One of the most striking similarities between the two tales is that in both the husband is old. January, upwards of sixty years old, is at his "pittes brynke" (E 1401).[9] Nicostrato is perhaps not quite so old, but he is "già vicino alla vecchiezza."[10] It has generally been thought that the old age of the husband was Chaucer's own addition to the deception story, but there is real question, I believe, that this was so. An Irish optical illusion story, for example, makes a distinction between the ages of husband and wife,[11] and so does the Spanish analogue of the blind-husband type.[12] Though Chaucer could have known neither of these in the twentieth-century versions we now have of them, either or both might descend from medieval versions now lost. It is important to note, however, that in neither the Irish nor the

state. In this version, a jealous rich man becomes even more suspicious of his wife after he becomes blind. When his wife learns that a young man is dying for love of her, she takes pity on him and arranges, by speaking through a long tube (so that her husband will not hear), to join him in a laden pear tree in the garden. As he waits in the tree, she tells her husband that she wants pears. After suggesting that she call for someone to climb for her, he reluctantly lets her climb it herself, then embraces the trunk so that no one can follow her up. God and St. Peter witness the scene. St. Peter suggests that God restore the husband's sight. God agrees, but tells St. Peter that the wife will find an excuse. When the husband sees his wife with her lover in the tree and accuses her, she immediately replies that if she had not done it he, her husband, would never have been able to see. The husband believes her, and is content.

[9] All references to Chaucer are from F. N. Robinson's second edition of *The Works of Geoffrey Chaucer* (Boston: Houghton Mifflin, 1957).

[10] Giovanni Boccaccio, *Decameron*, ed. Natalino Sapegno (1956; rpt. Turin: Tipografia Temprelli, 1966), 667. Subsequent page references to the *Decameron*, included within parentheses in the text, are from this edition. All italicizing is my own.

[11] See Wentersdorf, "The Enchanted Pear Tree Motif," 24.

[12] See Wentersdorf, "A Spanish Analogue," 320–21. In the Portuguese analogue it is the girl's father, not her husband, who is old.

Spanish analogue is the husband's age said to have any connection with the wife's motivation for taking a lover. In both Chaucer and the *Decameron*, on the other hand, the young wife is disappointed in her old husband's sexual efforts and *therefore* is attracted to a younger man. May's unexciting wedding night makes this only too clear in the *Merchant's Tale,* while in the *Decameron* version Lidia makes her motivation in seeking Pirro's love quite explicit when she speaks to her maid:

> Come tu vedi, Lusca, *io son giovane e fresca donna*, e piena e copiosa di tutte quelle cose che alcuna può disiderare; e brievemente, fuor chè d'una, non mi posso rammaricare, e questa è che *gli anni del mio marito son troppi, se co'miei si misurano*, per la qual cosa di quello che le giovani donne prendono più piacere, io vivo poco contenta; e pur come l'altre disiderandolo, è buona pezza che io diliberai meco di non volere, se *la fortuna m'è stata poco arnica in darmi così vecchio marito*, essere io nimica di me medesima in non saper trovar modo a' miei diletti e alla mia salute. (668)

In most of the analogues to the deception story no specific motivation for the wife is mentioned; her husband's only apparent fault is that he is blind. Even the slight motivation that the blindness might provide, however, is of course not present in Boccaccio's and Chaucer's versions. Lidia's husband is never physically blind, and May decides to accept Damian's love *before* January becomes blind. Are we to suppose that both writers independently hit upon the same idea—the husband's old age and resulting sexual incapacity—to explain the wife's infidelity? Such a supposition seems by no means justified when we remember that Boccaccio's version preceded Chaucer's version by some forty years and that Chaucer might easily have known it.

Also worthy of note in both Boccaccio's and Chaucer's tales is that the husband is rich and noble. Nicostrato is a "nobile uomo e ricco" (668), while the "noble Januarie" (E 2023) is a "worthy knyght" who lives "in greet prosperitee" (E 1247). In one of the other analogues (the *Novellino* version) the husband is said to be rich, and in one other (a Russian version) he is said to be noble, but in neither of these does the husband's comfortable station in life appear to serve any particular function in the story. In the two stories where the husbands are old, however, the husband's wealth serves the important function of motivating the young woman's marriage to him. This motivation is less obvious in Boccaccio's version, partly because Lidia is apparently herself of good family ("una gran donna" [667]), and partly because she is already married when the story opens, and so there is little need for us to know why she married. When we note Nicostrato's age and wealth, however, and Lidia's lack of either love or respect for him, it is apparent enough that, for Lidia, her marriage was almost surely in some sense a marriage of convenience. That May's marriage is one of convenience is only too clear. May is "of smal degree" (E 1625), and no mention is made of her bringing a dowry to her husband. Had old January been a poor commoner, May would clearly not have been persuaded to marry him.

The old husband's comfortable situation does more than explain why a pretty young woman, clearly not motivated by love, would marry him. It also helps to explain the accessibility of that wife to a younger man. Because they are both wealthy, Nicostrato and January have considerable entourages, comprising such lusty young men as Pirro and Damian. In most of the analogues, including even the *Novellino* version where the husband is also said to be rich, the wife's lover is not a member of the household; he is just "a man," "a lover," or "a student," the necessary figure in the plot with whom the wife cuckolds her husband. Only in Chaucer and Boccaccio is he a trusted member of the husband's household who has ready and relatively unsuspicious access to the unhappy wife.

Both lovers are entirely (perhaps stupidly) trusted by the husbands whom they eventually cuckold. That Damian is held in high esteem by his master is evident in January's description of him:

> "He is a gentil squier, by my trouthe!
> If that he deyde, it were harm and routhe.
> He is as wys, discreet, and as secree

> As any man I woot of his degree,
> And therto manly, and eek servysable,
> And for to been a thrifty man right able."
> (E 1907–12)

Boccaccio's Pirro is also fully trusted by the old husband:

> E aveva, tra gli altri suoi famigliari un giovinetto leggiadro e adorno e hello della persona, e destro a qualunque cosa avesse voluta fare, chiamato Pirro; *il quale Nicostrato oltre ad ogni altro amava e più di lui si fidava.* (868)

In both these versions, though of course in none of the others, an issue is made of the lover's loyalty to his master. Chaucer expresses the seriousness of Damian's disloyalty in an apostrophe:

> O servant traytour, false hoomly hewe,
> Lyk to the naddre in bosom sly untrewe,
> God shilde us alle from youre aqueyntaunce!
> O Januarie, dronken in plesaunce
> In mariage, se how thy Damyan,
> Thyn owene squier and thy borne man,
> Entendeth for to do thee vileynye.
> (E 1785–91)

In the *Decameron* version, also, Pirro's loyalty to Nicostrato is mentioned. Pirro rejects Lidia's original advances ostensibly because he will not dishonor his master: "io non farei a lui sì fatto oltraggio per la vita mia" (669). Later Lusca goes to considerable lengths to convince him, successfully, that he need not be loyal to Nicostrato (see 670–71).

Not only are Damian and Pirro both trusted and supposedly loyal members of the old husband's household, but each fears that the young wife will betray him. The subject of betrayal never comes up in any of the other analogues, perhaps because in none of them is the lover's fate in the hands of the wealthy and powerful husband. Damian's fears are expressed in an apostrophe:

> How shaltow to thy lady, fresshe May,
> Telle thy wo? She wole alwey seye nay.
> Eek if thou speke, she wol thy wo biwreye.
> (E 1871–73)

He expresses his love to May with the prayer:

> "Mercy! and that ye nat discovere me,
> For I am deed if that this thyng be kyd."
> (E 1942–43)

Pirro fears that Lidia is in conspiracy with her husband to test him ("io temo forte che Lidia con consiglio e voler di lui questo non faccia per dovermi tentare" [671]) and will trust her only after he has tested her sincerity by giving her three difficult deeds to perform. Both May and Lidia, of course, soon allay the fears of their lovers.

But what about those deceiving wives? There are certain basic similarities among all of the wives in the deception stories: they all seem to be young, pretty, resourceful, and eager for love. Only in the *Merchant's Tale* and in the *Decameron*, however, is the wife's love specifically said to be of such intensity that she nearly dies for it. We remember that May loves Damian so much

> That she moot outher dyen sodeynly
> Or elles she moot han hym as hir leste.
> (E 2094–95)

Lidia, similarly, thinks she will die if she cannot have Pirro. She tells Lusca, "se io senza indugio non mi ritruovo seco, per certo io me ne credo morire" (669). And while all of the wives are resourceful enough to think up acceptable excuses for their adultery, only May and Lidia are resourceful enough to pretend illness. The pretended pain in May's side not only conveys to the heirless January the implication that she may be pregnant, but also explains her sudden desire for the green pears:[13]

[13] For a useful discussion of the connection between May's pretended pregnancy and January's desire for an heir, see Milton Miller, "The Heir in the *Merchant's Tale*," *Philological Quarterly* 29 (1950): 437–40.

> This fresshe May, that is so bright and sheene,
> Can for to syke, and seyde, "Allas, my syde!
> Now sire," quod she, "for aught that may bityde,
> I moste han of the peres that I see,
> Or I moot dye, so soore longeth me
> To eten of the smale peres grene.
> Help, for hir love that is of hevene queene!
> I telle yow wel, a womman in my plit
> May han to fruyt so greet an appetit
> That she may dyen, but she of it have."
> (E 2328–37)

Might the idea for May's discomfiture have been suggested to Chaucer by Lidia's illness? Lidia pretends to be sick ("fatto sembiante d'essere inferma" [675]) so that she can request Nicostrato and Pirro to carry her into the garden as a diversion for her illness ("per alleggiamento della sua noia" [676]). Lidia does not use her illness as an excuse for her desire for pears, but she does, as does May, use it as part of her overall strategy in the garden scene. She, like May, is eager to elicit her husband's sympathy, partly so that she will be in a position to demand special consideration from him when she does ask for pears, and partly so that she can put her husband on the defensive and so head off his accusations. What husband, after all, would suspect, let alone accuse, an ailing wife of adultery?

The wives in the regular blind-husband analogues are sufficiently resourceful, when the accusations do come, to explain their adultery on the grounds that it was the only way they could restore their husband's eyesight. May uses this excuse also:

> "I have yow holpe on bothe youre eyen blynde.
> Up peril of my soule, I shal nat lyen,
> As me was taught, to heele with youre eyen,
> Was no thyng bet, to make yow to see,
> Than strugle with a man upon a tree.
> God woot, I dide it in ful good entente."
> (E 2370–75)

The suggestion that May was responsible for healing January's eyesight could, of course, have come from any of the blind-husband analogues. In none of them, however, does the wife refer to herself in such specifically medical terms. Not only does May claim "to heele" his blindness, but she also refers to "my medicyne" (E 2380) and pretends to great knowledge of blindness:

> "Right so a man that longe hath blynd ybe,
> Ne may nat sodeynly so wel yse,
> First whan his sighte is newe come ageyn,
> As he that hath a day or two yseyn.
> Til that youre sighte ysatled be a while,
> Ther may ful many a sighte yow bigile."
> (E 2401–06)

It is possible that Chaucer may have taken the suggestion for May's pretending to be a doctor from Boccaccio's Lidia, who, in an earlier scene, had pretended to be something of a doctor herself. In accomplishing her task to get for Pirro one of Nicostrato's best teeth, Lidia told her husband that he had a rotten one in his mouth that she could pull as well as any doctor ("senza alcun maestro io medesima tel trarrò ottimamente" [675]).

Whether or not Chaucer might have recalled Lidia's medical pretensions when he wrote the *Merchant's Tale*, it is important to note that each of May's counterparts in the regular blind-husband analogues is content to justify her adultery on the grounds that it would restore her husband's eyesight, and never thinks to deny that she actually engaged in adultery. May, on the other hand, insists that she did no more than "struggle" with Damian. January, she says, saw imperfectly what went on in the tree ("Ye han som glymsyng, and no parfit sighte" [E 2383]), and what he thought was adultery was no such thing. She finally convinces January that he did not see what in fact he did see. Might not Chaucer have taken his suggestion for this motif from the actions of Lidia, who denies completely that she has had anything to do with Pirro, who pretends to be angry with old Nicostrato for questioning her honor, and who successfully claims that what he saw never occurred? At any rate, it is worth noticing here that Chaucer has combined in the *Merchant's Tale* the best of two versions of the deception story. May not only claims that by her suspect actions she was restoring her husband's eyesight (as do the wives in the blind-husband stories), but she also denies that there was any adultery in the first place and convinces her husband that what he saw never really occurred (as do the wives in the optical-illusion stories).

In the matter of the husband's blindness, Chaucer has once more combined the best of two versions of the tale. In the blind-husband versions the husbands are blind throughout the story. The only exception is the *Novellino* version, in which the husband, already jealous, becomes blind and so even more jealous. Even here, however, the blindness comes very early in the story—in the second sentence, to be exact. In the optical-illusion stories, on the other hand, the husband is never blind. Chaucer's January is both sighted and blind. He can see perfectly well in the first 812 lines of the tale, and is blind for only 300 lines. For three-quarters of the tale, then, January can more fruitfully be compared with a sighted husband, such as Nicostrato, than with any of those in the blind-husband versions.

While old Nicostrato is never physically blind, as January is in the last third of the tale, he shares with January what might be called a mental blindness. Both old men, for example, are utterly blind to their own inability to satisfy their fresh young wives. Both are blindly unsuspicious of such younger men as Pirro and Damian, who, because they are members of the household, have easy access to those wives. And both, in the end, allow themselves to be blinded to the existence of an adultery, a copulation, that they see with their own eyes. This idea of mental blindness is made explicit enough in the *Merchant's Tale* through expressions such as the following:

> For love is blynd alday, and may nat see.
> (E 1598)

> For as good is blynd deceyved be
> As to be deceyved whan a man may se.
> (E 2109–10)

It is made most explicit, perhaps, at the very end of the tale when January, after his physical eyesight has been restored to him by Pluto, gradually relinquishes that eyesight to May's deception:

> He swyved thee, I saugh it with myne yen.
>
> . . . . .
>
> And by my trouthe, me thoughte he dide thee so.
>
> . . . . .
>
> I wende han seyn
> How that this Damyan hadde by thee leyn.
>
> (E 2378, 2386, 2393–94)

At the end, though he can once again see, January refuses to be anything but blind to the truth. This same sort of blindness is made quite explicit in Boccaccio's version also. At the very beginning Panfilo, the narrator of the tale, warns his lady listeners not to risk what Lidia will risk in the story to come, for not all men are so easily blinded as Nicostrato: "né sono al mondo tutti gli uomini abbagliati igualmente" (667). And at the very end, Lidia, in pretended anger, chastises Nicostrato for believing the eyes in his head when he ought to believe rather the eyes of his intellect (that is, his good judgment), which should assure him of his wife's innocence:

> "senza considerazione alcuna così tosto si lasciò *abbagliar gli occhi dello 'ntelletto*; ché, quantunque a quegli *che tu hai in testa* paresse ciò che tu di', per niuna cosa dovevi nel giudicio della tua mente comprendere o consentire che ciò fosse." (679)

The reader, of course, is well aware of the irony of her chastisement, for Nicostrato has just permitted the eyes in his head to be blinded by the eyes of his rather limited intellect. Do we not have recollections of Nicostrato's mental blindness, superimposed on physical blindness, in Chaucer's January? No detail more persuasively supports my thesis than this mental blindness. Here, in a version which antedates Chaucer's by forty years, Boccaccio makes explicit the idea that gives the *Merchant's Tale* much of its power in characterization and theme, an idea only implicit or ignored altogether in the blind-husband analogues.

It seems to me, then, that we should not overlook the *Decameron* version of the deception story in our consideration of the possible sources for the *Merchant's Tale.* The *Decameron* version is not, to be sure, of the blind-husband-and-the-fruit-tree type, but it could have provided Chaucer with significant suggestions and ideas that he could not have gotten from any of the extant tales of that type, and it is one of the very few analogues old enough to have been known to Chaucer in its presently available form. To overlook it is to be as blind as January to significant possibilities.

Comoedia Lydiae

Besides the *Decameron* version of the tale, there is only one other story of the optical-illusion type that deserves mention in connection with the *Merchant's Tale*: Mathieu de Vendôme's *Comoedia Lydiae.* The *Comoedia Lydiae* was almost certainly Boccaccio's source for his version of the deception story. Written probably in the twelfth century, this Latin tale might also have been known to Chaucer and might, therefore, have been a source common to both writers. The *Comoedia Lydiae* could, indeed, have provided Chaucer with several of the elements that we find in Boccaccio: a suggestion for the old age of the husband, the feigned sickness of the wife, her insistence that what her husband saw never really happened, the lover's position as a member of the household, his original distrust of the wife's motives. In many respects, however, the Latin version is more distant from Chaucer's than is the Italian. The husband's old age, for example, is merely hinted at, as in the following lines:

> Lydia posse negat; sed verum Lusca fatetur
> dente viruin vetulum sic iterasse negat
> Hic ex praeissis concludit Lydia: "Quare
> spes dabitur juveni, si datur illa seni?"[14]

[14] Quoted from Édélstand du Méril, *Poésies Inédites du Moyen Âge* (Paris: Librairie Franck, 1854), 370.

If the implied difference in age does motivate the Latin Lidia to seek a lover, this motivation is nowhere made explicit, as it is in the Italian and English versions. In the *Comoedia*, there is a fourth person in the garden. Lidia's maid, Lusca, goes along. Her function is apparently merely to make fun (behind his back) of the foolish husband. (Strangely enough, no one thinks to ask her about the adultery, though she was an eye-witness to all that occurred.) In both Boccaccio and Chaucer only three—the wife, the husband, and the lover—go into the garden. In the *Comoedia* the wife's feigned illness is apparently an excuse for her to walk into the garden, though she herself never asks for a pear. Her husband, apparently on his own, suggests that the lover climb the tree for the fruit. In both Boccaccio and Chaucer the wife herself desires a pear, and her prearranged request for one is what sets off the climbing of the tree. The husband in the Latin version, when he sees his wife and servant copulating, never upbraids them. Rather he debates with himself about what is going on, and himself concludes that he is the victim of an ocular deception caused by the pear tree. The guilty wife, then, has merely to agree with him. She does not, as do May and the Italian Lidia, have to convince an angry and accusing husband that she is innocent. Nicostrato and January both immediately upbraid their wives when they see the copulation. Nicostrato shouts, "Ahi rea femina, che è quel che tu fai?" (677). January cries out a similar question: "O stronge lady stoore, what dostow?" (E 2367). Both husbands need to be convinced by their wives that their natural suspicions are unfounded.

On the basis of our comparison, then, it would appear much more likely that Chaucer was familiar with the *Decameron* version than with its source. One cannot, besides, help agreeing with Germaine Dempster that Chaucer's contact with the *Comoedia Lydiae* "would a priori seem infinitely less plausible than his contact with the *Decameron.*"[15] The *Decameron* was more widely circulated and came

[15] Dempster, "On the Source of the Deception Story," 154.

from the hand of a writer from whom Chaucer borrowed more than he did from anyone else.

Decameron 2.10

Once we have admitted the possibility of Chaucer's familiarity with the *Decameron* pear-tree story, it is tempting to seek elsewhere in Boccaccio's collection for possible influences on Chaucer's *Merchant's Tale.* Of particular interest, especially in connection with the central portion of the tale (recounting January's senile love-making), is the last tale of the second day. In this tale a weak and emaciated judge named Ricciardo decides that he would like to marry a pretty young girl. Ricciardo's exact age is not given, nor is he specifically said to be an old man, but his position as a judge suggests at least a mature age, and the later descriptions and speeches of Bartolomea, his wife, make it quite clear that she is considerably younger than he is. Because he is wealthy, however, he succeeds in winning her hand. Upon discovering that he is just barely able to consummate his marriage a single time on his wedding night, Ricciardo devises an elaborate calendar of saint's days, fast days, and the like, on which, he tells his young wife, it is sinful to engage in intercourse. So complete is his calendar that he has to perform in bed only once a month, and sometimes even less frequently. Yet all the time he jealously guards his wife lest another man should serve her as he does not. One hot day, when Ricciardo and his wife, on vacation, are at sea fishing, a young pirate, Paganino, comes along, seizes Bartolomea, and carries her off. He soon teaches her to disregard her calendar, and the two get on so well that when Ricciardo finally discovers where she has been taken and comes to ransom her, she refuses to return with him. Having learned the true pleasures of love with Paganino, she chides Ricciardo for his inadequacies and sends him off. When, shortly thereafter, Ricciardo dies, Bartolomea marries Paganino.

The plot, of course, is far different from that of the *Merchant's Tale*, but there are some important similarities between Ricciardo and January. Ricciardo, like January, takes advantage of his wealth and social position to procure for himself a wife younger than himself. Like January—and unlike the husbands in the deception story analogues—he is specifically said to decide *first* that he wants to marry a young and pretty girl ("bella e giovane donna" [252]), and *later* settles on one who fits his preconceived specifications. The specifications of youth and beauty are ones he ought to have advised himself to avoid ("se così avesse saputo consigliar sé come altrui faceva, doveva fuggire" [252]). We recall that January similarly specifies a "mayde fair and tendre of age" (E 1407), and is cautioned by Justinus to consider carefully before insisting on precisely those two qualifications in a wife:

> "Avyseth yow—ye been a man of age—
> How that ye entren into mariage,
> And namely with a yong wyf and a fair."
> (E 1555–57)

Like January, Ricciardo becomes extremely jealous ("sì geloso che temeva dello aere stesso" [254]) and always guards her carefully ("sempre guardandola bene" [253]). Like January, he thinks of his wife as a commodity which, if he has enough money, he can keep for himself. And, like January, he appeals to his wife's sense of honor in his request that she be true to him ("non hai tu riguardo all'onore de' parenti tuoi e al tuo?" [258]; cf. *Merchant's Tale* (E 2171).

More interesting is a comparison of the sorry lovemaking of the two husbands on their wedding nights. Ricciardo, after a splendid wedding and magnificent feast ("nozze belle e magnifiche," "grandissima festa a casa sua" [252; cf. *Merchant's Tale* E 1709–31]), proves, like January, to be physically unexciting to his fresh young wife. May's disappointment is not directly reported ("God woot what that May thoughte in hir herte" [E 1851]), but her subsequent actions convey her feeling about January as effectively as does Bartolomea's more directly expressed disgust at Ricciardo's efforts to please her. Both husbands, after their wedding-night efforts, are quite weary. January tells May that

"My reste wol I take;
Now day is come, I may no lenger wake."
(E 1855–56)

Ricciardo's exhaustion is more explicitly detailed: "era magro e secco e di poco spirito" (252). It is especially noteworthy that both husbands feel the need to refresh themselves after their wedding-night efforts. January, after his "labor," takes "a sop in fyn clarree" (E 1843). Ricciardo, similarly, needs some post-coital stimulation: "convenne che con vernaccia e con confetti ristorativi e con altri argomenti nel mondo si ritornasse" (252). Indeed, so explicit are the nature and function of Ricciardo's refreshments that one almost suspects that they might have suggested the aphrodisiacs Chaucer has January take *before* his wedding-night labors:

He drynketh ypocras, clarree, and vernage
Of spices hoote, t'encreessen his corage;
And many a letuarie hath he ful fyn,
Swiche as the cursed monk, daun Constantyn,
Hath writen in his book *De Coitu*
To eten hem alle he nas no thyng eschu.
(E 1807–12)

Particularly interesting is January's "vernage of hot spices." "Vernage," Robinson's glossary tells us, is "a strong, sweet white wine of Italy." And what is that but Boccaccio's "vernaccia," that same Italian white wine? Not even the source Chaucer acknowledges, Constantinus Africanus's *De Coitu*, so specifically suggests one of the very aphrodisiacs that January uses.[16] We must note also that neither of the sources that have been suggested for this portion of the tale, that

[16] For discussions of the relationship between the *De Coitu* and the *Merchant's Tale*, see Maurice Bassan, "Chaucer's 'Cursed Monk,' Constantinus Africanus," *Mediaeval Studies* 24 (1962): 127–40, and Paul Delany, "Constantinus Africanus and Chaucer's *Merchant's Tale*," *Philological Quarterly* 46 (1967): 560–66. The *De Coitu* has been conveniently translated by Delany in "Constantinus Africanus' *De Coitu*: A Translation," *Chaucer Review* 4 (1970): 55–65.

is, neither *Ameto* nor the *Elegiae Maximiani*, suggests the use of aphrodisiacs at all, so Chaucer could not have taken the idea from either of them. The last tale of the second day of the *Decameron*, however, might have given Chaucer the idea for January's preparatory and restorative refreshments. In both stories, men richer in money than in sexual energy decide to marry women younger than themselves. Both men, after elaborate wedding feasts, fail to excite their lusty new wives, and resort to artificial stimulants to make up for those that nature no longer provides them with.

I cannot pretend to have proved conclusively that Chaucer's *Merchant's Tale* was influenced by Boccaccio's *Decameron*. The fact remains that we cannot know just what Chaucer's sources were. Either the true source is now lost or, as I rather strongly suspect, Chaucer so combined and changed and added to a number of the stories he knew that the precise nature of his original or originals is no longer accurately inferable from the distinctively Chaucerian work of art that he has left us. I do argue, however, that we should not exclude from our consideration of Chaucer's possible sources for the tale Boccaccio's *Decameron*. Because of its date, and because of the unparalleled closeness of certain of the details in some of its stories to details in the *Merchant's Tale*, the *Decameron* should be granted its rightful place alongside the *Miroir de Mariage*, the *Ameto*, the *Elegiac Maximiani*, and the *Novellino*, as one of the most significant of Chaucer's probable sources for the tale of January and May.

Lippijn: A Middle Dutch Source for the *Merchant's Tale*?

[I happened to sit next to Therese Decker at a Lehigh University dinner. We introduced ourselves—I from English, she from Modern Foreign Languages—and soon she was telling me about her translations of eight plays from fourteenth-century Middle Dutch. I listened with polite attention, but I really perked up when she described a play called *Lippijn*. It was about an old man who witnessed his own cuckolding but then allowed himself to be talked out of seeing what he had seen with his own eyes. I asked Therese many questions and asked her to let me see her translation. The result is this article that we co-authored about possible connections between *Lippijn* and the *Merchant's Tale*. She was responsible mostly for the translated text of *Lippijn*; I was responsible mostly for the analytical comparisons with the *Merchant's Tale*. Our article appeared originally in *Chaucer Review* 23 (1989): 236–50. Therese Decker and I went on to collaborate on two more projects involving short plays in the Hulthem manuscript. Both appeared as special issues that we co-guest-edited of *The Canadian Journal of Netherlandic Studies*: the Spring, 1995, issue on the Middle Dutch play *Nu Noch* and the Fall, 1997, issue on the Middle Dutch play *Boss for Three Days*.]

In the third quarter of the fourteenth century a series of eight verse plays were written, and presumably produced, in the Low

Countries.[1] These plays, generally referred to as the *abele spelen* and *sotterniën,* are in the Hulthem manuscript located in the Royal Library of Brussels. It is not known who wrote the plays, or even whether they were all written by the same author. Four of the eight Middle Dutch plays average slightly more than 1000 lines each. These four—the first secular dramas of the late Middle Ages—all deal with serious but non-religious subjects. At least one of them might be called a tragedy. The other four (one of them is unfortunately fragmentary) are short comedies, running to no more than 250 lines each. Clearly related to the fabliau tradition, these shorter plays are broadly humorous. Each was apparently meant to be played after one of the four longer, serious plays and to provide a few minutes of comic relief before the audience dispersed.

Although several editions of the plays have been published,[2] and although some of the plays—the longer and more serious ones—have been translated into English, they have been overlooked by all but a few scholars. Our purpose in the present article is of narrower scope: to call to the attention of students of Middle English literature one of the previously untranslated plays, to present a prose translation of it, and to discuss evidence that tends to support the possibility that this Middle Dutch play, never before mentioned in connection with Geoffrey Chaucer, may have provided him with a source for the *Merchant's Tale.*

Lippijn is about an old husband whose younger wife cuckolds him. Lippijn sees his wife making love with her paramour but is soon

[1] The manuscript dates from the very early fifteenth century, but internal evidence suggests a considerably earlier date of composition for the plays themselves. H. E. Moltzer, in *De middelnederlandsche dramatische poezie, Bibliotheek van middelnederlandsche letterkunde* (Groningen, 1875), 1: lvi–lvii, presents the most convincing evidence. Although scholars have dated the plays as early as 1280 and as late as 1400, present evidence suggests that a 1350–75 date is most likely. Chaucer's *Merchant's Tale* is usually assigned to the period of Chaucer's greatest maturity—sometime after 1385.

[2] Although more recent editions have been published of the four serious plays, the comedies have not been published since Moltzer's 1875 edition. All quotations from *Lippijn* in the original Middle Dutch are taken from this edition.

convinced by Trise, his wife's godmother, that what he saw was a trick played upon him by elves sent to deceive him. Printed below is a rather literal translation from the Middle Dutch verse. We have added, within square brackets, our own brief stage directions at what appear to be the appropriate places.

The play

LIPPIJN

HERE BEGINS THE COMEDY.

[Scene: Lippijn's home.
Enter Lippijn's wife.]

HERE BEGINS THE WIFE:
Hm! Say! Hm! God help it!
I want to revel
with my sweet love in the grass.
It has been a long time since I was there with him.
Hm! Say! Hm! Where are you, Lippijn? 5

[Enter Lippijn.]

LIPPIJN: I am here. What shall it be?

HIS WIFE: Lippijn, you go and get water and fire,
and I shall come back quickly
and bring something to eat.

LIPPIJN: By the death of our Lord, forget about it. 10
You stay out too often for too long.

HIS WIFE: Why, Lippijn, do not get angry.
Often I have a lot to do.
Before I hear my sermon
the day has already advanced, 15
and it is even later before I get to the butcher's hall.
I like to make a good buy.
Then I have to wait until my turn
comes up in the crush.

That is why I take so long. 20
Good Lippijn, you must know this.

LIPPIJN: In truth, you would cheat me,
and I do not know what to say about it.
Go on, I shall start our fire,
and get water and scrub the pot. 25
God help me,
I have given myself into slavery.

HIS WIFE: Good Lippijn, also wash the bowls
and sweep the floor nicely for us.

LIPPIJN: Dear, now hear, may God reward you! 30
And nothing more now. Even though I have been all my days your poor slave,
it seems to me that I shall be one all my life.

HIS WIFE: Be quiet! God give you shame.
I am sorry that you live so long. 35

[Lippijn leaves.
Wife goes to a different part of the stage.
Enter her lover.]

Well, is this not a nice coincidence?
Where can he be, the friend of my heart?
He is sick about having to
leave me thus as an orphan.

HER LOVER: Little love, different things kept me. 40
Have you been here long?

LIPPIJN'S WIFE: Indeed, my heart is so afraid
because I have not seen you for so long.

HER LOVER: Let us go and drink a good drink, my chosen little. love. 45
This evening we will yet be in joy. Now come here!

[They go off together, perhaps off stage,
perhaps to a concealed place on stage.
They embrace. Enter Lippijn, who sees them.]

LIPPIJN: Oh woe, Lord, is that true?
By God, I have seen them enough.
She lies with naked knees, 50
and he has crept between.
By the death of our Lord, he has crept in.
Look at it, that whore! She tells me
that she goes to market,
but she lies! She has fun with another man, 55
and makes a cuckold of me.
She says she goes to the meat market!
By Saint John, I shall repay her for this cheating yet tonight.
If I can get hold of a stick, 60
I shall beat her hide so much
that she will be sorry for this game
she has played with him.

[Enter Trise, godmother of Lippijn's wife.]

THE GODMOTHER: What, Lippijn, God give you a good day.
How is it with you? How do you feel 65

LIPPIJN: Oh, Trise! I think my heart will break
from the great sorrow I feel.
I never would have suspected my wife of
what she has done to me.

THE GODMOTHER: Lippijn, now make me understand. 70
How and in what manner?

LIPPIJN: I will be ashamed about this eternally.
She lies and plays with another man.

THE GODMOTHER: In truth, this is something I cannot
believe of your wife. 75
I know her to be so pure.
She would not do this for the world.

LIPPIJN: What a man sees with his own eyes,
you cannot talk him out of.

THE GODMOTHER: Lippijn, by my honor, 80
Many a person has been tricked by seeing.

LIPPIJN: What, no, this is not a trick,
because I saw her myself
lying with naked knees
and both labored hard. 85

THE GODMOTHER: Oh, Lippijn, you must not talk about this.
Your wife would be dishonored by it.
Your eyes are mistaken
from drinking and old age.
Good Lippijn, do not say such things. 90
Your wife would be shamed by it.

LIPPIJN: What the devil! Are you going to make me blind
about things which I saw myself?
I saw that she lay on her back,
and that he lifted up her skirts. 95

THE GODMOTHER: Oh be quiet, good Lippijn.
It was nothing but your imagination.
Have you never heard talk about elves
who trick people?
The devil often does tricks 100
in order to make trouble between husband and wife.
I would bet my life on it.
That was nothing but an elf you saw.

LIPPIJN: What the devil! Did God plague the world with elves
and fairies? 105
And would I not recognize my own wife?
That would certainly be unbelievable.
I saw that she went with him.
He took her in his arms and pulled her close.

THE GODMOTHER: Lippijn, tricks are never true. 110
I know your wife too well.
She has led such a pure life.

She would not do it for all the red gold in the world.
But deceit by elves is so great.
It makes many a person so blind 115
that he does not recognize himself.
How should he recognize someone else?

LIPPIJN: By the death of our Lord,
you are driving me completely crazy.
What the devil! What has happened to me now?
Am I blind, and do I not see? 120
I have never seen a wonder like this before,
and I see very well all these people
who sit here all around.
I am not blind,
even if you would like to make me believe it. 125

THE GODMOTHER: Lippijn, do you know what you are doing?
I beg you that you never say it.
You must cover your wife with honor.
It is an elf who tortures you,
who has confused your sight completely. 130
Your eyes are confused.

LIPPIJN: But my dear, are you sure that is what confuses me?
It seemed to me that I saw her.

THE GODMOTHER: It was an elf who was lying there.
I will swear it to you upon a cross. 135
Your wife is still at home.
I will bet you a beer on that.

[Trise here perhaps signals to the wife to hurry home.]

LIPPIJN: And she told me to get water and fire.
She said she would go for food.

THE GODMOTHER: Oh, Lippijn, do you want to know
the truth? 140

You certainly have been misled.
An elf has spread its net,
I know it well, in order to catch you.
Come with me. We shall go to your house.
Your wife will be sitting by her fire. 145

LIPPIJN: What! Am I drunk from the beer,
or do elves fly through the streets?

[They go to Lippijn's house.]

THE GODMOTHER: What, niece, do you not want to let us in?

LIPPIJN'S WIFE: Christ knows, sure. Who is there?

THE GODMOTHER: Well, Lippijn, did I not tell you true? 150

LIPPIJN: Blessed God of heaven,
I have never seen such a wonder!
I see well that the fault has been mine.

THE GODMOTHER: What did I tell you, Lippijn?
But you did not want to know it. 155
My niece is faithful and good,
even if you want to make her look like a whore.

LIPPIJN'S WIFE: God punch him in the jaws!
Did he complain of that about me?

THE GODMOTHER: Yes, and he complained to me 160
that you were lying with another man.

LIPPIJN: In truth, I thought that I saw it,
but I am satisfied now.
Trise must know best.
But, as realistically as if I had done it myself, 165
it seemed you had gotten up this morning
and told me to get fire and water.

LIPPIJN'S WIFE: Quiet, you dirty dog!
Are you starting to accuse me of other men?

LIPPIJN: Surely, to tell the truth, 170
then I saw it, or my eyes were wrong.
But Trise taught me
and said that an elf deceived me.

LIPPIJN'S WIFE: Then why did you lie about me
and shame me everywhere? 175

LIPPIJN: Oh darling, I shall make it good
if I said or did anything wrong.

LIPPIJN'S WIFE: You are going to get a beating for this,
you dirty, old, bad graybeard!

THE GODMOTHER: By our Lord, he surely deserves 180
that we knock him to the ground.

LIPPIJN: Dear wife, I shall never say it again.
I did not know that I was wrong.

LIPPIJN'S WIFE: Oh, we shall teach you a lesson now!

[Here They Fight.]

Good people, we have 185
played this peasant comedy.
They still live, as you
who have seen such things know.
Many common things happen
which nowadays cause no comment. 190
Furthermore, I ask that you receive
our comedy gratefully.
I beg the King full of grace,
who was born of the Virgin,
that no one will get angry 195
about what he has heard and seen here.
Get up. You may well go out now
because we all have to depart.
Our Lord God keep us all.

AMEN

Features shared with the *Merchant's Tale*

This play about Lippijn may not appear at first glance to be a promising candidate for status as an analogue, let alone a source, for Chaucer's *Merchant's Tale.* Lippijn, unlike January, is already married at the start of the play, is never struck blind, does not see his wife making love in a fruit tree, is not aided by a supernatural intervenor, and so on. Indeed, the Middle Dutch play does not even fall into one of the two generally recognized types of analogues for Chaucer's tale: (1) the "enchanted tree" type in which a wife caught with her lover persuades her husband that an enchanted tree had caused him to think he saw his wife making love, and (2) the "blind husband" type in which a husband's sight is restored by a supernatural power just in time for him to see a man in a fruit tree copulating with his wife, who then cleverly proclaims that the act had been her way of restoring her husband's eyesight. Remote as the connection may at first appear, however, *Lippijn* might have provided Chaucer with certain features that are found in the *Merchant's Tale* but that do not appear in any of the extant versions of either of these types of tales.

Before discussing the features that *Lippijn* shares with the *Merchant's Tale*, it may be well to remind readers that Chaucer had visited the Low Countries, and indeed that he had done so on a number of occasions. Chaucer made several diplomatic trips to the Continent, among them trips to Flanders in the 1370s. In addition, several of his trips to other countries—such as those to Italy—might have taken him through the Low Countries. There also is the indirect evidence of Chaucer's allusions to important commercial locations in the Low Countries. Some of those allusions suggest a rather specific knowledge of the geography and the commercial importance of those locations.[3] And it is interesting—though of course of questionable evidential merit—that scholarship has recently brought to light a brief

[3] We call particular attention to a fine article by Kenneth S. Cahn, "Chaucer's Merchants and the Foreign Exchange: An Introduction to Medieval Finance," *Studies in the Age of Chaucer* 2 (1980): 81–119. Cahn points out that Chaucer was very much aware of the intricacies of

sixteenth-century *vita* of Chaucer that begins: "He lyved some parte of Richarde the second his tyme, in the lowe cuntryes of Holland and Zeelande by reason of some disgrace that happenyd unto hym, as a man suspected to be spotted with the rebellion of Jack Straw and Watte Tyler."[4] Scholars must, of course, question the accuracy of this late suggestion, though at the same time we wonder why the earliest biographers of Chaucer would have mentioned Chaucer's stay in the Low Countries had there not been earlier traditions to the same effect. However that might be, it is virtually certain that Chaucer had traveled to and through the Low Countries, and that he would thus have had opportunity to learn something of the language and the literary traditions of the region.

The only evidence that Chaucer was acquainted with the *Lippijn* play, of course, rests in the parallels that can be found between it and the *Merchant's Tale.* Some of these parallels are interesting but carry little weight. It is perhaps worth noting, for example, that both Lippijn and January are old, whereas the husbands in most of the other analogues to Chaucer's tale are either young or of unspecified age. On the other hand, the deceived husband Nicostrato in Boccaccio's *Decameron* 7.9 is also an old man. Because of this, and because the old and sexually inadequate husband is a stock character in medieval comic tales, Lippijn's age cannot be said to be significant evidence for Chaucer's knowledge of *Lippijn.*

medieval financial practices, many of which were centered in Bruges and its nearby seaport town of Middelburg. It is interesting that Chaucer's Merchant, who tells the story of January and May, himself frequented Middelburg (A 277) and wears a beaver hat made in Flanders (A 272). Might Chaucer, in assigning this tale to the Merchant, have been giving a hint about where he (either Chaucer or the Merchant) might first have seen, read, or heard the plot about an old husband cuckolded by a young wife before his very eyes, and who then allows himself to be talked out of believing what he has seen?

[4] Robert F. Yeager, in "British Library Additional MS. 5141: An Unnoticed Chaucer *Vita*," *Journal of Medieval and Renaissance Studies* 14 (1984): 261–81, points out that this passage may derive from Speght's edition of Chaucer's works, published in 1598. Speght said that Chaucer, after "favouring some rash attempt of the common people," was forced to flee to "Holland, Zeeland." Speght's information may, in turn, have derived from John Bale.

More significant is that in both *Lippijn* and in the *Merchant's Tale*, but in none of the other analogues, we find two women characters, the young wife and another, older, more experienced woman who is willing, unasked, to share with less experienced women her knowledge about how to browbeat men. Might the idea for Proserpina—whose role is played by St. Peter in some analogues—have come to Chaucer in part from *Lippijn*? Whether or not Chaucer consciously converted the godmother from the Middle Dutch play into an underworld goddess in his tale, it is interesting that both of these worldly-wise women are more than a little willing to help other women find ready answers that will extricate them from compromising situations. Chaucer's Proserpina proudly announces that she will give May a "suffisant answere" (E 2266).[5] It may be more than pure coincidence that Trise had, in a play written not long before, given a sufficient solution to Lippijn's wife, who had also been caught in adultery by an angry and accusing old husband.

Other similarities in detail between the two stories are worth mentioning. For example, the lover is said to lift up the wife's skirts before he makes love to her:

> Ic sach dat si averecht lach
> Ende hi raepter op haer slippen.
>
> (94–95)

Chaucer is similarly blunt:

> And soddeynly anon this Damyan
> Gan pullen up the smok.
>
> (E 2352–53)

This detail which appears in no other analogue to the *Merchant's Tale* is an interesting one, for it suggests both the haste of the encounter—there is no time for a complete disrobing—and its generally unromantic quality: this is merely physical lovemaking, not emotional

[5] All quotations from Chaucer are from F. N. Robinson, ed., *The Works of Geoffrey Chaucer*, 2nd edn. (Boston, 1957).

or romantic love. More important, the lifted skirt is so graphic a detail that both Lippijn and January notice it. January comments on the lifted skirt: "Thy smok hadde leyn upon his brest" (E 2395). Is it likely to be merely coincidental that both foolish husbands, wanting to believe a version of the cuckolding that does least violence to their own egos, are willing to forgo the same piece of direct evidence to the contrary—the wife's lifted skirt?

Another feature that our two tales have in common is the vividness of the husband's perception of the cuckolding. Lippijn sees his wife's naked knees and the lover who has crept between them:

> Want si leet metten bloeten knien
> Ende hi esser tusschen gecropen;
> Bi der doot ons heren, hi esser in geslopen.
> (50–52)

He later tells Trise what he saw:

> Want ic hebse selve ghesien
> Ligghen metten bloeten knien
> Ende gingen hem beide te werke stellen.
> (83–85)

Chaucer uses similarly explicit language in describing Damyan's love-making with May: "and in he throng" (E 2352). He also makes it quite clear that January has seen this act. When May claims that all she did was "strugle with a man upon a tree" (E 2374), January is adamant: " 'Strugle!' quod he, 'ye algate in it wente! . . . He swyved thee' " (E 2376–78). In the other analogues there is no such explicitness. In the Italian *Novellino* version, for example, the husband merely looks up and "sees what the woman is doing." In the *Decameron* version the couple in the tree "frolic" and the husband merely looks up and "catches sight of them."

Another detail unique to *Lippijn* and the *Merchant's Tale* is the husband's being told that his vision is faulty. Trise tells Lippijn that, either because he was drinking or because of his advanced age, his vision is flawed:

U ogen sijn al verkeert
Van drincken ende van ouden dagen.

(88–89)

This suggestion is unparalleled in any of the other analogues, where no one thinks to suggest that the husband might have seen unclearly. In all of the other analogues the wife's clever answer is quite different. In the "enchanted tree" versions her answer is that the enchanted tree caused her husband to *imagine* that he saw something. In the "blind husband" versions her answer is that she had committed the act of adultery because she had been told that only by doing so could she cure her husband's blindness. Only in *Lippijn* and in the *Merchant's Tale* is the husband told that his vision is poor. The lines quoted above could have suggested to Chaucer May's words in her indignant harangue of January:

"Ye han som glympsyng, and no parfit sighte.

. . . . .

But sire, a man that waketh out of his sleep,
He may nat sodeynly wel taken keep
Upon a thyng, ne seen it parfitly.
Til that he be adawed verraily.
Right so a man that longe hath blynd ybe,
Ne may nat sodeynly so well yse,
First whan his sighte is newe come ageyn,
As he that hath a day or two yseyn."

(E 2383, 2397–2404)

Can it be mere coincidence that in only these two versions is the husband told that his sight may have been impaired, thus causing him to be mistaken in what he saw?

The most important evidence of direct influence, however, lies in the husband's gradual and dramatically vivid relinquishment of what his eyes have told him. Lippijn does see his wife *in flagrante delicto*. He tells Trise that he has seen it with his own eyes and there is no point in anyone telling him that he has not seen it:

Dat een man met sinen ogen siet
Dats hem nochtan quaet tongheven.
(78–79)

When Trise suggests that he may have been tricked into thinking he saw something, Lippijn quickly insists that there was no trick, because he saw his wife laboring hard with her naked knees showing (82–85). When Trise tells him that his eyes may have been mistaken because of drinking or old age, Lippijn insists that he is not blind:

Wat duvel, seldi mi maken blent
Van dingen die ic selve sach?
(92–93)

When Trise tells him it may have been elves who tricked him, once again Lippijn insists that he knows he saw his wife go off with her lover and saw the lover take her in his arms and pull her close:

Ic sach dat si met hem ginc,
Hi namse in sinen aerm ende tracse naer.
(108–09)

There can be no question that Lippijn saw, and that he knows what he saw.

Lippijn gradually, however, allows himself to be persuaded that he did not see. When Trise insists once again that elves can make a person blind, Lippijn begins to waver in his convictions by wondering whether he may indeed have been blind:

Wat duvel, es mi nu gesciet?
Benic blint ende en sie ic niet?
(119–20)

When Trise presses her advantage and says once more that an elf is to blame, Lippijn asks if she is sure, because it really did seem that he saw his wife:

Ey goede, eest dat, dat mi let?
Mi dochte emmer dat icse sach.
(132–33)

Trise then tells Lippijn that he is sure to find his wife sitting at home by the fire, as if that would constitute proof that she has been there the whole time and is innocent. Lippijn wonders if he may really be drunk or the victim of elves, and goes home with Trise. There he finds his wife waiting for him and decides that she has been innocent and that he has been wrong to accuse her: "Ic sie wel, die scouwen die sijn mijn" (153). When Lippijn's wife pretends to be angry, Lippijn totally capitulates and says that he merely thought he saw her, but that his eyes were wrong:

> Seker, woudic die waerheit lien,
> So saghic, of mijn ogen waren mi verkeert.
> (170–71)

And, finally, just before he is beaten, the weak and foolish Lippijn yields completely to his wife, admitting that he was totally wrong to believe his eyes:

> Lieve wijf, in en saels nemmeer setggen:
> Ic en wiste niet, dat ic was in dolen.
> (182–83)

There is no such gradual and dramatized capitulation in any of the other analogues, where the husbands yield almost immediately. In the *Merchant's Tale*, however, as in *Lippijn*, the husband is initially stubborn and sure, and then only gradually forgoes the evidence of his own eyes. When Pluto restores his eyesight, January looks up into the tree and sees May and Damyan making love. January cries out like a mother whose child has died and upbraids his wife, "O stronge lady stoore, what dostow?" (E 2367). May replies that she has "struggled" with Damyan because she was told that in that way she could cure her husband's blindness. January is absolutely convinced:

> "He swyved thee, I saugh it with myne yen,
> And elles be I hanged by the hals!"
> (E 2378–79)

January knows. He will pledge his life on it. May will not give up, however, and proclaims that her medicine must have failed, for if he could really see he would not talk such nonsense. He must have had an imperfect glimpse, not a real look, at what she was doing. Initially certain, January lapses into the uncertainty of merely thinking he saw what he saw:

> "I se," quod he, "as wel as evere I myghte,
> Thonked be God! with bothe myne eyen two,
> And by my trouthe, me thoughte he dide thee so."
> (E 2384–86)

May is indignant and pretends to regret that she was ever "so kynde" (E 2388–89). January capitulates with an apology that sounds very much like Lippijn's (see text above, lines 176–77):

> "Now, dame," quod he, "lat al passe out of mynde.
> Com doun, my lief, and if I have myssayd,
> God helpe me so, as I am yvele apayd."
> (E 2390–92)

This same January who had earlier been absolutely sure of what he had seen, then "thought" he saw it, finally decides that he had merely supposed that he saw it:

> "I wende han seyn
> How that this Damyan hadde by thee leyn,
> And that thy smok hadde leyn upon his brest."
> (E 2393–95)

May has argued well and, like the wives in all of the analogues to this story, emerges the victor in a dramatic contest over who shall control what a husband sees. Lippijn and January, however, alone among the husbands in the analogues, yield that control only gradually in scenes remarkable for their dramatic portrayal of male foolishness and female tenacity.

Nothing we have said here constitutes proof that Chaucer had ever read or seen the play *Lippijn*, or that this Middle Dutch play influenced the composition of the *Merchant's Tale*. Still, the probable date of the play, Chaucer's travel to the Low Countries, and a number of features that are common only to these two works, suggest at least the strong possibility that Chaucer knew of *Lippijn* and recalled certain of its features when he wrote his tale of January.

Chaucer's originality

In the end, of course, scholars are always more interested in what was most original about Chaucer's tales, not what was most derivative. Indeed, the primary justification for attempts to discover the sources and analogues of Chaucer's tales is that they give us a means of discerning what is uniquely Chaucerian about his tales. We shall leave to others most of the fun of seeing what light *Lippijn* sheds upon Chaucer's aims and emphases in the *Merchant's Tale*, and of discovering how it serves as a standard against which to measure Chaucer's own, quite different, achievement. We would, however, like to suggest three rather obvious ways in which Chaucer's version of the story differs from its Middle Dutch predecessor. In saying what we are about to say, of course, we intend no dishonor to the Middle Dutch play. The dramatic version, following as it does a longer and more serious play, had to be just what it is: slender, slight, and slapstick. All we have of *Lippijn* are the lines. We have none of the actions and improvisations the play would presumably have had on the stage.

Still, it is evident, first, how much richer the texture of the *Merchant's Tale* is than the texture of *Lippijn*. We find in the play a barebones plot involving only four people, one of whom is off stage most of the time. We find in the play no opening encomium on the joys of marriage, no advice from friends about marriage and selecting a wife, no clues about how or why the aging protagonist settled on the young wife he married, no wedding scene, no marriage-bed scene, no jealousy, no intrigue as two young lovers overcome obstacles so that they can fulfill their desires, no divine intervenors conversing in the garden, no wife pretending to be pregnant. *Lippijn* is to the *Merchant's Tale* as a paragraph is to an essay, and we are impressed, once again, with how much more Chaucer made of the possibilities inherent in the standard "cuckold comedy" than his predecessors made. Chaucer rewove the homespun of his sources into rich tapestries.

Second, characterization in Chaucer's tale is far more subtle than that in the play. Let us consider the wives. Lippijn's wife foolishly takes no precautions about meeting her lover, makes love to him in what is apparently a quite public place, and has no thought for the future. Chaucer gives May a more important role by making her smarter and putting her much more in control. May arranges for the garden meeting with Damyan, counterfeits a key, signals to her lover to climb the tree, and takes immediate charge when she finds herself caught. And instead of ending on a note of coarse slapstick with the beating of the henpecked Lippijn, Chaucer has May step back and let January lead her happily to the palace. May's strategy is to let January think exactly what he wants to think: that he is a fine husband and lover, that he has produced the heir he had so urgently wanted, that marriage will continue to be a paradise on earth, that his wife will continue to be faithful to him, and that he is still in charge of his marriage. May is a professional. She knows what she is doing.

Third, whereas the anonymous author of *Lippijn* was writing about peasants who, no matter how hard they tried to behave like their betters, still behaved like peasants, Chaucer was writing about upper-class men and women who, no matter how hard they pretended to behave as they ought, also behaved like peasants. That fact gives Chaucer's tale a thematic depth that the Middle Dutch play does not have. The play was designed to provide a few moments of bold, grotesque comic relief and to leave an audience laughing as they left the theater. Chaucer's tale is designed to make an audience laugh, yes, but also reflect on the inappropriateness of certain kinds of human behavior. We are not much troubled when Lippijn and Trise and the young lovers are gross and selfish and foolish, because that is what literary peasants are supposed to be. But we expect more of knights and their ladies. When Chaucer took a play about peasants and let some of its elements play themselves out on a stage peopled by the personages of romance, he set up a tension that makes audiences notice and think about human folly, selfishness, and nastiness. In that tension, absent from *Lippijn* and the other analogues to the *Merchant's Tale,* is the stuff of an enduring literature.

Noah and the Old Man in the *Pardoner's Tale*

[The mysterious old man who directs the three rioters to the pile of gold that unleashes their mortal greed has been a lightning rod for critical speculation—my own included. I think that the ancient traveler is a type of the biblical Noah—a good man who is permitted to survive the pestilence that has killed off men and women less virtuous than he. Researching the old man led me to larger questions about the reasons for the commanding presence of bubonic plague in the *Pardoner's Tale*. Those questions caused me to write a second article (see next). "Noah and the Old Man in the *Pardoner's Tale*" first appeared in *Chaucer Review* 15 (1981): 250–54.]

What are we to make of the old man in the Pardoner's *exemplum*, that mysterious, withered, sad-faced ancient who lets it be known that he is ready to go whenever it is God's will that Death carry him away from the dubious joys of this life? We have heard that he is Death, Death's messenger, the Wandering Jew, the Pauline *vetus homo*, Odin, a type of the Pardoner himself, old age, a pre-Swiftian Struldbrugg, simply a frightened old man, an agent of justice, a prophet, unregenerate man, etc.[1] Without further ado, I suggest that

[1] I see no point in tracing for readers of this journal the footprints of others who have written about the old man in the Pardoner's *exemplum*. Those who wish to will find a convenient place

when people in Chaucer's audience heard him speak about the strange old man, they may well have been reminded of the biblical Noah.

I shall not make here an exhaustive attempt to separate out the fruit from the chaff in previous explanations of the nature and function of the old man. I will say only that it is my view that there have been three major stumbling blocks in the path of too many of those who have trod this crooked way before me. The first is the notion that Chaucer's old man is somehow immortal, that he cannot die. Chaucer tells us no such thing. The old man is ready to die. He looks forward to the time when his bones will be at rest. He longs for his shroud. But it is not man's role to rush these things and he waits patiently "as longe tyme as it is Goddes wille" (C 726) that he remain alive. The second stumbling block is the notion that the old man is somehow evil in sending the young revelers to their death or that he somehow symbolizes mankind's sins. Chaucer, however, emphasizes the old man's meekness, politeness, patience, and piety. He emphasizes the old man's concern about the repentance of the three rioters and his warning that death awaits them if they do not change their course. The old man is consistently *contrasted* with the evil around him; and there can be no question but that the three evil rioters are responsible for their own prideful and avaricious rush toward death. The third stumbling block to a convincing interpretation of the old man is that virtually no one has considered the implications of the plague backdrop to the story.

The Pardoner's *exemplum* takes place in plague times. Death, we are told, "hath a thousand slayn this pestilence" (679). The plague

to start in the notes of Elizabeth R. Hatcher, "Life Without Death: The Old Man in Chaucer's *Pardoner's Tale*," *Chaucer Review* 9 (1975): 246–52. Curiously, Hatcher does not mention one of the most sensible of earlier discussions of the old man: John M. Steadman, "Old Age and *Contemptus Mundi* in the *Pardoner's Tale*," *Medium Ævum* 33 (1964): 121–30, reprinted in *Twentieth Century Interpretations of the Pardoner's Tale*, ed. Dewey R. Faulkner (Englewood Cliffs, NJ: Prentice-Hall, 1973), 70–82. All quotations from Chaucer are from F. N. Robinson, ed., *The Works of Geoffrey Chaucer*, 2nd edn. (Boston: Houghton Mifflin, 1957). Unless otherwise indicated, they are from Fragment C.

has ravaged a nearby village, only a mile away, carrying off to painful death "man and womman, child, and hyne, and page" (688). Because the plague has slain "so manye" (700), "al the peple" (676), and "alle oure freendes" (754), the three drunken rioters are moved to seek out the personified cause of all this destruction and kill him. The bubonic plague was a palpable reality in Chaucer's time. First appearing at mid-century, the plague reemerged in England periodically throughout Chaucer's lifetime. It carried off from a quarter to a third of the population and had a profound effect on the social, moral, and intellectual life of the nation.

In the absence of any knowledge that the bubonic plague was carried by rats and transmitted to people by fleas, Chaucer's contemporaries deduced a number of possible explanations for the terrible pestilences what were so much a fact of life in the second half of the fourteenth century: earthquakes, astrological misfortunes, poisoning of wells, and so on. The most common explanation, however, was a Christian one: that God had sent the plagues to punish men for their sins. There is ample evidence that this was the prevailing explanation. Boccaccio, in his famous account of the plague at the start of the *Decameron*, mentions the "iniquities which the just wrath of God sought to correct."[2] In England the Archbishop of York proclaimed that the plague was "surely . . . caused by the sins of men who, made complacent by their prosperity, forget the bounty of the most high Giver."[3] The Bishop of Winchester announced that it was caused by "man's sensuality which, propagated by the tendency of the old sin of Adam, . . . justly provoked the Divine wrath."[4] Langland, also, was among the many who attributed the pestilence to man's sinfulness.[5]

[2] Giovanni Boccaccio, *The Decameron*, trans. Frances Winwar (New York: Modern Library, 1955), xxiii.

[3] Philip Ziegler, *The Black Death* (London: Collins, 1969), 180.

[4] Ziegler, 145.

[5] See, for example, *Piers Plowman*, B-text, V.13.

There is evidence that the plague was seen in Chaucer's time as a repetition in small of the terrible flood that had swept to their death so many sinful men in the time of Noah. Noah's flood was, after all, the only other event in history with which most medieval Christians could compare the terrible pestilences of their own time. It was no coincidence, for example, that the chronicler of Louth Park, the Cistercian abbey northeast of Lincoln, wrote that the plague "filled the whole world with terror. So great an epidemic has never been seen nor heard of before this time, for it is believed that even the waters of the flood which happened in the days of Noah did not carry off so vast a multitude."[6]

There is no reason not to think that Chaucer shared the common view about the cause of the plague—that it was God's punishment for the manifold sins of mankind—and no reason to doubt that he would have expected at least some in his audience to draw a parallel between Noah, the old, old survivor of that first holocaust, and the old, old man in the Pardoner's *exemplum.* Both, presumably because they are good men surrounded by sinners, are survivors of God's retribution. Is there any reason not to see Chaucer's old man as a survivor? The three rioters meet him walking toward them when they are halfway to the village where Death by plague has his residence. Are we not to assume that the old man has been spared the destruction that has carried off so many of his sinful compatriots? Is he not a fourteenth-century Noah?

We find support for this suggestion when we look at the character portrayed in the Wakefield *Noah.* The play opens with Noah praying to God. He reviews some of God's accomplishments in creating the universe, the angels, the creatures on earth. He reminds us that both Lucifer and Adam were cast down from joy to woe because of their disobedience and sin, and tells us that, like Lucifer and Adam before them, Noah's own ungrateful contemporaries are now given over to sin:

[6] Ziegler, 179.

Bot now before his sight euery liffyng leyde,
Most party day and nyght, syn in word and dede
Full bold:
Som in pride, ire, and enuy,
Som in couetous and glotyny,
Som in sloth and lechery,
And other wise manyfold.[7]

This opening is paralleled by the opening of the Pardoner's *exemplum*, which is an account of the sinful words and deeds, by day and night, of the rioters:

In Flaundres whilom was a compaignye
Of yonge folk that haunteden folye,
As riot, hasard, stywes, and tavernes,
Where as with harpes, lutes, and gyternes,
They daunce and pleyen at dees bothe day and nyght,
And eten also and drynken over hir myght,
Thurgh which they doon the devel sacrifise
Withinne that develes temple, in cursed wise,
By superfluytee abhomynable.
Hir othes been so grete and so dampnable
That it is grisly for to heere hem swere.
(C 463–73)

Having established that the world is full of sin and so deserves any retribution God choses to visit upon it, Noah goes on, in a passage of particular interest to us for the parallels it offers with Chaucer's old man, to describe himself:

Sex hundreth yeris and od haue I, without distance,
In erth, as any sod, liffyd with grete grevance
Allway;

[7] *The Wakefield Pageants in the Towneley Cycle*, ed. A. C. Cawley (Manchester: Manchester University Press, 1958), 15, lines 48–54. Subsequent quotations are from this edition.

And now I wax old,
Seke, sory, and cold;
As muk apon mold
I widder away.
Bot yit will I cry for mercy.
(57–64)

Chaucer's old man, like the Wakefield Noah, is almost unbelievably ancient. He too lives in great sorrow and withers away: "Lo how I vanysshe, flessh, and blood, and skyn!" (732). Like Noah, he cries for mercy: "Leeve mooder, leet me in!" (731). Noah's age and general infirmity are emphasized again when he begins to work on the monumental ark:

A! my bak, I traw, will brast! This is a sory note!
Hit is wonder that I last, sich an old dote,
All dold,
To begyn sich a wark.
My bonys ar so stark:
No wonder if they wark,
For I am full old.
(264–70)

Like Noah, Chaucer's old man is bone-weary—"Allas! whan shul my bones been at reste?" (733)—and he walks with the aid of a staff.

I do not suggest that Chaucer's old man is Noah. I think it likely, however, considering the backdrop of the plague in the Pardoner's *exemplum*, the almost universal view that the plague was caused by man's dire sinfulness, and the parallels between the two old survivors of God's vengeance, that Chaucer and at least some in his audience would have thought of the Pardoner's old man as a kind of contemporary Noah who reminded them that sin does not go unpunished. Surely that "noble ecciesiaste" (A 708), the avaricious Pardoner, would have welcomed such an interpretation, for it would encourage his auditors to unbuckle their purses and give him their money so that he could pardon them from the sins that threatened, as they did in Noah's time, to destroy mankind.

The Plague and Chaucer's Pardoner

[The first time I taught the *Pardoner's Tale* in 1968, I was sure my students would ask me why Chaucer used the Black Death as a grim backdrop to the Pardoner's story of greed and murder. When they did not ask me, I asked them. Together we teased out some tentative explanations. That weekend I did a hasty review of research to see what Chaucer scholars could tell me about the fact that Chaucer, alone among the many tellers of the story, had set it in a time of bubonic plague. To my amazement, virtually no one had written about that. I decided years later to fill he gap. By the time I was finished, my footnotes threatened to dominate the article itself. "The Plague and Chaucer's Pardoner" first appeared in *Chaucer Review* 16 (1982): 257–69.]

The *Pardoner's Tale* is one of Chaucer's most widely read and discussed narratives, but because scholars have failed to consider the implications of the plague setting, the full richness and artistic unity of the tale have not been sufficiently appreciated. Most scholars cite the references to the plague simply as evidence that as an artist Chaucer was indifferent to the tragedies that haunted England during his lifetime.[1] To be sure, it has been noted briefly that the plague provides

[1] G. G. Coulton, for example, recognizing that the plague struck primarily the poor, suggests that, though Chaucer may have sympathized with the plight of the individual poor man, "with regard to the poor in bulk, he would only have shrugged his shoulders and said, 'they are always

motivation for the three rioters' seeking to destroy death.[2] There are other reasons, however, why a consideration of the plague setting is necessary to a full understanding of the Pardoner's *exemplum* and his motivation in telling it. Such a consideration may also shed light on Harry Bailly's violent reaction to the Pardoner's request for money.

with us' " (*Chaucer and His England* [New York: Barnes & Noble, 1963], 236). Similarly, Emile Legouis suggests that because Chaucer had little "interest in the reverses and internal troubles of his country," he "speaks incidentally and in no serious way . . . of the terrible plagues" that desolated England during his lifetime (*Geoffrey Chaucer*, trans. L. Lailavois [New York; Russell & Russell, 1961], 32). H. R. Patch tells us that there may be some truth to the notion that Chaucer was "untouched by . . . the horrors of his day," and suggests that Chaucer's "allusions" to the plague in the *Pardoner's Tale* "are only those of a spectator" (*On Rereading Chaucer* [Cambridge, MA: Harvard University Press, 1939], 187–88). More recently, J. F. D. Shrewsbury explains Chaucer's "timid reference" to the plague in the *Pardoner's Tale* by referring to what he calls the "superstition of the personification of pestilential disease—which was a common aberration of the public mind up to the end of the eighteenth century—in which case the less he said about plague the better it would be for his personal safety" (*A History of Bubonic Plague in the British Isles* [Cambridge, U.K.: Cambridge University Press, 1970], 41–42). And Barbara Tuchman, trying to explain why Chaucer gives the plague "barely a glance," suggests that "divine anger so great that it contemplated the extermination of man did not bear close examination" (*A Distant Mirror: The Calamitous Fourteenth Century* [New York: Alfred A. Knopf, 1978], 105). I hope to show in this essay that such speculations are wrongheaded. Chaucer was very much aware of the trials of his countrymen, and he did not fear to deal with them when they would serve the artistic needs of his storytelling.

[2] Germaine Dempster, for example, writes, "how much more tragic and intense if the three companions could be given a real reason why they should start on a mad and feverish . . . quest for death!" (*Dramatic Irony in Chaucer* [Stanford: Stanford University Press. 1932], 77). By and large, however, critics who mention the plague at all do so only in the most general of terms. Virtually no one devotes more than a few sentences to it. Robert Kilburn Root, in *The Poetry of Chaucer* (Boston: Houghton Mifflin, 1900), 227, says that the effectiveness of the theme of the story depends in part on "the terrible and mysterious force, the plague, death raised to its highest power." Marie Padgett Hamilton, in "Death and Old Age in the *Pardoner's Tale*," *Studies in Philology* 36 (1939): 574, says that in Chaucer the plague was made "the more ghastly when seen as a background for hollow revelry." Alfred David, in "Criticism and the Old Man in Chaucer's Pardoner's Tale," *CE* 27 (1965): 44, notes that the plague "motivates the action and provides a unifying symbol of corruption." Philippa Tristram, in *Figures of Life and Death in Medieval English Literature* (London: Elek Books, Ltd., 1976), 70, sees the plague as one of three warnings to the rioters that death awaits them.

Of all the early tellers of the famous story of evil men whose greed leads them to their death after finding a pile of gold,[3] Chaucer alone places his version in plague times. In doing so, he could count on calling up a host of responses from his contemporary audiences, most of whom would have known about the plague at firsthand. In 1348–50, and then again and again in the second half of the century, the plague raged through England, carrying off to a revolting and agonizing death certainly hundreds of thousands, possibly millions, of victims.[4] Whether or not this Black Death was "the greatest single catastrophe ever visited on the human race,"[5] surely Chaucer and his audience had all either witnessed directly or heard vivid reports of its terrible ravages. Therefore, when the Pardoner referred to the "privee theef men clepeth Deeth,"[6] Death, who had "a thousand slayn this pestilence" (679) and "in this contree all the peple sleeth" (676), he aroused in his medieval audience a set of associations and beliefs that we must reconstruct from the accounts by contemporaries who wrote about the plague more directly than Chaucer did.

An awareness of medieval attitudes toward the bubonic plague gives us answers to some otherwise rather puzzling questions: if there is a terrible plague, why are the three rioters having such a rousing

[3] Most of the non-Chaucerian versions are gathered together in *Sources and Analogues of Chaucer's Canterbury Tales,* ed. W. F. Bryan and Germaine Dempster (New York: Humanities Press, 1958), 415–38.

[4] The exact toll, of course, can never be known. Some contemporary accounts suggest that nine-tenths of the population was carried off—surely an exaggeration. Recent estimates have been more conservative, but even most of these put the death rate at between a quarter to a half of the population. Shrewsbury, the most cautious of recent students of the plague, puts it this way: "In the comparatively densely populated region of East Anglia, and in the larger towns that were afflicted by it, 'The Great Pestilence' may possibly have destroyed as much as one-third of the population; in the rest of England and Wales it is extremely doubtful if as much as one-twentieth of the population was destroyed by it" (36).

[5] Nathaniel Weyl, "The Black Death and the Intellect of Europe," *Mankind Quarterly* 15 (1975): 254.

[6] *The Works of Geoffrey Chaucer*, ed. F. N. Robinson, 2nd ed. (Boston: Houghton Mifflin, 1957), C 675. All subsequent references to Chaucer are from Group C of this edition.

good time in the local tavern? how does that mysterious pile of gold come to appear, unattended, by the oak tree? and who in the world is that strange old man who directs them to it?

First, why are those three rioters carousing in the tavern when there is so much human misery and death in the land about them? One possible answer comes from Boccaccio, who described the various responses of the citizens of Florence to plague times. Some survivors shut themselves off in houses where no one had yet died, eating and drinking moderately, listening to fine music, never discussing the plague. Others went about their life as usual, carrying with them flowers and sweet-smelling herbs to protect themselves from the poisoned air. Others fled the city and went to some spot in the country where the plague had not yet struck. Still others, like the revelers in the Pardoner's *exemplum,* engaged in riotous living:

> [They] held that plenty of drinking and enjoyment, singing and free living and the gratification of the appetite every possible way, letting the devil take the hindmost, was the best preventative of such a malady; and as far as they could, they suited the action to the word. Day and night they went from one tavern to another drinking and carousing unrestrainedly.[7]

This last, clearly, is the response of Chaucer's three rioters, a response that must have been all too familiar in Chaucer's time in regions where the plague had struck.

[7] Giovanni Boccaccio, *The Decameron,* trans. Frances Winwar (New York: Random House, 1955), xxv. Interesting corroborating evidence from another literary source is to be found in *Piers Plowman,* B. XX. 52–182. Antichrist, with many enlisted under his banner, carried by Pride, attacks Conscience. Conscience calls upon Nature ("Kynd") for assistance, and Nature sends into battle against Antichrist all manner of illness, including "pokkes and pestilences." Soon thousands of Antichrist's followers are dead. Conscience charitably asks Nature to let up a little to see if the evildoers will repent and become good Christians. Nature obliges. Instead of amending their ways, however, most of the survivors, like Chaucer's three rioters, give themselves over to assorted sins: Lechery, Covetousness, Avarice, Sloth, etc. It is interesting that here, as in the Pardoner's *exemplum,* plague is seen as a positive force, not only in destroying evil people, but also in providing motivation to do better for those who are not destroyed. Not all of those who survive, of course, mend their ways.

We should note that the boy in the tavern says that Death has slain a thousand people in "*this* pestilence" (679, emphasis added). This suggests there had been earlier visitations of pestilence in that area. If so, that fact is also relevant to the behavior of the rioters. One common contemporary observation was that after the plague had run its course in a given neighborhood the morality of those who survived worsened. Matteo Villani, historian of Florence, attests to this phenomenon after the Black Death of 1348–49, a catastrophe that might have been expected to improve the morals of surviving Florentines:

> Those few discreet folk who remained alive . . . believed that those whom God's grace had saved from death, having beheld the destruction of their neighbours . . . would become better-conditioned, humble, virtuous and Catholic; that they would guard themselves from iniquity and sin and would be full of love and charity towards one another. But no sooner had the plague ceased than we saw the contrary; for since men were few and since, by hereditary succession, they abounded in earthly goods, they forgot the past as though it had never been, and gave themselves up to a more shameful and disordered life than they had led before. For, mouldering in ease, they dissolutely abandoned themselves to the sin of gluttony, with feasts and taverns and delight of delicate viands; and again to games of hazard and to unbridled lechery.[8]

The same was true in England. William of Dene, a monk of Rochester, wrote in his chronicle of the decadence that ensued after the plague in Kent: "The entire population, or the greater part of it, has become even more depraved, more prone to every kind of vice, more ready to indulge in evil and sinfulness, without a thought of death, or of the plague which is just over, or even of their own salvation."[9] And

[8] Philip Ziegler, *The Black Death* (London: Collins, 1969), 270–71. Ziegler's book is particularly useful for its gathering together of fourteenth-century accounts of the plague.

[9] As quoted in Ziegler, 164.

Walsingham described the post-plague Londoners thus: "They were of all people the most proud, arrogant and greedy, disbelieving in God, disbelieving in ancient custom."[10] Such actions and attitudes were surely perceived by sensible observers as both sinful and suicidal,[11] but all accounts suggest that in showing his rioters carousing in a tavern, Chaucer was merely being a realist, for such behavior was apparently common.

In addition to explaining the behavior of the three rioters, the plague setting can explain the origin of the treasure they find. Critics have wondered how that gold got there[12] and whether it even existed.[13] There need, however, be no such puzzlement. The gold had

[10] Ziegler, 160. For further evidence of a sharp decline in morals in the aftermath of plague, see E. Carpentier, *Une Ville devant la Peste: Orvieto et la Peste Noire de 1348* (Paris: S.E.V.P.E.N., 1962), 195–96.

[11] The medical treatises of Chaucer's time suggest indirectly that the three rioters may be suicidal even before they rush to confront Death in the plague-ravaged village, for both wine-drinking and fornication were believed to render the body more than usually susceptible to the plague. Anna Montgomery Campbell, in *The Black Death and Men of Learning* (New York: Columbia University Press, 1931), discusses the view of Arab and Parisian physicians that the drinking to excess of strong wines was an unhealthy practice in plague times (75), and the prevailing view that "absolute chastity in time of pestilence" was a good idea (76). On this last, see also Johannes Nohl, *The Black Death: A Chronicle of the Plague*, trans. C. H. Clarke (New York: Harper & Row, 1969): "Nearly all physicians and plague authors warn earnestly against matrimonial relations, in the first place on account of the extraordinary danger of infection and then because they consume the strength and render the body liable and prone to attract the disease. *In peste Venus pestem provocat*, i.e. 'In times of plague the sport of Venus invites the plague,' was proverbial" (212). If Death had not found the three rioters under the oak with the pile of gold, he might have found them not much later, in the throes of a more prolonged and painful mortality, for they seem determined, one way or another, to poison themselves.

[12] Gerhard Joseph, in "The Gifts of Nature, Fortune, and Grace in the *Physician's*, *Pardoner's*, and *Parson's Tales*," *Chaucer Review* 9 (1975): 243, says that the gold is the gift of Fortune, and quotes as his authority one of the three rioters (who is, incidentally, wrong about just about everything else too).

[13] Root, for example, wonders. whether the florins are "real and palpable, or only a dreadful mocking vision" (230). The best discussion of the treasure is to be found in Joel Roache, "Treasure Trove in the *Pardoner's Tale*," *Journal of English and Germanic Philology* 84 (1965): 1–6, but Roache deals only with the legal aspects of the unclaimed treasure and does not connect it in any way with the plague.

belonged to a victim of the plague who, like Everyman, had discovered that he could not take it with him into the next world. There is evidence that dying plague victims were frequently forced to abandon their treasures. A Franciscan friar, Michael of Piazza, for example, described the effects of the plague in Sicily in 1347: "The houses of the deceased remained open with all their valuables, with gold and jewels; anyone who chose to enter met with no impediment, for the plague raged with such vehemence that soon there was a shortage of servants and finally none at all."[14]

If, as seems likely, the treasure was abandoned by a victim of the plague attempting to flee the infected village, then why is it still beneath the oak tree where it was abandoned? Why has no one else found it and carried it off? The answer would have been easy enough for one who knew about plague: the treasure itself might have been infected, and to touch it would have been foolhardy indeed. Geoffrey le Baker, writing about London at mid-century, said, "Scarcely anyone ventured to touch the sick, and healthy persons shunned the once, and still, precious possessions of the dead, as infectious."[15] The three rioters forget not only that the gold is morally infectious but that it can be physically infectious also. In their pride and greed they foolishly ignore the warnings of the old man who directs them to do so.

And what of that old man? Does a knowledge of the plague help explain him? One hesitates, of course, to propose still another hypothesis concerning that mysterious creature, but perhaps I may be forgiven for suggesting that he is a survivor from the village up the road a mile from the tavern. The rioters have gone halfway there when hey meet the old man coming from the direction in which they are heading. In a time when some villages were totally abandoned as a result of the ravages of the plague, it must have been no uncommon sight to see a lone survivor wandering about in search of a new home,

[14] Nohl, 19.

[15] Leonard W. Cowie, *The Black Death and Peasants' Revolt* (London: Wayland Publishers, 1972), 48.

wondering why his mother earth will not accept him, as it has taken his family and acquaintances.[16] I do not wish to press this suggestion too strongly, but it is noteworthy that the plague often sought its victims among the young, leaving as survivors the old and the weak. Geoffrey le Baker tells us that "the pestilence seized especially the young and strong, commonly sparing the elderly and feeble" an observation independently corroborated by other chroniclers.[17] The rioters' charge that Death has slain "us yonge folk" (759) in the current pestilence suggests that Chaucer knew the plague often tended to spare the elderly. This may be a sufficient clue that, whatever else the mysterious old man may have signified,[18] on one level he was simply a sad old survivor of a plague that had carried off almost every other "man and woman, child, and hyne, and page" (688) in his desolate village.

[16] Eyewitness accounts of such survivors, of course, would not normally find their way into the chronicles. I know of one exception, a "peasant driven stark mad with grief and wandering about the country" near the town of Durham after a plague. See A *History of Durham* in *The Victoria History of the Counties* of *England,* ed. William Page (London: A. Constable, 1907), II, 211.

[17] Cowie, 47–48; Ziegler, 78. Ziegler's skepticism as to the validity of such statements is refuted by modem medical knowledge. See Shrewsbury, 44, who observes that those between the ages of ten and thirty-five are the most vulnerable to plague, the very young and the very old being comparatively exempt.

[18] Elizabeth R. Hatcher, in "Life Without Death: The Old Man in Chaucer's *Pardoner's Tale,*" *Chaucer Review* 9 (1975): 248–52, provides a useful summary of the various interpretations of the old man. I find unsatisfactory, however, her own view that the old man serves to demonstrate the horrors of old age without death. To see the old man as "the aged person who cannot die" (250) is to misread the tale. He never says that he cannot die; he merely points out that he must remain alive "as longe tyme as it is Goddes wille" (726). Like any good Christian, he is ready to die whenever God calls him. There is no suggestion that God never will call him. Hatcher draws a parallel between Chaucer's old man and Swift's Struldbruggs. Both, she says, demonstrate the miseries attendant upon eternal physical life. A more appropriate parallel, I think, might be made between Chaucer's old man and Old Age in passus XX of *Piers Plowman.* The allegorical character named Old Age serves two closely-related purposes. First, he serves as the banner-bearer in Nature's army as it sets out to destroy the army of Antichrist, led by the banner-bearer Pride. As such, Old Age reminds the enemies of Christ that, however prideful they are now, their future lot is the humility of old age. Second, Old Age turns on the

A knowledge of contemporary attitudes toward the bubonic plague, then, helps us understand the events and characters in the Pardoner's *exemplum*. It also suggests that Chaucer probably viewed that *exemplum* not as supernatural or mysterious, but as realistic and contemporary.

Such a knowledge also helps us to understand the Pardoner—particularly his motivation in telling his tale. The plague setting makes the story of the three rioters who seek gold and find death more fearful, and because it is more fearful the story works to the benefit of its avaricious teller. To see why this is so, we must understand that in the Pardoner's *exemplum* Death is selective. Although it may *seem* that Death is indiscriminate, in the tale he carries off only the evil and spares the good. Of the characters who appear as individuals in the story, only the corrupt are slain: the three rioters, who swear, gamble, fornicate, and drink; and their "felawe" (672), who had apparently been one of the same stamp, for he was drunk when Death carried him off. Indeed, one of the rioters says Death slays "alle oure freends" (754). The taverner, the boy, the apothecary, and the old man survive, and these, so far as we can tell, are good men. The boy has learned from his mother to beware of Death and knows that men must always be ready to meet him. The tavern keeper, though he is not above swearing by St. Mary, knows it is best to be prepared for Death. The

dreamer. Old Age rides over his head so that he becomes bald, buffets him on the ear so that he becomes deaf, batters his mouth so that he has no teeth, ties him up with gout so that he cannot leave home, and cripples his privy member so that he cannot satisfy his wife. The dreamer needs this reminder from Old Age that he should devote himself not to the pleasures of the sinful concerns of this life, but to love and the rewards of the next life. The Pardoner may be doing something similar with the old man in his *exemplum*. Far from being the evil personage some critics have found him to be, the old man is a soldier in Christ's army to win the souls of evil men. "Look at me," the old man says in effect. "One day you will be old like me. Lo, how my body withers away. Why do you pridefully pursue physical things when you should instead humbly pursue spiritual ones?" But, just as the revelers ignore the warning of incipient death by plague, so they ignore the warning of incipient miseries in old age. That they pay the price for ignoring the warnings, of course, plays very much into the Pardoner's purposes. I have more to say about the old man in my note on "Noah and the Old Man in the *Pardoner's Tale*," reprinted above, pp. 280–85.

apothecary takes care to ask God to save his soul. The old man prays to God to save the rioters while he himself patiently awaits God's will. We are told nothing of the moral status of the inhabitants of the nearby village who have been swept away by the plague, but perhaps they were no better than they should be.

For the Pardoner's purposes his tale must clearly show that Death seizes the corrupt. The Pardoner underscores the point in a passage generally overlooked: it is the devil, he says, who gives the third rioter the idea to poison his two fellows: "the feend foond hym in swich lyvynge / That he hadde leve him to sorwe brynge" (847–48). *Because* the rioter has been living evilly, the fiend "has leave"—presumably from God—to poison his thoughts in such a way that he will bring himself and his fellows to sorrow. The point is clear: Death takes, by poison, blade, or plague, those who so live that they deserve to die. The Pardoner wants to warn his audience that if they are sinful, Death will take them. What more effective warning than the sinister image of the plague, the most frightening killer in Chaucer's time? What image would have made them more willing to heed the advice of the boy in the tavern—"Beth redy for to meete [Deeth] everemoore" (683)—by buying the pardons that would ready their souls to meet God?

Awareness of the plague background of the Pardoner's *exemplum*, then, reveals how very skillful the Pardoner is at extorting money. This Pardoner is diabolically clever. He plays on the fears of his auditors by proclaiming, in effect: "The end of the world is at hand. The deadly plague stalks sinners. The way to avoid it is to abandon your money, which can only infect you with death and damnation. But I can give you in exchange for that corrupting gold the pardon that will wash you clean from sin. Do not be like the three rioters who, because of their greed, died young and unready to meet God. Give your money to me."

If the Pardoner's *exemplum* is designed by Chaucer to show us just how clever the Pardoner is, then Harry Bailly's reaction may be Chaucer's way of showing that the Pardoner is too clever for his own good—or not quite clever enough. Again, a knowledge of medieval ideas about the plague helps us to understand what Chaucer may be up to here. Let me review briefly medieval notions about the causes of bubonic plague.

It was not discovered until the very end of the nineteenth century that bubonic plague is caused by an invasion of the human body by a bacterial parasite of the European black rat, a parasite conveyed to human hosts most commonly through the bite of a flea which has previously bitten the infected rat. Five hundred years earlier, men came up with considerably different explanations. Medieval men of learning deduced several possible causes for the terrible plague. Some blamed earthquakes.[19] Others thought it must be caused by an unfortunate conjunction of the planets.[20] Some blamed a Plague Maiden, who infected men by lifting her arm.[21] Some accused the Jews of poisoning the wells of Christian folk.[22] One man even ascribed the plague in France to the financial policies of its king.[23]

[19] Campbell, 16, 44.

[20] Boccaccio, xxii; Ziegler, 38. John Block Friedman has kindly called to my attention a contemporary account attacking ascription of the pestilence to planetary influences rather than to sin. The passage also offers further evidence for my notion about the prevalence of medieval comparisons between the plague and the biblical flood. The passage in question appears in the seventieth sermon of Thomas Brinton in *The Sermons of Thomas Brinton, Bishop of Rochester (1373–1389)*, ed. Sister Mary Aquinas Devlin (London: Royal Historical Society, 1954), II, 323: "But truly this particular pestilence and other misfortunes happen in these days. Those who ascribe such events to certain planets and constellations, rather than to sins, may say that sort of planet was in the ascendant at the time of Noah, when with the exception of eight creatures God submerged the whole world in the flood. . . . Therefore since sinful corruption and evil thinking are worse today than in the time of Noah, inasmuch as many kinds of sinfulness which did not exist then have been discovered today, and Sodomite sinfulness is widely prevalent, and the cruelty of the lords is greater today than in the time of David, let us not impute the scourge to the planets or the elements but rather to our own sins, citing this from Genesis: 'Deservedly we suffer these things because we have sinned.' " I am indebted to my colleague Edna S. deAngeli for help in translating the passage.

[21] Ziegler, 85.

[22] Ziegler, 97ff.

[23] Ziegler, 64.

By far the most prevalent theory about the ultimate cause of the plague, however, was that it was a punishment by God for man's sins. Boccaccio ascribed the plague to "our own iniquities which the just wrath of God sought to correct."[24] In Tournai the town council tried to bring the raging plague under control by forbidding men and women to live together out of wedlock and by prohibiting swearing and gambling.[25] The Archbishop of York proclaimed that the plague "surely, must be caused by the sins of men who, made complacent by their prosperity, forget the bounty of the most high Giver."[26] The Bishop of Winchester proclaimed that "man's sensuality . . . has now fallen into deeper malice and justly provoked the Divine wrath by a multitude of sins to this chastisement." A few weeks later he wrote to the people of his diocese reminding them as the plague approached "that sickness and premature death often come from sin and that, by the healing of souls, this kind of sickness is known to cease."[27] There can be no doubt, as we have seen, that Chaucer, too, assumed that there was a connection between morality and plague, and that those who were most sinful and least repentant would be its most likely victims.

Keeping in mind that most medieval people thought that there was a causal relationship between human sinfulness and the coming of the plague, we are ready to consider a new explanation for the Host's brutally personal insult to the Pardoner.[28] The insult comes after the

[24] Boccaccio, xxiii, and see Ziegler, 35–37.

[25] Ziegler, 81–82.

[26] Ziegler, 180.

[27] Ziegler, 145. I remind readers that the dreamer in *Piers Plowman* hears Reason preach that plagues are caused by sin. See B.V.13.

[28] Of the many explanations the most sensible is that the Host is simply angry at the Pardoner for singling him out as more sinful than the other pilgrims. George Lyman Kittredge proposed that the host responds to the Pardoner's request in "rough jocularity" (*Chaucer and His Poetry* [Cambridge, MA: Harvard University Press, 1915], 217). Other explanations are that "invincible simple-mindedness" motivates the Host's response (John Halverson, "Chaucer's Pardoner and the Progress of Criticism," *Chaucer Review* 4 [1970]: 199); that it is his "sense

Pardoner has told the Host that he should be the first to unbuckle his purse and come forward to pay him for the honor of kissing his holy relics. The Host lashes back with what bids fair to be the nastiest retort in all of literature:

> "Nay, nay!" quod he, "thanne have I Cristes curs!
> Lat be," quod he, "it shal nat be, so theech!
> Thou woldest make me kisse thyn olde breech,
> And swere it were a relyk of a seint,
> Though it were with thy fundement depeint!
> But, by the croys which that Seint Eleyne fond,
> I wolde I hadde thy coillons in myn hond
> In stide of relikes or of seintuarie.
> Lat kutte hem of, I wol thee helpe hem carie;
> They shul be shryned in an hogges toord!"
> (946–55)

I suggest that the Host responds so vehemently in part because he finds the Pardoner so full of sin that he invites the plague upon himself and upon all those who associate with him. The Pardoner, we must recall, is by his own confession a "ful vicious man" (459) who gleefully commits the very sins he preaches against—avarice, swearing, gluttony, and so on. His actions are based on "yvel entencioun" (408), and his preaching is utterly diabolical: "Thus spitte I out my venym under hewe / Of hoolynesse, to semen hooly and trewe" (421–22). If ever a man deserved to be punished by the plague, surely this Pardoner is he.

of social solidarity" (Barnard F. Huppé, *A Reading of the Canterbury Tales* [Albany: State University of New York Press, 1964], 217; and that it is his "competitive energy" (Donald R. Howard, *The Idea of the Canterbury Tales* [Berkeley and Los Angeles: University of California Press, 1978], 367). One critic feels that the Host reacts as he does because he has "latent homosexual impulses subconsciously feared" (George Williams, *A New View of Chaucer* [Durham, NC: Duke University Press, 1965], 149n.); another feels that he reacts that way because he sees in the Pardoner's request "a homosexual threat" (John Gardner, *The Poetry of Chaucer* [Carbondale and Edwardsville, IL: Southern Illinois University Press, 1977], 302). And so on.

Here the testimony of the English chronicler Knighton is relevant. He attributed the plague of 1348 to the presence at tournaments of women who dressed up as men:

> In those days there arose a huge rumour and outcry among the people, because when tournaments were held, almost in every place, a band of women would come as if to share the sport, dressed in divers and marvelous dresses of men—sometimes to the number of forty or sixty ladies, of the fairest and comeliest (though I say not of the best) among the whole kingdom. Thither they came in party-coloured tunics, one colour or pattern on the right side and another on the left, with short hoods that had pendants like ropes wound round their necks, and belts thickly studded with gold or silver. . . . There and thus they spent and lavished their possessions, and wearied their bodies with fooleries and wanton buffoonery, if popular report lie not. . . . But God in this matter, as in all others, brought marvelous remedy; for He harassed the places and times appointed for such vanities by opening the floodgates of heaven with rain and thunder and lurid lightning, and by unwonted blasts of tempestuous winds. . . . That same year and the next came the general mortality throughout the world.[29]

If the stories of these strange hermaphroditic ladies were as widespread as Knighton suggests they were, is it not possible that the Host, whose profession was to serve the itinerants who conveyed such tales, would have known of them? And is it not possible that he would have seen in the Pardoner of Roncevall, that effeminate "mare"

[29] Cowie, 18. The Pardoner's effeminacy has been well established. See especially Walter Clyde Curry, *Chaucer and the Medieval Sciences*, rev. ed. (New York: Barnes & Noble, 1960), 54–70. John S. P. Tatlock, in "Puns in Chaucer," in *Flügel Memorial Volume* (Stanford; Stanford University Press, 1916), 232n., has suggested that Chaucer may also be hinting at this effeminacy in having him be a pardoner of Roncevall, for a "rouncival" is a mannish woman.

who could grow no beard and who masqueraded as a man, another of the same type that had brought down upon the heads of those earlier sinners storm, wind, and finally plague? If God had provided a "remedy" for such evil by sending the plague in 1348, might he not do so again? And if so, are not the Host and the other pilgrims also in danger? Let us not forget in this connection that the Pardoner is associated with the hospital of St. Mary Roncevall at Charing Cross, a hospital that had been particularly badly hit by the Black Death at mid-century.[30] The Host might well have had reason to link with the Pardoner, who travels with the diseased Summoner, a certain taint of sickness, or even of plague.

I have one last tentative suggestion. It concerns the Host's refusal to kiss the Pardoner's old britches. The Pardoner has with him two pieces of cloth: a pillowcase that he claims is St. Mary's veil, and another fragment of fabric that he claims to be a piece of the sail that St. Peter used on the sea. Now, when the Pardoner invites the Host to come forth and "kisse the relikes everychon" (944), the Host recoils with his famous statement about kissing the Pardoner's stained britches. The Host's recoiling may be explained in part by the fact that it was commonly assumed that textile goods could transmit the plague from person to person and even from place to place.

Boccaccio, for example, tells us that "the mere touch of the clothes or any other object the sick had touched or used, seemed to spread the pestilence," and he tells the story of two hogs he had seen nose through the discarded clothing of a plague victim in Florence: "A little while later, after rolling round and round as though they had swallowed poison, both of them fell down dead upon the rags."[31] So fearful were people of spreading the plague through infected fabrics that in 1348 the city of Pistoia passed an ordinance forbidding anyone

[30] James Galloway in *The Hospital and Chapel of Saint Mary Roncevall* (London: John Bale, Sons & Danielsson, Ltd., 1914), 24, finds "very clear indications" that Roncevall "suffered severely" from the Black Death.

[31] Boccaccio, xxiv–xxv.

from bringing into the city any old linen or woolen garments.[32] It seems possible that the Host—having been reminded of the dangers of plague by the Pardoner's *exemplum*, having been made aware through the Pardoner's confession that the Pardoner is as evil as his three death-attracting rioters, and having been mindful of the precedent for a plague coming to destroy women who try to pass as men—might well be fearful of the false cloth relics of this Pardoner. God only knew what terrible contagion the Pardoner with his foreign connections[33] might have brought with him in those cloth relics when he came in from "Rome al hoot" (A 687).

Some of my argument has been speculative, particularly this last about the motivation for the Host's bitterly antagonistic reaction to the Pardoner's request for money. I do not feel, however, that we can understand the Pardoner or his *exemplum* if we overlook either the plague backdrop that Chaucer provided for the story or the evidence concerning medieval attitudes toward the plague. To overlook these is to be blind to important elements of incident, character, and theme. When we try to understand the Pardoner's remarkable performance as Chaucer's contemporaries might have understood it, we cannot help but be amazed, once again, at his consummate artistry.

[32] Campbell, 116. Shrewsbury explains why some outbreaks of the plague were correctly associated with the receipt of bundles of rags or other textile goods brought in from infected areas: "In the occasional event of the transport of [infected] fleas among clothes, rags, or other soft goods, the starving fleas would naturally, immediately they were released, attack the people handling the goods, with the result that cases of bubonic plague would suddenly appear in a village or town, which had previously been free from it, within a few days of the reception of the goods" (3; see also 29).

[33] The hospital of St. Mary Roncevall at Charing Cross was a daughter-institution of an ancient monastery in the Pass of Roncesvalles in Spain, and it continued in Chaucer's time to have frequent and important dealings with its mother house in Spain (see Galloway, esp. 6–10, 25–27). It is interesting to note that at least one medieval medical authority thought that Spaniards were, by national temperament, more than usually susceptible to the plague (see Seraphime Guerchberg, "The Controversy Over the Alleged Sowers of the Black Death in the Contemporary Treatises on Plague," in *Change in Medieval Society,* ed. Sylvia L. Thrupp [New York: Appleton-Century-Crofts, 1964], 219–20).

Index

This index lists the names of all persons referenced in the text—authors, editors and translators—scholars whose efforts have contributed to research of the *Canterbury Tales*. Also included are entries for important sources and analogues of the *Tales*. Sources are listed by title, by their authors' names (if known), and under the specific tale with which they are associated.

CPSIA information can be obtained at www.ICGtesting.com
227695LV00009B/44/P

9 781603 810753